Mary Gentle was born in 1956.
(1977), was a fantasy for young
the science fiction novels *Gold*
Light (1987). *Scholars and Soldiers* (
introduced readers to the White Crow with 'Beggars in Satin' and 'The Knot Garden'. The acclaimed White Crow books followed: *Rats and Gargoyles* (1990) and *The Architecture of Desire* (1991); *Left to His Own Devices* is the third.

In the classic authors' tradition, Mary Gentle has had several jobs, including Civil Servant and film projectionist. She currently lives in Hertfordshire.

Also by Mary Gentle from Orbit

SCHOLARS AND SOLDIERS

LEFT TO HIS OWN DEVICES

and

BLACK MOTLEY
WHAT GOD ABANDONED
THE ROAD TO JERUSALEM

MARY GENTLE

An *Orbit* Book

First published in Great Britain in 1994 by Orbit

'Black Motley' first published in *More Tales From the Forbidden Planet*, (ed) Roz Kaveney, Titan Books, 1990.

'What God Abandoned' first published in *The Weerde Book 1* (ed) Mary Gentle and Roz Kaveney, Penguin Books, 1992.

'The Road to Jerusalem' first published in *Interzone 52*, October 1991.

A CIP catalogue record for this book is available from the British Library.

ISBN 1 85723 203 8

Typeset by Solidus (Bristol) Limited
Printed and bound in Great Britain by
Clays Ltd, St. Ives plc

Orbit
A Division of
Little, Brown and Company (UK) Limited
Brettenham House
Lancaster Place
London WC2E 7EN

Contents

LEFT TO HIS OWN DEVICES

Chapter 1:	Masters of Defence	3
Chapter 2:	Programmed Sunlight	12
Chapter 3:	Simulations	22
Chapter 4:	The Language of Angels	30
Chapter 5:	Johanna	44
Chapter 6:	Criminal Proceedings	48
Chapter 7:	'The Wondrous Architecture of the World'	58
Chapter 8:	No Sword No Intention	66
Chapter 9:	Earlier that Same Morning	81
Chapter 10:	Owls and Other Birds of Prey	84
Chapter 11:	Brutal Isolation	92
Chapter 12:	In the English Renaissance Memory Garden	102
Chapter 13:	The Armour of Light	114
Chapter 14:	Games Software	123
Chapter 15:	Street Fighter	132
Chapter 16:	Mephistophilis	136
Chapter 17:	War Games	143
Chapter 18:	A Grave and Gallant City	146
Chapter 19:	*Omnia Mutantur*	155

BLACK MOTLEY 169
WHAT GOD ABANDONED 217
THE ROAD TO JERUSALEM 247

LEFT TO HIS OWN DEVICES

CHAPTER ONE

Masters of Defence

Eighty feet above the London pavement, rapier strikes against dagger.

That sound echoed across the flat roofs with a sliding crash. Cymbals. A salt taste leaked down to Valentine Branwen's lips. She squinted against the sun, accentuating the lines at the corners of her eyes. Flexed her hand, still feeling the tingling impact through her dagger's blade to its hilt.

'Not close enough.' Valentine grinned.

A young woman in a loose tank-top and shorts faced her. The young woman switches on. Valentine watches it: the slight shift of spinal muscles, the replacement of foot position, the vaguely blank look in the eyes. Valentine felt her opponent's tension in her own muscles; let it wash through without touching her. They began to cautiously circle.

The young opponent – and she *is* young, no more than eighteen – holds a swept-hilt rapier in her right hand, and a thirteen-inch dagger in her left hand. The 80 degree sun flashes from the windows of Centre Point. Another young woman sprawls against the door to the stairwell, paging through *Cosmopolitan.* Voices come up from the street below, with the smell of warm lager.

Take it all in. See without seeing. Everything equally important. The bleached blue sky leeches colour from the brick stacks on the roof. Paint peels on the waist-high iron railing at the edge of the building.

Her opponent's rapier lunges.

It has happened before Valentine considers it: the cut-away parry that she does with her dagger, stepping in close to the younger woman's body, and how she places the blade of the dagger (the sole weapon she is using at the moment) quickly against the young woman's belly.

'You're still *thinking* about it, Frankie.'

Frankie Hollister's rounded shoulder muscles shifted. She smelled pleasantly of sweat. Her thick, gold-brown eyebrows scowled. 'You're a lousy tutor!'

Valentine moved away, the concrete gritty under her bare feet. Sun burned her shoulders under her loose white tank-top vest. She let herself become aware of the Gothic plainsong hissing out of her other student's Walkman, and squatted down beside the teenager, her wing of dark red hair falling across her shoulder.

'Start a work-out routine.'

One headphone temporarily lifted. 'It's too *hot*.'

'Rue...'

'Well, I didn't want to be here *any*way. I only put in for it because *she* did.'

'Please yourself, sweetheart.'

A rapier *whicked* through the humid air. Nothing extraneous left her mind. No spurt of adrenaline. Valentine still thought: *eleven o'clock Friday morning and already too hot to practise, there's iced tea in the flat below, drama students are a pain, Rue Ingram is ignoring me out of nothing more personal than idleness.* Only her hand, cued by the sound and Frankie Hollister's ink-blue shadow in her peripheral vision, moved the dagger strongly up to catch the rapier blade between guard and ricasso, before it struck her back.

'You *do not*—!'

She drove sideways and down from her crouch, hitting the concrete with her left shoulder and rolling, and put her right hand into the hilt of her own rapier, and came up gripping it.

Grit clung to her bicep and back, and her knee under her cut-off brown denims. The sun lasered off windows, off car sunroofs far below; pooled shadow at her feet. She took one stride, another: positioned her back as much to the sun as could be.

Hearing only the sound of blades, she missed a metallic groan. The iron fire-escape creaked.

She feels the disparate weights of a blade a yard and a half long, three quarters of an inch wide, in one hand, a blade fifteen inches long in the other. Her dagger foot is advanced, her dagger hand forward; her rear hand and rapier raised, point steadily aimed at her opponent's eye—

'—*do* not *mess about with swords!*'

Frankie Hollister's blade thrusts, low. Valentine hacks it down viciously with her dagger. The younger woman is holding her sword far too loosely, expecting a dojo's usual mannered duelling. Expecting theatre combat.

Valentine's blow bounces Frankie's sword's point off the concrete. The girl yells, her right hand slipping off the hilt and tangling in the steel loops of the curved guard. Valentine steps forward, body-charging. She collects Frankie's sword with her dagger and hammers it left, trapping it across Frankie's body. Her impetus slams the young woman back against a brick stack, trapped by Valentine's weight.

The air jolts out of the young woman's lungs. Her face is pale and shiny. *I may have broken her wrist,* Valentine thinks.

Rue Ingram dropped her magazine and stood up, black mass of hair falling over her pale face and pale shoulders. A girl in a red flower-print dress, with a satin elastic hair-band worn around her wrist, and Walkphones jerked out of her pierced ears. She is looking beautiful, in the way that they do. 'Leave her alone, you cow!'

Valentine pushed her face into Frankie Hollister's, sheathing her dagger without looking, still holding her sword with the blade pointing down. 'I am teaching you to fight for the stage. I can teach you the real thing if you prefer. With live blades.'

A drop of blood bulged on the young woman's arm. Pressure behind it broke the meniscus: it dropped down to her elbow in a sudden run of red.

Valentine flicked her nail contemptuously along Hollister's practice blade. The rebated or blunt edge was flat. A burr of bright steel, knocked up where the blades had made contact, pricked like a metal thorn.

'File that down. Then we'll try again.'

'Cow!' Frankie said. She licked the blood from her arm.

A new voice spoke from the top of the rusting iron fire escape.

'She's right. "Cow". And, I may add, "bully".'

A fat man stepped delicately from the iron platform to the roof. His age indeterminate, he appeared somewhere between thirty and forty. He stood over six foot four inches tall. His white cotton shirt sleeves, rolled up, bulged over bolster-layers of flesh. Great patches of sweat soaked his underarms. His hair shone copper red, bright as fuse wire.

Valentine stared for whole seconds. Caught, she decided dazedly, by seeing him out of context. Hell, he shouldn't be back in this *country*. For something like a minute she took in the vast bulk of him without ever formulating his name.

'I must apologize,' he said gravely to the two younger women. 'She has a fierce temper. God knows I have cause to know that – but do I complain?'

The fat man carefully placed the ivory jacket of his suit on a brick stack, lowered himself on to it, and struck an attitude.

'I do not,' he concluded. 'Although I have been a martyr to this temper of Valentine's—'

'Class dismissed,' Valentine said absently. And when there was no movement in the corner of her eye, she projected her voice without raising it. '*Now.*'

A whiff of sweat drifted across the hot roof. The sun shone on his copper-red hair, curling in a hacked-off crop. Too-blue eyes surveyed Valentine from a fat, freckled face. The man mopped his chins with the tail end of his tie, ignoring the sweat mark that resulted.

'You aren't even going to introduce me,' he said mournfully. 'And such pretty ladies, too.'

'Yeah, introduce us!' Frankie Hollister looked up from massaging her wrist. Valentine noted absently that it was functional, that the girl looked grim, that Rue Ingram was supporting her friend with an arm around those bare shoulders.

'Frankie Hollister, Rue Ingram, two of my students from the London College drama course.'

'I apologize for remaining seated. Most impolite. The effort of the climb.' He gestured with one fat-padded hand at the fire-escape steps. For all that, his immense chest and belly did not rise or fall rapidly, and despite his size he was not panting. He favoured the eighteen year olds with a beam. 'I, of course, am your instructor's husband.'

'You're *married*?' Frankie grunted at Valentine.

Rue only watched, dark eyed.

Valentine was not yet used to the road silence. No noise of engines, of gear-changes and horns. Only faint voices came up from the street, and out of a window somewhere there was music. It would be the silence weighing on her that made her reluctant to break it, and put an absorbency of sweat across her forehead.

'This,' she said, 'is Baltazar Casaubon. Now *go away*.'

'But I've only just got here,' he protested in hurt tones.

'I don't mean you!'

'Oh, good. You want me to stay, then.'

Valentine Branwen took a deep breath, then another. Hyperventilation and the sun made her dizzy. She sheathed the rapier she still held by touch, left thumb at the mouth of her scabbard, right hand guiding the blunt blade home. 'Rue, Frankie; same time next week.'

Baltazar Casaubon lumbered to his feet and began gallantly helping Rue Ingram pack her gear into her sports bag. Valentine folded her arms and watched all the small delays of departure. The sun was heavy on her head. A thirst rasped in her mouth.

When their footsteps had died away down the interior stairs of the building, and Baltazar Casaubon turned away from the roof door, she stared at him for a long minute. He yanked his tie loose. A shirt collar button pinged.

'Shouldn't you be home in the States,' Valentine Branwen said acidly, 'with your *wife*?'

The pedestrianized cobbles of Neal Street run south towards Covent Garden. Baltazar Casaubon indicated a café a few yards further on, as he breasted the waves of shoppers.

'You don't want me in your flat,' he said mournfully. 'I understand. That's your home ground. I don't feel hurt. I can understand that you want to talk on neutral territory. Public, even.'

He seated himself under a meagre London tree at one of the pavement café tables, cramming his bulk with difficulty into one of the uneven-legged plastic chairs. He leaned his elbows expansively on chairs to either side of him, ignoring the glares of overcrowded tourists.

'A mineral water, I think.'

The woman dumped a ski-bag of swords beside him. Although concealed, they rattled metallically. His own meagre luggage – an augmented portable PC in an ABS plastic case – he kept clamped firmly between his swollen ankles.

'How did you find me?' She gestured at the computer. 'That?'

With pudgy fingers he searched in his shirt pocket. He proffered a business card now soggily wet with sweat, curved where it had rested against his chest. The lettering was still legible. *White Crowe Enterprises. Swords and Software.*

'I expected something a bit more high-tech than chasing down my business card!'

'Your changing IDs are hard to follow.' He beamed. 'But I can always find you. Even when you abandon the software industry to become a fight instructor, God save us.'

He let her bring the drinks out, and when she did, he said nothing, only burying his face in his glass and lifting it. His eyes slitted closed against the sun. Clear water spilled down his neck. His chins jerked. He lowered an empty glass.

'Ah...' One fat finger scraped around the inside of the glass, collecting the slice of lemon. He put it in his mouth and chewed.

A lingering odour of petrochemicals and dog-turd pervaded midday. The woman sitting opposite him leaned back into the dappled shade of the sapling. Her white tank-top hung loosely about her shoulders. Her knees under her cut-off brown denim shorts were scabbed. She smelled of exercise-sweat. Sun gleamed from chained bicycles beside her, a man's earring beyond, and her own shadowed eyes.

When he saw her last, her hair was dark red and her eyes tawny. Now her hair has silver at the temples. Her eyes are silver, too. She is wearing mirrorshade contact lenses. He sees himself, white and copper and incredibly small, reflected therein.

'You are my wife,' Baltazar Casaubon observed mildly. 'I distinctly remember the wedding. I wore white. You didn't.'

'*Casaubon!*'

Loud enough for two small Japanese girls to startle as they walk past the table. Baltazar Casaubon graciously inclined his head and murmured, '*Hontō ni sumi-masen.*'

One giggled. '*Dō itashimashite!*'

Baltazar Casaubon's empty glass was almost lost in his huge hand. He jiggled it hopefully, turning to Valentine.

The red-headed woman leaned back in the white plastic chair. Her tone, vehement, nonetheless pitched itself under the ambient street noise.

'I just don't believe this! Remember me? I'm the one whose lover and father of her children turned out to have a wife he was still married to – except you didn't tell me this at the time, and you certainly didn't tell me when we were getting married. Or indeed, afterwards.'

'Oh, *that* wife,' he acknowledged cheerfully.

'You lied to me! You never told me. You never *told* me!'

Casaubon broke eye-contact. Valentine closed her eyes. A time passed in silence.

Giving up on her theoretical generosity, he hailed a waiter, and ordered several bottles: some water, some wine. 'I still don't understand why you're angry.'

'What do you *want*?'

He opened his mouth, but before he could speak, she cut across him.

'No, no, don't bother. I know what you want. You want me to do something for you. I don't know what it is, but you want me to do something for you. You always bloody do. Well, you can just bugger off!'

He attempted an injured look. Not sure of its success, and deciding that the extreme heat must be putting him off, he unscrewed the cap from one of the bottles of water and upended it over his head.

'Oh, *Je*sus.' Valentine Branwen brushed fruitlessly at her sprayed bare arm and tank-top. He distinctly noticed her shift around in her seat and face away from him, staring at the shop windows opposite. Her body language said volubly that she did not know him, had never met him, was nothing to do with him.

He scrubbed a hand through his soaked hair. 'Valentine—'

'Excuse me, miss, is this man bothering you?'

Both Baltazar Casaubon and the red-headed woman looked up at the café's waiter.

'You'll never know ...' Her voice was uneven. 'Thank you. No. It's fine.'

They sat for a while. Lulled by the rhythm of people walking past, up and down Neal Street, into shops and out, and lulled also by what proved to be a quite reasonable wine, Baltazar Casaubon lurched with a jolt out of a half-doze. His water-soaked shirt front and trousers were almost dry. Valentine had leaned her elbows on the unevenly balanced plastic table and was watching him.

She said, 'You went back to her.'

'You asked me to leave,' Baltazar Casaubon riposted, with great dignity. Then he frowned, lips pursed. 'I might almost say, you threw me out.'

'What gives you the right to even *speak* to me?'

The whole street smelled of summer heat. In between the people wearing cotton skirts and jackets, the bare arms and sandalled feet, Casaubon picked out a man looking into the window of the bookshop opposite. The man wore casual jacket and trousers. He also knew which window commanded a reflection of the outdoor café tables.

Quite neutrally, Valentine said, 'I know you're still doing US Defence work.'

'You do keep track of me!' He smiled, smug.

'Not especially. I stayed in contact with a few of our – *my* colleagues, after I left. Sometimes your name gets mentioned. That's all.'

He scratched at his great belly, under his shirt. Another shirt button came away in his hand. He regarded it thoughtfully. 'I don't have any accommodation in London at the present.'

'Now *there's* a surprise.'

'I knew I should have taken you to bed first. That way you'd have been far more amenable.' He frowned. 'What are you laughing at?'

The woman had always had a bark of a laugh. It turned heads at the nearer tables.

'No.' Her mouth was an odd shape. 'No, you don't charm me into whatever it is. I know how you work. After all these years, I know.'

He threw his arms wide, exposing his great belly. Several café patrons ducked. Another shirt button pinged. 'Do it, then! Leave me to sleep on the streets! Why don't you hack into the Home Office and have me deported? Why not—'

Her finger placed on his lips silenced him. He took the hand, pressing each of her knuckles in turn to his lips.

'You're not going to walk away,' Casaubon said reasonably. 'You might as well sit down and let me tell you all about it.'

Valentine Branwen shoved her chair back with strong wrists as she stood. She leaned her knuckles on the table, and her body-weight on her arms.

'Sweetheart, it isn't enough to be funny, and charming. You know, I used to think there would be some way I could tell when you were lying to me? But there isn't. It's just how you are.'

A flash of light reflects from her mirrorshade lenses.

'I don't think you understand why what you did hurt me. That frightens me, because I can't *make* you understand. It frightens me, because I'd take you back tomorrow. Just stay away.'

Baltazar Casaubon leaned back. The plastic chair creaked. Absently, one of his fat hands slid down round his belly to scratch at his crotch. He frowned, sniffed at his fingers, and looked up at her again.

'I would stay away. But I need your help.'

*

The man watching window reflections dawdles back towards the café. He is wearing a different jacket, and sunglasses, and a small child holds his left hand. It is his own child, but then, his particular government department commonly employs such methods.

He sees the unknown woman's palm hit the plastic café table, bottles jolted and rolling. Her voice is loud enough that it turns heads within a radius of thirty metres.

'*No.* I started White Crowe Enterprises to get away from all that. Jesus Christ! I don't see you for eighteen months, and you come back, and it's *this*?'

CHAPTER TWO

Programmed Sunlight

Four days later, on the Monday that they officially closed London, Rue Ingram stood in the narrow court behind Shaftesbury Avenue and Neal Street and burned her wedding dress.

Moisture steamed up, drying in the early dawn heat. Piles of satin fabric lay on the rain-wet cobbles. The wedding dress's cream-and-peach sheen crisped in the flames, consumed, turning black. A stink of paraffin stung her nostrils. She wiped the back of her wrist under her nose.

'Are you sure you know what you're doing, miss?'

The voice interrupted her thoughts. Her head lifted sharply. Old brick buildings surrounded her, four and five storeys high; the iron fire-escape clinging to the wall at the end of the court.

Under its pierced metal steps, a man leaned against the far wall.

A man in his thirties, perhaps; blond, hairy, shambling, scruffy, *big*. Boots laced up to the ankles. Slightly bloused combat trousers and a sand-coloured sweatshirt. A cluttered web-belt locked around his waist gave some further iconographic suggestion of the techno-military.

'What are you doing?'

'What business is it of yours?' Rue Ingram rubbed the heel of her hand into her eye socket, tears slick against her skin. A waft of smoke caught in her throat and she coughed, thickly.

'I'm a cameraman.'

She raised black eyebrows at that.

'For the rolling-news satellite channels.' He tapped his web-belt equipment.

'Yeah? Which one?'

'All of them. Some. A fair proportion. I'm a freelance.'

'Oh, *sure.* I know what *that* means. And before you ask, no, I don't do "modelling".'

Her hair plastered the back of her neck, above the scooped neckline of her black cotton dress. The fire's heat added to the already-hot summer morning. Pain tensioned the cords of her throat.

As if bewildered to find herself there, she said, 'That's it, now. That's it. Finished. The deadline's passed. Oh, hey, I wanted London closed as much as anyone! But he *could* have got residence. He *could* have applied. Bastard.'

The man shifted his back from the brick wall, straightening. Maybe younger than thirties, the beard makes it difficult to tell.

'I'm Miles Godric. Why don't you come for a drink after I'm done here?' He glanced up at the strip of sky visible between buildings, that now glowed a yellow-white, pregnant with heat-wave. 'You look as though you need one.'

Rue Ingram stared at the smouldering cloth at her feet. Bodice and veil burnt to ashes, but the vast panelled skirt barely half consumed. She kicked at it with a sandalled foot. 'Rolling news. You want eye witness stuff. Reactions of the public to Fortress London. You can just go—' she sniffled.

'But you could use someone to talk to.'

'A more foolish man than I—'

The voice cut across Miles Godric's. Rue glanced upwards. Up where the fire escape passed a fourth-storey room, a fat man leaned large arms comfortably on the windowsill. She said, 'Who?— Oh. We met a couple of days back?'

'A man more foolish than I,' Baltazar Casaubon revised, no more grammatically, 'would ask you what you were doing.'

The slightest lift of tone made it into a question.

'I'm burning my wedding dress,' Rue Ingram said dourly, 'what does it look like?'

'It looks like a mess,' he observed, 'and in my backyard, too.'

A conviction of tragedy turning by some sleight of hand to farce took hold of her. The red-haired man leaned out of the window, vastly fat shoulders and torso filling almost all the frame. He pursed delicately-chiselled lips, staring down at the burnt cloth.

'I suppose you and your invisible friend wouldn't like to come up here and talk about this?'

Rue Ingram, bewildered, was about to speak when the shambling man ducked out from under the stairs and stood in the court, where he became visible to the fourth-floor window.

'Would you be Casaubon? Mr Baltazar Casaubon?'

The older man leaned several chins upon his hand, and his elbow on the windowsill, and gazed down at the court as if he gave the matter serious consideration.

'I might be,' he conceded. 'Who are you?'

'Miles Godric; you faxed me to meet you in this ... yard.'

'Godric ...? Godric! Ah. I *know* I faxed you. You were the only name in her address file that looked like a media person. Hate media people,' Baltazar Casaubon concluded diffidently. 'Hungry little rats out for their own aggrandizement.'

Miles Godric shrugged large shoulders, as if he only took in the surface of what the fat man was saying. 'Is that fair?'

'You came, didn't you? I suppose you'd both better come up. Top flat. Go around to the front – the stairs back here are less than safe, I warn you.'

The fat man vanished back inside. Rue Ingram gaped up at the empty window. 'Wh—?'

Miles Godric took her elbow, staring up in the same direction. His grip felt strong. 'I think you should come in. You need to sit down.'

She ran a finger round under the neck of her dress, the black cotton already wet with perspiration. A soft smell of skin made her breathe in sharply, in pain. It seemed that her lover's own smell, incised upon her body-chemistry, remained with her in his absence.

'What's your name?'

She snarled, 'What's it to you?'

The last licking tongues of flame died. The wedding dress, a heap of black-and-cream cloth, lay marked with smoke and dust. She stirred it with her foot, then bent down to rip a section from the hem free and stuff it in her pocket. 'Oh ... Who *is* he, anyway?'

'You don't know Baltazar Casaubon?' Miles Godric pushed damp blond hair out of his face. His eyes, meeting Rue's, were pale, throwing the pupil into sharp relief. Lion-eyes.

'I met him for two minutes last week. If I knew who he is, I wouldn't ask.'

'Last week? I didn't realize he'd been in the country that long. He's – I'd rather explain afterwards.' Godric smiled, broad shoulders unconsciously hunched as if he were attempting not to loom over her. 'It gives me an excuse to ask you out to dinner.'

'Oh, get *real.*' She swung on her heel, the brick walls towering above her; walked out into the street, steeling herself against the blows of the sun's heat. Her eyes automatically slitted. She felt the front vee of her dress for the UV shades hooked there, hurriedly putting them on.

Miles Godric caught up with her as she lost impetus at the junction with Neal Street.

He edged her a few steps down, past shops and cafés, to an entry-phone and entrance, the door already clicking open.

Miles Godric found the tiny fourth-floor kitchen smelled of toast and cat urine.

His gaze slid across the closed door that must lead to the rest of the apartment, took in window, fire-escape, and a man built large enough that manoeuvring between table and sink required his total concentration. Baltazar Casaubon. A man whom he has never met. He knows his reputation. And Miles Godric once had the man described to him closely enough that all is familiar.

Miles hooked his thumbs over his web-belt. 'You don't mind if I record this.'

The small recorder locked to his belt was already online; the larger shoulder-slung one he now set down among the piled dishes on the kitchen table.

Baltazar Casaubon sighed sweatily. Standing, he looked down from what Miles Godric guessed to be six foot four or five; over chins, towering chest, and immense belly only just constrained by his trouser-belt. With a sudden effort he tugged his shirt-tail free of voluminous white trousers and pulled the shirt off over his head.

Momentarily muffled by shirt, the fat man observed, 'Burning your *wedding* dress?'

The dark-haired girl snatched her anti-UV shades off and glared at him as he emerged, ruffled. '*So?*'

Baltazar Casaubon wadded his shirt, regarded it for a moment, then scrubbed his neck and under his armpits with it, and tossed it into a corner of the kitchen. Fine red hairs protruded through the string vest that he wore.

'Well, really,' he said mildly, 'if you must—' And then held out his arms.

Miles watched the girl allow herself to be enveloped in an ursine embrace. Fists clenched at her mouth, she sobbed and bubbled. Miles's eyes stung in sympathy with her gut-wrenching sobs.

He checked his light-levels.

'She a friend of yours, Mr Casaubon?'

'It would seem so.' Looking down, the fat man added, 'Have some hummus.'

The girl stepped back out of his arms and regarded with suspicion the dish of elderly chickpeas that he held out.

'There are—' She coughed, losing throatiness. 'There are whole micro-ecologies evolving in there.'

'Do you know, you remind me of a dear friend of mine. What do you want, boy?'

Miles Godric, at least a decade too old for that 'boy', rested his hip back against the kitchen windowsill. A faint air, already warm, slid into the room; smelling of dust, vinegar, and dog-shit. A less perceptible, more metaphysical scent impinged itself on his instincts. The smell of something happening, times upon which events pivot.

'I got your fax. Yes, I want to record a public announcement by the greatest link-architect of the decade. The greatest renegade link-architect, I should say.'

'Hhrrrmmm...' The fat man scratched in his copper-red hair, studied his nails for scurf, and flicked it on to the floor. Straggling sweaty hair fell over copper brows. A search through his trouser pockets elicited a rubber band. He smoothed his hair back in one ham-hand, fastening the band around the tiny pony-tail at the back of his neck. He met Miles's gaze with guileless blue eyes.

'Even with the advantage of youth on your side,' Casaubon rumbled, 'you may still meet someone whose nerve is of a better quality brass than yours.'

Miles schooled his face to cool interest, moving across the kitchen. Window light cast the fire-escape's angular shadows across Baltazar Casaubon, the leaf-shadows of an iron forest. Good introductory shot.

The nameless girl, sucking a finger loaded with hummus, mumbled something inaudible; removed her finger; concluded, '... *really* don't know why I'm in here ...'

'You're in here because I invited you in.' The link-architect sighed. 'Both of you. For my sins. Do you drink lemon tea?'

Miles nodded agreeably. 'Sure. Tell me—'

'Because if you *do*, there's tea in the cupboard, and a lemon around here ...' Plump-fingered hands waved at the tiny cluttered room. '... somewhere.'

Miles hooked the big recorder around to face the closed door, crossed the room, tried the handle, and pushed it open.

'Good grief,' he said mildly.

He walked through into the long, wide room beyond. Its street window opened to the roofscape across Neal Street. Sun slanted in, hot and white, bleaching the floorboards.

And, hard and harsh, and at right-angles to it, *other* sunlight slanted in from a 'window' filling all of the partition-wall between the room and the next building.

Miles padded forward, the boards creaking under his booted feet, staring at a second sun. At blue sky and a warm sandstone cityscape below; domes, pillars, colonnades, piazzas ...

And touched the finger-thin flat screen monitor fixed to the partition wall. Even close, perfect definition fooled the eye; his stomach churning with the apparent drop outside the apparent window.

He smiled. 'That's what I *call* a monitor.'

The girl passed him, walking to get to what breeze flowed in through the streetside window. Her heeled sandals clicked on the boards, picking a way between a jumble of High Street-available hardware: Apple Macs, Amstrads, old Spectrums, keyboards lashed together in a tangle of wiring; telephone cables running in bundles; monochrome PC monitors stacked three high and a dozen wide.

Miles Godric looked past the gash High Street stuff to the ex-GLC Crays, guessed at the remaining room being similarly occupied, surmised in a moment of sheer amazement the high bandwidth of information going into and out of this flat.

The girl eyed the hardware with momentary interest. 'Hey, I bet you can do stuff with this! But what a kludge.'

'The gear may be a kludge, but the programming must be elegant.'

'I have to go ...' Her suddenly tear-heavy voice bounced dissonances against a background track he at last identified: Tull playing *Said She Was a Dancer*. Her hair, loose and with braids in the tangles, hung down black about her rounded, tanned shoulders; her skin smooth and odorous with summer. Her young, pale face shone with sweat.

True and false windows cast double shadows on the floor. On the big monitor, small green figures over Brunelleschi's dome read 07.45 a.m. Miles focused through the garage-clutter at disc-strewn desks in front of the main window.

'I rarely contact the media,' the large man began, consideringly, from the kitchen doorway.

He was interrupted by the sound of footsteps hammering up the stairs. Miles turned his belt-recorder to the room's further door, letting its arc take in hardware, monitor, and the stained double mattress in the corner.

The door banged opened, hip-shoved by a woman with her arms apparently full of cloth bundles.

Miles Godric felt heat climb up his fair-skinned face with one heartbeat, drain away in the next.

'*Valentine?*' Casaubon startled.

'Hi, Ms Branwen,' the girl snuffled, apparently unsurprised at the woman's presence in the flat.

The newcomer dropped what she carried on the pale floor-boards, in a patch of programmed sunlight. The light blazed back from her clothes: a muddy doublet and black breeches. A fisted hand rubbed the small of her back. Her black hair, obviously a wig, flashed with the blue gleam of a crow's wing. It was styled just short enough to rub the edge of her white linen collar.

'Baltazar ...? What the *fuck* are you doing in here? Jesus Christ, I told you to get lost! I meant it. You're *not* staying here.' Her eyes slitted. 'Did you break in over the weekend?'

'Of course,' the fat man said equably. 'What on earth are you doing dressed up like that?'

Godric thought, This isn't *his* flat. And then he thought nothing, only stared. He registered her voice. The way she stands. Saw her gaze move around the room as immediate anger faded and she realized she was not alone.

'Rue, this isn't a Friday, what are you doing here?'

And then, finally, her gaze intercepted Miles. Her mouth shut up like a trap.

'How very useful,' Casaubon said, 'that you should have a freelance cameraman as a friend.'

'"Friend" isn't quite the word for Miles and me,' the woman said grimly. 'How are you, Miles?'

You didn't return my calls, how would you know how I am? Miles hooked his thumbs under his web-belt and watched her. 'I didn't know you'd moved to Seven Dials, Val. Do I take it I was contacted at random?'

Tiny crow's-feet crinkled at the corners of her eyes as she stared at Baltazar Casaubon. 'By someone poking around in my secure files.'

The woman tugged at her black woollen sixteenth-century knee-breeches, unbuckled a belt from her waist, and let belt, scabbard, and a long sword clatter to the floor. Her fingers fumbled at her scalp. She pulled the black wig off, shaking free a mass of dark red curling hair. It fell across the shoulder rolls of her quilted Renaissance doublet.

'I do a lot of this,' she said coolly. She might have been addressing Casaubon or himself. 'Not that it isn't more trouble than it's worth, with London closed. You should have seen me coming back. I got stopped at every customs post and passport check on the Northern Line.'

A thin *skree* of steel: she squatted and drew her blade and sighted along it, her arm at full extension. 'And if I have to explain one more time that this isn't "a medieval sword", it's a Renaissance military rapier with a swept-hilt, then I swear I'll make a kebab of the person that asks me!'

The girl, Rue, stepped forward. The movement catching Val's eye, she lowered the blade's point to safety. A curious smile tugged at her mouth as she stood.

'To what do we owe the pleasure of *your* company, Rue?'

Baltazar Casaubon said, 'She was out in the court. She was burn—'

'I don't want to talk about that!'

In the silence left by the girl's tearful outburst, Val sheathed her sword.

'Let no one say I don't take my games research seriously.' She scratched her sweaty hair, and smiled sweetly at Baltazar Casaubon. 'Elizabethan historical re-enactment. Wars of Religion. There weren't enough Papists to take the field this time, so I had to leave the heretic Protestants and join them – can't disappoint the public. At least we won. They won. Well, you know what I mean. Somebody won.'

The fat man waved his arms. The floorboards flexed under his advancing weight. '*Damn it, Valentine, you quit because you said you wouldn't do any more simulation war games!*'

'Different games.'

She stirred the cloth bundles with her foot. A cloak, a black leather doublet, a wig, a purse ... effectively a disguise: the more so because it appears to be not disguise but costume.

Miles Godric met her eyes. Silver brilliancies. Deliberately professional, he said smoothly, 'How long have you been back in contact with Baltazar Casaubon?'

She inclined her head, as if to an opponent's touch in fencing. 'It only feels like centuries. Exactly which channel are you with these days, Miles? I've lost track.'

Baltazar Casaubon remarked, 'Primarily with *Hypershift!*, I believe, but not on a contract. One can't choose one's wife's lovers, of course, but one would have thought a better-quality channel ... Damn it, I suspect we're about to star in some gutter-press extravaganza.'

He paused.

'At least, I hope so. I demand to *star*, at the very least.'

'"Demand" to star?' Miles queried.

'In exchange for your presence here. At, if I may say so, one of the great historical events of the decade.' Another pause. Baltazar Casaubon absently dug a finger in one nostril, removed it, and wiped the result on his trouser-leg.

'Event of the century,' he corrected himself. 'If not of several.'

'I want to talk to you,' Val said. Miles winced at the tone that meant trouble. The fat man remained impervious.

The woman walked across the room and squatted by a kettle that stood on the floor, plugging it into the only singly-used power point in the room. A thin steam began to rise. She busied herself with mugs and some black granules from an unmarked paper bag.

'I am *not* going along with this. You're on your own. Both of you,' she added sourly. 'Rue, you want a cup?'

'Uh, no.'

Miles's fingers checked sound-and-vision levels, swiftly and automatically. Excitement over and above the professional flared, without cause or evidence; his breathing shallow with anticipation. He kept his gaze on her bright face. 'Never mind the bloody tea, Val. I never could get a straight answer out of you—'

'Know exactly what you mean,' the fat man rumbled.

'*What* are you not going along with?'

Squatting, she rested her forearms across her knees; tea-spoon in one hand, chipped mug in the other. The soft hairs at her temples were dark red, with strands of purest white. She tapped the bowl of the tea-spoon softly against her full lower lip, only her eyes shifting up to meet his.

'Whatever it is, I'll bet he can't do this without me.'

'Don't be ridiculous,' the fat man said loftily. 'I merely wished to give you an opportunity to participate.'

Spoon clattering into mug, Val threw both down, straightened, crossed the room in swift strides, and was seized up out of her path into an embrace by massive arms; Baltazar Casaubon's face buried in her neck, her arms about him, his hands grabbing her so that the linen shirt rode up out of the back of her breeches.

She removed herself with two practised blows from her elbows.

'Oh bloody hell – Miles, we're out of sugar. Suppose you go out and get some. We'll talk when you get back. Talk *alone*.'

'But it was Mr Casaubon I was to film!'

'*Miles, don't argue.*'

Miles Godric collects cameras, recording equipment, and his shaken thoughts.

'Sure,' he says. 'Twenty minutes.'

CHAPTER THREE

Simulations

Rue Ingram was barely aware, through swallowed weeping, of the door banging behind Miles Godric.

The fight instructor flopped on to the mattress, on the floor. She rolled up her sleeves, dabbing a clear liquid from a bottle on to the bruises on her arms. Then she took off her woollen breeches and silk hose, stretching her barefoot legs. Her linen shirt covered her to mid-thigh. One large yellow and purple bruise marked her shin, lesser ones spreading in a chain from thigh to knee.

Hurts, Rue thought.

'That was *my* interview! How dare you interrupt?'

'That was my ex-lover! Who gave you the right to poke around in my encrypted files?'

'*I* shall make tea,' the fat man said pointedly, removing himself and the kettle to the kitchen.

Rue picked up and unsheathed Valentine's military rapier and swung it experimentally. Fake sunlight from the big monitor flashed. Knuckleguards scraped her fingers. The weight of it pulled at her wrist.

'You really *fight* with this thing? Not stage fighting? Not to a script?'

The older woman said, 'Yes, I fight.'

The blunt edge chilled Rue Ingram's thumb. She let the sword fall on the stained mattress. Tears pushed over her lower lids. She pulled back from emotion.

'What's that smell?'

'Witch hazel,' the woman said. 'It helps bruises heal faster.'

Not the usual Friday tutor. No professional *hauteur*, only a pragmatic intention to treat her minor injuries, regardless of dignity. The woman's eyes were edged with faint lines, and the bones of her cheeks stood out under taut skin. Her body under the loose skirt moved with a compact energy.

Rue wandered aimlessly across the cluttered room, the bevelled screens of old monitors reflecting her a dozen times. The rattle of crockery and muffled curses sounded in the kitchen.

'See this?' Rue reached into her dress pocket. Her hand cupped the thin weight of a cut-throat razor. She flicked it out and open. Metal snicked. Valentine Branwen came instantly alert, with a tremor of complete responsiveness to the position of the knife.

Slightly shaken by the difference in her, Rue said, 'See that? When I fight, I don't mess around with blunt blades. I'm not *playing*.'

'You'd be better off if you were.' Inevitable laughter, sardonic and slow, faded from Valentine's voice. 'You've never used it.'

'I will! If I need to, I will. I might need to. It's protection.'

Rue wrist-flicked the razor shut and dropped it back into the pocket of her dress. The weight gave the black cotton one more unnoticeable crease. She paced restlessly. From the kitchen came an increasingly pointed rattle of crockery.

'Jesus, Ms Branwen, don't you ever walk down the street? Half of Former Europe is living rough on your doorstep! It's *why* they've closed London. To keep the refugees out. You ought to be on our side, you have to live here too!'

Valentine Branwen pulled the linen shirt off over her head. She shook her hair loose, emerging from her sole remaining garment. She stood, naked, muscle-weary, arms raised; the room's double sunlight blazing back from her white skin. A few dark red hairs feathered the aureoles of her breasts, and her triangle of lush hair further down glittered reddish-black. Rue's breath caught under her sternum.

Valentine said crisply, 'Do you want to know the only thing I learned from playing soldiers? It's how *often* you die ... and don't get up again when it's game-over.'

Grief wiped out momentarily by anger, Rue had no vision of how all the subdued language of her body shifted, transmuted to a hard power and determination; a metamorphosis from grub to skull-winged black butterfly. 'This city is my home! These people should go back where they came from!'

Dark oblate bruises marked Valentine's upper arms, and the outside of her thighs. The older woman fingered each reflectively, ticking them off, and glanced up. 'There comes a distressing tendency to total up lumps and bruises as if they were real battle scars.'

She felt under the mattress on the floor and pulled out a sleeveless white t-shirt and a crumpled pair of white Levi 501s. Standing to dress, she added, 'Not that there haven't *been* scars. It's when you catch yourself becoming proud of that, that you know you've lost it.'

From the open kitchen door, the fat man's voice rumbled, 'Damn it, Rose of the World, you have a macabre taste in relaxation.'

'*I told you to get out!*'

'*And* you know better.'

Turning abruptly, the woman's bright face shone against the monitor-skies over Florence. Rue almost looked for the breeze that swayed the cypresses to move the woman's hair. The multiple humming of hard discs sounded thick, like honey.

'Rue, sweetheart, someday I'll show you some of the stuff I'm working on.' The woman's thumb slides along a shelf of labelled discs. *Shatterworld. Lace and Leather. Tactica.* 'For now, you're going to have to love me and leave me. I need to talk to—'

'You can't— ' Dizzy, breathless, balance gone from that centre that lies at the base of the skull, Rue Ingram forced herself to begin again. 'You can't have all this and just write *games* software with it! It's obscene. Nobody over twenty-five ought to be allowed to handle technology. You don't understand what it's *for*.'

'It's for commercial interactive multi-user Virtual Reality games at the moment,' Valentine said grimly, 'and it's for paying my bills. There are worse games.'

Rue suddenly snivelled.

Baltazar Casaubon, with a tray, in what he obviously supposed to be an undertone, rumbled, 'She's *upset*. I found her outside, burning a wedding dress.'

'A *wedding* dress? Why the hell would she – oh, never mind. Not now.' Valentine sighed. 'Here. Have this tea. Sugar's good for shock.'

Casaubon, whose tea it was, looked momentarily affronted. Then, with a grand gesture, he shoved a teetering stack of machine code printouts from a chair. 'Sit down, Rue. I shall not ask questions. I am not an inquisitive man.'

Alone, in someone else's flat, not wanting to think, not wanting now to be alone, Rue doggedly continued.

'You just spread *crap*. I've played VR games. All this bullshit about multi-national corporations with artificial intelligences, street runners with surgically implanted data ports. It isn't going to *be* like that.'

'No. It isn't going to be like that. It already isn't like that.' Valentine seated herself cross-legged on the sun-warmed floorboards by Rue's feet, moving with a fight instructor's grace. 'Do you know what I used to do for a living?'

'What?' Rue stared.

'I flew virtual F16s. Or, I should say, I *wrote* virtual F16s. And virtual M1 Abrams tanks, Apache helicopter gunships, aircraft carriers, satellite submarine detectors, cruise missiles. Half of the UCS military's SIMNET is mine. And I wrote the landscapes for wars. The reason the landings in Iberia worked at all is because the infantry knew the Virtual country backwards, forwards and sideways before they ever got there in the flesh ...'

Valentine smiled.

'I used to talk to brat-hackers in the States. They'd harangue me about Drexler and the nanotechnology revolution, and how we're going to send Von Neumann machines to the stars, and meantime down here there's going to be nothing but corrupt and outdated nation states powerless before the subversive hacker anarchy ... It makes good copy for commercial games. And I like it.'

'You're sad,' Rue sneered.

'I know the alternative. You start off with smart shells – and you end up with bolt-action rifles, making your own ammunition. Former Europe. Urban civil war, where the water and the power and the medical supplies break down; and you won't be programming anything because the telephone network doesn't function, and the dark fibre cablenet has been blasted sky high, and even the high tech sensors on military equipment have degraded ...'

'My – this guy I know – he's in the Forces ...' Rue rubbed the heel of her hand across her eyes, and then under her nose. '*You* don't like the information revolution because it's wiping out your world; how they did things in your day!'

'I wasn't aware my day was over,' Valentine said, not waspishly. 'Sweetheart, I think your cyberpunk dystopias are ... infinitely fragile and valuable. Looking at technology on its own is naive. The old power structures can swallow hacker anarchy and never burp.'

Baltazar Casaubon, returning with his own tea mug, stated, 'The last thing that child stands in need of at the moment is a lecture.'

Caught up in the argument – anything but think or feel – Rue yelled, 'But they don't understand it! They don't understand how the world *is* now.'

Valentine Branwen buttoned her white jeans taut across her flat stomach.

'Sweetheart, they don't have to understand it. You don't have to understand something to exploit it. And now, if you'll excuse me, I have an intruder to throw out of *my* flat.'

Gridlocked, abandoned cars blocked Monmouth Street and snarled into a metal kaleidoscope around the pillar of Seven Dials. Closed London's sparser crowds dotted the street. Miles Godric identified the nervous, card-clutching men and women in bright clothes as foreign tourists, and those mixed in with the locals as refugees.

His boots jolted on the hot, cracked paving stones.

Warm air moved against his face. He touched the microphone attachment on his web-belt shoulder strap.

'Val Branwen, ex-star of the US Department of Defense, is back in contact with her husband Baltazar Casaubon, notorious hacker, data-thief, and possibly the 90s' most versatile and intelligent constructor of hypermedia architecture. It seems neither deliberate nor willing. But does it imply she's doing more than write commercial games software? What announcement does Baltazar Casaubon want to make to the public ...? Is this connected with rumours of an explosion of discoveries coming out of the Multi-Net as more of it comes online? Val hasn't changed. I've heard far too much about Baltazar Casaubon from her. Am I only seeing him through her eyes?'

'Spare some change, please? Spare some change, please?'

A woman in filthy man's overalls leaned out of the gaping door of a BMW. Her red-rimmed eyes fastened on Miles. Her hair shone pepper-and-salt through the shattered windscreen, bright with sunlight and grease.

The inside of the car was draped with old cloth, rucked up into rat's-nests on the back seat. No sign of who might have owned it, once; it took on the contours of the homeless now.

Miles Godric met her flat gaze; saw a tinge of anger in the woman's face. Curious refugees: leaving a six-bedroomed house and two Mercedes cars abandoned in the wreckage of Paris or Florence; inarticulate, dispossessed of the middle class.

'Spare-some-change-sir-please.'

On the opposite side of Earlham Street two men in late middle age shared the contents of a bottle in a brown paper bag. Their blotched red scalps almost met, bent over it. One's gaze flicked up, met Miles's and skidded across him as if he left no retinal image.

'I don't carry money,' he explained, his voice gentling, 'I'm not a tourist. Sorry, love. Look, try down Shaftesbury Avenue.'

Her hand closed over his forearm, broken nails digging into his skin. Fast and without fuss, he dug his own nails into the joint of her wrist, forcing her fingers to release.

The usual unhappy thought went through his mind: Someday *I* shall end up like this.

The Seven Dials pillar gleamed, its faces blue and gold in the rising sunlight. Counting exits, Miles Godric crossed two streets, entered a Chinese supermarket, and emerged a few minutes later with sugar, rice, noodles. Those who lived in the abandoned cars looked dully at him as he passed. He thumbed the smallest belt-camera online, relying on picture compensation to edit out his movements, and scanned the long line of cars.

Background material, he tells himself.

Finally frustrated, he checks his watch, sits on the bonnet of a broken down Jaguar, and takes his subnotebook PC out of his backpack. Practised hacker access to the MultiNet via a mobile phone link gives him, within a quarter of an hour, tax and health records on Val Branwen (uninformative), the telephone bill for modem use to the Neal Street flat (phenomenal, but still less than it should be), bank statements that feature regular small payments to odd sources (unspecified), and no information on Baltazar Casaubon whatsoever. Querying a civilian and a military subNet in California adds nothing.

No record of her marriage. No record of any association with Casaubon. Some mention of himself, twelve months ago. Otherwise squeaky clean.

'Someone's interested in you, Val ...'

He has seen this kind of thing before when hackers tamper with their own records, but this goes beyond that. The marks of absence are over everything. It appears to be very similar to what happens when security forces encrypt information because they themselves are interested in it.

For a minute it bothers him more that his name and the address in Docklands are on file than it does that the PanEuropean Security Services are obviously monitoring Val Branwen, and have been for some time.

Since before Baltazar Casaubon went 'missing' in the USA, in fact.

Miles Godric walked back up out of Earlham Street. A sudden stench hit his nostrils. He looked down and swore, and scraped his ankle-boot against the curb, scraping off the worst of the wet horse manure.

Up ahead, where Neal Street and Monmouth Street come to an intersection with Shaftesbury Avenue, a rider slumped along on a hack mare with the motion of a sack of potatoes. Ban the internal combustion engine and they'll use anything.

A dozen or so tourists, bright in crimson and azure shirts, raise their cameras to photograph the horse and rider.

He leaned his shoulder against the entry buzzer.

No answer.

Checked his watch: thirty minutes.

No answer. At all.

The outer door closed behind Rue Ingram as, finally, she left.

Silence in the flat. Early morning sun.

'Why don't you,' Valentine asked, pronouncing each word with individual precision, 'just fuck off and die?'

Baltazar Casaubon grabbed at his throat with both hands, fingers sinking into multiple chins. He gurgled. His body stiffened from head to heel. He tipped backwards, and fell.

Pivoting on his heels, he pitched backwards and hit the floor, rigid as a board. Three desks, a monitor, and two filing cabinets jolted six inches into the air and crashed down. Dust shot up from between the floorboards. A stack of discs ricocheted down the metal shelving.

Valentine, simultaneously thinking *I am* not *going to laugh* and *Is he hurt?*, snorted uncontrollably. She wiped snot and spit on to her bare wrist. Her eyes watered.

Baltazar Casaubon remained suspiciously still.

'I hope you *have* cracked your skull,' Valentine snarled.

Casaubon lay still. Without moving, he murmured, 'They'll never get me down those stairs on a stretcher. I shall starve to death on your floor.'

Amusement vanished in irritation. 'Casaubon!'

'After all the effort I go to, to entertain you...'

'I don't want to be entertained, I want you out of my life.' She sighed and sat down on the mattress. 'That's not true, of course. What I want is you back in my life, but without all those annoying little faults. Bigamy. Burglary. That kind of thing... How's that for irrational? You are what you are. And if you attempt to seduce me while I'm in this mood—'

Casaubon's hand scuttled back to his side.

'—I shall rip your testicles off, varnish them, and wear them as ear-rings. Who knows, maybe I'll start a mass trend.'

'How many testicles do you think I've *got*?'

His mock alarm brought her close to laughter.

'Perhaps you could re-grow them for each occasion,' she said whimsically. 'A new fashion line. Baltazar's Balls. Look, this is all very nice, but now you're leaving.'

He lifted his head, regarded the room, and flopped back to the horizontal.

'I could try, this thing is more important than both of us?' he said hopefully. 'I guess the troubles of two little people don't amount to a—'

'Don't you dare!'

Valentine rested her arms on her knees, sitting foetally; after a while she pulled her discarded linen re-enactment shirt into her arms and sat with her nose buried in it, smelling the ingrained scent of wind and turf.

'Are you going to tell me what this is all about?' she demanded.

'Of course not,' Casaubon said reasonably. 'Somewhere out on those roof-tops is a vibration-sensitive laser microphone trained on our windows – do you want me to tell the whole *world*?'

Valentine sighed.

'I suppose we can always go for brutal isolation.'

CHAPTER FOUR

The Language of Angels

'Civilians talking about war,' observed the PanEuropean Minister of Defence, 'is like virgins talking about sex, I have always thought.'

Flight Lieutenant Wynne Ashton hesitated. The middle-aged woman sitting in the co-pilot and gunner's seat of the Mark 7 Lynx helicopter turned her head and smiled at him. A helmet hid her blonde hair. Her voice sounded through his headphones again.

'I wonder what civilian *experience* of war counts as? Heavy petting, perhaps?'

'Uh, yes, ma'am. No, ma'am. I mean, I don't know, ma'am.'

Ashton unnecessarily repeated the last three items on his flight check list, thumbed the cut-out to advise the tower that he was ready, and glanced back once over his shoulder. The cramped interior of the Lynx, made even more cramped by the very basic eight-man seating riveted in, was full of men in suits with shades and, he suspected, Heckler and Koch P7s and MP5s. The roar of the turning rotors a foot or so above the cabin roof meant non-radio-mediated speech was impossible.

Acknowledgement came through from the tower. The sun sparkled across the canopy; the leather seats were hot to the touch. Ashton, without fuss, lifted off from the French airbase and up and forward into the July sky.

'Good machine,' her voice said.

'The Mark 7's OK.' He eased the cyclic forward.

'You've flown combat missions.'

Nose down, to obviate at least some of its forward visibility problems, the Lynx drove ahead. He took the helicopter up to two thousand feet, gaining a few degrees of welcome coolness, and the machine dropped a step in the air as they came over the edge of the hills outside Rouen.

'Yes, ma'am.'

'Tours of duty in Central Europe, in Iberia, and West Africa.'

Ashton thought at first that, being a politician, the woman had taken a quick flick through his file to make him feel noticed. However, the likelihood – or *un*likelihood – of the PanEuropean Defence Minister bothering about the good opinion of a Rapid Reaction Force chopper pilot who is purely taking her from Rouen to London with appropriate cargo of security people...

'You didn't take out residence in London in time, Lieutenant.'

'No, ma'am.' Awkward, he wanted to vocalize a set of confused feelings that had been clear at the time. That it had seemed unjust to use his military qualifications to get him residence when that would be the only reason for his acceptance. That he would feel exposed and isolated in London.

'Although,' the woman's voice changed slightly, 'you were engaged to be married, Lieutenant Ashton?'

The Lynx drifted sideways a little, and he corrected, corrected again, and found himself with the first pilot-induced oscillation since training school. Behind the mirrored visor of helmet and HUD he could feel his skin grow hot.

'You obviously know a lot about me, ma'am.'

She ignored that effortlessly. 'Engaged to a girl called Rue Ingram. I don't want to know why you decided not to marry her, Lieutenant. I do want to know about Rue Ingram. What she does. Who she is. I thought you might be able to tell me.'

The air thrummed, and the grey disc of the rotor blades held steady in their apparent position towards the top of the windscreen. The Lynx chuntered north across the void at a hundred and eighty miles per hour; sky clear, no wind, rising thermals.

'I don't know what you want to know,' Ashton said. 'She's a drama student. She works part-time in a London shop. A theatrical costume shop, round the back of Shaftesbury Avenue. She lives in Seven Dials as a resident. She's going to be nineteen this year. She doesn't drive. She's not very mature, ma'am – I mean, she doesn't understand why I couldn't be in the UK all the time, or see her all the time. I don't think she wants to do anything much except talk to her girlfriends.'

Curiosity overcame military formality.

'Ma'am, why do you want to know about Rue?'

Johanna Branwen, the Minister of Defence for an area from the Carpathians to Carthage, said, 'I like to know what company my daughter is keeping.'

Water hissed, creasing back from the slow prow of the *Carola.* A smell of rank Thames water permeated the deck of the tourist riverboat. The smell of the estuary, not of the sea.

Casaubon, in view of the public nature of the place, had let himself be persuaded into wearing a shirt. Now he was not entirely certain whether the oversized, short-sleeved silk garment with the red hibiscus-flower pattern was a mistake.

'They'll know you're in England.' The woman watched a big Saab paralleling their course on the Embankment. She wore her hair differently, and two years longer. 'I've got used to having my phone tapped and my electronic mail monitored.'

'They will know I'm in England. I'm counting on it.'

'What?'

A computer with no modem, no incoming fibre or data discs, cannot be hacked into or corrupted: it is in brutal isolation. Casaubon pitched his voice under the racket of a hundred and fifty *bona fide* tourists, driven out of central London's canyon-streets by the reflecting hammer blows of heat. Difficult to pick individual voices out of the ambient noise background. When faced with the subtlest surveillance techniques available, old-fashioned physical isolation often works.

'No one will touch *you.*' Valentine sounded cynical. 'You're the leader in your field. They'll cut you a lot of slack before they pull the plug. They think there isn't anyone else who can do what you can do.'

'The same was said of you.'

Sweat stuck his shirt to his back between his shoulder blades, and clung warm and damp where it was belted under his trouser waistband. Sweat left Valentine's face shiny, where she turned it up to the sun. The red flush of a burn already marked her cheekbones and the tops of her shoulders.

'I'm taking a chance, little one,' he said. 'I think that when you did what you did—'

'Which was what, exactly?' she bristled.

'You ran away from California and stuck your head in the sand,

and decided to let mummy protect you while you piddled away your life on PC games...'

'I don't have to hear this!'

'You can hide here under your mother's security blanket for as long as you like, but you're not living! Damn it, woman, you have responsibilities!'

Buildings seemed to jut up directly from the flat water. Sun-coloured brick warehouses, office buildings with the interior walls scraped out, and goldenrod and birch saplings growing from the crevices. The river here smelled of dust. The noise of the riverboat engine echoed back from the walls of Docklands.

'As I say,' Casaubon continued, 'when you ran away, I don't think it was because of the little differences we were having.'

'About whether you'd actually married me or some bimbo, you mean?'

'She isn't a bimbo, she's a perfectly respectable doctor of medicine. You shouldn't let your natural jealousy warp your judgement. But I digress... I think, little one, that the reason you left California wasn't the "project failure" you told the Department of Defense had occurred. I think you *solved* the particular problem you were working on. I think you solved the algorithm. And then you ran.'

Nothing, then, for three quarters of an hour; nothing but trying to soak in every whisper of coolness from the river water. They chugged further downstream, in a wider river, in sight of the Thames barrier. He saw her shading her eyes against light off the water too bright to look at.

She said at last, 'Why travel so many thousand miles...?'

'Because the same thing has happened to me. I made a breakthrough in the area *I* was working in. And, like you, I destroyed all records except my personal ones, evaded security, left the US, and... vanished.'

The tourist commentary crackled unheard over speakers. The boat reversed its course. Women in cotton dresses smelling of sour perspiration changed their children's nappies. The White Tower floated by on the bank, lost in leafy tops of plane trees.

Baltazar Casaubon gave a smile of surpassing sweetness.

'Besides, little one, I assumed that you would still have all your contacts at the Yates Hospital research department.'

They came back almost as far as the pleasure boat dock before she nodded an ambiguous *yes.*

*

Miles Godric woke, still huddled waiting into the doorway of the Neal Street flats. There were a few pennies in his lap, and one of his lighter camcorders was missing. He swallowed the foul taste in his mouth and scrumpled his sun-hot hair. The skin on his nose was crisp.

'You took your time.' He focused on his watch. 'Jesus, it's three o'clock in the afternoon!'

Their two shadows cooled and covered him. Miles saw that the fat man now wore a scarlet shirt, and a pair of scarlet cotton shorts, with which his copper hair seemed expressly designed to clash.

Val Branwen unlocked the street door. 'You'd better come up.'

Baltazar Casaubon cupped a huge and protective hand around the woman's shoulders. While not appearing to be appreciated, he was not immediately rebuffed.

Miles Godric stood and followed. His belt camera panned angles, searching the sunlit stairs as he climbed up after them to the fourth floor flat. Liquid soaked the centre back of his t-shirt. The air seemed liquid also, like breathing mud or fur. He leaned against a landing window, breathing hard, sweating harder. For a moment he remained, head down, resting his forearms on the sill, until the pain of the sun-hot wood made him move. He lifted his head.

No smell of exhaust. No noise of vehicles.

From a mile south the sweet sourness of Thames water drifts to him; that and the dung-and-cooking-oil smell of the streets. The heat hollowed his lungs. Visions of the dirty green river and the cooler air over it haunted his flesh with tangible desire.

One summer when we all lived on Neal Street…

Possible opening words for the video commentary spooling through his head. Variant styles. Sweat stung his eyes as he blinked at the pale sky, the world held in a translucent bubble of heat: 90°F and rising.

Hard rock music pounded through the third floor flat's door. It cut off abruptly when the door to Val's flat closed behind him. The woman balanced on the balls of her feet; a lithe stance ready to take off in any direction. Heat slicked the red hair damply to her temples and neck. Sweat darkened the white t-shirt between her breasts.

'Smile for the cameras.' A demure sarcasm sounded in her voice.

'Miles, I've set up a demonstration.'

'But you haven't been back here.'

'I borrowed the Yates Institute's terminals. They're used to seeing me there for story research.'

'Sorry. Not awake. I – that's a private medial research facility?' Belatedly, he gave her the statutory hypermedia warning. 'You're online and on record.'

'Good,' Casaubon approved.

Miles straightened, hands at his belt, touching to check, automatically, the standard levels of light and colour. The online code burred under his fingers, home base responding. Metal and plastic slicked his wet fingers. He walked through into the apartment's double sunlight.

'I'll talk you through some of it,' the woman said.

'Mmmmrgh!' Casaubon protested, wandering back in from the kitchen. He slumped into the swivel chair in front of the wall monitor, a bowl cushioned in the crook of one arm, from which he ate with a tablespoon. He waved the spoon mutely.

Valentine Branwen licked a spatter from her bare arm. 'Oh, you're welcome to it if you prefer to—'

She made a face and interrupted herself, looking over the link-architect's shoulder and inspecting the contents of his bowl, which appeared to be lumpy and consist of various shades of pink. 'What *is* that?'

Baltazar Casaubon removed an emptied spoon from his mouth. 'Loganberry icecream and tuna-fish.'

'Oh.' The woman paused. 'Fine.' She added thoughtfully, 'I see.'

The fat man put another loaded spoonful into his mouth and said indistinctly something that might have been, 'With tabasco sauce.'

Val glared at him. 'It's *your* damn demo. *You* do this.'

'Oh, very well ... I, ah, am a link-architect. I do the architecture of information space; that is, a database cross-indexed to within an inch of its life.'

'We can assume some background knowledge among *Hypershift!*'s viewers,' Miles said more acidly than he intended. 'Tell me what's new.'

The link-architect, Casaubon, put his bowl down on the floor and padded amiably over to stand beside Miles Godric, resting his bolster-arm across Miles's shoulders. 'You understand, it's the freedom from linear text. When it's possible to access texts at any point instantaneously, we have what is sometimes called information-flight. *All* information co-exists, simultaneously ... the creation of indexes, cross-indexes, and maps to where one is in the information-space become crucial, hence,' he inclined his head, 'myself. Minds become disorientated when information comes in no linear progression. That's why one needs link-architecture – the creation of ordered multiple links between pieces of information.'

The fat man paused.

'Is that good, do you think? I can do it again, if you like. Do you think,' he peered at Miles's belt, 'that you caught my good profile?'

'The channel will do their own voice-over in any case.' Miles took a deep breath. 'That way it won't sound stilted.'

He needed both hands, then. Val Branwen threw him a headset and gloves, and he stood, dangling the goggles in his hands for a minute and looking at her quizzically. A red tendril of hair was plastered to her forehead by sweat. In her sallow face, her eyes gleamed reddish-gold.

'Put them *on*,' Val said, overly patient. He couldn't help but grin. He cabled the set into the most powerful of his camcorders. As he pulled the goggles over his eyes, he saw her have the grace to give him her own most self-mocking smile.

VR space.

A pale light glows in the depths, grey and glittery, with a hint of wings. The airless room tightened about his throat. He swallowed. The gloves are hot on his hands.

'How does it operate?'

'No different from any other. Hold on, let me just ... oh fuck it – wait a minute ...'

A faint tremor of his flesh argued a movement cancelled before it began: the hooking of his thumbs under his belt. The solid web-belt, with its comforting heaviness, from which direct-line cameras and sound detectors hang like weapons. His boots are hot on his bare feet, but their heels sustain him. His uniform a carapace to bear up and shape what lies within.

A breath of hot wind touched his cheek. From the window? He tensed.

Around him the pale light opens. A gothic roof arched up into vaults of darkness. He squinted at the stained-glass windows, eyesight adjusting, moved forward and cracked his knee against clear air.

'Sweetheart, you're too old to walk around when you're in VR...'

Valentine Branwen's voice comes from frighteningly close at hand. The other side of a high definition image in which the walls are fifty feet away and the wide tombstone-studded floor between Miles and them empty.

He grinned approvingly, moving his hands. Jerkily, the nave of Westminster Abbey shifts around him. The pixel images are blocky, geometric, cartoon colours. The marble busts that clustered in niches along the walls began to speak. He pointed a gloved finger.

'... hypertext and the problems of information flood...'

'...late nineteenth-century Romantic poetry...'

'... steam engine, and the homogenization of Time...'

'... food additives addressed...'

'... battle of Plassey and consequent colonial expansion...'

Miles turned his head, knowing the field and focus of his hardware independent of his movements. The busts of appropriate statesmen, poets and soldiers, scientists and academics mouthed their particular subjects, white marble lips moving simultaneously in animation.

Light slanted down from the gothic windows, casting rainbow shadows on the flagstones. Each tombstone set flat into the floor had a named subject. Miles pointed his gloved finger at the one nearest to him.

The cathedral shifted, jolting as if a hand-held camera swung round and pointed downwards. The tombstone rose up, with a gritty squeak, and the high-definition viewpoint jolted down the steps into a crypt beneath, where each coffin was labelled with subsections of that subject. He grabbed at air, his balance gone, and bashed his knuckles against something in the invisible apartment.

A rumbling voice murmured, 'Let me follow up a few flight-paths for you.'

Inner ear fooled by the eye, he feels his muscles tense and relax. The crypt floor drops away. The world folded up and poured itself into one of the labelled coffins, that unfolded out into structured shelves, ladders, webs...

He flew.

Fast as snowflakes in a blizzard, word- and image-menus flashed up before his eyes. A storm of pictures, sorted so rapidly that he could not comprehend. Information flight through video tracks, sound recordings, statistical charts, novels, and dense texts.

'As far as I can see,' Miles spoke blindly, 'this is standard Art-of-Memory indexing: you find your way around Virtual Reality by associating icons.'

'It's a little more sophisticated than the standard version, but the principle's the same.'

'This isn't the breakthrough you indicated.'

Val's voice said, 'This? Oh, this was just Baltazar proving to me that what he's got, works. The breakthrough isn't anything to do with Art-of-Memory indexing. Look, I'll run my demo.'

He slips off one glove for a minute and checks his belt equipment. It is downloading this quite happily. Glove on.

'Running *School of Night*,' Val's voice says, and the audio hiss runs over her voice, and becomes a tacky lutes-and-sackbut introductory track. Val never did think much of music, he remembers that.

The glittering greyness becomes a room with white walls and a low, beamed ceiling. The boards are bare. Men in stockinged feet move about the floor. They are men in ruffs, doublets and knee breeches, practising swordplay. Three, five, ten figures at least, in a dazzling display of multiple virtuals.

Miles recognized Val's preoccupations. He thinks he knows, has seen in one of her books, the woodcut she has chosen to animate here. It gives him an odd stab of familiarity, and then a moment of insecurity: he is, after all, blind with goggles and deaf with audio playback, in a room with his ex-lover and her husband whom he cannot see.

The pixel quality has little of the geometric blockiness of most commercial VR. Only a faceted quality remains: the walls, the swords, the faces of the duellists glitter as if covered with fish scales. Miles pushes his hand forward. The specifically engineered tolerances of the pressure glove give him a feel, albeit muffled, for the hilt of the sword on the bench beside him.

Red letters run across the top of his vision, exactly where (he notes wryly) a military HUD would run. ALL THE WORLDS A STAGE™. *A ShakespeareWorld Franchise Production.* It blips out before company and copyright details appear: obviously not pasted in yet.

'You must never,' a main character says, walking into his field of vision from the left, 'grip your man's weapon unless you have upon your left hand the *guanta da presa,* which is to say, a gauntlet with fine mail rings sewn upon the palm of it. Then you may catch at his sword-hand wrist when you will, and pull it across your body to twist and break the small bones of the elbow.'

'That,' says another main character, who seats himself on the bench at Miles' right, 'is Master George Silver, who is our chiefest exponent of the Art of Defence. And yet, sir, there are other arts, for those who would investigate them.'

The sound quality is good, although to his ear it is perfectly obviously Val's voice run through a synthesizer.

'You may parry to strike down his sword arm,' says the grey-haired, stocky man in Elizabethan dress, swinging a sword with a simple cruciform hilt as if it weighs nothing, demonstrating upon the empty air. 'And when you have struck his arm down, strike your hilt up full into his face, and send the bones of his nostrils up into the brain and so slay him. Or kick up his heels with your left foot, and throw him a great fall. Good day to you, Master Marlowe.'

Miles turns his head and the viewpoint world adjusts itself with no lag at all. Now this one *is* an animate portrait: the painting of a red-haired twenty-four year old in a flashy doublet, arms folded, eyebrows black, cheeks red as a young boy's. The poet and playwright Christopher Marlowe.

Experimentally, he quotes, '"All who love not boys and tobacco are fools".'

'Sir, I could have heard you quote other of my words with more satisfaction, but few with more pleasure.' The 'portrait' Marlowe is different full-length, stockinged feet stretched lazily out, a long-stemmed pipe in one hand, the implicit smile become a grin. 'Now, sir, to business. Are you initiate in the Art you see here, or would you become initiate in others? The play of swords is sweet, the play of minds sweeter; sweetest of all, sweet magick, tis thou has ravished me.'

It is commercially obvious which the cue words are. Miles Godric suggests. 'An initiate in magic?'

'A true science magick is, master; full of lines, characters,' a blip here, which Miles guesses to be an ill-remembered quotation, and the audio track picks up again, synchronized with the red lips, 'and many do practise it here in Gloriana's kingdom. Abjuring the illusions of the common day, we enrol ourselves a School of

Night, wherein we may seek all knowledge, forbidden or no.'

Voice track cuts out. The airless grey abruptly returns. In mid-air a crack opened into emptiness. Into unbearable brightness – the sunlight of Neal Street. In peripheral vision he saw more. Her hands lifted the goggles. The dark glowing air was patched with unreality.

Miles Godric stripped off the gloves, his skin sticky with the summer heat. He blinked at Val with the feeling, familiar from commercial VR games, of having been gone a long time somewhere indefinable.

'*Some* of your enthusiasms wore off on me,' Val Branwen commented. 'I'm calling my expert system "Marlowe" ... It's a follow-up to the big game I did last year; I had an expert system, "Virgil", games-mastering INFERNOWORLD™.'

Baltazar Casaubon muttered, 'Oh *dear*.'

'Rumour on the MultiNet has it that—' The feeling of having been gone a long time, flying through information space, stayed with him. '— that what you're talking about is DNI. True?' he persisted.

The woman's gaze immediately went to Baltazar Casaubon. The big man sat monitoring the Virtual Reality programme on the wall monitor.

'We OK?'

'Of course.'

An almost imperceptible excitement tensed the line of her shoulders. Miles caught it on camera. The hairs on the back of his neck hackled. Framing a question, he opened his mouth to speak and was interrupted.

'How long do you think it took me to key in and cross index that particular association-tree?' Valentine Branwen asked. 'The physical programming of the data, and putting it on to a database?'

The sun blazed in that quiet room in Neal Street. No traffic noise or fumes, no music; only the quiet.

Miles, statistics at his tongue-tip, guessed. 'Images, sounds, animation ... I'd say something on the order of six to eight months.'

'I'll tell you,' Valentine Branwen said. 'Four hours. But, true, that doesn't include time spent setting up the CAT-scan and magnetic resonance equipment.'

A chill touched him, and the trigger of adrenaline-rush, and hope. He did not say *that isn't possible.* With some deliberation he touched the stud at his belt that would give him direct voice-comment over the video. He panned in on Val.

'Let me just make that clear. You're saying that you constructed that VR sequence within a space of *hours*? Today?'

'Yes ... Let me quote something to you. The president of the Royal Information Society, on June fifth of last year.' She opened a video file on the wall monitor. A dark man behind a rostrum.

'The task we face in translating the collected knowledge of human-kind on to computer databases is as great a task as the construction of paved roads, where once there were only footpaths. When we have done this, the speed at which we can use information moves from walking-pace to high-speed racing-car mode. But the sheer time taken in constructing programs, and the architecture of indexes that will link them, and most of all the sheer physical effort of scanning in the data, means that decades will pass before we have any true realization of what information-flood means, and what it will do to our society. It is unfortunate, but there is no way around the physical facts.'

Miles nodded. 'Yes. The President said that at Rouen. I was there. And you're saying that there *is* a shortcut? That you can load data in hours that, even with teams on full time, it would take months to get online?'

With the sting of adrenaline-rush comes a kind of switching on. He caught without effort the best camera angle: the small, red-haired woman with the window's light blazing back from her white jeans; and at her back the immense form of Baltazar Casaubon hunched over gimcrack monitors.

'Oh, the hardware isn't that difficult. Medical laser scans, magnetic resonance – the technology has existed for years. But not the ability to process the result. Not the link-architecture to deal with the sheer volume and complexity of direct-brain data.' He saw her look, a little bemused and wondering, at the fat man.

'A prototype, working, safe method of direct neural input of information from a human mind into a computer.' He stated it flatly. 'Direct neural input. DNI. Would you confirm that, Mr Casaubon?'

'Hhrmm. Yes. Obviously.'

'You're saying this at the moment without any proof. Tell me,' Miles said. 'What do you need the hypermedia news for?'

'I would have thought that was obvious. We need to get this out into to the public domain. We want commercial offers.'

'Out?'

'It is, at the moment,' Baltazar Casaubon said gently, 'technically – legally – the property of the US military.'

Miles Godric stared.

'But you won't, immediately, mention that.' Valentine Branwen shook the hair back from her face and stretched, arching her back. One fisted hand reached up towards the ceiling. Joints and tendons popped. She gave a long, rested sigh. 'We need a massive campaign for multinationals to come in and buy the system.'

Rather blankly, his mind racing, Miles asked. 'And then?'

'Then?' Her voice changed. He saw her stroke the grained wood of the windowsill, touch being the ultimate test of reality; and put her fingers to her mouth, still with the tactile memory of wood. 'And then, one supposes, everything is different.'

'You think people will just come and—' He shook his head. 'You think I'll *tell* people they should come to this project and get their brains minced?'

Baltazar Casaubon leaned back from the bank of monitors. He scratched through his greasy copper hair, beaming. He ignored the provocation, and waved an expansive hand.

'Of course they will. *You* will. Especially after all the hypermedia news coverage, when you volunteer to be the first man read by DNI in a public demonstration for all the scientific, medical, and IT establishments.'

'When I *what*?'

The fat man abruptly stood up from the monitors, rising to his full height. 'Good *God,* what's this country coming to? The government in power when I left would never have tolerated this! I bring this back to PanEurope and some piddling little cameraman whines that it isn't *safe*? Where's your guts, man? True, the National Security Association and Federal Bureau of Investigation have us under surveillance – but I assure you, they won't be able to interfere if the media acts quickly enough.'

Miles raised his eyebrows, recognizing a wrong intonation in the genuine anger. There is more to be uncovered here. This is only the surface.

Casaubon rumbled, 'Your place – your *business* – is to help us get this story out. We're not obliged to give explanations of every little qualm we may have.'

The woman sat down in Casaubon's vacated chair, one bare foot up on the desk. She smoothed the white denim over her knee and glanced up from beneath copper-red lashes, smiling slightly.

'Miles, it's a prototype. These are adult games we're playing. Weigh it up – is this something you want?'

The fat man muttered: '... plenty of *other*...'

Miles looked at his hands. The fingers just perceptibly shook. He is twenty-nine this year. In one holistic flash he sees it: all the city, all doors opening, the respect and resentment that success forces.

Notoriety. Status.

Reward.

CHAPTER FIVE

Johanna

The PanEuropean Minister of Defence stared at the walls of the unisex toilets in the Federal PanEuropean Defence building. *Johanna Branwen eats babies!* someone had scrawled. Under it, neatly, someone else had printed *yes but at least she peels them first.* Johanna Branwen smiled appreciatively. When the plumbing in one's office breaks down, one discovers such treats.

She left the cubicle and paused in front of the full-length executive mirror. The habit of fifty years is not advisedly broken: she checked her image for how it could be read.

The yellow interior illumination shone kindly on her face. It softened the lines of her plump chin. Businesslike, she flicked steel-and-silver curls out from under her tracksuit collar; repaired her scarlet lipstick; dabbed on a little more of her distinctive musky perfume. A wide, thin mouth, with only a hint of fullness in the lower lip. Her eyes are long and tilted, her lashes fading.

'Mmm ...?'

She pushes her fists back and plants them on her hips, the black fur-collared jacket swinging open. Under it she wears a scarlet track suit, Nike trainers, large amounts of subtle gold jewelry. It does no harm to be seen to be losing the battle against plump flesh, not at fifty-three. It relaxes people. A soft body indicates a soft mind.

She checks her wrist. Rolex watch-and-wrist-VDU. She clip-locks the jacket, remains staring down at her fingers. They show her age: brown-spotted, with raised veins and the blue tinge of poor circulation. She wears warm, clumsy, brown wool fingerless gloves – but not when observed. Now she strips them off, takes one last mirror-check.

'You'll do, girl. You'll do.'

The security guard fell in by her side as she left the washroom. She climbed the flight of stairs back up to her office. The plate glass bullet-proof windows glittered. Siesta weather in London. Not ten in the morning and the sun made the lowrise cityscape outside shimmer. Finials of white Baroque stone pierced a deep blue sky above the complex's major courtyard. Polarized ogee windows burned back light. She noted the guard sweat, despite the air-conditioning. She rubbed her own hands together to warm them.

'Files,' she said, passing through the outer office. Her Principle Private Secretary Morgan Froissart hastened to stand, smartly, abandoning a clutch of microdiscs. 'See that I'm not disturbed.'

'Minister.' The second secretary began diverting calls.

'Put that stuff back on screen, Morgan.'

Morgan Froissart followed her into her inner office. 'Certainly, Minister.'

She sprawled into her padded leather chair and sank her chin down into the fur of her jacket collar. Customarily, the air-conditioning is turned off in her office. She began to feel warmed. She watched the man sweat across his face and under his arms, and smiled. Life is full of small satisfactions, if one knows where to look.

'And these are?'

'The initial reports from the diplomatic bag from Washington, dated two years ago. I've isolated mentions of Professor Branwen, Minister.'

She gave a lizard-smile. 'Play it, Morgan. Play it.'

She leaned forward, resting her lips against her thumbs. Her fingers still blue-white with circulatory disease.

'These premises are secure.' Morgan Froissart gave the obligatory reminder. He voice-keyed the first report.

Johanna Branwen fingered the fur at her collar. Small body-language movements that are less a giveaway than a deliberate broadcasting of uneasiness; a warning, as it were, that someone might suffer the side-blast of this one.

The wall-VDU bloomed into colour. An image of a small, white-walled interrogation room. She would have recognized the style even without the recorded head-up display figures. The Confederate American States.

'The security complex at Dallas, ma'am.'

'Yes.'

'"I know nothing about a fire supposed to have destroyed data. I know nothing about any fire supposed to have destroyed records. You have all my computer time logged. You know how much time I've spent in the department, you know exactly what I've been doing. What else is there to say?"'

A thirty-something woman, voice ingenuous to the knowing ear. Sitting on a plain chair with one knee hooked up and her hands clasped around it, the red hair pinned back from her sharp-eared face. This is two years ago: she wears her hair differently now. Valentine Branwen does not physically take after her mother, to any great degree. But there are similarities.

'"I'm quitting because I have ethical problems now working for the military. I don't expect you to understand that. You can debrief me as much as you like – I'm clean."'

'So that was her story, at that time. She was never proved to have undertaken, ah, extra-curricular activities. I imagine, however, that she did.'

'Probably, ma'am.'

'She must have known at that point that she would be removed from Confederate government custody. Extradited back here.' Johanna rested her chin on her thumbs. 'Morgan, take a note. The custodial sentences on the escorts who failed to bring her back to Rouen should be increased. Say, four years. No: five. It seems this is more serous than was at first thought.'

'Yes, ma'am.'

'Run *Casaubon.* The interrogation in March of this year.'

The fat man, sweating, in a room in San Jose.

'"Why try to persuade me to implicate the people at the Department? Ridiculous. I may have misused materials and worktime, but nothing has come of it that need concern you."'

'Are they talking about the same thing, Minister?' Morgan ventured.

'One has to assume so, but ...' Johanna shook her head. 'What do we have from April to June?'

'Various sections of the Defense Department being shut down due to "compromised security", and their staff being pretty roughly investigated.'

Her secretary voice-cued sound and vision. After a moment he decreased the sound of the beatings. Johanna Branwen recovered it to full stereo.

'Their security people are right, of course. Something like this can rarely be put down to the invention of any one person, even if he is,' Johanna Branwen said distastefully, 'a "computer wizard". Morgan, make sure that we keep unofficial access to Confederate records. There will be no overt cooperation with us, I think.'

'No, ma'am.'

The PanEuropean Minister of Defense stood and moved to her window. The undulating London cityscape rolled away from her, low-rise windows flashing back the sun. She shivered and pulled the furred jacket closer around her neck.

'Why are they stupid enough to seek *public* exposure? My damn daughter,' she said. Her Principle Private Secretary, hearing that, heard for the first time the speech-patterns of Valentine Branwen from her mother's mouth.

'We know where her husband is now, but legally, Minister, we can't do anything about it. Nothing criminal has yet been proved against him here or in America.'

'What I want you to do,' Johanna Branwen stated clearly, 'is to lay false information in her records. Criminal acts, mental instability, whatever seems appropriate. Both of them; the man too.'

'Minister. Ah ... That kind of disinformation can be very difficult to eradicate afterwards, Minister. And the security services themselves are much better placed to excuse such an action, if it ever became known it had taken place.'

Johanna Branwen tucked her cold hands up into her armpits. She did not bother to look at Morgan, knowing how the light from the unpolarized windows made her a black silhouette against the sun's glare.

'I want it done under my control, and I want it done *now.* I see only one hope for this situation. My daughter and her colleague must be completely discredited, to the point where no one – least of all the commercial corporations and the scientific community – will believe a word they say.'

CHAPTER SIX

Criminal Proceedings

A horn blared ceaselessly, jammed on. Barking dogs answered it. Rue Ingram skirted the gates of the British Museum – washing flapped on lines strung between the NeoClassical pillars, and a gang of eight-year-olds played football with tin cans in the courtyard – and ducked into the tiny noon shade of a plane tree.

'So that's your tame video journalist boyfriend,' Frankie Hollister said.

Rue stretched, heat-sticky. The bark of the tree rubbed dust against her bare shoulder. 'He's not my boyfriend!'

'He shows you advance videos of the news.'

'He came round to the refectory because he heard her say what college I was at. He's a journalist. He just wants me as a source.'

'Yeah!'

Seeing Hollister's grin, Rue abandoned what she had been going to say. The car horn rasped. They walked on under the summer trees.

'So all this was when?'

'Monday.' Rue added. 'That *was* her on *Hypershift!* news this morning.'

'Give you that one,' Frankie Hollister drawled. She jerked her head, flipping the short gold-brown hair out of her face. Her hands, fisted, dug deep in baggy cotton dungarees pockets. 'She *undressed* in front of you?'

Rue Ingram nodded.

'Gross.' Frankie shuddered theatrically. The black cotton strap of her overalls slipped down her bare, dark shoulder. 'She's *got* to be over thirty. Wrinkles and bags. Urrgh.'

The smell of sun-washed flesh stayed in Rue's memory, her own or the woman's, she was not sure which; together with the slow beat of *Said She Was A Dancer* and the glitter of light from the whole-wall monitor.

'Yeah, it was pretty gross. I wasn't thinking about that. What it is, she was all over bruises. From real swordfighting.'

'C'mon, don't kid me. He beats her, right. They do that.'

'Nah. And I don't think she thought anything about undressing.' Rue stopped. Her long, slender black brows came down into a scowl. 'I think she was just ... unselfconscious.'

Frankie Hollister snorted. She swaggered ahead down Great Russell Street, fists still in her pockets, not waiting for Rue's half-run that brought her up level. They walked across to Tottenham Court Road.

'Maybe *we* could go on one of these battles,' Frankie said.

'Oh, *swords*. You and swords. *Again*. The swords aren't the *point*. The bruises ...'

Heat blasted back from the walls of buildings and the windows of shops, stang up from the metal carapaces of abandoned cars that paved the road four lanes wide.

'Does she know you're one of us?'

The sun beat down on Rue Ingram, on the back of her neck; and she swallowed nausea. She slitted her eyes against the sun's light reflecting from walls and pavements. 'She knows. I told her.'

Frankie, small and bouncy, strode ahead as if heatwaves couldn't touch her. 'Guess I ought to ask her some questions, then. Make sure we got nothing to worry about.'

Summer's brilliance forces the gaze down. Down from the deserted windows of Centre Point, diamond-bright against the sky; down from the roofscape against the cloudless blue. Down to the street, the people, the parasols and icecreams.

'Christ, they've even got up this far!' Outraged, Frankie Hollister jerked her head at a refugee Basque woman with three ill-dressed children, sheltering from the heat in a gutted dormobile. A scatter of possessions marked it as an inhabited vehicle. 'We're gonna have to do something about this. And *soon*.'

Four hours later, across London, Miles Godric stands talking to a newscaster colleague, Eugene Turlough, in the garish corridors of an independent research hospital.

'The process is based on a multiple magnetic resonance scan of the brain, modelling a holographic representation of synapse activity. That's experimental, but it isn't new – what's new is the architecture of the master program that interprets the raw data as memory.'

'Yeah ...' Eugene Turlough wiped his hand across his red face. Sweat soaked his t-shirt, blotting the *Hypershift!* logo. Miles' senior editor (talking across the crowded room to the senior editor of *Newsbytes*) flanked his other side. The hospital gown left Miles paradoxically chilled and too hot under the lights of the cameras.

'So the medical side's a souped-up brainscan.' Turlough, morose, cradled a glass in the palm of his sweaty hand; a half-inch of yellow media party wine slopping. 'So it's ... Miles, if you volunteered for this, you're mad. See *why* you're doing it. You're going to be able to ask your own price for freelance work after this. But that's assuming you don't get your brains fucked here.'

'At least I'll make main headline spot – either way.' Godric spoke with a new confidence that he saw raise hackles up Eugene Turlough's spine.

A nurse in pale blue that could have been an informal, if severe, day dress touched Miles's arm. He nodded, smiling, and walked across to the trolley and lay down. The noise of voice-over commentaries sparked like wildfire through the room. He heard Val Branwen's urbane irony, being interviewed. The clipped webbing about his waist was comforting: sound and vision linked to base, his words to be recorded in realtime.

In the cold whiteness of the theatre anteroom, he lay absolutely still. Medical staff moved smoothly from machine to machine. The competence of professional practice seemed unostentatiously but clearly written in their movements. A memory came into his mind of Val sighting down the length of some damn antique sword: the movement of her wrist framing that same competence.

'Miles.'

Her voice spoke so appositely that it was a moment before he turned his head. 'Come to see if I've changed my mind?'

'Have you?'

'With the entire London hypermedia corps out there?' Miles Godric looked at her from under long fair lashes. 'You know me better than that. I guess you know me better. Baltazar Casaubon didn't assume I'd do this without talking to you first.'

'You think? Well, maybe you're right.' Offhand, as if what she says is routine; her thoughts quite different.

'I hear there have been representations from the American embassy this morning. Will your mother make any comment on this?'

The woman mirrored his own professional expression. 'Keep trying. My answer to that is still *no comment.* I just wanted a word with you before the scan.'

Irritated at his momentary heartfelt gladness in having her to talk to, Miles Godric said, 'Which particular word would that be?'

She choked on laughter. 'I knew hanging around Baltazar Casaubon wasn't doing you any good! Ah well. The word, I suppose, is flexibility. Don't be surprised. When the neurons start firing, you'll get side-effects that aren't easily attributable to memory-readout. You may feel some sense of interaction with the structuring program – the linking-architecture – but Baltazar assures me it's because this is a prototype, there's still some odd feedback. I've felt it myself. It's a bug we'll iron out.'

She leaned up as one of the nurses moved across and swabbed his arm, injecting a syringe with almost-painless smoothness.

'Remember, if you've done any meditation or relaxation, practise it as you go.' Val touched his arm. 'The beta-blockers ought to do it. Memory's a fragile thing, and what controls learning and reading is chiefly levels of tension. We won't get much out of you if you're in a chemical state of anxiety. But Casaubon told me you test out low-aptitude for fear.'

'You mean—' His voice slurred. He felt for the beltcorder, adjusting sound levels by touch. 'You mean this is a highly public occasion, so don't fuck up my chances by being terrified?'

She chuckled. 'That's what I mean. What did you choose for a subject-reading?'

'*Tamburlaine.*' He saw her dark red brows indent. 'Baltazar knows. Well, you put Marlowe into my mind. I don't know if I ever told you, back when I did my media degree, it had the videos of Olivier's *Tamburlaine* and *Doctor Faustus* on it. Not a thing one admits to in journalism.'

He played for a smile: got it. She touched his cheek with the pad of her index finger.

'So we'll get lit. crit. out of you, will we? Now that I do have to see! OK, I don't think there's anything else. Go for it, guys.'

His attention shifted, charming the medical staff; a word and a smile distributed here and there, until the hard base of the scanner was under his spine, his shaven skull under a cap, and firm in the padded clamps. A faint *whirrr* was the only sound of the scanner sliding into position.

He opened his mouth to start a commentary and gave a small, dry cough, the ridges of his mouth desert-dry with tension. He began again. 'The process of the scan has been fully explained to me, as has the theory of memory data reading. Baltazar Casaubon is as yet not ready to disclose full details to the public, although specialists in his field are studying his evidence – are subjecting his evidence to intensive study—'

He stopped. *Live* transmission, not a tape for editing. Well, too late now. And to have some (not unprofessional) evidence of tension here ...? Maybe no bad idea.

'My first question, naturally, is: does DNI work? And my second? That's another question entirely ... If direct neural input is possible, I want to know – is what it reads the objective truth, or a subjective lie?'

A silence spiked behind his eyes.

He began quite consciously to let go of fear.

'Let's see what we can get.' Valentine Branwen cued the Sony wall monitor to montage, and it split between the theatre where Godric's body lay motionless, the skull encased in a vast wheel of machine; the medical staff calibrating read-outs; and Baltazar Casaubon, sweating between keyboard and icons. The audio track piped through his continual mutterings.

Fortunately they were, Valentine reflected, too mumbled to be decoded, even if English had been the first language of most of those present in the Yates Institute teaching room.

Keiko Musashi sipped coffee. 'Thank you for a most interesting demonstration.' The Japanese representative for Sony-Nissan kept her eyes fixed on the monitor. After a moment she added, 'There is no representation of the downloaded data?'

Valentine split the screen again to display rapid lines of machine code. 'Regrettably, this will be of little value until structured in analogue form.'

'Ah.'

'*Hontō ni sumi-masen.*' Valentine bowed her head briefly.

The screen divided again to give a blurred and jerky image. She heard a mutter behind her. The image was perfectly recognizable as a shot of the main reception area of the Yates Institute, but a cinéma vérité shot: point of view Miles Godric.

'Such an image might be reconstructed from the security cameras,' Pyotr Andreyev said, speaking for the Pacific Rim consortiums.

'We have some pre-arranged data to download, to avoid any possibility of fraud.'

The man from Kazakhstan sank back into his chair. Curiously, in this room lit only by neon tubes, the walls surrounded by channelled white marble slabs, and smelling of disinfectant, he did not seem out of place. Valentine had downloaded his data and found no medical training.

'There are many implications to this new technology,' Keiko Musashi said, 'if it can be brought past the prototype stage. For entertainment, for teaching skills, for financial dealings, for legal affairs. It is quite breath-taking.'

Valentine Branwen seated herself on the edge of the table and poured herself coffee.

'I may,' she said, 'have had more to do with the entertainment division of all your corporations during the past two years. Prior to that, as we all know, I was one of those unworldly researchers desiring only knowledge, working for the Confederate government.'

A small, ironic laugh acknowledged what she said. She nodded at Pyotr Andreyev.

'Being unworldly, you comprehend, I may not understand commercial matters. However, I do have some understanding of patent law, company law, and the necessity of dealing adequately with it, which is why all Mr Casaubon's agreements will be finalized through Fisher, Pitman and Trott, here in the City. And you will appreciate, also, that other multinationals apart from the Pacific Rim will be approached.'

'Of course,' Keiko said.

'Baltazar Casaubon will sell on what seems the best promise of development,' Valentine said, 'and on no account will he sell this process to a company which is buying it to suppress it. That's his only condition. Let's begin the discussion.'

'*Kso!*' On screen, the fat man swore aloud, and began to reprogram the secondary sequence from the beginning.

The late evening sun shone in through the hospital's high Victorian windows, slanting light and lessening heat on to the hypermedia crews, ubiquitous in black jeans, track suits, sweat-shirts; no face much over thirty. Valentine Branwen let her gaze slide past them to the editors in summer suits and dresses. Older. She shrugged her shoulders back, a movement that loosened muscles and tension without being obtrusive.

'You,' Baltazar Casaubon said, 'would rather be in the field.'

With his words came a sensory memory so strong as to be almost hallucination: the smell of grass, sun on dried dung, mud and wool and linen; black-powder gunshot. Her eyes automatically narrowed. She shrugged, this time for effect.

'Why do you think I do re-enactment battles? They have solvable problems. Easily solvable.'

'But the implications of them are no less ...' The link-architect paused for a word. '... questionable.'

She put her fingers on the creased arm of his white suit, thoughtful, aware of an implicit distance between them that only might be to do with the occasion; a distance forgotten in the last few days' frantic work, but now remembered.

A camcorder whirred online. Eugene Turlough's over-heavy stomach drooped over the waistband of his black tracksuit bottoms. He spoke with alcohol-fuelled clarity. 'Mr Casaubon, can you tell us why this is such a significant invention?'

The fat man beamed. 'Significant? *Earth*-shattering! I have, here, successfully married together medical technology with a hardware system capable of recording, accurately, the hard-memory levels of the human brain. And, crucially, with a software system of link-architecture *capable* of dealing with that amount and complexity of information.'

'So you can turn electronic slush into eidetic memory record.' Turlough's eyes had a slight glaze, counting footage-seconds. 'Why is that "earth-shattering"?'

Valentine Branwen raised her head. The window light dazzled her vision and struck a brilliant red from her hair, an entirely selfconscious gift for the camcorders – saint in a shaft of heavenly light, Joan at the stake, Prometheus in the self-bought fire.

'What we do,' she said, 'is keep inventing the wheel. There was a time – I think it was somewhere around the year 1250, some of you may remember it—'

A chuckle went round the crowded room. Her eyes crinkled as she acknowledged that.

'A time when you could learn everything there was to know

about one given subject. And perhaps know a little about most others. That time was over by the end of the Renaissance. The Scientific and the Industrial Revolutions brought us more knowledge in any one field of study than any one person could assimilate. And more fields of knowledge than the Middle Ages could imagine existing. In our own century ... any specialist field has divided and sub-divided, there's no way I can know my field, and know about – say – link-architecture in detail as well.'

The room was quiet but for the subliminal whirr of camcorders. Urbane irony touched her tone.

'I can't explain this in soundbites. When you put it out on hypermedia, you'll flag references for what I've first said, so that anyone who's interested can follow up what I'm saying now. What I will say. And what the Yates Institute has said; what the PanEuropean Ministry of Defence claims; what the beginnings of hypermedia invention was ... And that's the way the human mind works. It follows expanding webs of knowledge. And in the cracks between the webs – if you'll pardon a mixed metaphor – is the wheel we keep reinventing, and the wheels we haven't invented yet.'

She rubbed the back of her wrist across her face. Her long-sleeved white cotton shirt hid bruises, trapped heat.

'Somewhere in what the human race *already* knows are the Big Science answers to cancer, crop failure, a technology that will take us out of the solar system, and the answers ... The answers to questions that we don't yet know enough to ask, because the concepts themselves are still hidden down those cracks. We don't find them, except on rare occasions, because the human mind is too small. Self-programming DNI computers will *not* be too small.'

A man raised his hand. Baltazar Casaubon indicated him with a wave of one broad-palmed hand.

The questioner spoke with a northern accent. 'None of this is new, Mr Casaubon. We've been promised information flood for years now. What's different about this?'

'Time,' Casaubon rumbled. 'Simply time. The limitation was always the speed at which knowledge could be physically got into computers. And then the time that it takes to put in all the cross-links, the roadmap-architecture necessary to read it. Crudely, sir, this system reads the human memory as fast as the human memory works – holistically, almost instantaneously. That means information flood within a few years, rather than fifty or a hundred.'

'Accurate information? Doesn't memory blur facts, forget them?' *Newsbyte*'s prime news reporter: Pramila Aziz.

Casaubon's ponderous head inclined. 'A reasonable objection. Knowledge input through the human brain might be more sketchy than that scanned in from print and video, and more prone to error. However, the advantage of this hardware is that it reads at the *eidetic* level of the brain, where everything is photographically recorded.'

Aziz said, 'So this process could read the mind for, say, evidence in a criminal trial?'

'Only under certain very limited circumstances, Ms Aziz. The mind must be relaxed, trusting, unanxious. Or else the result is neurochemically-ruined garbage.' Baltazar Casaubon clasped his hands over the head of his ivory walking-stick. 'Of course it can't read minds for interrogation. What a supposition. As if I'd write link-architecture for a program that could. I'm not a fool, you know.' He beamed encouragingly at Valentine Branwen and the assembled journalists. 'Intelligence is not making the same mistake twice. Genius is not making the same mistake *once*.'

A voice from behind the bank of camcorders and lights said, 'Is it true that the US Defense Department is claiming joint ownership of DNI, Mr Casaubon?'

Casaubon smiled. 'This is mine, to do with as I choose – and I choose to sell it to the highest bidder.'

A man stood. Valentine recognized Eugene Turlough again, his eyes fixing on hers.

He said, 'Professor Branwen, is it true that in America you first worked for, and then disclaimed all connection with, the Department of Defense? That two years ago you fled the US? Now you're with a man rumoured to have stolen data on three continents. Ms Branwen, is it true that you have been clinically treated for regular psychotic episodes?'

An irresistible smile spread across her face. Valentine Branwen laughed. She saw the clear, relaxed sound diffuse a little of the room's tension. 'You *have* been listening to my commercial competitors, haven't you?'

Eugene Turlough looked past her. 'Mr Casaubon, may I ask you a question?'

The large man leaned his immense weight on one hip and the

walking-stick, and gestured expansively with his other hand. The camcorders duly took in white suit, sweat-stained shirt, his greasy red hair still fastened in a tiny ponytail with a rubber band.

'Is it true,' Eugene Turlough asked, 'that there are six paedophilia charges still outstanding against you in PanEurope for offences against the Revised Child Protection Act?'

CHAPTER SEVEN

'The Wondrous Architecture of the World'

'Don't you dare walk out on me now!'

'You have not,' the large man said, miffed, 'gone out of your way to make me feel welcome. Now you tell me *not* to go—'

'*Casaubon*!' Valentine Branwen glared. The strong urine smell of the Gentlemen's toilets made her blink. Her voice, forced low for secrecy, bounced off the tiled walls.

Baltazar Casaubon reached down and under and unzipped his trousers, facing the urinal. 'You said to me, I distinctly remember, when we came here at the beginning of the week, that you would help me up to a point, and then I was on my own. I'm just on my own a little earlier than I anticipated. It is not,' he said, 'a problem.'

The sound of his running urine echoed. Valentine absently hit the button of the wall hand-drier, in case of microphones, and spoke under its roar.

'You do *know* what kind of a tightrope you're walking here? You're trusting to the fact that the NSA and European Security won't cooperate. For how long? You're trusting Johanna to protect me, and protect you by default. For how long? You're assuming that six multinational corporations won't care that they're buying something you don't actually own—'

'They don't care. If I'm not mistaken, they're in the process of attempting to steal it even as we speak.'

Casaubon shook out the last drops, zipped up his trousers, and moved to the washbasin. Halfway there he stopped, glared downwards, and eventually shook one ponderous leg.

Valentine turned the tap on for him. 'I thought we had ten days maximum. We made it to six. Time out, game over. I'm not going back out there on my own!'

'They won't hurt you, little one.'

'Hurt me! *Hurt* me? They're spreading all the dirt they can think of over me, and I've got a business to run! How long do you think White Crowe Enterprises is going to last once some of the mud starts sticking?'

'I'm sure your other contacts in interactive media will be only too pleased to make you a *cause célèbre.* You can always,' he said pointedly, 'ask your lover Miles.'

'He's not my lover! He's a lousy fuck! There: are you happy?'

Like most taps in hospitals, these had long spatulate handles enabling them to be pushed with an elbow. Baltazar Casaubon pushed off the tap, moved to the hand-drier, and dried his plump fingers through two cycles of warm air.

Footsteps sounded outside in the corridor. A hand tried the locked door, despite the OUT OF ORDER notice she had tacked up. The footsteps moved away. Common garden-variety stupidity.

'Is he a lousy fuck?'

'No, he's quite good, actually. Out of bed, though, he's piss-boring.'

Baltazar Casaubon, somewhat smugly, remarked, '*I'm* never boring.'

'*He* was never a bigamist!'

'You do harp on things, little one. I've noticed that. It could be a mistake, all this obsessing. You might become—'

'—boring,' Valentine said in unison with the fat man. 'Yes. Very witty. I've heard it before. *I thought this was important.*'

'You're a businesswoman. I've given you my power of attorney. Johanna will protect you up to a point. I'm sure I can leave the financial and contract side in your capable charge.' Baltazar Casaubon unlocked the door, surveyed the corridor, and looked back at her. 'Or not, as the case may be.'

'Baltazar, don't you dare!'

The door clicked shut behind him.

Silence. Two minutes. Three. Five.

She swung around, paced two steps forward, two steps back,

constrained by the small space and slippery tile. '*Shit!*'

A startled *Newsbyte* editor and a Sony-Nissan aide collided coming in together. The OUT OF ORDER notice was not now in evidence on the front of the door.

Embarrassed, Valentine Branwen walked quickly out of the Gentlemen's toilets.

Through the hospital windows, the last light drained from the sky.

The outer wearing of clothes has its effect on inner confidence. Back in combat pants, t-shirt, and camera belt, Miles Godric regarded the crowded room with only slightly disturbed ease, and broke away from the other journalists, practised at the ending of interviews. His newly-shaved scalp itched and he rubbed it, making a wry mouth of wounded vanity. But it is a visible and honourable campaign scar. He moved swiftly across to Eugene Turlough while replaying the previous two hours' hypermedia record. Towards the end of the disc:

'*—regular psychotic episodes?*'

'Oh shit!'

'*—paedophilia ... offences against the Revised Child Protection Act?*'

'Eugene, you asshole, so what! They're *Hypershift!*'s story!'

The man's jowls were red and wet. 'If it's a scam, we have to have been seen to ask the awkward questions first. Yeah? So don't tell me my job, shitbrain.'

Miles grunted, shaking his head, and turned his back on Turlough. His camcorder focused in on Val's face, now slack with concentration, almost ugly in its absence from exterior stimuli. Slowly brilliance returned.

'I'll take you guys through some of the text version first,' Val Branwen announced, 'that's probably easier. And we seem to have some pretty clear bits. Miles, are you coming over to see what you produced?'

He walked across to where she stood.

'I'm into the Yates mainframe. Take a look at this. I've run the raw data through the particular form of link-architecture invented by my friend here—' The red-headed woman looked up. Miles Godric automatically glanced up as she did. There was no sign of the fat man.

'Where's Casaubon?'

'In the washroom, I suppose. Avoiding any more awkward

questions.' Valentine Branwen straightened up from her terminal, hand in the small of her back. She seemed oblivious to the hypermedia journalists crowding the bank of monitors, jacking in their own systems. A kind of careless confidence emanated from her, arousing a – memory?

Something speared his head from eye to cortex. Not a pain, but a memory, a memory of—

He shook his head, and scratched his shaven scalp.

Eugene Turlough pounced. 'Disorientated?'

'To tell you the truth, hangover. Christ, I knew I shouldn't have gone out drinking last night!' He fixed a convivial smile in place, faking it from the eyes and not the mouth, and leaned one arm on the monitor, so that he could see past Val's elbow.

'Up and running,' she announced.

A muted sound went through the journalists, part excitement, part scepticism. Miles's automatic smile widened. The muscles of his face felt stiff.

'Take you through the prepared version of the text...' The woman clicked icons. He leaned down to study the section of page presented:

> in sharp contrast to *Doctor Faustus,*[23] whose internal dialectic is concerned not with the acquisition of knowledge,[24] but with the damnation of free will and NeoPlatonic magic,[25] *Tamburlaine,* its eponymous hero, the peasant conqueror of Asia, is a thought-experiment in will, ambition, and achievement (shorn free of Christianity, Renaissance ethics, and all plot save the protagonist's headlong, bloody rush into victory) set free to play in the Elizabethan theatres, and to remain (for reasons about which it may not be valid to conjecture) a money-spinner and byword, quotable to the point of parody for a generation, and surpassed by only one other play.[26] The shepherd-general of Asia

---

[23]*The Plays of Christopher Marlowe,* ed. Roma Gill, Oxford University Press, 1971

[24]*Radical Tragedy,* Jonathan Dollimore, Harvester Press, 1984

[25]*The Occult Philosophy in the Elizabethan Age,* Frances Yates, Routledge & Kegan Paul, 1979

[26]Marlowe, *The Spy at Londinium,* 1610, ed. Jeremy de Cossé Brissac, Cyprian Press, 1910

'I'll get the database to check that against the original.' The woman shifted small, muscled shoulders under her white shirt. He saw how, without appearing to, she kept her attention on the room; taking in the reactions of the editors and journalists. 'OK, there's the text-page, from a standard university database. And here's what we got from you.'

His text scrolled through:

> in sharp contrast to *Doctor Faustus,*[23] whose internal dialectic is concerned not with the acquisition of knowledge,[24] but with the damnation of free will and NeoPlatonic magic,[25] *Tamburlaine,* its eponymous hero, the peasant conqueror of Asia, is a thought-

'Yeah!' Miles hit his fist against the console.

'It could be a set-up,' *Newsbyte*'s Pramila Aziz said ungraciously.

'It could be. But it isn't. At the moment,' Valentine Branwen said, 'DNI recording needs all the help it can get. If you're expecting perfection – not yet. OK, let's take a look at Miles's independent visuals ...'

Miles Godric stared at the wall VDU.

At first the image seems a substandard graphic. Then it shifts into near-photographic focus. A man in golden Renaissance armour, on a stage backed by sky-cloth; other actors around him in armours of stark white, red, and black. Val keyed in sound:

'Nature ...'

The actor's voice boomed with theatre-projection, false in any video recording but here reverberate with power:

> '... that fram'd us of four elements
> Warring within our breasts for regiment,
> Doth teach us all to have aspiring minds.'

Eugene Turlough, at Miles's shoulder, protested, 'That's not the video. But there aren't any live recordings of ... it could be virtual. It could be a fix-up, virtual cut-and-paste.'

'That would have been about the time I was at Oxford. He was an old man, but – Jesus Christ. Is my memory *that* good?' Miles said wonderingly. 'It was a pretty naff evening, there was this girl; I wasn't really paying attention ...'

Val Branwen smiled, nothing faked in it, the flesh around her eyes creasing warmly. 'But this has everything Miles Godric knows about Kit Marlowe. Play texts. Textbooks. Performances. Especially performances.'

'Let me through.' A blonde woman with sharp blue eyes elbowed her way in beside Miles.

The face, vaguely familiar, he identified after a second. 'Louise de Keroac?'

'The year above you,' she said crisply. 'I went to that performance. There aren't any live recordings. But there's something I remember – something he did. Is there more of this? Keep it running.'

On the wall VDU, the actor abruptly swung around and put his back to the audience; his voice nonetheless sounding out clear and yearning:

> 'Our souls, whose faculties can comprehend
> The wondrous Architecture of the world,
> And measure every wand'ring planet's course,
> Still climbing after knowledge infinite,
> And always moving as the restless spheres,
> Wills us to wear ourselves and never rest
> Until we reach the ripest fruit of all...'

The figure raised armoured hands to the great sun at the back of the stage, drowned suddenly in a flood of yellow light:

'Why, this is Hell, nor am I out of it!'

'Yes.' Louise de Keroac shook her head. Her blue eyes swam with tears; her hand on Miles's shoulder was warm with sweat. 'That's what he did, that last night. That's not from *Tamburlaine*, it's from *Doctor Faustus*. That's how it *was*.'

'Damn it, it works!' Eugene Turlough rested a hand on Miles's other shoulder. 'Miles, first, for *Hypershift!* readers – you went through a whole battery of medical tests before and after, and we'll get the results through soon, but subjectively: have you had any ill-effects from your experience?'

He saw Val spread hands (bruised olive and brown across the knuckles) in a gesture of assurance.

'Nothing to speak of,' he lied.

He hooked his thumbs under his web-belt, weight on both hips. Decisions, always taken in some split second between the webs of chronology. Decisions, and what are their motivations?

'Professor Branwen, I realize this is a prototype.' Miles smiled publicly. 'I've been Mr Casaubon's guinea-pig. You owe me first rights to a hypermedia feature – let me have first access to the complete version of that recording.'

Val nodded. 'Sure, Miles.'

The editor of *Newsbyte* was the first to take him aside.

'As I understand it, Mr Godric, you're not on exclusive contract to *Hypershift!* Our channel network would be very interested. I'm thinking of a figure in the area of three hundred and fifty thousand pounds initially. Then royalties.'

'I'm thinking of a seven figure sum,' Miles Godric said.

Darkness.

The landing outside the Neal Street apartment creaked under a cautious, massive weight. A shade slid across shadow: the door closing.

Baltazar Casaubon clasped a briefcase to him as he bent to lock the door. A scrabble of claws, and a rat – pale in the light from Neal Street's one remaining streetlamp – peeked out between the folds of his white suit jacket.

'Sssh,' the link-architect advised.

He padded heavily down to the entrance.

Outside, across the road in Monmouth Street, a bonfire burned in the wreck of a van. Dark figures swarmed around it. The link-architect moved, for his bulk, surprisingly softly; skirting the fire's light. He tucked the case under one arm, carrying his ivory stick lefthanded.

Newly-planted surveillance cameras suffered inexplicable breakdowns in their programming, blanking out realtime and replaying shots of an empty street.

Towards the end of Earlham Street a noise startled him. He gripped the swordstick's handle and pulled. A slender blade shone in the city darkness. The sounds stopped and did not resume.

The link-architect Baltazar Casaubon padded away down narrow alleys. Above, visible in newly carbon-dioxide-free skies, a full moon burned.

She knew as soon as she put her key in the lock that the flat was empty.

Empty places have a sound to them. Unmistakable. She went in and shut the door behind her, and stood in the room for a time, in the orange radiance of the streetlamp outside the window. Little licks of orange reflected back from dull monitor screens. Red and green LEDs blinked on timers.

I guess that's it, then.

She checked, just the same. No portable. No clothes. Even the rat's cage gone – although not the pungent, pleasant smell of it. Not yet. Give it a day or two.

Sometimes (the right biorhythms, her own excitement, something) his skin has a dry, fuzzy, electric quality to it. Then, she can spend hours roaming his body; not that there isn't enough of it; lying in the sun, their uncurtained window not overlooked, time to grow sweaty and then dry.

She logged on to an old Powerbook, one of the five machines connected into a net within the flat, and ran a check on her own security systems. Tampered with. This one is probably US Military Intelligence. That one is MI6. The MI6 one is almost an old friend: She knows the operator's tricks of thought. These are probably commercial taps. This one here is very good, but it can't crack her public key encryption.

Besides, there is nothing here to find. Her multiple redundant back-ups are thirty jumps away, through telephone exchanges, hidden under false names on university databases. She always has liked universities.

Knowing she won't sleep, she downloads the latest trawl of files from the MultiNet, answers her e-mail, plays with bulletin boards. Tries for her own amusement to crack her way back in to the database at San Jose. At least manages to hide her identity from the tripped security expert systems. Tinkers with some of the ramifications of ALL THE WORLDS A STAGE™. Kit Marlowe, playwright and spy and games master, bringing the player character to the rooms of Elizabeth I's chief minister, Walsingham. Her voice synthesized to that of a dry old man:

'"It is white angel-magic, surely, that which you do seek. Our great magister, Doctor John Dee, sought it for many years in his Enochian congress with the spirits of God. It is the language of the angels of God, in which tongue men may speak to one another only the truth".'

She leans back from the keyboard mike.

And thinks, *I wonder if I did the right thing?*

CHAPTER EIGHT

No Sword No Intention

Two weeks later, in the PanEuropean Ministry of Defence:

'Minister, you have parliamentary debates on Tuesday and Friday. Two meetings of select committees, one this morning and one this afternoon; reports are in the appropriate multimedia files for presentation.'

Her Principle Private Secretary continued to read the diary file aloud.

'You have an official dinner on Wednesday, and you have been asked to speak; the speech department are delivering that for your final approval this evening. Your club holds its AGM on Thursday. You have meetings with delegations on Wednesday and Friday mornings. There are some other appointments I'm holding off on confirming until I have your approval.'

Johanna Branwen swivelled her chair round to face the office's full-length, bullet-and-bomb-proof window. The dawn sunlight gilded her face. She sat with her right arm hanging down, monotonously opening and closing a Hawkeye II lock-knife. Practising without looking the single-handed finger-coordination of the movement to open, and the manipulation of the lock-release to shut. The blade's edge shone rainbows.

'In the days when I was my own secretary I kept this sharp for opening letters. There were jokes about its other uses.' She let her lips curve. 'Useless for e-mail, of course.'

She snicked the blade shut and laid it down flat on the desk, ignoring Morgan in favour of the other man present. 'What advice does the department have for me?'

Her latest military adviser, a young man with shaven hair, observed, 'We can leave the conflict in Germany to the news media, ma'am. Nothing decisive is anticipated in the next week. I've advised your speech-writing department to make some pronouncement on the casualty rate – it's well below the expected ten per cent, which you should capitalize on immediately. It will rise to fourteen per cent as soon as we have to fight for Bonn.'

She watched him. A broad-shouldered boy in his early twenties; boots polished, brown fatigues tailored and pressed. He answers not quite by the numbers, but that possibility is always there.

'I could certainly put that into the speech for the Japanese trade delegation at the Guildhall. Our better morale, superior training. Then revise it to underdogs fighting against the superior firepower of tyranny, if it comes to Bonn.'

'It must come to that, ma'am.'

Pleasantly mild, Johanna Branwen said, 'But I think it may be expedient for there to be peace. A temporary cease fire.'

He frowned. 'Ma'am, with respect, if you don't carry the military victory through, the campaign will have been pointless.'

'Ah, the single-mindedness of the soldier's view ... I must thank you for your help.' She sat back, in an attitude of dismissal. 'Your commanding officer will be receiving a full report from me. Joinville, isn't it? It's unfortunate that you're not of the right calibre to become a permanent military adviser to a minister, but I'm *sure* this won't prevent the forces using your no doubt excellent capabilities in some other respect ...'

She had the minor pleasure of seeing him colour a splotchy red and white. The boy saluted and left. She chuckled to herself, making a note on the e-pad.

'They will send me these idiots,' she said cheerfully. 'Morgan, call up the files, will you.'

By the time Morgan Froissart had done that, the cheerfulness faded. Dawn's slanting light showed up the lines of her face, and there was nothing soft or humorous in that hardness.

'I have the latest update, ma'am.' He slid a microdisc into the console. She swivelled to watch the wall-VDU. Very little of the displayed schematic graphic is now green. Some sections are amber. By far the most of them are red.

'These are our breached security systems,' Morgan said. No drama in his voice. 'As you are aware, Minister, in the past two weeks we've experienced increasingly massive leaks. Multiple users who shouldn't be there.'

'We *must* order a new system.'

'With respect, ma'am, we can't order a new system. This one has been makeshifted and adapted over the years. By now it's unique. We wiped and went to back-up tapes, but they are corrupted too. It's been suggested to me that the operating system is corrupt, and not the software.' Morgan appeared unusually frustrated. 'None of the experts can explain to me, ma'am, why all kinds of security have been breached. All they tell me is that, even if we close down, we don't know what else has been planted to be activated later.'

Her hand went to the desk and wrapped around the warm metal of the lock-knife. Absently she slid the blade open, clicked it shut. 'We can work on isolated systems – but hermit computers have their limitations. Certainly the Ministry can't be run that way.'

'This has progressed appallingly quickly in two weeks, ma'am.'

She clicked her fingers and the wall-VDU darkened. No light in the big office now but the dawn, orange in the east. She shivered and keyed the daylight-fluorescent panels, blinking in the welcome additional blue-white light.

'I have some little appreciation of the field,' she said. 'The sheer degree of complexity required to breach all the different kinds of security we have... And yet we can't *not* put data into the system.'

She turned away from the window, looking philosophically at the big man, who stood with his broad shoulders straight and his back erect; and Morgan Froissart looked back at her. Practised enough to school his expression away from panic.

'No single attack should work against all systems,' he said, because of the multitude of different operating systems. And yet it is.'

'The stages of technology,' she said ruminatively. 'You see, we're past the stage of new technology being used to do the old technology's job but faster. We're well past that. New technology does things now that can only be done with new technology. And we depend on it. We *have* to use the databases. We *have* to use the nets. We can't close it all down. Nor can we risk continued data corruption. Everything would grind to a halt. Chaos.'

'Apparently our virus-killer software programs are useless.'

A silence followed. He added tentatively:

'It's beginning to show up in other ministries' databases. The news will break—'

'I *know*!' Johanna Branwen put the lock-knife into her jacket pocket. She shrugged the jacket collar up, and brushed silver-grey curls out from under its edge with both hands. 'Is it a virus? That is the mark of the man my daughter married. I believe he must have generated this program-corrupting virus. And ... I don't doubt but that she is assisting him.'

'We can pick up your daughter whenever you give the word. US Military Intelligence has gone back on standby.' Morgan shrugged. 'Admittedly it would happen in the full glare of publicity, during this direct neural input affair, but it could easily be done.'

'"The full glare of publicity"? Really, Morgan. You've been watching too much satellite news. The question is, how much of that kind of "publicity" can we bear? And – actually, I think we can stand a great deal, Morgan, provided no one permits this to be made into a *cause célèbre*. It's probably useless to further discredit Valentine. It's certainly becoming essential that we have her husband.'

'Do we assume she knows where he is, ma'am?'

She can, with a little effort, think of Valentine as someone else. Someone else's daughter. Whether she can do this when she sees the woman, she doesn't know. But certainly she can act without compunction where Baltazar Casaubon is concerned.

Johanna Branwen says, 'Find them.'

The wall of the docklands apartment came into focus. A hazy sun shone in, warming the painted brickwork. Two weeks mostly without sleep, interrupted by cat-naps and unconsciousness. Miles automatically groped towards the keyboard for morning tv. He rubbed his eyes. Sleep-gritty vision gave him the time on the wall screen's inset chronometer: 05-03 a.m.

'Shit! I'm wasting time.'

He rolled over, under dirty sheets, aware of the early satellite news, paying minimal attention to the local headlines.

'The Prime Minister today stated that there will be further financial incentives offered by the government to those residents of London willing to sell their houses in the dormitory towns. Next: another customs post has been set up on the Victoria Line, owing to the high influx of tourists this July. Our special report—'

'Ah, *shit!*' This time he means *Hypershift!*'s early morning magazine slot.

Frustrated, he hit his forehead with the heel of his hand; rolled over, and punched the pillow. The white cotton indented; slowly relaxed. He sat up, struggling into crumpled combat pants and staggering from the bed to the balcony, the wooden planking already warm from the dawn sun.

I'm losing it. I'm losing the money. I should have had this taped and ready to go. Christ, two weeks!

A breeze raises the hairs down his back.

Two dogs snarl at each other in the alley between the warehouses. He leaned over, looking to left and right, seeing the rusting cars that blocked each of the crossroads; some smoke going up from a cooking fire in the gutter near a Fiat Uno. A dark hand reached out of the car body and turned a skinned rat upon a spit.

Too early for the streets to be safe. Too late to try to go back to sleep.

He turned, staggering back into the sparse apartment, picking up the diary-corder off the top of a stack of printouts. His voice sounded odd even to himself. Worn down to the bone.

'Further notes on my direct neural input recording ... I can't make this make sense! Everyone knows that Christopher Marlowe never wrote a play in 1610 called *The Spy at Londinium.* It isn't even recorded as a lost text. Hell, Christopher Marlowe *died* in 1593, May 30 ... But here it is, in the databases. And I can't find even *one* academic record that doesn't take it for granted that the play exists, and that it had its first night in the year 1610.

'Could it be a lost play? But they quote from it. All of them: Boas, Ellis-Fermor, Bradbrook ... And there's no way the play can have been discovered after I left Oxford. Some of the references go back to 1905. I don't *understand.*

'All of them say it's a genuine Marlowe play. But that isn't the important thing. The only thing is. Is. *Fuck.*

'Only schizophrenics get personal messages from the tv set. Is that what's happening here? Was Eugene right when he said it would fuck my mind? Do schizophrenics think sixteenth-century plays were written to give them personal messages? Is that what I am?

'Do I, honestly, think that this is some sort of a *communication* with me? Because that's what it felt like, I swear to God: like something *talking* to me.'

The satellite news soundtrack blipped, breaking his concentration, and he glanced up to see a still graphic of a man. Caught leaning on an ivory walking-stick, free hand scratching at the seat of a pair of white cotton trousers that strained to encase his bulk; the light from the research hospital's windows striking copper fire from his hair.

'UK headline news. There is still no news on the missing American scientist Baltazar Casaubon, last seen at the June launch of the controversial direct neural input method of computerized mind-reading. Michael.'

'Thank you, Eugene. Direct neural input, or direct-brain reading of data, has aroused protest world-wide from civil liberties groups. A ministry spokesman said today that it is not government policy to interfere with commercial developments of multinational corporations not based in the UK. Sony-Nissan and Pacific Rim representatives were unavailable for comment, and representatives of the US Department of Defense issued no statement after seeing the Prime Minister yesterday. No arrest has yet been made of the controversial computer scientist Baltazar Casaubon, rumoured to have been charged with child sex offences. Eugene—'

Two weeks.

Am I going crazy?

Miles Godric stood still for a moment. Outside, a quarrel of sparrows skittered across the opposite warehouse roof. Their noise ceased and he threw down the diary-corder, picked up the webbing and clipped his camera-belt about his waist as he ran for the stairs, grabbing up a sheaf of printouts as he went.

'Block,' the older woman advised.

Rue Ingram gripped the hilt of the bastard sword in sweaty gloved hands. The canted blade hung in her vision, unfocused. Trying not to look at the woman, the woman's eyes, the woman's smile; but to take in passively the whole field of vision: backyard court, flagstones, brick wall, building, fire-escape, woman, sword.

Movement flashed to her left. She dropped her guard position, and caught Valentine Branwen's sword. Halted: slammed into the angle between cross-guard and blade. Blocked.

'Hey!' She grinned, wide enough to hurt the muscles of her cheeks. 'Hey ...'

'Aw, Jesus, it was about time. We been here three days running and that's the first time she's let you use the thing properly.'

Frankie Hollister sat across the bottom rung of the fire-escape, in the diminishing shade, bare feet up on ironwork, ankles crossed. One sweaty fist pushed the hair out of her eyes.

'You're just jealous because you can't afford private tuition now,' Rue needled.

'I will not,' Valentine Branwen said, 'teach this to you, Frankie, so that you can take some irresponsible gang of children out on the street with it. Term's over. It's not my business any more.'

'You're teaching *her*.'

'So I am. But she has more sense than you do.' The woman smiled lopsidedly. 'In another day and age I would have taught sword. Now all I know is how to create two-edged swords of another kind entirely ... OK, OK. Practise with the quarterstaff, Frankie. The drill's the same.'

Rue rubbed moisture out of the hollows of her eyes.

Brilliant light sleeted down into the court, shadows shrinking towards noon. Thirst dried her lips. She frowned, squinting the blaze out of her vision; bounced on the balls of her feet, and swung the hand-and-a-half sword in a cautious, pulled blow.

Silver darted. Valentine's blade flashed in a half circle, parrying her own sword through. The shock of metal scraping metal tingled in her hands. Her grin remained, wide and wider.

The woman said, 'So are you thinking of re-enactment, Rue?'

Concentration never missed a beat. Rue Ingram moved smoothly back, evading a strike, came in again; was suckered to the right for a block, and the woman's sword tapped her lightly on the meaty part of her thigh.

'"Think of it as a three-foot iron bar",' Frankie Hollister quoted, bored. She rested a wooden bokkan over her tanned shoulder, ignoring drill. 'That's what it looks like the way you guys are using it.'

'Because at the moment she has to think about it. Engrave reflexes on her unconscious mind. Input instinctive programs.' Valentine moved springily, her body at ease with the motion of the sword. Each pulled blow landed with no apparent effort, no strain on her wrist. 'Get the unconscious programs running, trigger them with an attack – which I won't do at the moment, Rue; that comes much later – then the whole thing moves faster.'

Safe within the circle of teacher and pupil, Rue Ingram thought block, parry, blow. Not wanting to think but to feel, react.

'I couldn't get out to – ow. Shit, you had me there. I couldn't get out to do re-enactment now. Not now they've closed the borders.' Rue hitched up the strap of her dress. 'My father's talking about taking the government grant for selling our house, and moving up to Manchester or Bristol or Newcastle. But London's still the information capital. He won't move out knowing we can't move back in again later.'

'I been in and out since they closed the borders.' Frankie's voice came from behind. 'S easy. You just got to look like a tourist, is all.'

'What, you, an incomer?' The older woman's voice was lightly teasing.

She put in an attack and Rue swooped to parry it through, metal on metal, a clear ringing sound that Rue had thought she would love and in combat mentally filed under *extraneous noises.*

'If you moved out would you meet your fiancé again?'

Rue blocked, wildly, catching a knuckle against the cross-guard of the woman's blade, and stepped back to strip off her leather glove and suck the finger. Pain or something like it started tears that she blinked back.

She rested the rebated sword back against her shoulder. 'If he couldn't stay here for me, why would I want to leave and go out to him?'

A *thukk!* sounded at her right side, and Rue looked, and her own arm was up, and the sound had been metal against wood. She froze, staring at Frankie's bokkan, that had whistled in at head-height and was now stopped, held by her own raised blade.

'I don't ... I didn't ...'

'First there is *no sword.*' Silver eyes glinted. The older woman even ignored Frankie. 'When the blade becomes an extension of your arm. You don't strike "with the sword", you just strike your opponent's body. And then there is *no intention.* You're not even conscious of seeing the weakness, the blow; you just find you've moved. No sword, no intention. Rue, I think you're starting to learn. Hollister—'

'Val! Val Branwen!'

Rue Ingram automatically lifted her head. The voice came from the entrance to the court. The glint of video lenses caught her gaze. She put the hair back from her hot face. 'Miles?'

Almost not recognizable: the shaven scalp grown out into a yellow-silver crewcut that has the paradoxical effect of making him seem more broad-shouldered. His pale skin reddens with sunburn.

'What is it?' The red-headed woman knelt to lay her military rapier flat. She stood up, stripping off sweat-softened leather gloves and shading her eyes with one arm. 'What's the matter?'

Learning how to see, Rue studied the line of Valentine Branwen's shoulders, silhouetted against inner-court windows, seeing how the muscles relaxed into honesty. *She isn't really that surprised to see him.*

Brown shadows lined his cheeks, hollows thick with stubble a shade darker than his hair. Rue thought *he's older*, and then *no, he's ill.* A belt pulled his combat trousers in to gaunt hip-bones. He cradled a bundle of printouts in his arms.

He ignored Rue, ignored Frankie; spoke to Valentine Branwen as if no one else was there. 'Where's Baltazar?'

'I wish I knew. To tell you the truth, I'm surprised *I'm* still here.'

Rue Ingram sat down on the flagstones, resting the medieval bastard sword across her lap. A bar of light from the flat blade flashed across the man's face. Nothing registered.

'I need to see him!'

'You and every other hypermedia. Not to mention the Ministry of Defence.' Valentine Branwen frowned. Her tone changed. 'Real problems?'

'Oh, sure. Yeah, that's for sure.' He rubbed his face with the heel of his hand and, as if startled, felt the rough stubble with his fingers. His brows lifted. He moved his mouth as if he tasted something stale. Rue saw his pale eyes were red-rimmed.

'I need to speak to him about the link-architecture on direct neural input data,' Miles Godric said.

The woman stared back at him. 'Really?' Blankly unconvinced.

He changed tack. 'I can tell you *most* of what you've been doing.'

Rue, listening for glibness, heard honesty.

'The Yates Institute – half its funding comes from the Confederate Department of Defence. I checked up before your press launch. Now the Defense R & D boys have got your DNI systems back to play with, so they're happy. *Except* – so have the European Ministry of Defence. And so have the commercial companies. In Europe, the States, the Far East – No one can sit on it now!'

Rue slid her fingers down the blunt sword blade. Sun made the metal hot and harmless.

The man said, 'I've got contacts. You were right; no one was going to go public on this at all. You forced the military's hands. Successfully. Now they *want* Baltazar Casaubon.'

The woman raised a red eyebrow. 'If all this were so – and with cameras online, I'm not going to say anything about it – *if* that were true, then it's just the mechanics of the arrangement. You knew what we were doing. It succeeded: end of story.'

'*You look at this!*'

Miles's voice rang off the narrow court's walls. Rue winced, startled.

'*You look, Val.* This is a printout. From the data you recorded off me at the press launch. Listen—' He flourished the paper. It rustled in the noon heat. 'I don't remember any of this. I wouldn't. It's crap. Marlowe never wrote a play in 1610 called *The Spy at Londinium.* He was *dead* by 1610, dead fifteen years! OK, I thought, so it's a program glitch, Casaubon fucked up, DNI doesn't live up to its claims. And then I started reading this.'

Rue Ingram rested her cheek against the blade of the sword. Its blunt edge indented her skin. She sighed for the training, impatient now for the interruption to be over.

'You too, Ingram. Listen.'

Startled, she sat up. The man's eyes, rimmed with sepia shadow, fixed on her. He held up the printout and read aloud:

'"The Spy at Londinium, by Ch. Marlowe, Gent. Act One, enter Lady Regret."'

His voice echoed flatly in the narrow court. Frankie Hollister rested her nose down on her crossed forearms, back curving, shadows marking every indent of her spine. The red-haired woman began to pace, slowly. Rue swallowed with a mouth suddenly dry.

Miles Godric said, 'This is Lady Regret's speech:

'"Under fair nature's eye, within this yard,
Now Phoebus' chariot mounts the morning sky,
I'll make a pyre of every gift he sent.
This gorgeous robe of tissue, like the moon
Glazed over with the silver of the stars,
Its bodice trimmed with fine embroidery—"'

'What?' Rue said. And then, 'Burning a dress. It's talking about burning a dress.'

Miles startled, then nodded. 'That's right; drama student. Checked you out a couple of weeks back. Listen.

"Its bodice trimmed with fine embroidery,
And every panel of it figured o'er
With pictures of the happiness I lack—
I mean, the scene of my defeated love;
My marriage to this faithful-faithless man.
Here let it lie. And I will set my tinder
To cloth as fragile as my delicate flesh:
So let it burn—"'

His halting delivery faded on a dry mouth. He added, 'Then there's a stage direction, "She fires the cloth. Enter a spy." Then the spy says:
"A strange sight, e'en for these degenerate days!
What do you, maiden?" ...'
Rue dropped the broadsword. Metal clashed, echoed back from the high buildings. She snatched the printout from his hands, tearing it, and looked down at the paper:

SPY: A strange sight, e'en for these degenerate days!
What doe you, maiden, wailing in this place
Like Hecuba?
REGRET: Say whats your business here?
I feele no urge to speak of this defeat.
I'lle warrant you your business is far off
From questioning mee, who know not what you are.

'Original spelling.' Rue became aware of Frankie craning to read over her shoulder.

SPY: Madam a scribe is what I am. Or if
You like it better saye I am a spy.
News is my business, sought amongst the court
And retailed at a price that is aboue
The jewelled stars that hang at heauen's ear.
(I would haue heauen's ear too, an I could,
To hear thatte newes which I myself create.
I must discharge my poison where I can.)
Now speak: what strangenesse is this?

REGRET: O regret!
I rue me that I answer what you ask.
As you may see, I burne my wedding dress.
Our cittie is besieged (you know that well)
Like to a landlock'd island, girt about
With greedy hands that seek to rauish us.
My once-sworn loue now dwells without these walls.
I cannot be cojoin'd with him in loue
Because he left me ere the gates were shutt
To follow warres in lands I do not know;
An *Icarus* vpon the fields of blood,
High o'er the land of our most ancient foe.
Go tell it to the court, tis news enough:
Him I cannot follow. This my grief.
Of my life's joys I call him now the thief.
SPY: You burn all colour. Blacks youre funeral pall,
And yet the colour may become one faire,
As it is said, jett lacks not opulence
Because he has night's hue, so grief adorns.
Drink with mee lady it may ease your minde
To tell your grief—

Enter the fatte clowne

CLOWN: A man more fool than I
Would seek, fair child, to know your cause of grief.

'That's us.' She stared at Godric. 'The first time I met you. *That was us*. Here. What the *fuck* do you think you're doing? I didn't ask to be put into any play! That's private!'

Valentine Branwen's hand on her neck, flesh against warm flesh, steadied something of the dizziness in her head. Rue looked a question at the older woman.

Who said, 'If this is a joke, Miles—'

'You look at the bibliography I've printed out. If it's a joke, I'm getting academic references for it that go back nearly a century!'

Breath failed the blond man. His pale eyes screwed up, as if pain clamped around his temples. He hit the printout, ripping the top sheet of paper. Rue read *THE SPYE AT LONDinium by Ch. Marlowe Gent. Printed by Master Rich. Alleyn at St Pawles Churchyarde 1610.* The man thumbed through, sticky-handed, and slapped another page into Valentine's hand.

'Read that! It's a fucking eight-page bibliography. *Where does that come from?*'

Valentine's hand slid away from Rue's shoulder. The woman tapped her bottom lip with her thumbnail. 'You checked this out against university databases, obviously. Did you look at any early print sources?'

'Print? Where would I get time to do the legwork? I called it up through databases—' Godric stopped dead. Rue saw him nod, once, and a shadow leave his eyes, to be replaced by anger. 'Primary sources. Original print books. They won't say anything about a new Marlowe play – because it's a fucking electronic *forgery.*'

Rue reached out and tugged the printout from his grip.

Valentine spoke slowly. 'Miles ... it couldn't ... but I can't see any other explanation – I think the program must be somehow recasting your DNI recording in the form of a four-hundred-year-old play. Christ alone knows *why.* Maybe something corrupted the data.'

'Val, it *isn't* all my recording. There's stuff here *I* couldn't know! She never told me about this guy she was supposed to marry!' He turned away from the older woman. 'Rue. Is there anything in this that's about him? That *you* didn't tell me?'

She searched the paper. Letters blurred in her vision, loss of concentration unfocusing her eyes. At last she said, '"To follow—" *wars,* is it? "— in lands I do not know." Icarus. I never told you he was a helicopter pilot. I never told you he was posted to France.'

The printout concertinaed out of his hands, spilling across the dusty flagstones. Rue fell to her knees between them, knocking against the older woman's muscled leg; scrabbled among the papers as Miles Godric squatted beside her, and Valentine at last went down on one knee to rummage through the coffee-marked, half-torn pages of text.

Frankie Hollister, still sitting on the fire-escape, grunted and watched.

'How long have you been snooping on me?' Rue demanded.

Miles Godric sat back on his bare heels. An edge of one camcorder on his belt grazed her arm. 'How much did you talk with Baltazar Casaubon about your boyfriend?'

'I didn't. Are you saying this is *his* idea of a joke?'

The older woman gazed at Miles Godric. She let what paper she held fall to the flagstones. Her eyes squinted against the sunlight. 'The play's incomplete.'

'It's all fragments. It doesn't,' he said, 'it doesn't actually read like Marlowe. It reads like every Renaissance dramatist I ever had to study for my degree, in collaboration.'

'It could be just that. Your memories of reading them. A freak arrangement of data.'

'How did the program learn to do that? And where does the other data come from! And, Val, that isn't what it feels like. It feels ... like there's something there. When I play it back. Something ... there.'

The silver lenses blink. A tremor of genuine disquiet? Or something else? Dazzled, Rue dropped her gaze, seeing the mess of papers through green and purple after-images.

Godric said, 'I need to find Baltazar! There's more about the "clown" in here, listen:

"Go bid the spy devise most cunningly
A plot by which we may o'erhear the man:
This clown's a very oracle for news.
And all who wish their Delphic questions answered—"

Then a lot of mythological references, then:

"He hath a room, more fell than Faustus's,
In which he practises a rare conceit:
Devices like to Bacon's brazen head
That spoke and said, *Time is, was, and will be,*
Speak unto him, and tell him far-off news.
This clown, master of witty devices,
Perils his fat soul: spy, go seek him out ..."'

Rue sat, legs sprawling under the thin, hot cotton of her skirt. Valentine shook her head.

'*Where is he?*' Miles demanded.

'I don't know.'

'Bullshit!' a female voice interrupted. Rue, startled, stared over her shoulder at Frankie Hollister. The short girl sprang up, letting the bokkan fall, and shoved her fists in her dungarees pockets as she swaggered over to Valentine.

'I seen you two together that time. Don't tell me *you* can't find him. Not if you want to. Don't give me that crap!'

With some satisfaction the blonde girl squatted and rested her arm across Rue's shoulders.

The weight of flesh made Rue sweat in the noon heat. She shrugged free and knuckled Frankie's arm. 'Get off!'

'I want two things understood, Miles,' Valentine Branwen said softly. 'The first is that you turn your video equipment offline now, and you put it back online when I tell you to, and that's the way it is.'

The man reached to his belt controls. She watched him.

'The second thing is, Rue, you and your little friend will have to come too. Just for the moment, I don't want anyone sneaking off to the news media.'

She touched the spilled printout.

'Maybe ... I can find him if I can think like him.'

CHAPTER NINE

Earlier that Same Morning

A liquid plop sounded.

Baltazar Casaubon wiped his massive hand across his face without bothering to open his eyes. A sticky substance smeared his fingers. He wiped it down his shirt, and sat up. His eyes opened.

Pigeons wheeled over Trafalgar Square.

The sun, not high enough to have burned off the dew, struck against the sides of buildings all down gridlocked Whitehall, and flashed in gold from the spires of the House of Commons. He wrenched his neck one way, then the other, creaking; and grunted.

The ABS plastic computer case jabbed into his massive flank. He got slowly to his feet, and stretched. One shirt-button pinged, losing itself among the pigeons grazing on early tourist grain.

'*Mon pauvre ami*!' A coin clinked on the guano-spotted pavement.

The link-architect Casaubon yawned jaw-crackingly wide, stretched his bolster-thick arms, and swooped to pick the pound coin up. He looked, but the tourists had wandered off towards Nelson's Column.

'*Merci bien*,' the large man rumbled. '*Mille fois*.'

No traffic sounded in the Square. All the air shone clear, sun delineating the NeoClassical columns of the National Gallery with a pristine grace. He grinned widely, and wiped the remains of the pigeon droppings off his faintly-freckled face. He belched. Rummaging under the lip of the fountain found him the shoes and jacket he had used as a pillow.

'As to that ...' His voice rumbled, deep in the morning air. He hooked one shoe on, a finger under the trodden-down heel; then the other; and shrugged himself gratefully into the creased and stained jacket. '... *now* we shall see what we shall see.'

He made a faint gesture by way of brushing himself down, and strode off across the square, and then down an alley, past St Martin-in-the-Fields church into Adelaide Street.

'Hey, mate, got any change?'

He took his absent-minded gaze off the Victorian Gothic roof of Charing Cross Station, the sun sliding down its spires as morning advanced. Two men in dirty sleeping-bags lay half-sitting in a doorway; a girl with cropped yellow hair squatted beside one, a cigarette hanging from her fingers.

'I do believe I ...' The pound coin came easily to his searching fingers. He proceeded to turn out each pocket, slinging his case by its strap over his shoulder.

'What you got there then, mate?'

'That's his change of clothes,' the girl said. 'Off for an interview, he is. "You've got the job, what's your address, then?" "Er, third cardboard box on the right, Trafalgar Square." "Well fuck off then we ain't got no job for you!" That's about the size of it, innit?'

'You.' The link-architect pointed a massive, fat finger in her direction, and beckoned magisterially. 'Come with me.'

'Oh yeah. Want me to do that, do you?'

The girl glanced at the younger of the two men, who shrugged to his feet. His sleeping bag had split at the end. He wore it as a robe. They followed as the fat man, head high, walked down past the entrance to the Underground station.

'It's obvious when you think about it.' Baltazar Casaubon waved his free hand. 'How ridiculous the damned thing is. You know what's being taken away from you? *Time.* Time for the important things like making love, and good food, and arguing about what kind of Art is truly moral. Don't you agree?'

The man scrubbed at his stubbled cheeks with a hand upon which the nails were blue and blackened. 'I think you're a fucking nutter, mate.'

A dozen men and women were gathered around the standpipe at the corner with the Strand. Baltazar Casaubon queued to take his turn, and cup plump hands to hold the freezing water, and rinse his face and neck.

He looked up, copper-red hair sleeked wetly to his forehead.

'I'll show you,' he said.

Another two or three people joined him on his majestical promenade along the pavement of the Strand, appearing out of abandoned cars and shop doorways. By the time he reached the bank fifteen or so men and women crowded his heels, hacking coughs into the morning air.

'So now what?' the blonde girl demanded.

The link-architect thoughtfully picked his nose, and wiped his fingers down his once-white shirt. He looked about him helplessly. Then he beamed, and bent over (knocking an older man three steps back with the collison) and picked up an abandoned pencil from the pavement.

He walked along the bank's frontage to the cash dispenser, and, on the white marble above it, carefully inscribed two numbers. He entered them into the cash point, fat and dirty fingers poising delicately to tap each numeral. And then he stood back.

The machine whirred.

A grinding sounded, down in the depths; vibrating through the paving stones. A harsh ratcheting sound started, stopped, and picked up again. The cash point cover slid up.

Twenty-pound notes slid down the rollers, jammed, and slid out, pushed by the force of notes behind them. Ten, a dozen, a hundred, two hundred...

A flick of wind caught them, and the ten- and fifty-pound notes that followed, a whole stream, darting up into the air above the Strand like birds; and the street-sleepers at first stared, then grabbed, then chuckled, and bellowed, waking others, frightening the first businessmen coming in from the station; and all the while the link-architect Casaubon leaned back on his ivory sword-stick and watched the notes pay out: the financial artery cut and spouting into the street.

The blonde girl saw him go, but – both hands, all pockets, and the front of her t-shirt crammed with notes – didn't bother to follow. With a biro she carefully wrote on her arm, in blue ink, the numbers inscribed above the cash point.

By midday the knowledge of the numbers had spread as far as Southwark, and by two o'clock the banks suspended business.

CHAPTER TEN

Owls and Other Birds of Prey

The noise of a drill echoed down from dusty heights, drowning out a clock striking three. Valentine Branwen glanced up at the scaffolding and plastic-shrouded building at the end of Monmouth Street, and then back at the outside of *The Greene Lyon.* A cardboard notice in the pub window neatly lettered NO WORK BOOTS OR OVERALLS.

'OK, OK, I'm *going.*' Frankie Hollister pushed her way rapidly back out through the swing doors.

'Can't find a working phonebox hardly anywhere these days.' The short girl glared. 'I got through, though. The woman says you can come over. Sounds a right old bag to me.'

Valentine Branwen raised an eyebrow.

From inside *The Greene Lyon* a voice shouted something undecipherable but hostile. Swaggering a little, Frankie caught up with Valentine's rapid walk. She said, 'I can't go in half the pubs round here.'

'Why not?'

'Because I'm a Hollister.' A pause, as if it should be self-explanatory. 'Hollister Construction, yeah? See the sign back there? My father's sacked half the labourers on this site. So there's pubs I can't drink in because there's too much hassle. Not trouble, I don't *mind* trouble; just hassle. And then there's other places I can drink because I *am* a Hollister – there's a lot of us. Me mum was the only girl among nine boys, so there's all them, and my sisters' husbands. See?'

Valentine nodded with something that might have been

nostalgia. She remained aware of Rue Ingram hovering at the girl's elbow, and of Miles Godric walking as if the solid pavement were rubber under his feet. A horse-drawn dray loaded with cladding rumbled up St Martin's Lane towards the building site, in a slow weave between burnt-out vehicles cleared to the sides of the road. All conversation ceased until the noise passed them.

'We're not that rough,' Frankie Hollister said. 'There's some of our lot I wouldn't mess with. There was one got sent down for GBH and armed robbery – he didn't *do* the armed robbery, but the law came round and did his place over and said he assaulted them. They didn't have any evidence and they were deliberately winding him up. But he wasn't a Hollister, he was one of me brother-in-laws' cousins, I think. They think I'm dead thick, going to college.'

The short girl shrugged her dungarees up over her shoulders, the cloth showing gaps where safety-pins held the straps together. Grime ringed her neck, London's black dust. Valentine looked from Frankie to Rue.

Oh, Frankie. The original, of which the other is but a pale copy. But my time's run out, I think.

They turned into Long Acre, the street shining in the afternoon heat, tourists scanning those shop windows not boarded up. Mark Knopfler on lead guitar sounded from a ghetto blaster. Below the Victorian brick skyline, glass and steel frontages glittered. She tasted air growing cleaner by the day.

'Miles ...'

Camcorder lenses glittered, mechanically alert. The man walked hunched in the heat, fingers whitely gripping the pile of printout. She withstood an impulse to put her arm around his muscular torso.

She shook her head, feeling her sun-hot hair brush her shoulders, shuddering with a kind of physical realization of the city itself: brick, stone and mortar, river and gulls and burnt-out cars; still thronged with people, still the heartland of her soul. 'You've got first rights on the inside story of DNI: you can ask your own price for your next career step. You're *OK*.'

'Not if I hand in a story that sounds like a schizoid hallucination!'

He gripped the mass of paper he cradled. The pallor of his skin glowed in the high afternoon light.

'Direct neural input had powerful enemies. They've gone

quiet,' Miles Godric said, surprising her with his coherence. 'Or have they?'

She looked at his hair, roots growing out very fair, and the thin beard that lined his cheeks; and met his pale eyes, with a vision of how he would be in twenty years time, older, confused, compromised; but undefeated.

He said, 'You didn't use e-mail because hackers read e-mail. You used a public phone, not the one in the flat. You really are trying to get out from under.'

'For a couple of hours, maybe.'

'Jesus Christ, woman, did Baltazar even *think* about what he was doing? Direct neural input – it's a secret policeman's wet dream! We're close enough to a fascist police state as it is. Yes, OK, fear screws up the reading, and it's fragmentary, but it'll be improved, there'll be drugs—'

Seeing that he would speak piecemeal, she did nothing but make a small prompting noise.

He said, 'That's if anything genuine is coming out of it. *If* it is.'

She came to a halt as they crossed the top of Neal Street, the two younger women some yards ahead, and he stopped with her; and lifted his head to stare at the clarity of the summer sky.

'But when it turns out garbage like this—!' Miles hugged the printout tighter to his chest. Valentine watched him: heat-stricken, eyes rimmed with sweat. His hands pressing flat against the paper, as if that meant he would never have to read the words again.

'I almost hope it is garbage. Even if I never see any money out of it if it is.'

'But is it garbage?' she said. 'Where does a "play" come from, how can it exist? Does it invalidate DNI?'

Valentine Branwen fisted her hands and stretched, shoulders relaxing in the pressure of summer's heat. Still ozone summer; and the horizon a hazy white-blue. She licked her lips, this time tasting grit. The entrance to Covent Garden tube loomed.

'It's one of two answers,' she said. 'It does. Or it doesn't. And, believe me, I want to know which one it is just as badly as you do!'

After an hour and three-quarters of changing lines on the Underground, Rue Ingram stood in an outside yard watching a big copper-haired woman bite into a peach. Juice ran down the woman's muscular forearm, blotting the faint gold fuzz of hair. The woman wiped her mouth with the back of her hand, and put the peach-pit between her back teeth and cracked it.

'Baltazar who?' she enquired. 'Never heard of him.'

Rue looked tentatively at Valentine Branwen.

Who shoved her shirtsleeves up, and pulled the tail of her shirt out of her jeans, flapping the cloth to circulate air over hot flesh. 'How are the kids behaving?'

The big copper-haired woman spat out the fractured peach stone. She appeared to relax. 'The boy's fine. I left him reading the *Financial Times*. The girl's an unholy terror.'

'*Tell* me about it ...'

They seemed to overflow the small yard behind the wooden fence: Rue with Frankie, the cameraman with Valentine Branwen, and the big woman in dungarees. Rue craned her neck. The afternoon sun gleamed on the woman's hair (the colour of fuse-wire), on pale and freckled flesh. A face that is young except for crepe-skin around the eyes: forty or so.

'And White Crowe's still collecting cute little girls.' The large woman winked at Rue Ingram. Frankie gave her a blistering glare. 'And reporters?'

Rue glanced at Miles Godric. The camcorder lenses glinted at his web-belt, his knuckles were white around the sheaf of paper.

The teacher of sword, the sun bright on her bush of dark red hair and on her white shirt, prodded the large woman's denim-covered belly.

'Are you going to let us in, or are we going to stand out here and fry?' Valentine asked acerbically.

'Baltazar hasn't been here, you know. She thinks you know where he is.'

A voice from inside the block of flats called, 'Dorothea!'

The big woman pushed the front door open and led the way in.

Out of the sun, indoors, Rue blinked retinal after-images out of her vision. A council flat front room full of furniture and perches. Something stank.

'My mother keeps owls,' the large woman explained, just as Rue realized that the copper eyes staring at her from every corner blinked. A pointed wing lifted, stretched. 'And other birds of prey. It means the place stinks of droppings, we keep very odd hours, and the fridge is full of dead mice. Have some icecream?'

Her surprisingly delicate hand appeared out of the dimness.

Rue Ingram stared at the dish of chocolate-chip icecream.

'You don't want any?' The big orange-haired woman walked past Rue. She hitched one large haunch on to the edge of a desk, snagging her torn denims on the old wood. She rested the dish against her large cotton-shirted breasts. Through a mouthful of icecream she said, 'Waste not, want not!'

Rue watched how the tiny room, hot despite all open windows, made the woman's fair skin flush pink; freckles deepening across her wide forehead and cheeks. Her massy orange hair was escaping from its braid, sneaking tendrils across her heavily muscled arms.

'Really, Dorothea, where are your manners?'

'Sorry, Mum.'

'Pour the tea.' A white-haired woman, tiny in this family of large, self-indulgent redheads, spoke from an armchair. She frowned critically at Dorothea. It was unclear, at a second glance, whether this glare was intended for her daughter or for the Scops Owl, fully grown and barely five inches tall, that gripped her own outstretched finger. She turned to Rue Ingram. 'My name is Luka, my dear. Please sit down. Your friend too.'

Frankie remained recalcitrantly standing, fists buried in her dungarees-pockets. Rue held back something that might become hysterical laughter and took the teacup Dorothea passed to her. She tasted the appallingly weak tea. 'Um, thanks. Yeah. Thanks.'

The old woman began feeding something yellow and red and furry to the Scops Owl from between her withered lips. She could be no taller than four foot six. Her silver hair hung down her back in a braid as thick as her daughter's arm. A few bright hawk feathers had been woven into the strands.

She abandoned the Scops Owl reluctantly. 'Valentine, my dear, with all respect to the way you and Izumi choose to bring them up – I simply cannot cope with both your children! Not even with Dorothea's assistance. And she can hardly be absent from work for ever.'

Rue balanced the fancy tea-cup and saucer. She looked to Valentine Branwen for a cue.

'Izumi will have them back in California soon. I've booked a flight. I need to show Baltazar something before he goes back to her.' Valentine hesitated. 'Miles, if I can take the printout—'

'No!' The man blinked in the indoor summer dimness. He locked gazes with Valentine, ignoring everyone else in the room.

'I want to see Baltazar Casaubon *now*.'

Valentine halted for a half-second, her gaze sweeping the room. She did not take notice of Rue. She grinned, winked at Miles Godric, said, 'Don't go away!' and vanished back out into the corridor.

'She doesn't believe he's not here. I'll keep an eye on her.' Dorothea rose up and slouched out of the room, still carrying her bowl of icecream.

'Well, now.' The old woman, Luka, turned back. 'I don't believe I know your name, young man.'

'He's Miles Godric.' Rue said, when she saw he wasn't going to. She put the cup and saucer down on a spindly table. 'Are you Baltazar Casaubon's mother?'

'Yes, my dear.' The old woman beamed. It was time-faded, and aided with dentures, but Rue recognized it: the link-architect's benevolent, unselfconscious beam.

'Do you know, I grew up on an estate like this?' Miles Godric suddenly gave an absent, cut-off chuckle. 'Flat blocks, no gardens, and always knowing out there it was *London*...'

He took an automatic foursquare stance, catching all the room within the range of camcorders, adjusting contrast levels.

'I knew the way out when I was eight – university, networking, technological specialization. I made it.'

'Oh fer Chrissakes!' Frankie moved with a swing to her elbows that threatened every ornament, dresser, coffee table, and hooded hawk in the tiny crowded room. Belled jesses jangled. The low mutter of bird sound rose to shrieks. She strode across to the back window. Rue saw a square of common grass beyond the glass. 'Let's stop pissing about. We don't have to stay here. C'mon, Rue.'

'And you must be the young lady I spoke with on the telephone. "Frankie".' Luka lifted the Scops Owl. It blinked amazingly large furry eyelids at Rue, opened its beak, and hissed. A thin strip of leather held one of its legs, wound between the old woman's fingers. It threw itself forward ferociously, straining the leather, hissing. A dropping splashed white-and-black on the hem of Rue's dress.

'I love it.' Rue grinned. 'A little pitbull owl.'

The heat did not lessen. It altered in quality from stunning to stifling. Lulled, the hawks stood motionless on their perches. Miles Godric, with one careful fingertip, stroked the back of the Scops Owls' head. 'Val brought us a long way round to get here, but I could find the place again. I'll just keep coming until I find out what's going on. Until I find Baltazar Casaubon.'

'I haven't seen my son. The police have asked me the same questions.' Luka stood up, placing the owl on a perch and her empty cup on the one table that seemed out of place in the room. A stout desk, covered in paperwork, with a battered large monitor and keyboard. The monitor displayed a 3D exploded graphic of architectural plans.

Rue sauntered over, eyeing the incomplete drawings. An inset in one corner of the screen showed what was presumably the finished plan: a spired and multi-floored anachronism large enough to be an office block or major museum. Luka's voice at her elbow said:

'Dorothea has no sense of the Classical virtues. No order, harmony, restraint. She will persist with these Baroque monstrosities. They're so ...' The old woman sought a suitable classification. 'So flamboyant.'

'I like 'em.' Rue picked up the 1996 desk calendar. Still on June.

'He's *not* here?' Miles sounded dazed.

Rue walked across and shook Miles's shoulders. His muscles hardly tensed against her. 'Of course he's not here! Haven't you been listening? Aw, for fuck's sake!'

'Language,' Luka said critically. 'You young girls are much too excitable, 'I've always said so.'

Rue fisted her hand and punched Miles in the ribs. He grunted, pained, rubbing his side; and suddenly focused. 'You're not too old for a good shaking—'

'We need you to be with it!' she snarled. The heat of the afternoon made her sweaty, breathless, short-tempered. 'I don't understand what's going on. I'm in this too! That play ... Valentine acts like she doesn't know, but it's just an act. I don't believe her! I want to know what's happening!'

'Yeah!' Frankie hefted her slipping dungarees straps up over her shoulders.

'Ah.' The small white-haired woman tsk-ed. A flurry of wings in the sun-dark room came from a tethered peregrine hawk. Rue, turning, flinched from movement, and felt claws prick her own scalp. She reached up with over-controlled patience and coaxed the Scops Owl on to her forefinger.

'"Ah"?' Rue said. 'What does *that* mean?'

'People often react to my daughter-in-law that way. If I were

Baltazar I doubt I would permit – but there: old women become interfering old biddies. I won't interfere.' Her thin face creased. Rue watched all the parlour's light shine in her eyes.

'I don't get it.'

The old woman moved her gaze quite deliberately to Frankie. Frankie Hollister wiped at the back of her sweating, dirty neck; and suddenly looked confused.

'Really,' Luka said.

Stillness came, suddenly catching up: the long, hot walk over; the flat dim and shining. Rue replaced the owl and put her hands up, and smoothed her straggling black hair back from her face. Her palms felt hot. She ignored Miles Godric's stare, concentrating now on the old woman's face.

'I think you'd better tell me what you mean.'

'I'll put it as plainly as I can,' Luka said. 'My dear, if you're sleeping with my daughter-in-law, she won't leave Baltazar for you.'

Valentine stood in the kitchen, regarding the street through the window, her face blank.

'The police have been here several times,' Dorothea said. 'I think my brother has been very careful not to come here.'

'But a message? He has to have left a message somewhere!'

A rhythmic noise intruded itself over her attention threshold.

Dorothea moved back down the entrance hall, looked, and then came to lean her immense bulk against the door-jamb, finishing her icecream. 'Something's up.'

'Not the kids?'

'No. They're safe.' Dorothea straightened broad shoulders. 'But I think you'd better come out now and deal with it.'

CHAPTER ELEVEN

Brutal Isolation

A twinge of hunger surprised Valentine as she paced down the corridor behind Dorothea. She glanced at her watch and found it after six. The summer afternoon light streamed in through the open front door. She squinted against the rising dust.

An olive drab Lynx, rotors heavily turning, stood on the piece of common grass between the flat blocks. Soldiers in woodland camouflage ringed the perimeter. She could just make out, through the helicopter's windscreen, a man in a suit.

She showed teeth in what might have been a grin, raising her voice over the idling engine. 'OK, Dor. I know who it is. You want to take the kids out to Covent Garden for an icecream?'

The big woman nodded. 'Jay already told me to. He's smart, your boy. Weird, but smart.'

A brown-haired boy of perhaps eleven stood waiting quietly on the path, ignoring the helicopter, his black trousers neatly pressed and his white shirt buttoned up to the neck. A three-year-old girl crouched by the fence, sun bright on her orange curls. Her summer dress was rucked up around her chest, and she squatted, chuckling. She was peeing ornamental patterns in the dust.

'I haven't really seen them long enough this time. It'll take them a while to get used to me again.' Valentine looked wistfully at the little girl. 'Phone before you bring them back here.'

'Trust me.'

Luka entered the hall, closing the door to the front room behind her with a cold deliberation. Her blue eyes were milky as the sky. '*That person* has come here. Tell me when she leaves.'

The old woman stalked towards her kitchen.

Somewhere in the next flat a sound-system plays *Your Latest Trick*, and Valentine paused for a second, slowing her pulse to the beat. Then she turned and went into the front room.

Rue and Frankie stood together by the open window; Rue whispering uncomfortably in the smaller girl's ear; Frankie leaning back against the sill with her ankles crossed. Miles Godric sat bolt upright on the sofa.

Johanna Branwen sat at Dorothea's desk. Her gloved fingers flicked across the keyboard. The monitor glowed faint rainbows under sunlight. 'Interesting ...' Johanna leaned back and stretched her arms out wide. The white fur collar of her jacket framed her plump, lined face and steel-silver hair.

Valentine looked her up and down. The woman wore a startlingly white tracksuit and Nike trainers. Gold bracelets clinked on her wrists; gold flashed at her ears and fingers.

'I was just discussing with Luka the inadvisability of having illegal anti-surveillance equipment in your house,' the woman's familiar voice said. 'She chose to leave. You're sending my grandchildren away. Permit me to send these other children with them.'

'You took your time getting here.'

No surprise at that comment showed on the middle-aged woman's face. Caught in the automatic power-plays of conversation with Johanna Branwen, Valentine suddenly sighed. 'I *didn't* expect you in person. Let's talk. Really talk.'

'I don't believe I'm familiar with that experience where you're concerned.'

There was a smothered laugh. Johanna Branwen glanced over her shoulder at the two girls.

'You find that funny? Mmm. Interesting. Frances Amy Hollister, aged eighteen, student, four juvenile convictions for – let me see – driving without a licence, arson, being in possession of proscribed substances, carrying an offensive weapon. To wit, one sharpened steel comb.'

'Aw, *what*? Fuck you, man.'

'And Rue Ingram. No criminal record, as such; but there was that abortion you had last year. Did you ever tell your lover that you had become pregnant, before he was posted overseas? No, I beg your pardon, this was your previous lover. The married man.'

'That's a lie!'

'It *is* a lie,' Frankie Hollister wailed. 'I'm her mate. I should know.'

'Perhaps you should. But obviously you don't.'

'That's enough.' Valentine Branwen walked across the small, hot room. Birds of prey stretched, hooded beaked heads questing. She put one hand on Rue's shoulder, one on Frankie's. Feeling the hearts beat through sweat-sticky flesh. Holding the two of them. 'So she has access to Home Office records. That's not exactly surprising.'

'"She." You don't call me "mother",' the older woman stated. 'You don't call me anything, I notice. Not even "Johanna".'

Valentine squeezed Rue's shoulder, then Frankie's. 'Go.'

'Yeah.' Frankie Hollister swaggered across the sunlit room, reached down and took a handful of biscuits from Luka's plate as she passed, stuffed them in her mouth and went out spitting crumbs. Miles Godric got unsteadily to his feet.

At the door Rue turned her head. Valentine met her gaze. A tall, leggy girl; black hair falling on to sun-golden shoulders; her creased black dress marked with the droppings of owls. One of the merlin hawks cried. Valentine looked away from the intensity of Rue's stare, and moments later heard the door close.

'Shit, why do you always do that? Why try to destroy people?'

'They'll have forgotten it by tomorrow. Turn round and let me look at you.'

'Don't say "it's been too long". You know what I look like. You'll have seen enough security tapes of me over the last couple of years.'

Slowly, she turns. Aware of grime on her white jeans and shirt; aware of sweat-patches under her arms, and the summer smell of hot flesh. She tucked strands of dark red hair away behind her ears.

'You look older,' Johanna Branwen said.

'How much heavy support did you bring with you?'

'They don't let me go anywhere without security, I'm afraid. One of the penalties of being a cabinet minister. Morgan is in the helicopter. The rest, I assume, are where they usually are. I think it's more than time that I spoke to your – to Baltazar Casaubon.'

Valentine looked down at her own callused hands. 'Sometimes, when I wonder how I got to be such a bastard, I think about you. Then I know. I learned it from an expert.'

'That's pathetic.' Johanna Branwen got up from the desk. An inch or so smaller than her daughter, but somehow giving the impression that her sight-line is an inch or two taller. She walked across and closed the louvre window. The sun-dim room grew hotter and more stifling. The hooded birds became quiescent.

She said, 'The truth is, that what we find out, as we get older, is that we are not nice people. It may be the last illusion one loses. Only pride restrains us from cruel and immoral acts. Pride in not being that sort of person.'

She undid the belt of her jacket, and drew off her pale leather gloves.

'And some of us, as well, when we learn enough about ourselves to stop pretending we care about injustice, go further and learn that we love gratuitous cruelty for its own sake. And the thing is—'

Valentine felt her arms gripped. She looked levelly into the older woman's eyes.

'– the thing is, *it doesn't matter.*'

Hands grip her, hands that are older than hers but the same shape. Blue-white at the fingertips. Raynaud's Disease. The smell of these hands is familiar from memories too deep to despise: memories of when chairs were tall, and the ground close and interesting, and hands were there to wash you clean. The hands of someone tall, who settles the frightening world into intelligibility. The hands of a smart, strong, beautiful mother; to whom (as it should) the world comes to listen.

Valentine reached up and detached the older woman's fingers. She held the cool hands for a moment. 'Casaubon's not here. Hasn't been here. And there's no message.'

'Really?'

A tremor in those cold hands. The fragility of older flesh goes through Valentine like a knife of pity. She loosens her grip. 'I used to – worship you. I wanted to be just like you, in control of everything, making everything do what you wanted. It would have frightened me, then, to think there could be something you don't know about. Or that if you do know – which wouldn't surprise me – you don't know what it means.'

Valentine held out her hand to Miles Godric, who had remained standing. She took the scrolled-up printout, reversed and scrolled it the other way, flattening the paper out.

'I expect,' she said, 'that you will have seen this.'

Rue looked at the soldiers who lay with their rifles around the perimeter of the common ground. She walked down the path, skirting the yellow grass beaten down by the military helicopter.

The blonde girl said, 'Is it true?'

'Frankie, you're *Catholic.* What was I going to say to you?'

There were several men, not in uniform, wearing jackets despite the heat. Two of them began to walk around the path. The noise of the idling rotors made it difficult to speak. Rue went with them when they reached her.

'Just a few questions,' one shouted. 'Purely routine.'

The other showed an ID that seemed official.

She believed them, being realistic about it. *They'll have checked us out, down to dental records. If she's a cabinet minister's daughter, then I guess they know all of what Frankie and me have been doing at the dojo. This is just procedure.*

It was not until she was climbing awkwardly up the step into the body of the helicopter, smelling hot oil and metal, deafened by the rotors, that she properly saw the pilot. His mirror visor was pushed up.

Her automatic glance at the plain-clothes officers made her think, by their faces, that this was not a surprise to them.

'Wynne?'

Flight Lieutenant Wynne Ashton said something to his helmet mike. Sweat pearled his skin, what she could see of it under the equipment and flight suit. That skin that smells of spices.

'Well, Jesus,' Rue Ingram said, her voice breaking at every word, but her head up, 'isn't *that* just wonderful?'

'Not now,' Ashton muttered, obviously painfully embarrassed.

'"Not now."' Rue from ignorance or pain could ignore the idling rotors, the turboshaft engine, the weight of the aircraft and the accidents that might happen if the pilot's attention wandered. '*You* can tell *me* "not now"?'

'Rue...'

'Oh, you can remember my name. *That's* nice.'

The visor curves down, blanking her vision of his eyes, and sunlight slides across it as his head moves away.

'Go fuck yourself,' Rue said. And then, 'How could you just *go*? You didn't even speak to me!'

His head did not turn.

'Shit...'

She was unsure whether he heard her. She moved, stooped, to sit on one of the bolted-in metal benches. One of the plain-clothes officers fastened a lap-strap across her body, and leaned back wiping owl-shit off his cuff.

Frankie Hollister reached over and held her hand tightly.

The heat of the airless room dizzied Valentine. She leaned over Johanna Branwen's shoulders, watching the older woman's face as the woman began to read.

'A play.' Her eyes slid down the cast list. She looked at Miles Godric. 'With a "Ladie Johannah". And a "Valentinia". This was a poor joke.'

Miles Godric wiped his face, hand rasping over his scruffy beard. Valentine waited for him to say something.

'Ah.' She grinned at Johanna. 'I forget. You terrify me because you're my mother. I was never afraid of you as a cabinet minister. Other people are. Miles, she's seen this already. I'd put money on it.'

'Wait outside.' Johanna Branwen watched Miles Godric to the door. As it closed behind the big man, she began to read aloud, quickly at first, and then more slowly. 'Let me see: "the Ladie Johannah" has a speech here . . .

"My damnèd daughter fled the Western Land
As sly thieves flee, my agents circumventing—
And mark me, servant, those must be abused
In keeping with my curious wit's desire:
Condemn them to a lower prison cell
For five long years; and for my daughter's fate
Let her be calumniated with all vile
Rumour, and her feckless husband too.
The world must well believe that they are mad,
That done – and other lies which I'll suggest—
They'll speak in Sphinx's riddles to the world,
And not a world of words will be believed."'

Johanna gave a chuckle. 'Interesting. I would have sworn the security systems around my office were impregnable. But then, of course, there's no such thing as an unsurveillable target. But why this doggerel? And why try to pass it off as direct neural input?'

Valentine said, 'You're not shocked that I now know you were behind the smears.'

'I'm hardly ever shocked, you should know that.'

'Yes.'

'And if this is an attempt to do it—'

The older woman broke off. Valentine looked up from the coffee-and-guano stained papers. Johanna held two sheets of printout in her hands. She sat down, without looking behind her, on the sofa. A Tawny Owl blinked at her with flat, back-lit gold eyes.

'And that,' she said, 'is one of the penalties of an extremely rapid reading-speed. One takes things in too quickly. Takes in the poison with the apple, as it were ...'

Valentine sat beside her. The soft sofa threw them together, hip to hip in close proximity. The cool of the woman, in that summer afternoon heat, brought back other, older memories. Valentine traced down the page with her fingertip. 'Let's see? Um ... a "Secretarie" says:

"Ambassadors from foreign potentates
Would speak with you; and you yourself will speak
And dine with those who curry favours from you ..."

Then "Johannah":

"See you this blade? It hath an edge so sharp
Nought in this world may match it, save my wit,
Which so excels the common run of men
That you may rightly say, I rightly rule."'

Valentine raised an eyebrow. 'Oh. Your knife. Did you say that?'

Johanna Branwen leaned forward, her hands clasped together in her lap. 'After a fashion, I may have ... implied that. But one would have to know me better than most to guess at it.' She began to pull on soft leather gloves.

Valentine read on. 'Stage directions. "Lady Johannah as in a dream. Enter to her her child Valentinia, attended by demons, at several doors." Demons?'

The older woman said, 'We all have demons.'

Valentine read aloud. '"First demon":

'"We come as heralds of the coming day
When Dies Irae is loosed upon the world.
All that men know, all men now shall share—"'

She stopped, and began again:

'"All that men know, all men now shall share,
As once Pandora loosed upon the world
All ills and sores that tetter on your skins.
O Man! Beware. At her hand, hope was left.
What hope for you?"

Then "Mephistophilis" ...

"All in the balance lies.
Whether this be the work of my Dread Lord,
Or whether it shall be that after this
Man shall partake of angel qualities
Having the angels' knowledge of the earth,
Remains unknown until this fruit is tried."'

The sun's warmth filled the room, filtering in golden. The smell of droppings and dead meat stuffed the nostrils. Luka was in the kitchen, banging pans. Starting with the old peregrine on the corner perch, the hawks screeled. Wasps buzzed. Valentine breathed out a long breath. '*Did* you dream?'

'Good God! In the middle of a heavy day with parliament sitting? No, I did not dream.'

'I... You had me worried there for a minute.'

Johanna snorted. 'This is pure fiction.'

'Is it?' Valentine said. 'Is it? Impure fiction, at least. Oh, I *see*.

"VALENTINIA": "We make the world anew. Not shame nor pity
Stays our hand. What though disaster come?
Power's not bred without pain, nor love from mirth.
We choose to loose the dogs upon the world:
Heralds or hell-hounds, let Time choose their courses."
"MEPHISTOPHILIS": "How is this different? How is this the same?"
"JOHANNAH": "The governing of man, for good or ill,
Is mine. Such a Medusa's art it is,
It hardens we who wrestle it to stone.
Pity I have not, love I never knew.
Thus you'd excuse me, daughter of my womb,

For actions taken when my course is plain.
How then, for actions similar, excuse you?
Necessity we both claim for our god."
"MEPHISTOPHILIS": "Bred in one cradle, sister more than mother;
Fighting the world behind the self-same blade.
How could you fail but recognise the other,
Mirrored in action, thought, desire and deed?
But like likes not its image painted well:
Avoids it as it were the mouth of Hell".'

Valentine paused again. And then, as if it were not the first thing in her mind, said, 'So this never actually happened. So what? There are personal database records. Psychological profiles. *That's* what's going on here. Some process is synthesizing data.'

'Synthesizing?'

'Extrapolating. Creating. That's my guess. It's like the "Spy" and "Lady Regret" scene between Miles and Rue – it isn't what did happen, it's what *should* have happened. It would have helped Rue to talk, then. And this—'

Johanna Branwen interrupted. 'You realize, this kind of interpolated fictional conversation makes the more genuine sections useless for blackmail.'

'If I'd ever wanted to use them for that, yes. Is that what you thought?'

The older woman said sharply. 'Don't be ingenuous. It was always one of your worst faults.'

Valentine let out a long, relaxing sigh. 'I admit it.' And, after some seconds' thought, let the remark stand on its own.

Johanna Branwen said, 'Who created this recording? Whose idea was it to use surveillance techniques to produce, for want of a better word, a psychodrama?'

'This is what Baltazar Casaubon's system architecture produced out of what the medical scans read from Miles's brain activity. Nothing more. Nothing less.'

'Perhaps something more.' Johanna gripped Valentine's arm. 'What is being that creative? Is there anything else you want to bring to my attention before I find your Baltazar Casaubon?'

Guard down, pretence abandoned: the immediate feel of total honesty is heady. Drunk with it, Valentine said, 'Only that I think he dislikes you with as much reason as you dislike him. You're jealous. And he has to deal with the parts of me that are you. Because, oddly enough, I won't abandon them. They are part of me.'

After a moment, Johanna Branwen said, 'Personal matters aside, one of the matters I urgently want to take up with your husband is the current plague of database security corruption. I take it he's responsible? No, you needn't answer. No matter. This is more ... more than I had anticipated.'

The woman brushed the fur of her collar back from her scarlet lips, murmuring into the Rolex comlink. Steel-and-silver curls plastered her forehead in the enclosed heat. Nonetheless, as the middle-aged woman stood up, Valentine saw her shiver.

Valentine started to speak: thought better of it.

Johanna Branwen regarded her daughter. 'You worked on artificial intelligence projects for the American military.'

'Yes, everybody did, at one time or another, but we didn't get anything. Just complex expert systems. You think *this*—' Valentine stared. Her mirrorshade lenses obscured as she blinked, rapidly. '*Be real.* Things like artificial intelligence don't happen by accident!'

'No.' The older woman stood. 'They don't, do they?'

CHAPTER TWELVE

In the English Renaissance Memory Garden

Early heat echoes from the enclosing brick walls of the Garden of Scents.

Miles Godric typed, with one unsteady finger, *Ten mins. flying time north London. No border checks. Security safe house? Ministry of Defence? Ministerial w/end retreat? No contact media*! and encrypted the file on his subnotepad.

Another blazing morning's sun is hot on the cloth of his combat pants, already burns his fair-skinned muscular arms under his short-sleeved t-shirt. He feels bare and unbalanced without his video equipment.

'Of course I'm scared,' he admitted. 'I'm not stupid. You're a very influential woman in this government. I've already stretched things about as far as I can go. Technically I'm an accessory to industrial espionage, if the US ever decide to prosecute Baltazar Casaubon.'

'Military espionage,' Johanna Branwen corrected mildly. 'I think you'll find it carries a higher penalty.'

Miles rubbed the socket of his right eye, hard, and blinked through retinal sun-blotches. His palm rasped against his beard. 'It hasn't been declared an illegal act, yet, Minister. And I've got a contract. Despite your forcing me to sign the Official Secrets Act.'

'Purely a formality,' the minister says, with a note of humour in her voice that Miles reinterprets at least twice. 'Curiously enough, I'm still not adverse to you making a substantial and satisfactory amount of money out of this, Mr Godric. It's merely that the national interest will have to be satisfied before you do. Otherwise, regretfully, I will authorize your extradition to the Confederate States.'

Carrot and stick.

Madam a scribe is what I am. Or if
You like it better saye I am a spy.

He remembers how Val's expert system 'Kit Marlowe' grinned at him, a morphed portrait of the past in a VR future world. Doctor Faustus. More than anything, Miles thinks, I need to understand what has happened to me. No access to databases, MultiNet, his own neural recordings. He feels bereft.

'You'll have to let me go in first,' Val Branwen said, not to him. 'First. Alone.'

She knelt on hot flagstones, face bent close to the sparse camomile that covered an area around a sundial, inhaling the plant's scent. She wears a pair of expensive spectacles with thin gold rims, mirrorshade contact lenses abandoned in their compulsory trip north. Even Val's stuck without cleanser. Miles Godric grinned, leaning his large body further back on his bench, under the mild shade of a palmate-leafed creeper.

Two ornamental stone fish fountains spouted water, splashing in the silence.

'"Go in"? Impossible. Even if he were located.' The minister, Johanna Branwen, stood unprotected under the blazing sun. A middle-aged woman with expensive perfume and high-quality sports clothes. Familiar from morning studio briefings, but never known. He may have processed a feature on her about three years back, it isn't clear in his mind. Until yesterday he has never spoken to any politician outside of his technician's role.

This is too much, too high, too dangerous.

Try as he might, he can see no physical resemblance between the two of them. Val might take after some hypothetical father, he speculates, assuming anyone had ever dared engage Johanna Branwen in anything so carnal as coitus; and his rambling mind snapped back into focus after twelve hours of lights, caffeine, interrogation, stimulant drugs, and a small cream-walled office with heavy-duty recording equipment that hadn't seemed to belong in the house here.

The Elizabethan candy-stick brick chimneys are all that can be seen of the palace, over the green tops of the pleached lime walk. Miles breathed in lavender, camomile, roses, and a hundred other plants of whose names he would never bother to become aware. Plants cared for by people who exist to function, not to be noticed by those with power or privilege.

He *wants* that privilege. Has he wanted it so badly he has permitted something terrible to be done to him?

'If Baltazar has any sense he'll be out of the country by now,' Miles said.

Both the women turned their heads to look at him with identical expressions.

'Ah. Now I know what it feels like to be *completely* superfluous.' He eased back, brows raised, and dropped his hand down to the bone china cup of coffee in which (despite it not being past nine in the morning) he had required a lacing of brandy.

Val sat back on her heels. 'Shut up, Miles. OK, Baltazar might have run. I don't think so. I think he's still in London. He will run, if you send MI6 and the Met and the army down on him like a ton of bricks. Let me handle it.'

'Ridiculous. Even the supposition that you might do that is ridiculous.'

'You'll frighten him off, you'll never find him. I know what he's like! If he's *really* interested in not being found, it'll take you months. Years, maybe.'

Miles hears an unspoken conclusion to that sentence: *You haven't got that long.*

The early sun coloured the brick walls peach. Heat beat down on the garden, in whose thickets of leaves and fleshy stems some dew remained still moist. Birds called. The bright colours of nameless flowers shimmered. A bee drifted past, body hanging at an angle in the air. Lack of sleep and close interrogation left him with a mind able to slip its ratchet. The coffee and brandy bit at his duodenum.

The younger woman rose without swaying, balance utterly sure. He flexed blunt fingers. The feel of her shoulders and curved back, taut under the white shirt, is not so distant from his memory. He finds himself thinking, without any real sense of connection, of her thin waist, and the Ingram girl's thin arms, and the huge solidity of Dorothea Casaubon. Flesh to be romped over, kneaded, dived into.

'Withholding information on a matter of national security would be an indictable offence in peacetime. As matters stand, I'm afraid it's rather more serious than that.'

'I don't know where he is!'

'Yet you assume that you can find him.'

'It helps that I know what I'm looking for. I was married to the man, remember? That beats a security services psychological profile any day!'

Miles abandons the empty cup and the bench, lurching to his feet, scuffed combat boots trudging the brilliance of the garden walks among flower beds. White Classical statues haunt the undergrowth. He notices that the sundial is wrong by an hour: PanEuropean Standard Time. Its verdigrised copper glows.

This place is full of *but.* The military helicopter landed on the gravel car park in front of the hall unchallenged, but. No perimeter security is visible, but. His interrogators did not state what department authorized them, but.

No one has said he is under arrest. But.

He can't hear a rifle cock, but every time he comes within a certain distance of Johanna Branwen a small red dot appears on his chest. A red-dot laser sight. The same dot appears, too, on Val's white shirt if she approaches the limits of secure distance.

'It's *my* Marlowe play!' he calls. 'Recorded from in *here.*' Hitting the side of his head with the heel of his hand. Wincing. 'Jesus H. Christ, do you *know* how much I'm going to lose in income if I can't use this?'

'Please be quiet, Mr Godric.'

Something flicks past him with a whirr of feathers. A bird, he realizes, and straightens up from a low flinch with embarrassment.

'I'm sick to death of *shut up, Miles.*' He walked to Val, looking down at her sun-caught face. She blinked. 'I want to know what you've done. Whatever the status of direct neural input software, that isn't all that's going on here, is it?'

The woman shrugged.

Miles closed his big hands on her shoulders. 'No. No, you don't do that to me. I know that most of the medical tests I've been put through in the last twelve hours are to do with neurological damage.'

'Oh – no, that isn't it. There's nothing.' The red-headed woman shrugged again, a little helplessly, backing off; and snatched off her spectacles, clutching them in her palm. Her gaze went briefly to her mother.

Johanna Branwen seated herself on the wooden garden bench. She inhaled scent from the lavender beds.

'As far as my people can find out,' she said, 'the public auction, if I may call it that, of direct neural reading of the human brain, preceded by only a few hours the sabotage of security in government, City of London financial, police, military, medical, university and social services databases.'

'Sabotage of security?'

'Beginning with my own ministerial database.' The older woman looked at Val.

'Police? Military? ...' Miles said.

'Across the board,' Johanna said, distastefully, in verbal quotes, as if the cliche were painful to her; and added with no more stress, 'I hardly think it to be coincidental. Since my government has as yet had no ransom demands, and no political leverage from ... elsewhere, it seems to me that Baltazar Casaubon, having surfaced here, is a likely candidate for such irresponsible sabotage.'

'Sabotage,' Miles repeated for the second time, and caught himself with an impatient shake of the head. 'Security compromised. Government files, Defence projects, bank accounts, industrial patents, credit records—'

We come as heralds of the coming day
When Dies Irae is loosed upon the world.
All that men know, all men now shall share.

'Anyone else would have made capital from it before now?' he speculated.

'I cannot imagine otherwise.'

'This is going to break!'

'Of course. It already is. People talk,' the minister said dismissively. 'We are containing the problem, but cannot continue indefinitely, which is why I am not willing to allow Baltazar Casaubon any chance of leaving the country.'

The sun makes the stone of the sundial hot under his forearms where he leans on it. The hot metal bites at his skin. Miles Godric breathes deeply of the scents of the garden. His eyes follow the flick of bees across the marble whiteness of nymphs, fauns, satyrs.

'That many different databases? Could even Baltazar come up with something that would crack the security of so many different operating systems?' He frowned. 'There's a theoretical easy back door into Unix, but that doesn't apply to ... and there are so many ways to encrypt data!' He held up his subnotebook in Johanna's direction. 'Ok, you can run an algorithm that will crack the password on my public key encryption files, but it won't give you a result within the lifetime of this galaxy! The possible numbers are too huge. You're talking encryption depending on two *eight-figure* prime numbers.'

He sat down, spine to the stone sundial, careless of the camomile crushed under his boots. The scent drowned him. 'Unbreakable security codes. It's the classic mathematical thing – the travelling salesman formal Non-P problem. You have a map of PanEurope and you want to work out the quickest route by which the salesman can visit every city once only, without backtracking or crossing his route. Two cities gives you two possible routes. Three cities gives you six routes. Four cities gives you nine ... no, twenty-five ... no: I forget. When it gets to sixty cities, forget it. The factors involved are so complex that the processing required to work this out would take several lifetimes of the universe, and even then you wouldn't know if it were the best route, or just 98 per cent best ...'

A voice chuckled. It was Val, but Val watching Johanna Branwen.

'Now I feel like little Rue,' the red-headed woman said, 'telling you *but you don't understand the information age!*'

'I have people to do that for me,' the cabinet minister said tranquilly. 'Besides, I do know the mathematics of Non-P problems. Why does one's child always assume one to be living in the past? I know that without unimaginable amounts of processing power, which no one has, data security cannot be breached. And yet it is.'

The shadow on the sundial imperceptibly moves.

'What you do,' Valentine Branwen said, 'is, you spend four years working on security projects for the US military. You don't work out a way to solve Non-P problems. Eventually you develop an algorithm that *converts* a Non-P problem into a P problem – makes it solvable in a feasible amount of time, with a best-case answer. Which is the same thing, really.'

Her hand touches Miles Godric's muscular shoulder. He stares.

Johanna Branwen glances at empty air. It is the first and only sign Miles has had to confirm that they are being recorded.

Val says, 'I put the algorithm in a piggyback program with the direct neural input software. I knew that was going to get spread round a *lot* of databases. I wanted everyone to have access to it. I'm good at viruses that virus-killers can't detect. I put the code-breaker algorithm into a self-replicating worm virus – with an expert system to activate it at random intervals.'

Silence in the garden.

Miles Godric, weakly, said, 'Oh, Jesus.'

'Not unless he's an expert programmer.' Johanna Branwen's voice is deeper, richer, dropping into notes of irony and unbelief that Miles has never yet heard. 'Baltazar Casaubon could be this stupid, this irresponsible. But that *you* could. Valentine, Valentine. You knew what the implications were. Are. *Why*?'

'Because I can,' Val Branwen said. 'Somebody told me – we're not nice people.'

'A software program that opens encrypted files, disseminates information,' the minister said. 'I begin to see the shape of this … artificial intelligence program.'

'Mother, there is Baltazar's architecture, and there's my algorithm; there *is* no artificial intelligence project!'

The heat swells a bubble of scents: shrub, border plant, climbing vine, flower. Miles Godric sneezes once, minutely, like a kitten. Wiping his nose, surprised, he said, 'There could be.'

He saw that both of them were staring at him.

'Something,' he said, 'produced *The Spy at Londinium.*'

Johanna Branwen walked through the palace rooms as if they were her home.

Valentine carried her shoes in her right hand, bare feet padding over the parquet flooring. This seemed to be one of those Elizabethan country mansions, just short of a royal palace, that had ceased to be fiddled about with in the eighteenth century. If she cared about it she could have identified it. Portraits looked down from pale green and white walls on to white-and-gold furniture.

In the high-ceilinged, sunny drawing-room that they entered, men in suits quietly vanished into corners, except for one burly man with a Parisian accent who matched his steps to Johanna as she moved to close the French windows. He spoke rapidly to her. Valentine looked out at blue sky, tree-tops. No traffic, no twentieth-century buildings. The occasional military vehicle.

Heavy desks occupied one side of the room. She wandered over to a workstation, dropped her shoes, and attempted to log on to whatever political, military or security mainframe might be available.

'There is,' Johanna's voice said beside her, 'the matter of your children. My grandchildren. I think they should stay in England.'

'With you.'

Valentine ran an immediate self-check on the system. It gave her, almost incidentally, their geographical location.

'Neither your bigamous ex-husband nor his first wife, admirable though her genetic research programmes may be, seem capable of raising motivated children.'

Valentine sat back. Her gold-rimmed glasses slid down the sweat on the bridge of her nose. '"Motivated."'

'I should hardly like them to grow to adulthood resembling their father. Or, indeed, their mother.'

Valentine swore and attempted to hack into the Land Use Registry by a different route. That failing, she abandoned it for import and export registries. Data flicked by on the active colour screen.

'Whatever makes you think I'd let you take Jared and Jadis?'

'I can't imagine. Unless it's the way you let their father have custody, and leave their upbringing to his family or to Izumi Teishi's family.'

'I wouldn't give a dog into your care, never mind my children.'

'Oh, *Val*entine.'

Specialist medical equipment orders gave her the first clue. She hacked into the London hospital administrative databases. Some of the dates on the orders seemed reasonable. Metropolitan police records? Abandoning the connection with Land Registry, still unavailable, she resorted to transport firms. Guessing, she ran several quick data searches. She sat back in frustration.

'Izumi's maternal. They like her. California's – well. California, I suppose.' Valentine glanced up. 'I won't have Jared and Jadis anywhere near the PanEuropean war.'

'Not even vicariously, when Jared hacks into SIMNET? He is quite bright for an eleven year old.'

Restricted information, pride and oneupmanship become, Valentine thinks, sickly in private matters, no matter how effective in the public sphere. Bloody old woman.

The hum of hard discs behind her, and the conversations of Johanna's staff, made no more than a surface impression on her mind. For the sake of it she took a broad scan through Social Welfare mainframes, and blinked at the ease and quantity of files available. An alarm went off somewhere behind her. Johanna quieted the voices with a gesture.

'Is that really relevant?' A waspish note in the older woman's voice. 'Or are you merely curious as to the damage you've done?'

'Merely curious. As to my children ... I would rather let Izumi have them. They love her. It's safer.'

'Than me?'

'Than *me*.' Valentine hacked into her own small network back at the flat and ran a retrospective on modem use by anyone other than herself.

'Now that's odd,' she mused. 'OK. I know where he is. Even if I don't know why he's there.'

There was a silence from the rest of the room, and a second's startled glance from Johanna. Actually startled. Valentine smiled.

'Oh, come on. I know the man. I know what I'm looking for.'

'Are you certain?'

'Of course not. But it's my best-guess result. You can see for yourself ...'

Johanna leaned over, one soft cold hand gripping Valentine's shoulder. Her perfume drowned the smell of sunlight and cigarettes. She was shorter than Valentine remembered.

She said, 'He's in a theatre?'

Rue Ingram and Frankie Hollister walked down the steps together from the anonymous modern office building. They did not look at each other. When, as if by mutual decision, they halted on the pavement, neither spoke to the other.

Gridlocked cars stretched away down Whitehall from the Ministry of Defence building. Summer nights are cold enough to wake pavement sleepers at four a.m. Snotty-nosed children, up for hours, watch Rue, watch Frankie. A man in blue slacks moves away from the side road as if he has been waiting for them. A clear-complexioned young man with short hair and a skinny, muscular body.

'Rue?'

She recognizes what the flight lieutenant wears when he's off-duty.

'Rue, are you all right?'

Frankie Hollister begins to plod away east. Back towards home. Rue follows. She ignores the building beside her, only her shoulder on that side is tense, as if she is hunched slightly away from the concrete and glass.

'I knew you'd be released.'

She makes no answer.

'Rue.' A hand on her arm, stopping her walking. She looks down at it.

'I brought you this,' Wynne Ashton says. What he holds is an old, very creased piece of paper. She unfolds it. Poster-painted. Childishly painted.

He says, 'My mum – my adopted mum – she keeps some drawings I did in primary school. That's her, my dad, and me.'

All three the same: blobs with yellow hair, pink skin.

'They know one of them has to be me because it's the smallest.' He watched her closely. 'Twenty-five years ago, if you wanted to adopt a baby, you could only get babies of colour. That's why I won't take Closed London citizenship. It's a fraud. The only reason *I* qualify is because I'm serving in the armed forces. Do you understand, now, why—'

Rue Ingram tore the painting across once and dropped it, and walked away.

His resonant voice behind her said, 'Bitch!'

An hour in the Garden of Scents sunburned his forearms painfully, and reddened the tender skin at the nape of his neck. Miles Godric sprawled on gravel, his back against the walled garden's brick wall, smoking a French cigarette he had bummed off one of the security guards at the wrought iron gate.

'He's in a *theatre?*' Miles stared up.

Val's face against the sun was invisible, her hair a red corona.

'What the hell is he doing there?'

'A disused theatre,' Val corrected herself. She squinted behind her UV spectacles. The faint throb of a helicopter echoed from all points of the horizon. 'I suppose because it's the least likely place.'

Miles stood and ground out the cigarette under his boot. Its scent mingled with the scents of the garden. A soft, large white rose brushed his face. He saw Johanna Branwen standing on the steps leading down into the garden, conferring with a secretary. Shadows pooled at their feet. He longed for the shade of the lime walk behind them.

Now Phoebus' chariot mounts the morning sky...

'Let me guess. The minister *now* says she plans to keep you and me in protective custody until the security teams snatch him?'

'Something like that.' Her hand, browned from long training in the sun, stroked the petals of the rose. She sniffed at her fingers. She swung round, facing Johanna.

'If something goes wrong, if he's hurt, shot, how are you going to explain that!'

'Don't be ridiculous, Valentine. I'm fully aware of his value as a resource, if nothing else.'

'By the time you can mount a security operation, he won't be there. For Christ's sake, Mother, your data security is fucked! Every time you use a phone, a modem, shortwave radio ... He can watch what you're doing, while you're doing it!'

Devices like to Bacon's brazen head
That spoke and said, Time is, was, and will be,
Speak unto him, and tell him far-off news.
This clown, master of witty devices,
Perils his fat soul: spy, go seek him out...

'There is,' Miles Godric said, 'something I have to tell you.'

Neither of them paid attention. Val Branwen, face taut, fists clenched, body-language of a fourteen year old, yelled, 'He'll see who's coming in, and the only person he'll stay still for is me! You have to let me go in alone and talk to him. Jesus Christ, I want to know what's happened as much as you do!'

'And have both of you vanish?' The minister spoke softly. 'I'm sure I can convince your ex-husband that your future happiness depends on his cooperation.'

... Whether it shall be that after this
Men shall partake of angel qualities
Having the angels' knowledge of the earth...

Whatever it is, it talked to me.

Still missing the weight of cameras at his belt, Miles walked forward until the red dot sight appeared on his sand-coloured t-shirt. He scratched through his dusty hair, and tried not to loom over the older woman.

'If government security is falling down around your head, that has to be a primary concern. Maybe as a newschannel man that's what I should be most interested in, but ... Minister, it's *my* neural input that was used here. If there *is* an artificial intelligence, or the slightest beginning of something that could lead to one, then that's what I've been interacting with.'

Johanna Branwen watches him in the Renaissance garden.

'I've gotten tired,' Miles says, 'of being told things are not my concern. I'm doing my job, Minister. Wire me up. I'll go in with Val. I'll tell Baltazar it's a live link out to the rolling news media. Online and on record. Tell Baltazar Casaubon that's how you'll guarantee his safety – nothing can happen on camera. I'm sure you can make it *appear* that the broadcast is going out.'

A half smile appears at the corners of her mouth. Familiar from satellite news broadcasts, from hard copy paper news.

He said, 'Baltazar Casaubon created the software for direct neural input, and Val solved the code-cracker algorithm, and do you know what, Minister? If this is a true artificial intelligence that's come out of their project, you need to be first with it. You need to go cautiously. You *cannot* afford to lose either of the people who created it.'

CHAPTER THIRTEEN

The Armour of Light

Baltazar Casaubon was not in the riverside office-block basement that did duty as the Rose Theatre Museum.

Valentine Branwen gave the museum's PR equipment a cursory glance, left Miles puzzling, and walked towards the fire exit.

'Val—!'

Valentine walked outside. The stink of river mud hit her. Midday sun blazed down. She welcomed the heat, the smells; all equally enjoyable to her sensual appetites.

'Down here!' a muffled voice called, as the fire door clanged behind her.

She walked across to a wall and leaned her arms on the brickwork. A breeze blew off the river Thames and into her face. Barely cool. And smelling of fish, of weed, and of diesel-engined tourist boats. She lifted a hand and waved to a passing passenger cruiser. Distant hands waved back.

She leaned further over and looked down.

Sitting with his buttocks overflowing a sunken oil-drum, and his white trousers rolled up to his vast knees, Baltazar Casaubon sat spread-legged with his bare feet in the river. Scum ridged his ankles. He wiped a muddy hand through his copper-gold hair and beamed up at her.

'Hello, my little one. Thought you'd turn up before long.'

The mud smells of mortality. Here the wooden wharves crack with the heat, and green-shrouded rocks jut up from the shoreline. A few yards away in tidal mud, a half-sunken bicycle trailed weed from its rusted spokes. A gull swooped low, calling.

He seemed, physically at least, to be unharmed.

She warned, 'I've got Miles Godric with me.'

Baltazar Casaubon stood. His feet sucked deep into the mud.

His head down, ponderously watching where he stepped, he began to make his way ashore. She reached down one arm, impulsively, and when he had gotten ashore he reached up and took it, smearing her wrist with cool mud.

'If I were you, I'd hurry,' Valentine said.

'Oh, I think Johanna – it is Johanna? – will contain her impatience, don't you?' He picked his nose magisterially. 'This is a most wonderfully insoluble conundrum!'

Valentine glared at him with tawny-orange eyes. 'I'm glad somebody thinks so!'

Miles Godric thought, Don't I remember this from a school trip, once?

The surviving parts of the Elizabethan Rose Theatre – post-holes, pit floor, and audiences' hazel nut refuse, mostly – seemed crushed under the low concrete ceiling of the office-block basement. A clerestory window let some sun trickle into the stuffy room. Around the walls, hologram projectors and Virtual Reality stations cluttered the bare boards. Tacky strip-plastic labels advertised (erroneously, he noted) *Shakespeare's Rose,* together with live actions of *Doctor Faustus: The First Night.* His mouth quirked, reading that.

'The hologram equipment?' the red-headed woman suggested. As if she had guessed the right answer to a problem without knowing why it was the right answer.

'The hologram equipment.' Baltazar Casaubon stripped rapidly to his string vest and underpants, and seated himself at a table with his immense back to the museum exhibit. He hunched over a keyboard and flat-screen monitor; a half-empty bottle of Lambrusco Rosé at his elbow.

Miles rubbed at his face. Sweat filmed his skin. He panned automatically, sweeping the piles of equipment it was obvious did not belong to the museum: old monitors, chip circuit diagrams, camcorders, other stuff. The implant mike behind his ear approved: '*Lots of anti-surveillance gear in there, Miles.*'

Morgan Froissart's voice.

'*I'm keeping you on realtime recording.*'

He thumbed the acknowledgement key.

'Baltazar. You're online and on record.'

'Oh yes. I know.'

Miles walked across the room and dumped a printout into the

fat man's lap. He ignored Baltazar's startled yelp. The stack of paper slid, concertinaed, and began to cascade to the floor.

'I know about the algorithm. I want to know what else is going on!' Miles hooked his thumbs in the back of his camera belt, watching Casaubon's flushed, startled face.

'Algorithm?' the man squeaked.

Val squatted down on her haunches. She swept the printout into a pile, picked it up, and dumped it back on Baltazar Casaubon's table.

A small smile, instantly extinguished, crossed his fat features. 'You did it. You actually did do it.'

Baltazar Casaubon glanced back up over his shoulder. The woman nodded once, only a slight movement of the chin; her expression preoccupied. Something between the two of them cut Miles out: a communication as wordless as it was exclusive.

'I thought it must be you,' he said smugly.

Miles snapped, 'Have you read this?'

'In part.' Obediently, the fat man thumbed up the first page. His delicately-shaped lips moved silently as he read.

The small, airless room made Miles ache for rain; for cool drinks in a bar; for forgetfulness. The long silence was broken only by the flick of pages as Baltazar Casaubon skim-read the remaining verse.

Miles snarled, 'Never mind the bloody play! I want to know why it exists. What it means!'

Baltazar Casaubon lifted his nose out of the stage directions and gave him a pained look.

'I think it's a damned nerve! "Fatte clowne", indeed!'

'Never mind your vanity.' Valentine wiped a blotch of bird-shit off one sheet of the printout. 'Re-access the original neural record. I want to look.'

'And I don't even get more than fifty speaking lines in the whole—'

'*Casaubon!*'

'—play. Psychodrama. Whatever term you prefer. I have *finally* got the system up and running again,' he added, with more hurt dignity than seemed possible for one man to accrue. 'I was merely pondering my next action when you arrived.'

'The "play" is a fake.' Miles spoke quietly. 'And it could be said, couldn't it, that that discredits direct neural recording?'

Baltazar Casaubon regarded him with a glacial calm. 'No one

said information technology was going to be one hundred per cent reliable. There will always be lies, and misinformation, and primary sources are few and far between, and even the provenance of *those* is not proven. To think otherwise is to be technophile and simplistic.'

'I—' Miles spluttered.

'And besides, this is not direct neural architecture as I structured it. What it has produced is an electronic data forgery - of a kind. The question is,' Baltazar Casaubon finished magisterially, 'what nature of forgery? Done how, and for what purpose?'

A crackle broke the silence. Miles looked to see Val Branwen, one hip resting up on the rail that surrounded the sixteenth-century architectural remains, tinkering with the tuning of her wrist VDU. It was quiet enough in the museum that he heard the broadcast clearly.

'— and the stock market panic brought on yesterday by the major High Street banks closing their public services shows no sign of abating. Tokyo and New York are expected again to follow suit when the markets re-open.

'A government spokesman strenuously denied that the integrity of confidential data in MI6 and the Department of Social Welfare has been compromised.

'Rolling news channels this morning carried excerpts from the confidential medical records of Members of Parliament, Chief Constables across PanEurope, and the Royal family. A High Court injunction failed to—'

'Sabotaging the banking system was a mistake,' she observed.

'I don't make mistakes,' the fat man said loftily. 'Although I admit sometimes my timing may leave something to be desired.'

Val snorted. 'You're telling me! You're sitting here, and I know what you're thinking about. US security snatch squads. European SWAT teams. The Ministry of Defence and the metropolitan police. You're scared shitless.'

'Far from it,' the link-architect said loftily. He sat before monitor, phone, fax, and modem; glancing shrewdly up. 'Far from i— That wasn't a siren, by any chance, was it?'

Miles saw the woman momentarily let her hand rest against the greasy curls of hair at the back of the fat man's neck, as if his flesh warm against her knuckles comforted her.

'All this is probably just an expert system run wild.' She sounded unconvinced. 'That's all.'

The link-architect rested his immense elbows on the desk, and his chin on his interlaced fingers. 'The trouble with you two,' he mused, 'is that you worry too much.'

Valentine cuffed him smartly across the side of the head.

The midday sun slanted down into the room, scattering across the improvised control desk. Smartcard modules lay in heaps. Casaubon made a long arm across the desk and picked up a sandwich, spilling jam across a keyboard as he bit into the bread.

'Whatever it is ... it seemes to be an integral ...' The fat man spouted crumbs. '*Integral* part of direct neural architecture.'

Miles reached down a finger and touched the spilt jam, and lifted his finger to his lips. Strawberry. A movement flickered in the corner of his eye. A fat white rat, its fur spiky with jam and butter, sat up beside the corner of one keyboard and cleaned its spring-wire whiskers. Baltazar Casaubon snapped his fingers. The rat ran, jumped, clung to his shirt, and scuttled up to sit on his broad shoulder, scaly tail dangling. Casaubon put his finger up for it to chew on.

'The question is, of course, why a sixteenth-century play?'

Miles stared him down. 'No – the question is, where did the additional input-data come from?'

Casaubon reached up across his expansive chest to scratch the pet rat behind its ears. Val Branwen leaned across him to access the system.

'The question is, why isn't it a plain recording of data? Let's find out,' she said.

Movement glinted in the corner of Miles Godric's eye. He fell silent.

The museum stage equipment began to show active tell-tales. A pale hologram light bloomed in the centre of the cramped room. Grey and glittery, with a hint of what might have been wings ... The airless heat tightened about his throat. He swallowed. The holograms focused.

The Rose Theatre, reconstructed from a few fragments of wood and stone: octagonal white-plastered walls surrounding them, blue sky over their heads and over the peaked, thatched roofs of the galleries. Polished, painted wood gleamed.

Sunlight blazed out of invisible sources, glaring so that his eyes ran. He wiped the back of his wrist across his eyes. The hologram projection machinery vanished, hidden by three-dimensional images of raised stage, pillars, galleries crowded with Elizabethan play-goers (mouthing conversation in silence). The bare stage's back wall was painted so that it appeared, *trompe l'œil*, as carved and columned; rioting with cherubs, Greek deities, angels, clouds, mythical beasts, and golden suns. The interior of a painted temple...

He shook his head and looked away. At the hologram's edges his vision skewed; then museum door and desk were plain and clear. The fat man had his head bent over the keyboard, muttering.

Val Branwen, dazzled, stared past him at the hologram scene with rising excitement. He turned back.

On the stage wall, among painted Renaissance cherubim, a despatch bike rider in leathers leans his way through the celestial traffic. Below, a train-rail gleams in the hills of Arcadia.

'Tampered with,' Casaubon announced, with satisfaction. 'Now we shall see...'

Miles stepped forward. A blot of dark light appeared an apparent few feet in front of him.

He focused his eyes on a tiny image that hung in mid-air, wings beating furiously. Minuscule blue eyes gleamed in a face surrounded by brown curls. The pink, naked *putto* sketched a bow, mid-air.

'Very funny,' Miles Godric said acidly.

The voice that issued from the speakers sounded several feet to the right of the *putto*'s not-quite-synchronized lips.

'Baroque cherubs aren't to your taste? I can alter that. Remember, you contain *anima* and *animus* both within you.'

The voice itself...

'You heard a recording once. Very old. Of the last *castrato* singer.'

...a truly strange voice, one for which he has no referent; too low for a woman, but with nothing at all of a man about it.

The hologram blinked. An androgynous image grinned at him, hair auburn, eyebrows black, cheeks red. It quoted, 'A great reckoning in a little room...'

The VR 'Kit Marlowe' – and yet, not quite. Miles Godric screwed up his face, striving for concentration. The image of a young woman, or a young man, sat on the edge of the raised wooden stage. Across its black t-shirt was printed THIS IS NOT A REHEARSAL... As it twisted around to look into the wings, he read the back of the shirt:... THIS IS REAL LIFE.

A demon peeped out from the uncurtained wings of the stage, and darted back.

'This is – you – you're Baltazar's link-architecture. I ... *remember.*' His throat felt sore, constricted as with influenza. He swallowed several times without releasing that feeling. 'It *is* an artificial intelligence system.'

'Not precisely.' Now its hair is lion-yellow.

Sweat ran down his back. Seen close up, the resemblance is undeniable. His own face: reversed, as in a photographic image rather than a mirror, the image the way the world sees it. Leaner, younger, but none the less his own. A feather of hair shone, plastered to its forehead by apparent perspiration.

'You can call me system-name *Mephistophilis.*' A light-slip, disorientating as a landslip. His androgyne-self slid down to stand in front of him, dressed now in a sixteenth-century scholar's long buttoned black gown, still with the same appallingly familiar face.

'This shape becomes me best...' It surveyed him with guileless pale eyes. 'Shall I tell you what I am? And then we'll move on to the interesting stuff. Lines, circles, signs, letters and characters: Ay, these are those that Faustus most admires. Can you record me?'

Too deep a voice, too many harmonics and familiarities in it for ease of mind. Miles put his hands on his belt. 'I can record holo-images.'

He turned his back on the creations of light. 'Who wrote this program?'

Baltazar Casaubon leaned back in his chair, which creaked alarmingly. The white rat still squatted on his fat shoulder. 'Miles, my boy, this is your neural recording. It appears to have altered again.'

Val muttered, 'Miles, speak to it. Try to trigger another sequence.'

Miles turned back. The illusion of depth stretched the museum room out to the back of a bare stage. On the edge of hearing, Baroque music played. The androgyne sat again on the edge of the stage, legs jutting out from under the scholar's gown, heels kicking against the boards.

Miles rubbed his hand across the back of his neck, feeling sweat, and muscles tensed as hard as rock. 'Explain, then. You're what – a computer-analogue written into the system, to make it accessible? Part of the link-architecture. A talking index. An expert system.'

The androgyne hooked its arms about one raised knee, resting its chin on its arms. Behind it, decoration crept up the pillars that supported the stage canopy: strapwork, cartouches, cherubs. The underside of the stage canopy glistened gold and blue, painted with sun, moon, and astrological constellations. The soundtrack mocked. 'Listen to the man who talks to architecture!'

Miles hesitated. Val's arm brushed him as she came to stand next to him.

'Anthropomorphism. It isn't the first time I've treated a reactive system as intelligent.' He grinned. 'What always got to me about the Turing test isn't how many programs pass it, but how many human beings fail it.'

Val chuckled, her tone for a moment almost as low as the hologram-image's. 'It sounds so self-directed. I swear it, Miles, it could be. It just could be. A real artificial intelligence ...'

Morgan Froissart's voice prompted in his ear: '*Mr Godric, ask about the database corruption that's going on – ask if this is responsible. Ask if it's a side-effect of this program.*'

Miles opened his mouth to speak.

The hologram said, 'No, it isn't, not in the way you mean. And it isn't corruption, Miles Godric. Corruption is the last thing it is.'

Baltazar stared. Val Branwen took a sudden step forward. Sun leeched into the museum hall. Distortion whorled in the image's hands. Used now to that photographic but altered resemblance, Miles began to feel some control coming back to him.

'It's accessing transmissions. It *is* using the code-cracker.' He demanded, 'Self-test. Explain what you are.'

The androgyne figure gathered its legs under it and stood, hands spreading out, taking in all the stage.

'I gave you the printout,' it said, in that low rich voice that was his, but somehow neither a man's or a woman's. 'Did you ever see a play? And then did you ever go and see the same play put on by some other company? The words are the same, but the play is *different.* The experience is different. If you like, the text of the play is the stage upon which the experience takes place. The text remains the same, the play – the result – is different. Does that answer your question?'

Miles, a little blankly, said, 'No.'

The programmed hologram continued to speak. 'What you had

recorded was eidetic memory, Miles. Memory from, if you like, the left hand side of the brain. Hard memory, like hard text. And what you get back from me is the play ...'

It smiled. 'I'm not an Artificial Intelligence. I'm an Artificial Unconscious.'

CHAPTER FOURTEEN

Games Software

Johanna Branwen sits in warm sunlight, blinded by goggles. The minutely-faceted VR image she regards is that of Francis Walsingham, spymaster to Queen Elizabeth I. She recognizes his features from one of the portraits in the gallery here.

'Neural networks?' She spoke over the VR game's soundtrack.

Morgan Froissart's voice concealed less of his exhaustion than his unseen face. 'It's one of our department's theories, Minister. You asked them to expedite possible models. If the architecture for the code-breaking algorithm were to have spread, corrupted a neural network experiment somewhere, that might account for what Mr Godric is currently interacting with.'

'It sounds unlikely to me.'

The virtual room she sits in is low-ceilinged with lead-paned windows, and a show-off pixel sunset going on outside over Elizabethan London. A tavern in Deptford. She has not, in two attempts at the game, managed to avoid historical necessity: the games-master expert system 'Kit Marlowe' lies once again dying through a stab into the eye. The player is on her own.

Walsingham says sadly, '*Master Marley could not be allowed to live and speak of this white magick. These Cabalistic wonder-working words are not for the common people. It is a secret of state, which we cannot allow freely to be known, for if all men knew and spoke the arcane tongue of angels, and thus spoke nothing but truth, how then might government be accomplished?*'

'My daughter fancies herself a satirist,' Johanna remarked.

'Another theory, Minister, is that direct input of brain activity into data storage, once it reaches a certain level of complexity, achieves consciousness spontaneously in the same manner as the human brain.'

'"Philosophy is odious and obscure,"' Johanna quotes, within the game and outside it.

Walsingham's trunk-hosed agents, feminine in ruffs, but with nothing effeminate about their thick-bladed chopping swords, move to guard the door of the tavern's upper room. One says, '*She knows the language of the angels. Shall I silence her mouth for ever, master?*'

Morgan Froissart, edgy and unseen, says, 'Quite, Minister. Another theory is that your daughter used the same expert system to structure the virus that dispersed the code-cracking algorithm as she did for SHAKESPEAREWORLD™. That would have incorporated her expert system into the architecture structuring direct neural data. But not, however, the historical period bias.'

Johanna moves the VR glove, triggering a games token she acquired early in the sequence. Her virtual hand removes the velvet mask from her face. Cleverly, a mirror on the tavern wall behind Walsingham shows her her own virtual features. Chalk-white maquillage. Tight, dyed auburn hair. Tudor nose. Her own yellow-tawny eyes.

Walsingham's jaw relaxes behind his thick beard. Amazed, he blurts, '*Your Majesty—*'

Morgan Froissart said, 'However, Minister, Miles Godric is known to have played the prototype version at your daughter's flat, before his neural output was recorded. Therefore, an interaction between his DNI and the original expert program ...'

'Well done, thou good and faithful servant,' Johanna says lightly, and the virtual Walsingham bows his head in smiling relief. Removing the VR headset, she surprises an identical expression on Morgan Froissart's face.

'Minister?'

'It's of no consequence.' Johanna Branwen stops laughing. 'This theory accounts for the downloading of Godric's neural data in verse form, is that it? What are they doing?'

Morgan crosses the drawing-room towards the cluster of suddenly agitated technicians. A sky even more flamboyant than that over virtual Deptford lights the room orange. Johanna clicks her own monitor to the surveillance channel, studies the raw unprocessed camcorder image.

The screen abruptly blanks.

'I'm no tool of a police state. You can no more interrogate me than you could interrogate anybody's creative subconscious.'

The hologram display of the Artificial Unconscious grinned, mimicking conversations in voices a shade deeper than its own resonant tones.

'"Where were you on the night of the tenth?" "Fish!" It won't *work*, Miles.'

Its hologram lips continued to move just out of synch with the sound.

Bewildered, Miles Godric threw his hands up, gesturing helplessly. He turned to do a camscan that took in the dusty reality of half the museum hall: the fat man bending to let the rat scuttle down off his shoulder and into the pocket of his jacket hanging on the chair, and Val Branwen with her hands fisted and resting under her chin, an expression on her face that defied deciphering.

'What use is an Artificial *Un*conscious?' Miles demanded. 'What fucking use is a *subjective* database?'

Mephistophilis's image laughed. 'As well ask what's the use of any kind of creativity.'

Val Branwen leaned her small, muscular shoulders back against the room door. 'Do you know, you haven't triggered the same sequence again even once?'

Miles repeated, 'What use is an Artificial *Un*conscious?'

The contralto-tenor voice said, 'Miles Godric, do you want to hear what more I have to say? Shall I make spirits fetch you what you please? Resolve you of all ambiguities?'

He looked into the hologram of his own face, the image younger and more ambivalent. Taken from personnel records a decade ago. Acknowledging a limitless curiosity, he nodded in consent.

The speakers say, 'But this play will run without an audience.'

A dead channel hissed in his ear.

All outgoing transmissions of his camera equipment appeared to be functioning. But no response to the query key. And no voice of Morgan Froissart in his ear-mike. Nothing but dead air.

Instantly, he envisions the panicked transmissions among the soldiers and security officials, from however great a distance they are surveying the Rose Theatre; pictures the howling sirens, alerted marksmen, cordons thrown around the South Bank.

'Oh, shit,' Miles Godric says, fruitlessly attempting to punch a signal through. '*Shit.* This is where the roof falls in.'

*

Morgan Froissart held out the secure video-phone. 'It's the PM for you, Minister.'

Johanna Branwen nods, absently.

He said, 'With the Home Secretary, on a conference line.'

Johanna takes the phone. 'David. Richard. Yes ... I concur. No. Regrettably, no. You are aware that there are no transmissions at the present moment that can be considered secure?'

The phone quacked.

'Oh, absolutely,' Johanna Branwen agreed. 'Only in person.'

The link-architect Casaubon lowered his head ponderously and sniffed first under his right armpit, and then under his left armpit. He beamed with amiable surprise.

'Oh, good ...'

He got to his feet and padded across the room, and bent down to rummage in his discarded white jacket's pocket. His hand came out wrapped around a container tiny among the massive folds of his flesh. Cheerfully he upended it into his other hand, and began to pat and smooth handfuls of talcum powder under his arms, across the deep creases of fat at his chest and stomach, and between his tree-trunk thighs and behind his knees.

The air turned momentarily white.

'The heat,' he explained to Miles Godric.

The slick, sweat-abraded flesh at his elbows, chins, balls, and buttocks eased with application of the cool powder. He sneezed, inhaling by mistake, and put the tin of talcum back in his jacket pocket. He continued to prod through his heap of discarded clothing.

Godric waved his stocky arms. 'How can you be so calm! There are armed SWAT teams, police cordons around Southwark—'

'In which case I see no reason not to look my best, and be comfortable.'

Baltazar Casaubon, head bent, concentrated on pulling on the pair of white cotton trousers that, although marked with Thames mud and pavement dirt, were the cleanest garments in the pile.

'You used me! You let them think they could keep you under observation through me!'

'I used you,' Casaubon agreed.

Knowing that agreement can short-circuit anger. Or give a few useful moments of shock to manipulate. Memories of days arguing on committee, back-stage politicking, smoke-filled rooms and deviousness are clear in his mind.

'And I have no objection to being under observation. I merely prefer it to be a little more personal.' Baltazar Casaubon straightened and turned. He looked at the sharp, hungry face of the man. The sunlight slanted in through the closed shutters. Through the clerestory windows, the river gleamed in the heat that just now began to lessen. The edges of the hologram projection twisted vision. Casaubon looked at the frozen image, then back at Miles Godric.

'Are you angry?' he marvelled, voice rumbling deep in his chest. 'This is a story some men would give their life to see, *boy*, and you're complaining that I chose you?'

He slitted his eyes comfortably in rolls of flesh, watching the younger man. Miles Godric moved with explosive sharp gestures.

'It's all out of control! Isn't it? What happens now, Baltazar? Do you know? No. Does she? No!'

'No,' Casaubon confessed. He sat down at the desk. The white rat poked twitching whiskers out from under a collection of micromonitors. He winked at it. The rat turned tail and vanished.

'They're going to blame me,' Godric said. 'I'll never get a freelance commission again.'

'My heart bleeds!' Casaubon got to his feet, towering a good six or eight inches over the younger man. He pointed with one pudgy finger at the frozen hologram, the androgyne figure in the archaic scholar's gown. 'Never mistake the nature of Mephistophilis. Do you hear me, boy? No matter how good a deal it seems – the nature of Mephistophilis never changes. I offered you a story. More than *a* story: *the* story. How direct neural input will happen and why the world won't be the same any more. And you have it, and you tried to command money and power by having it. But then you made a deal with Johanna. Now,' Baltazar Casaubon rumbled, 'she's collecting. Godric, I want you here, I want your recording equipment working, I want no argument about it.'

'I can't get a channel out!'

'You can still record.'

'Record *what?*'

Valentine's muffled voice, from the museum door, looking down Park Street, said, 'Here they come!'

Casaubon surveyed the room rapidly. He hooked his sandals out from under the desk and slipped them on, treading down the heels; and moved to position himself in the slatted sunlight from the clerestory windows. He listened for the faint whine of Godric's camcorders focusing.

The door banged open, one black-hooded man breaking to the left, the second to the right, and the third barrelling straight across the room to end up with his back slammed into the far wall, machine pistol trained on Casaubon. Casaubon made no extraneous movements. The door swung on its broken hinges. An order cracked out, outside. There are also the ones you don't see.

Valentine Branwen walked in, escorted, beside a plump, middle-aged woman.

The SAS team continued to cover entrances and exits.

Baltazar Casaubon returned his attention to the armed man nearest himself. 'I regret,' he said, 'that I can't offer you any refreshments. But I suppose you can't drink on duty anyway?'

Something that sounded suspiciously like, 'No, sir,' came from under the black wool balaclava. The remainder of the team twitched.

'Johanna!' Casaubon drew himself up to his full height and directed a smile of wonderful sweetness at the woman following Valentine in. 'A pleasant surprise.'

'I think, neither.'

'Well, true,' Casaubon admitted. 'Even you had to realize – the more that secrecy becomes impossible, the more the powerful must do things in person. I thought you might be along.'

The woman rucked her jacket collar up around her ears, shivering, and regarded Miles Godric. 'What is the point of that, Mr Godric? None of your transmissions are being broadcast, as I have cause to know.'

'He can record,' Baltazar Casaubon said mildly. 'It's historic.'

'It's irrelevant,' Johanna Branwen said. 'There is, regrettably, no way to put this genie back in its bottle; however, there are successful measures that I am empowered to take.'

The plump woman glanced briskly from Casaubon to her daughter. 'City finance, medical records: these are minor inconveniences. The fact remains that, temporarily, you have caused a breakdown in the systems of government. The Prime Minister is of the opinion that the only option remaining is to put the country under martial law until things can be controlled.'

Valentine blurted, '*Martial law?*'

Johanna Branwen walked across the museum floor and stared up at the hologram theatre, and the still image.

'Regrettably, I have had to inform the Prime Minister that I cannot exercise that option. My advice to him is to sit on things, cover up, and hope no one realizes how destabilized things are until we have them back under control. Given the war in Europe, we can't afford any more upset.' She spoke crisply. 'Administrative chaos is one thing, the market crashing is another; civil unrest, on the other hand, is absolutely not allowable. Fortress Europe only retains the UK and small areas of France and Spain; we *cannot* afford unrest here.'

Casaubon leaned on the back of the chair at his desk. It groaned but took the weight. He moved to seat himself comfortably in it, belly slumped down on his thighs, the rolls of flesh on his back bulging over the back of the chair. He hitched up the knees of his white cotton trousers. A cooling breeze blew in through the clerestory windows.

'Martial law.' He beamed at the armed team surrounding them.

'I have said that is not an option. Much as I regret it. The Prime Minister concurs.'

Valentine, voice unconsciously high, said. 'You can't avoid social unrest!'

Johanna smiled. 'I can avoid being out of office at the end of it. A combination of "open government" ideology broadcast by us, combined with apologies for the system breakdown, ought to do it. Now.' The woman swung around. 'You will release flawed copies of the codebreaking algorithm into the system to muddy the waters. Hopefully that will devalue the original to some degree. You will then work on encryption until either you achieve new security measures, or it becomes apparent that you are unable to do this; in any case, we have a safe and secure location in which you can pursue your research.'

Valentine shook her head. There was a noise Casaubon thought might have been a snuffled laugh. When the red-haired woman raised her face, it was very drawn. Johanna Branwen turned towards him.

Casaubon lifted a copper-coloured eyebrow.

She said, 'This is not a central European regime. Therefore, unless you do resist arrest, you are unlikely to meet with an accident resisting arrest. I think that is something of a shame. You will, however, cooperate with the authorities in analysing the nature of this artificial intelligence, produced however accidentally, and in continuing your research into direct neural input.'

Swivelling his chair, Casaubon spotted the half-eaten sandwich on the desk, seized and bit into it, and through a mouthful of bread and jam observed, 'Not all my software is contaminated with the little one's expert system. What the multinationals have bought will work very well recording eidetic data. Information flood will happen. Openly. From now, we live in glass houses, Johanna. Glass houses.'

She ignored him.

'*You,* however—'

He saw the shambling big man flinch, Godric's hands seeking reassurance at the controls of his cameras and not receiving any. Pale eyes blinked.

'— I don't need.'

'I'll sign whatever you like. You can have my files. This film.' Miles Godric's voice shook. 'Look, I'll sign the Official Secrets Act, I don't want anything to do with any of this, I just want to go back home and do my job. You can trust me to be responsible. There's no way I'm going to disclose anything. It wouldn't be in my interests, would it? I'm not going to be that stupid, am I?'

Casaubon wiped his fat hand across his face.

'Well,' Johanna Branwen said. 'Mr Godric, you can be the public face of the government here, if you want to.'

Ah. Yes.

It compromises him, and it gets him reward. He consents to be their public apologist and broadcast on behalf of the government, to keep things under control. He becomes part of it, Baltazar Casaubon reflects. And thus safe? Who can tell.

Godric shook his head and scratched at his beard. His eyes were small, bright. 'Thank you, Minister. I'll try to justify your trust in me.'

Casaubon heard Valentine snort. The big man coloured.

'Baltazar, it didn't even occur to you not to do this, did it?' At *this,* Godric's jerked thumb took in hologram, troops, the entire concept by implication.

Casaubon slitted his eyes against hologram sunlight. He wiped his forehead ponderously, and then wiped his hand down his trousers. He gave a great, honest laugh. Genuinely puzzled, he asked, 'Why would I not do any of this?'

'"Never mistake the nature of Mephistophilis"!' the man quoted. 'Fucking hell, Baltazar!'

The armed guard with Johanna, at her nod, escorted Miles Godric out of the museum. Casaubon watched the departing recording equipment with a sigh.

He swallowed the last of his sandwich and rose to his feet. Noon blazed from the hologram stage, from Elizabethan Southwark, and he reached down with sticky fingers to poke at the keyboard. The arrested image of the androgyne jerked into movement, stopped again. The remaining armed men in the museum room became alert to it, without it being possible to say how this was apparent. He swore under his breath.

'Damnable thing ...! I spend three quarters of my time trying to get it to give me anything at *all.*'

The armed Special Forces soldier beside him, with an appearance of instantly-regretted curiosity, asked, 'What does it do when it's not dumping data, sir?'

'It writes reasonably good modern song lyrics.'

Silence in the sun-dim museum. Valentine: her narrow shoulders hunched, thumbs hooked over the back pockets of her white 501s, all her posture that of a sullen brat. He could not stop the smile that creased his face. And the steel-and-silver woman: Nike-shod feet braced apart, arms wrapping her jacket over her thick crimson tracksuit; gold earrings catching a heavy spark of sun.

'No one,' he said gently, wonderingly, 'has ever seen anything like this before.'

He sequenced numbers, symbols, and operant codes in rapid order; entering where necessary the identity of the person to be addressed. 'System-name *Mephistophilis.*'

The woman wrapped her jacket more tightly around her body. 'The program intercepts audio-visual transmissions. And taps data sources. Then it synthesizes an end-product, with which one may, to a limited extent, interact.'

Hurt, he protested, 'You're simplifying something of stupendous complexity. Why, I don't fully understand it myself, yet. You may be interested to know, Johanna, that it defines itself.'

He watched her flinch, very slightly.

'What we have here,' he said, 'may be the prototype of something definable as artificial intelligence, but it calls itself – calls *itself,* mark you – an Artificial Unconscious.'

It halted her momentum. He saw that. She lowered her head, jaw down, looking up from under her brows, and it went through him like a blade: Valentine's gesture.

'Artificial *Unconscious*? I... see. Do I? No. No, I don't believe I do.'

'I'll show you,' Casaubon offered.

'No! No. Send me a report. I don't need to see.'

And then the hologram image moved.

CHAPTER FIFTEEN

Street Fighter

Ten o'clock and the light beginning to die.

Footsteps picked a sharp rhythm down the Tottenham Court Road Tube Station corridor, hesitated, slowed further; and then picked up speed again, heading back in the opposite direction.

Rue Ingram glanced up from where she knelt, lacing on her combat boots, and glimpsed a vanishing back. No one else came up the steps towards this exit. She grinned, feral. Holding down a hard tension.

At her side, a voice said, 'Aw, shit. Anybody got any tape?'

Instantly and without looking, she handed the boy a roll of black insulation tape; which he began to wind around his boot to keep the loose sole on.

Some nine or ten youths rummaged in innocent rucksacks. The last sun slanted down the steps from Tottenham Court Road Underground entrance, picking out the filth and graffiti on this first landing, shining on the Soldier-Saints as they geared up. Rue spared a glance for the electronic newsboards above her head, glimpsed ... *DATABASE CORRUPTION CONTAINED, PAN-EUROPEAN MINISTRY OF DEFENCE CONFIRMS ... GERMAN SKIRMISH REPORTS TO FOLLOW* ... and turned back to fastening her combat boots.

'OK!' Rue stood. She tugged the black assault vest down, tightening the fastenings; checking the handle of the commando knife in its sheath. The buzz of illegality ran through her. Tonight is different. Because of what has gone before: different.

Beside her, Frankie grinned with more than usual manic enthusiasm. 'Another tour of duty! Here we go!'

A tall, fair boy shrugged into an expensive but too-small blue flak jacket that barely came down to the bottom of his ribs;

oblivious to their mockery. 'So are the south river guys here?'

'Maybe.' Rue fastened the web-belt and pouches around her waist. She shook out the folds of the long black skirt she wore over ripped tights. In a warning undertone, she said, 'Frankie's mad tonight.'

'Fuck, that girl ain't ever been nothing *else* but mad.'

Two brothers marked each other's faces with camouflage paint, green and black on brown. The rest – putting on shirts tightly buttoned to the neck, solid boots; webbing, headbands, ragged strips of cloth tied about their biceps – yelled at each other, voices rising.

'Move out.' Frankie touched Rue on the arm. 'Let's *do* it, guys.'

The roof of Rue's mouth tasted fizzily dry. She picked up her heavy sports bag. She swallowed and ran, boots clattering, up into the last evening light and Oxford Street. The pounding of her boots seemed to contain and shape her anger, making a fierce rhythm out of humiliation.

A tourist turned a whitened face as they flooded out into the open, his mouth a square of shock. Junction of Oxford Street and Tottenham Court Road. Gridlocked taxis, long-abandoned, shone with chitinous black carapaces. Further down she saw vans, trailers, a burnt-out bus. Rue kicked a waste-bin on its steel pole, laughing to hear the noise echo.

'Hey *fucker*!'

'Yo, Frankie!'

Rue shucked into the sleeveless leather jacket, newly painted on the back with the sword-that-is-a-crucifix insignia of the Soldier-Saints. Feeling suddenly outclassed, for all its expense, by the gang of crop-haired young men and women in overalls, boots, and black headbands that surrounded her and Frankie.

She shook the hair out of her eyes, tying her own ragged headband on. It is peach and ivory silk, scorched at the edges. 'Let's go!'

The short girl swaggered past, her eyes squeezed into slits against the western light. A bottle of brandy cradled in her arms, the red of her cheeks could have been alcohol or remembered anger.

'We going to do a sweep.' Frankie's free arm swung out. 'Mark this fucking street. Clean the shit out of it for good, while they're drugged out of their fucking brains!'

The sky was a darkening clarity over high roofs. Somewhere an audio news broadcast sounded: ' – *unsuccessful attack on the city of*

Bonn at 2 a.m. this morning –' She recognized the anchorman Eugene Turlough's voice.

Control slid away, willingly abandoned. Rue Ingram linked arms with Frankie and the tall black youth with her; beginning the rhythmic chant, the stamping; the slow, dangerous progress that kicked over bins and the last rug-displays of the street traders; kicked in one unbarred shop window in a glorious scythe of plate glass; marching up the wide street.

Furtive figures slipped from abandoned cars ahead; vanishing into the half-light.

'Flush 'em out! Extended line!'

The street-wide linkage of arms dissolved into a scatter of kneeling figures.

Rue dropped down and scrabbled the gun out of her sports bag. Blued metal. Heavy. Hopper magazine. She worked the lock-and-load, lifted it, sighted along the crude metal sights and pulled the trigger.

The gelatine-and-paint missile scarred orange down the side of an abandoned Mercedes.

'*Mark* them!' Frankie yelled. She lifted her own paint-gun and fired rapidly, repeatedly; dying a shop window in an arc of blue spatters; and hit a man in a decaying parka.

Two other men moved off, swearing. Rue aimed, felt the thunk of recoil, and one yelled and slammed his hand into the side of his head, and took it away orange. Indelible orange.

'We *know* what you are!' Her voice ripped her throat. 'Everybody can *see* what you are!'

She shot again, branding another for public recognition, public abuse. The magazine rattled, emptying, empty.

'Hey—' She caught Frankie's arm. The short girl jerked loose.

'What's *that?*'

Voices from up ahead: screaming and shouting. Rue poised for flight. 'Is that the police?'

A laugh from the short girl stung, acidic, and Rue coloured.

'Shit, no! Sent the south river guys along to Oxford Circus, they're coming up towards us now. Hey, Dinnie!'

A sandy-haired boy stopped, knelt down, and carefully took from his pockets two plastic bags, kept upright. He unwrapped half a dozen bottles filled with clear liquid, and with wet cotton strips trailing from their neck.

'Shit, Frankie!' Aghast. 'Shit. That isn't what we do.'

'It's what *I* do.'

Light bloomed in the young woman's hand. Rue noticed, by contrast, how the sky above was velvet blue. A yellow circle of light. Twilight.

And will they still be in that flat on the estate?

The tingle of Rue's blood slowed, chilled, and she met Frankie's eyes soberly.

'You're going to hurt somebody.'

'That's right. I am.'

And then the bottle sprouted a tongue of fire as Frankie hurled it in a half-arc, and shattered ahead in a spreading semicircle of flame. Hot air blasted back in Rue's face, singing her eyebrows. She swore.

'Aw, fuck it, I can't throw the damn things far enough!' Frankie Hollister sat down on the pavement, legs apart, gasping through laughter for breath. 'I can't – throw them away – from me!'

'Christ, you're a mess when you're pissed.'

'Yeah, an' you too, sober.'

'We've done enough. They've called the police by now. Let's go.' She raised her voice. 'Bug out! ERV! *Bug out!*'

'Oh, I don't think I want to, just yet.' Her precise imitation of Rue's accent was cruel.

'I don't care what you want, Hollister. You're coming with me.'

'I want to do some more of these. Yo. One more guy won't beg off of tourists. Or steal my tax money for Benefits. Yo . . .'

'For Christ's sake, who cares about money—'

'Not *you. You* don't have to. You got your sugar mommy, that fucking middle-class dyke. And *why* didn't you tell me about that married guy?'

The tiny flame bloomed again, kissed the rim of a bottle. Rue saw Frankie's eyes bright in the light, fascinated, staring affectionately as the cotton rag burned down. Holding the burning bottle in her hand.

'Oh for – just throw – *throw* it!'

Panic spilled bile in her throat. She reached down and grabbed and threw in one smooth motion, made efficient by terror of fire and explosion. The petrol bomb wobbled in its flight, thunking through the window of an abandoned van. The shatter of glass and the *woof*! of flame loosened fear in her. She fell down on to her knees and stared at the burning vehicle.

A hand waved silently, trapped behind the glass.

CHAPTER SIXTEEN

Mephistophilis

There are armed men cordoning off the Rose Theatre museum, helicopters over the streets, Special Forces troops in the auditorium. Johanna Branwen flinches, nonetheless, when the hologram image moves.

The stage speakers broadcast, in broad Confederate, '*Yo, marine!*'

Johanna endures the inside-out shift of vision that a change of holograms causes. The Elizabethan theatre becomes gunmetal grey: the scene the interior of a Chinook troop-carrier helicopter. Taken from newsreel clips, translated into three dimensions. Tropical sunlight blazes from nowhere into its open belly.

She wiped the heel of one hand slowly across her eyes. English heat is different. 'That's ...?'

'I said *Yo*! You deaf, soldier?'

The strident voice's Confederate accent is not native. Johanna focuses on the hologram figure's face, briefly reminded of young Rue Ingram and then revising her impression. This face is much younger than its original is now.

The military kit is out of date. Green combat fatigues. Ammunition pouches. Cloth-covered helmet. Grenades hanging from outdated webbing. Jungle boots.

This is what they copy, the children, from films and T/Video. War games fought with the paraphernalia of the war-before-last. As always.

She hesitates.

'Hey, Jo, they *your* files, man.' Not androgyne now, the figure sprawls against a metal airframe, one foot up on the bench, an M16 assault rifle resting across her plump hips. She wears combat fatigues open to the waist; under that a green t-shirt stained with sweat. Dog-tags. Soft black curls plaster her forehead. She grins, wide-eyed. She is young. Nineteen. No lines of fat around the chin; but her hands are white and pinched.

'This is a joke.' Johanna pauses in fastening her jacket against the evening chill. Watches, fascinated.

The *castrato* voice rasped, 'No joke. It's Mephistophilis, man. None other. All things that move between the quiet poles shall be at my command ... But her dominion that exceeds in *this* stretcheth as far as doth the mind of man.'

There are microphones in the interactive museum technology: it must be accessing them. '"This"?'

'Knowledge. Power. *War.*'

The voice spoke just out of synch with the lips. Johanna moved to one side, then to the other, her eyes fixed on the three-dimensionally solid hologram on the Rose Theatre's non-existent stage. 'You're stealing – co-opting – system-space. That's coming through a satellite-delay.'

'Via the Confederate West Coast. It's a simple principle.' The sweating fat man beamed. 'How pleasant to have an intelligent audience. I confess I don't entirely understand this military ambience.'

'I served abroad,' Johanna Branwen cut him off. 'When young.'

The hologram figure stands up, slinging her M16 from one shoulder by its strap. Her shoulder patch is that of the European Volunteer Force. The curly black hair that will one day be steel-silver is tied back with a headband, ripped from one of the combat jacket's torn sleeves. Her eyes are bright. 'And I will be thy slave and wait on thee, and give thee more than thou hast wit to ask. How much wit you got, grunt?'

Johanna, testing, repeated back, 'And I will be thy slave ...'

'And I will be thy slave and wait on thee, and give thee more than thou hast wit to ask. How much wit you got, grunt?'

The same words, the same intonation. Johanna relaxed slightly into a self-referential checking of her image, a deliberately-softened tone of voice.

'This is not from a direct neural recording. The Defense Department personnel records, I assume? It's an interesting simulation, Baltazar, I grant you, but—' The self-deprecating, I'm-ordinary-folks chuckle. '— we don't have time for it.'

The hologram-figure threw up her hand, appealing to the skies. 'You princely legions of infernal rule, how am I vexed by this villain's charms! From California has he brought me now, only for pleasure of this damned slave.'

'I am hardly a slave,' Johanna said drily, and then, '*California?*'

Mephistophilis chuckled. 'Constantinople, in the original, but what's a quote between friends?'

Testing again, Johanna Branwen repeated with her original inflection, '*California?*'

'You some pisspoor excuse for a politician, you know? Never knew no politician that wasn't. We'd've won if you politicians had let us.'

That *you politicians,* from that young, unforgiving, known face...

'Hey, I got to make the best I can with what I find in here. California mainframe battle simulations, future war tech stuff. You know all about that, Jo. No use for it – yet.' The figure hunkered down, tapping a global map that now glowed under her feet, superimposed on to the steel stage flooring. 'Local wars. That's all there is these days. Local wars. Skirmishes and insurrections. Too bad, huh?'

Consenting to interact, Johanna said, 'A war economy would boost prosperity. However, one can never *regret* the lack of war.'

Mephistophilis raised her head. Beads of sweat slid down her face; darkened the torn combats. One hand came up to brush the hair from her forehead. 'Don't *give* me that shit. Is it not passing brave to be a king, and ride in triumph through Persepolis? You love it! We

never rest
Until we reach the ripest fruit of all,
That perfect bliss and sole felicity,
The sweet fruition of an earthly crown.'

So. Not Faustus, for me. Tamburlaine.

'Clear the room,' Johanna said, projecting her voice without raising it. With articulated and smooth precision, the armed men vacated the room for the twilight of Park Street. 'This ... particular interaction could all be electronic fakery. My daughter writes games software, after all.'

'Nothing to do with me.' Her daughter shrugged. 'Your files have been cracked, I guess.'

The hologram light-slipped, returning for a brief moment to its

Godric/Marlowe figure in a scholar's gown.

'All electronically stored knowledge, free to all.' The amused, multi-sexual voice soared as the figure threw up his arms. '"Why, this is the Invisible College, nor am I out of it!"'

The fat man raised an eyebrow, and peered thoughtfully at the voice recognition codes on the monitor. 'Of course, there was nothing to say it wouldn't have a sense of humour, too.'

Johanna shook her head, and raised the Rolex communicator to her mouth. 'Morgan, I'm about done here.'

Light flared as the hologram interior of the Chinook helicopter reappeared on stage. The hologram figure swung to her feet, one slender hand resting protectively on the shoulder-slung M16. Green eyes gleamed. Dirt and sweat marked her face. 'It's happenin'. You could'a used this – got right to the top – but you blew it. Man, you are *history*. Old woman, get your dumbfuck ass outta here!'

Old woman. Watching that scorn, that so long forgotten young face, she really has only one thought. *Why couldn't my daughter be like this*?

The fat man remarked mildly, 'I must say that one gets entirely fitting responses from Unconscious software. You're not impressed?'

'By the technological achievement? Infinitely. By the result? An oracle is useless if it tells one only what one already knows. I don't need to be told that I enjoy my work. Or that I'm ambitious.' Johanna met her daughter's gaze cheerfully. '*Quelle surprise.* Pious warnings, I regret, won't alter me now. Is this what you wanted Mr Godric to record, to make some attempt to coerce me? Do you think I'm worried about the disclosure of some ... some pop-psychodrama? I'm sorry to disappoint you. The satellite channels will no doubt make their usual meal of all this, and good luck to them, if it takes their small minds off more important concerns.'

'More important?'

'Let us merely say, I would sooner hear my private life broadcast than, for example, the firing codes for our nuclear deterrent.'

She pressed the communicator again.

'You will both, I may add, be kept in custody separately.'

'Oh, don't be ludicrous!' the fat man snapped, testily. 'The little one and I will have to work together on this.'

Valentine looked at him. A cool breeze blew in through the

shutters. Johanna inhaled the evening odours of the river, and the distant café kitchen smells of cooking. The fat man's stomach audibly growled.

'Preferably before dinner,' he added.

She rubbed her numbed hands one against the other. 'You don't question this "oracle", I notice?' she said to her daughter; and watched the old expression come to the child's face.

'But what have you ever done,' she continued gently, 'except run away?' She looked at the hologram. '*Deserter.* Do you know, I thought you might eventually make something of your life? I got you dual citizenship; I thought when you followed me into the Forces ... but there. I never expected any child of mine to make such a sprawling *mess* of her life.'

Her daughter shrugged.

Her child Valentine has crow's-feet at the corners of her eyes, behind the gold-rimmed spectacles; a few white hairs. Her child is over thirty. Over thirty-five. What does that make me? she wonders. Old? I am not yet ready to give it up, any of it.

'Of course,' the fat man ruminated, 'there was no guarantee that the collective unconscious would be a pacifist.'

'Collective unconscious?'

The fat man grimaced. She assumed it to be a smile: on his flesh-drowned features it is difficult to determine.

'Don't you think? What else would you call an artificial intelligence that works randomly, on dream-logic, and can access and download any data? No conscience and all creativity. The collective unconscious of the information age. I am uncertain,' he confessed tolerantly, 'whether this is the original program we're accessing, or one of the copies. Mephistophilis appears to have proliferated.'

'Baltazar, I could just have you disappeared,' she snapped. 'There are probably any number of people who can duplicate your research.'

'"Our" research,' her daughter corrected her. 'However accidentally. I solved the algorithm. I wrote the virus. I estimate five months to infiltrate ninety-five per cent of global databases. Whatever this is, there's going to be a lot of it about – and there isn't one damn thing you can do about it.' Her voice took on a thoughtful note with which Johanna was long familiar. 'I suppose you could call this data corruption. Corrupted with change. But the world always is.'

The fat man belched, and gently massaged his vast stomach.

'These devices would have been invented anyway, in the course of things, but gradually, and subject to prohibitions, and you people would have found ways to preserve government security,' Casaubon said. 'I'm putting all of this into the open at one go. Victory here belongs to whoever gets in first, before countermeasures can be devised. You knew you were too late, Johanna, when you were able to find me this easily.'

'I don't know if you're clinically certifiable.' Johanna shook her head. 'Megalomania? Delusions of grandeur?'

'Hardly delusions,' he said. 'Johanna, Johanna. Sometimes the important thing is not the message of the oracle, but merely the fact that it is *here*.'

Johanna Branwen stared at the stage. At the hologram figure: the girl's unlined face, active body. Her potential for what, forty, fifty, sixty more years?

Abruptly, she flailed at the theatre equipment control board, hitting it with her gloved fists. The projection equipment squealed. The hologram sun vanished. Johanna blinked at the dimness in the endlessly-long falling of the summer's night.

'And what do I do with you now?' she mused.

'Nothing.' Baltazar Casaubon's fat features became perfectly serious. 'What you cannot do, as the Artificial Unconscious says, is coerce creativity.'

She looked at him.

'Without undue modesty, I must confess that there are probably two or three men who could do what I've done here. Who could fully understand it. Who may be able to replicate, constrain, control it – eventually. Is *probably* good enough, Johanna?'

'Possibly,' she said.

'I got the algorithm out successfully,' her daughter Valentine said. 'Now you're desperate for new security measures, and I'm damned if I'm going to help you. This is the window. This is where everything happens, in the space between now and when you do get secure encryption again. You can have my files, if you don't already. Work on counter-measures. See how long it takes.' Her eyes are red, golden, bright; with a brilliance that is more than a reflection of the hologram. 'That's just inevitable technology: invention and counter-invention. But there *is* going to be open government, information flood, chaos. People *are* going to know what they're not supposed to.' She added quickly, 'What he had developed was dangerous. What I had developed was dangerous. And someone else would have developed direct neural recording or a decryption algorithm in time. Putting them out *together* – that's the only way I could see of doing it safely.'

'Safely!'

'And you cannot,' Valentine said, 'coerce me. Simply, you can't make me work for you, because I'm not afraid of you.'

'I never wanted that,' Johanna protested.

'You couldn't even make a secure facility to hold me, now. Not if you want me to work. That must cut you down to the core.'

They stared at each other.

'Well.' Johanna picked thoughtfully at the fur of her coat collar. 'There is physical violence.'

'I'm walking out of here. With Baltazar. With Miles, if he wants to come. You can stop me if you're willing to hurt me.'

Johanna rapped her gloved knuckles against the hologram projection machinery. Without the illusions of light, the museum was dingy. Only the cold stone floor of the Elizabethan theatre remained. Outside, she could hear radio transmissions squawking.

'Yes, I thought it might come to this,' she said. 'It isn't over yet.'

CHAPTER SEVENTEEN

War Games

The last light leaves the sky over gridlocked Oxford Street. Rue Ingram shudders.

'Oh fuck. Oh fuck.'

Burned, crisping black, the flesh melting...

'*Jesus.*'

Careless of whether there might be petrol left in the abandoned vehicle's tank, careless of the fire's heat beating against her face, Rue knelt on the pavement and stared ahead. The broken-down van held fire: a glass and steel bubble. The stench and smoke of burning upholstery threaded the night. Footsteps sounded, Soldier-Saints running towards her.

'I...'

Flesh melting, trailing slime down the inside of the windscreen. No scream, no sound. She coughed, surprised into vomit that stained the front of her dress.

'...no!'

The tall youth, holding himself with laughter, pointed at her.

'What...?'

Rue Ingram stood, brushing embedded grit from her knees.

The van burned smokily. Still it was possible to see, through the van's windscreen, the tangled straight arms and legs of Oxford Street shop window dummies.

Melting wax, burning wax.

'I'm going home.'

'Oh, what!' Frankie Hollister rested an arm up across her shoulder, leaning, breathing alcohol into the night. 'We haven't finished yet. I want to find a car with some of those bastards still living in it. I want to do that to them.'

Rue put her hands against her own hot cheeks. 'That's going too far!' Her eyes caught movement. 'What's ... *police*!'

Far down Oxford Street hooves clattered, mounted police coming up at a canter. The light from burning cars shone on their visors and clubs, slid down the horses' gleaming flanks.

'You and me, we can't – if they get us again – Scatter!' Rue yelled.

Frankie, hot-faced, shouted over the noise. 'Regroup at Covent Garden!'

Six or seven teenagers loped across Oxford Street and away into side roads that Rue knew would take them up Tottenham Court Road, round the back of the British Museum and then south. A dozen of the Soldier-Saints ran with her and Frankie. Rue ran, boots pounding the pavement, leading the rest down into the alleys back of Soho Square.

Breathless, harsh whispers:

'Oh, shit I ...'

'Frankie!'

'Little motherfucker's crazy ...'

'Gear down.' One of the brothers spoke. 'They're gonna be here soon, let's go.'

'Did you see what she —!'

'Christ Jesus!'

Nervous laughter echoed off the walls of buildings. Behind them the stink of burning tyres choked the road. The churning black smoke covered the last of their retreat.

Rue Ingram slid the zip of the sleeveless leather jacket up to cover her assault vest and the hilt of the commando knife. The webbing she unclipped, looped over one shoulder. The weariness of relaxing tension unstrung her muscles, so that her legs were glue and rubber.

'Oh god ...'

Frankie leaned back against a brick wall, face upturned, sweat running channels of dirt down her skin. Without directly looking at Rue, she said, 'You're shit at this. You know that?'

In the night-neon of Soho, among gridlocked cars and blaring strip-joints, Rue hears something. The road smells of horse dung. She kneels, going into cover behind an abandoned car. *He* taught her this. Passed on snippets of bootcamp training, amused at her interest. Wynne Ashton, amused and derisory.

'I'm not shit! Wynne taught me!'

'Guess that's about *all* Wynne taught you.' Frankie Hollister does not move to get into cover, but she lowers her head and looks bright-eyed at Rue. 'Last Easter I told him you'd never leave London.'

'You told him —'

'I told him you were sleeping with another guy. He didn't even ask for a *name,* Rue.'

'Oh, Jesus, Frankie.'

Rue stares up, neck hurting, from beside the car.

'Waste of time.' The blonde girl stripped off her jacket, dropping it on the pavement, over the crumpled bin-bag in which she had concealed her paint-gun. She moved slowly. No more rapidly, she walked off south-west into Soho.

'What do you mean, a waste of *time*—?'

Vanished: gone into streetlamps and neon and the darkness between tall buildings.

Crouched at her elbow, a tall fair girl said, 'You wanna go on somewhere else, Rue? Mark some more of them?'

'Wait!' Rue held up a hand for silence. She glanced over her shoulder. None of the Soldier-Saints visible, and that's how it should be: all in cover. She strained her hearing.

Frankie.

No.

No...

'There!' She pointed. 'Fuck, they've got police horses round the back of us. Let's get out of here!'

Rue Ingram runs. Hard behind her, and faster, a horse canters across closed city streets.

CHAPTER EIGHTEEN

A Grave and Gallant City

The light shines blue, with a cold clarity only seen at dawn. Miles Godric gazes up at the cloudless sky over Adelaide Street. The haze will come later, after dawn: for now it is 3–30 a.m. and sparkling.

Street refugees, mostly middle-aged men and women, sit around a brazier. The coals glow, almost invisible in the new sunlight. Far overhead, pigeons wheel whitely over St Martin's Church, vanish down below the skyline to settle in Trafalgar Square.

'Val – where are you going? What are you doing?'

The red-haired woman grins at him. Her eyes are puffy with lack of sleep, and she walks with a slack-boned step, but she is, nonetheless, grinning. 'You'll find out. You can broadcast it for Johanna.'

'*Val.*'

'Oh, I don't mind. Why would I mind the open society? I invented it, after all.'

'Not so much of the *I*,' Baltazar Casaubon rumbled.

The big man – and he stood a good two inches taller even than Miles, as Miles was once again reminded, standing beside him – coughed, and pulled his creased white jacket around his massive shoulders. He absently poked a finger down towards his pocket.

A pink nose and vibrating whiskers emerged from the top of the pocket, nipped Baltazar Casaubon's questing forefinger severely, and vanished back into the voluminous folds of silk.

'I don't think Spike likes cold mornings ...' The fat man sucked his bleeding finger.

'For God's *sake*!' the red-headed woman said. 'Keep that animal out of sight!'

Casaubon anxiously regarded Miles Godric, the refugees, and the paying customers across the street entering an all-night vegetarian café. 'You think there'll be a panic?'

'I think we'll have everyone crawling over you going *eeuuw! ain't it cute!*' Valentine said grimly.

Baltazar Casaubon instantly assumed the demeanour of a man who was not carrying his pet white rat upon his person.

Miles, exasperated, demanded, 'But where are you *going*?'

The fat man's eyes lowered, gazing south down Adelaide Street to Charing Cross Station. Miles wonders if he is envisaging the Surrey countryside invisible beyond: Surrey and Sussex and the Channel, whose tunnel opens in countries where other languages are spoken.

Where other wars are fought.

They have been back to the Neal Street flat. Miles does not know what they have packed; except, of course, for the bundle of swords. By this, knowing Val, he assumes she is not returning.

He nodded a greeting to the men and women clustering round the brazier, and scrubbed at his cropped yellow hair with dirt-rimmed nails. The early sun warms his skin. Easy enough for the government to turn him into a babbling nobody, the kind of crazy in a dirty parka who stops you on street corners with stories of cover-ups, conspiracies. It's only a matter of perspective. Down here among disbelief, drugs, violence; how long before it would be true?

His belt cameras record.

Miles Godric turned to face Val Branwen. She stood at the door of the vegetarian café Cranks, looked back over her shoulder, and beckoned as she went in.

'You know that I'm recording this officially.' He spoke to the fat man beside him. 'You don't even care, do you?'

'Food, boy,' Baltazar Casaubon growled, clamping a huge hand on to Miles's shoulder. 'There's always time for food.'

'But—' But *Johanna*. Does she really just want me to record these two? Not stop them? And then do what?

Through the plate glass of the café he can see Val, sports bag from the Neal Street flat slung over her shoulder, vanishing into the restroom.

'Perhaps it's time I took up my responsibilities again. I am not,'

Baltazar Casaubon confessed, 'a young man any more. Make no mistake, I'm not *old.* By no means. But it is past time I settled down, chose something to do, and did it with some effort, because otherwise,' the big man said, 'I shall have done nothing but wander.'

'Nothing! Direct neural input architecture is nothing, I suppose. And the Artificial Unconscious?' Miles shook his head, muttering. '"Nothing"!'

'That? Mere playing with gadgetry. Nothing of much importance. You wait,' Baltazar Casaubon promised, 'now that I have *real* access to research, and let me loose on art and architecture in this country; on mathematics and military engineering, music and the stage: *then* you'll see something. Assuming I am ever heard of again. Johanna is not a woman of her word.'

'What will *she* do?'

No need, between them, to specify who is meant by that *she.* Baltazar Casaubon's head swivelled to the door through which Van Branwen had entered Cranks.

'I don't know. I have never known.'

Miles Godric understands in those words a history between the two of them longer than he can understand, no matter how many hours of interview he may have with Casaubon, or how close he has been to Val.

Through the plate glass window he sees her emerge into the café again.

She wears a white shirt that moulds itself to her narrow shoulders, and brown wool breeches, and she carries a brown, gold-studded leather doublet slung over one shoulder. Rapier and dagger dangle from her sword-belt, nothing awkward in her management of the hardware. Dark red hair pinned up. He sees that she has woven white-feather earrings into the hair at her temples, gleaming in the morning sun.

'Excuse me,' the large man said. 'I believe that it's time that I went and changed.'

The fat man edged himself around Val Branwen where she stood in the doorway, shading her eyes against the light. She beckoned. Miles walked as far as the street corner. Arm's reach away. 'Are you going with him? Or are you just seeing him across the London border? Are you going together?'

She smiles. There are lines in that smile. She is old enough that a night without sleep lets him see how her face will look when she is fifty. Sallow, warm skin. Some of the lines around her mouth are new since he and she were lovers.

'All these questions. For *Hypershift!*? For the Ministry? That's the same thing for you, now.'

'Yes. I suppose so.' He reached down and touched the controls on his belt pad. Main camera offline. Main transmission offline. Backup visual record offline. Store transmission offline. 'I can stand being a highly-paid government spokesman. It sounds safe. I was never what you might call an investigating reporter, Val. But – I don't have to start the job until working hours.'

She reaches up to touch him, touch his face; and he catches her hand. It is small, held in his stubby fingers and large palm.

'As my mother said, it isn't over yet.'

Her hand is cold. Colder than one would expect, and he considers that Raynaud's Disease is inherited.

'I'm going home,' he said. 'I can't record if I'm not here. And I can't say where you're going if I don't know. I'm sorry to miss the end of this.'

She grips his hand once for goodbye. Flesh to flesh. 'But you will know everything. Ultimately. We're all behind glass walls now. I'll tell you the stuff I never told you,' she said whimsically, 'before you go to the bother yourself. My father died when I was four. Johanna has always been Johanna. I ran off at thirteen, got myself a false-age computer ID, worked, worked as a hooker, put myself through university, went into military training, went with mercenaries to Central Europe, went to the US – every time she caught up with me, I ran. Until one night I realized the solution to the Non-P algorithm was staring back up at me off the screen. And then I ran back home.'

'And now?'

'Oh, now. That's the question ...'

'Don't tell me,' Miles said. 'There are already things I wish I didn't know.'

'Then I guess you'll have learn not to ask. If you can.'

Miles turns and walks away into the streets around Charing Cross. Looking for unmarked helicopters, for plain-clothes security operatives, for anything that will tell him what is happening.

Warm air drifted out through the open café fire-doors. Rue Ingram slipped inside Cranks, bone-weary, two of the boys and the youngest girl at her heels.

'That's it. We're safe. Sit,' She pointed to one of the stripped-pine tables. They collapsed into the seats. She made her way towards the counter.

'Two decafs. Two orange juices.' She felt around in her skirt pockets for change. Used to paying for the others; to be the only one able to pay for the others. But the difference now is that it is by her choice. A kind of weariness that is not of the body possesses her: a pleasant melancholy.

She took the two decaffeinated coffees to the table and returned to the counter for the juices.

Four a.m., and those half-dozen men in the corner are the first of the market traders, coming up in allotment carts that smell of veg and dirt. Four a.m., and the groups down in the main part of the café are the last of the has-been brat-hacker drinkers, hanging out into the early hours; black leather and mirrorshades and faces too old for their clothes. She nodded to a couple of her father's friends there.

'Yo, Rue...'

The black youth's soft murmur reached her. She followed his glance to the door. A dozen or so men and women came into Cranks by twos and threes, greeting each other as they passed the door; coming up from the Underground or across from Covent Garden.

Plumed hats bobbed. She noted their long jerkins, breeches, bandoleers, belts cluttered with draw-string purses, and lace-collared shirts; and hardly had to look for the muskets and swords they carried rolled in blankets.

'Oh, *what*,' the black youth, Pete, muttered.

Rue Ingram eased down into the curve-backed chair beside him. She rested her elbows on the table. The belt and webbing were uncomfortable zipped under her sleeveless leather jacket. Slowly she pulled down the zip and shrugged the jacket off, careless of who might be watching. Rolled it and shoved it in the sports-bag with the paint gun.

'Looks like the Protectorate Civil War Society. Or the Carolingian Sealed Knot, maybe. I always forget which is which. They'll be going out of London. I forgot: she told me there was going to be a muster somewhere down south this week.'

'She? Aw, your "Valentine Branwen", I suppose.'

''Sright.'

After a few minutes pause another group began to drift in from outside. A clatter drowned conversation: plate armour set down beside tables. The men wore fifteenth-century doublet-and-hose, those without gowns shivering in the dawn's chill; and the women walked bundled up in kirtles and shawls. Queen Carola's army ignored them. Rue Ingram leaned into the aisle, looking at the scabbarded swords in their blanket-bundles.

'You won't like them,' a voice said behind her, 'they're a War of the Roses society that go under the name of *Sir Nigel's Company*, and they don't permit women to fight.'

'Oh, what!' Rue swivelled round in her chair. Two tables away, no longer screened by the market traders, Valentine Branwen raised a decaffeinated-coffee mug.

'Valentine?' She stood; took a brief look at the other three Soldier-Saints – Alice, Mike, and Pete half-asleep – and walked back to join the red-haired woman. The woman's shirt was creased linen, the collar and cuffs a foam of dirty lace. Doublet and breeches were brown. Rue saw that she wore her sword-belt, the blade tied into its scabbard with peace-strings. She looked weary.

Rue said, 'You told me there was going to be a muster. You might have told me when. When will you be back?'

Valentine said, 'Rue, you're very beautiful, do you know that?'

Rue blushed. 'Aw, c'*mon*. Get real.'

The woman had her elbows on the pale pine table. She rested her chin on her interlocked fingers. Light showed the crepe skin at her throat, the lines fanning out from the corners of her warm eyes.

'Sweetheart, you're not doing anything with your life here, are you? Have you ever thought about California? Or mainland Europe – I used to hold a commission in the PanEuropean Forces before I went to the UCS, you'd be perfectly safe with me. Or there's Nihon.'

'You *got* to be joking!'

Valentine stared.

'And what,' she said acidly, 'is so laughable?'

'Jesus, you're thirty-*six*.'

'You bothered to find out.' One red-brown eyebrow went up. 'Hellfire. Sweetheart, you think anyone over nineteen is an old fart, don't you?'

Rue stood hesitant, confused.

'I take it,' the older woman said gently, 'that you're not interested in going on a trip with me?'

'No!'

The woman's mouth moved. Sun through the café window shone in her dark red hair, in the feather-decorations at her temple, and from the hilts of her weapons. Rue looked away, wiping at the paint-ball stains on her skirt.

'Why do that?' the woman said suddenly.

'Why? Oh – it's an excuse. All of this. Mark the refugees for deportation, and they'll open Closed London again. An excuse. They'll never do it. But ...'

Rue lifted her head, pushed her fingers through her now-lank hair.

'But, it's so difficult to stop. Because what no one told me is that – despite *everything* – I'd enjoy it so much.'

'You should keep up with the swordfighting.' The woman reached down. 'Here's something. To remind you of the virtues of blunt blades. Here. Take it. I'd move soon, if I were you. I understand the police check out the all-night cafés after street fights.'

A toilet flushed loudly in the Gents, and Baltazar Casaubon walked out. In costume, Rue saw, bemused. The fat man wore white silk knee-breeches that didn't do up over his capacious belly. The cloth was stained with slops from the bottle of red wine he carried. His calves and feet were stockinged, but otherwise bare. He carried a pair of heeled court shoes tied by the laces and slung around his neck, resting in the folds of a silk shirt and badly-tied cravat. Something sky-blue and silk and voluminous over his arm might have been a coat or a cloak.

He rumbled, 'Damned health food. Turns my guts.'

'That,' the woman said, 'is because you never let yourself become used to it. If you're good, I'll buy you a burger at the station before you go.'

'Really?' He perked up. 'And chips?'

Rue looked at her gift. She weighed on her outstretched palms the heft of Valentine's drop-hilted parrying dagger. The diamond-sectioned blade glittered in the dawn light. She slid it into her left hand and the pommel nestled against the heel of her hand, fitting perfectly.

'I guess I better go find Frankie. I didn't tell her yet, she's got a rep job to see her through the summer to next term.'

'Good luck,' says the fat man.

When she lifts her face she is, through wetness, smiling with a brilliance to equal the early light. 'But when will you be back?'

The morning chill froze Johanna Branwen's fingers. She halted in the entrance of Cranks, standing in the down-draft of warmth from the door heater and lazily surveying the café.

'Ah...'

She made her way steadily between the tables. Her thick-furred jacket snagged against wrapped sword hilts and the sleeves of badly-made doublets. The men and women who glanced up found themselves muttering involuntary apologies. She drew up a chair and sat down at an empty corner table.

Just faintly through the soles of her feet she felt the passing of the first Underground trains.

'Valentine.'

Her daughter looked across heads from the counter queue and met her eyes. Johanna beckoned. Valentine Branwen muttered something to her fat ex-husband and walked across to stand with her fists on her hips. 'What the fuck are you doing here?'

'I have something to say to you and your husband.'

The early summer morning glitters through the plate-glass windows. 4–30 a.m., pavements still dark with dew; the sides of buildings white with roosting pigeons. The smell of the river drifted in: mud, and dead weed, and diesel. Johanna slitted her eyes momentarily against the brilliance, anticipating the longer, hotter days of the continent as soon as unfinished business could be concluded here.

'You don't...' Her daughter's face creased into a frown. 'Look, you're not here to – apologize, or anything? I don't want this to get embarrassing.'

A small smile curved Johanna's lips. She shook her head, filled with a contrary liking for the woman her girl has become. She reached over and tapped the pommel of her child's sword. 'You look ridiculous wearing that in public.'

'Only because it's not a live blade, Mother.' A smile. 'How do you *expect* me to carry it? It was designed to be worn.'

'Bring your ex-husband over here.'

Her daughter's heeled period shoes clicked on the wooden floor. Johanna watched her back as she moved. Narrow shoulders in a white shirt; brown knee-breeches and hose; the dark red hair braided over her head in barley-rows, and white feathers wound into the hair at her temples. Vivaldi played on the café's sound-system. She felt a chill, precise melancholy; and at the same time a sprightly joy. She rested her plump chin down on her gloved hands. Her daughter, returning, put a mug of apple-tea in front of her. Steam coiled upwards.

'Sit down,' Johanna said crisply.

The fat man, following, beamed. He inspected the nearest chair, mug in one hand and a plate balanced in the crook of his elbow. Finding the chairs all too fragile, he put his back against the wall and slid down into a sitting position between her and Valentine, near a small pile of bags and cases. He dug one finger into the plate of lemon cheesecake, sucked it, and made a purse-mouthed face.

'Heavy on the lemon,' he remarked. 'Johanna! There was absolutely no necessity for you to come and see me off. None at all. I assure you, my time-keeping may not be superb, but I shall have no difficulty in ensuring that I catch the cross-Channel train.'

'Two things,' she said.

The fat man scratched at his head, leaving traces of cheesecake in his orange-gold hair. She watched him steadily for several seconds, turning then to look at Valentine. She put out of her mind's eye the superimposed memories of a younger girl, in the holidays from boarding school, with that same sober, ironic wariness in her eyes.

'And this is the first.'

The café doors opened behind her. A large woman entered, seeming taller by virtue of the orange hair coiled up into braids on top of her head, and wearing a smart ivory silk suit. She carried a notebook PC clamped between one fat elbow and flank.

'Now. About this Alexandria Project,' she said.

Dorothea Casaubon seated herself at their table.

CHAPTER NINETEEN

Omnia Mutantur

'There are more violent forms of intimidation and coercion,' Johanna said thoughtfully. 'I thought, however, that what I would do is bribe you. You specifically, Baltazar.'

She watched her daughter. The younger woman's face froze. The large man choked on a mouthful of cheesecake, spraying brown fragments on her scarlet tracksuit. She brushed them off.

'*Bribe?*'

'Like so many people,' she said as she watched him, 'you are under the illusion that there is nothing you want that badly. Dorothea, please?'

Dorothea Casaubon's large hands flipped up the cover of her notebook PC. Working the tiny keys with difficulty, she accessed and displayed a sequence of screens. A large baroque public building. Optical disc storage units. Dark-fibre communications networks.

'A storage and access facility for information. I think,' Johanna said lightly, 'that they used to be called libraries. I forget how many terabytes of storage capacity are planned for installation. Certainly it will be globally unique. This is only the first building, the whole complex will be the size of a small city. Accommodation, entertainment complexes, fully equipped research laboratories – you'd be surprised what you can do with a Defence budget when you try.'

Dorothea Casaubon pushed up the ivory silk sleeves of her suit jacket and leaned back in her creaking chair. 'You *are* paying me. Good. I was beginning to wonder.'

Baltazar Casaubon looked up at his sister. He jerked a cheesecake-covered thumb. 'You design for her?'

'I do now.'

'Ah.'

The copper-haired woman wiped sweat from her face, smearing her lipstick. She blithely crowded Johanna with her elbow as she removed a mirror compact from one pocket. Lining her mouth, she muttered indistinctly, 'Why "Alexandria", though?'

Baltazar interrupted Johanna before she could reply.

'Good grief! Does no one have a classical education these days? The Library at Alexandria! One of the seven wonders of the world. It contained all the books in the world,' he said softly, 'and it was burned.'

Johanna smiled.

'I've come from arranging shared funding with Confederate America, the Japanese trade-sphere, and Australia. I have also arranged a Middle Eastern site for the storage facility. Quite near the historical Alexandria – a genuine publicity coup. Building can start in three weeks.'

She rubbed her fingers together and felt the painful pricking of returning circulation.

'I shall use it as a flagship. We must ride the wave of information-flood.' She tried the phrase out on her tongue and smiled. 'I must have Morgan contact the speech-writing department. Open government. A due concern to ease the transition to new forms of society. And what could make me appear more liberal than funding the re-established Library at Alexandria? "Information for all." There's a slogan. I'm sorry to say,' she concluded, 'that there will not be a place on the staff for you, Valentine.'

Her daughter's shoulders moved in the slightest shrug.

'However, Baltazar, I should like you to consider taking the position of Director.'

The fat man's freckled face reddened. For once he said nothing at all.

Johanna continued, 'The salary is one hundred and twenty thousand pounds per annum. Duties won't interfere with your own research. A full staff at the Library at Alexandria will handle heavy publicity, concentrated work-schedules, and – let no one say I'm changing sides to be with the winners. No, indeed.' She put her fingers into her hair at her temples, smoothing the slick curls back over her ears. The café lurched with the momentary dizziness of sleeplessness.

'A few years ago I could work through the night and never

think about it.' She gave a blurry smile. 'Well. What do you say?'

'Keiko Musashi offered me a position with Sony-Nissan.' He avoided her daughter's gaze when he said it. 'Continuing neural architecture research.'

'*And?*' Valentine demanded.

'I told Keiko-sama I should not, as it transpired, be joining her.'

The red-headed woman frowned. 'What did she say?'

Baltazar Casaubon dug his finger deep into his ear and examined what he had extracted. '"*Bakame!*"'

'"Bloody fool".' Valentine chuckled.

'Ah ...' Johanna began to pull on a pair of soft leather gloves. 'But that isn't the point, is it, the research? The point about the Alexandria Project is that it will have a staff of three thousand, and an associated staff of twice that number. In effect, a small city – and you can run it. If you want to. Say the word.'

The fat man said quietly, 'It's redundant.'

'What?'

'Before it's built. Johanna, who needs a physical library? What's the point of storing information, of concentrating it?' He shrugged. 'When you can have it all, now, anywhere, independent of geography.'

Dorothea Casaubon nodded vigorously.

'It's the mistake of thinking knowledge can be restricted to one head.' Dorothea eyed her brother's cheesecake enviously. 'You're all running around in pointless circles. I was getting the codebreaker algorithm off *public* bulletin boards as shareware ten days ago.'

'*What?*' Johanna stared, appalled.

'Hackers are like that.' Dorothea shrugged, her immense breasts moving under her ivory silk jacket. 'It won't be that long before there are bootleg copies of direct neural input architecture. Johanna, you never did understand the hacker mentality. We don't care about all this authoritarian garbage.'

'Neural architecture is worth hundreds of thousands of pounds!'

Dorothea said, 'We just want to see how he *did* it. Play with it ourselves. Money doesn't matter.'

'If hackers are so bloody subversive,' Valentine demanded, 'how come they're all employed for vast salaries by multinational corporations, and they can't organize a union worth a damn? If young hackers are going to change the world, why do they spend all their time playing multi-user dungeons and worrying about how high-level their wizard is?'

The fat man murmured, '"Shoot the liberals".'

'I say shoot the techno-liberals – what did you say?'

'Nothing,' Baltazar Casaubon said. 'Nothing at all. I wouldn't dare.'

'I'm *right*,' her daughter Valentine said.

'I'm hungry again,' Casaubon said. 'Do you think there's any remote chance of concluding this and getting some more food?' He turned bright eyes up to Johanna, beamed, and in an undertone said, '*I* knew we could trust the hacker network to distribute the software. It seemed a reasonable fall-back plan.'

'Thank you, Dorothea. You can leave the files.'

The big woman rose, awkwardly. Her gaze skated over Johanna's daughter. She looked down at her brother. 'It's time you did something you can be recognized for, Bal. Make the family proud. Don't you think?'

The fat man grumbled under his breath.

The café door swung closed behind Dorothea Casaubon.

Johanna Branwen removed her gloves and cabled the notebook PC into her mobile phone with hands upon which the fingers were pinched white and purple. 'Whether it's redundant or not, Baltazar, you want it.'

'No.'

'No? Shall we see,' she said, 'what the idiot-savant of the psychological world has to say about it?'

At the touch of her finger, software began to upload on to the notebook PC.

'Although I must say,' Johanna added waspishly, 'that if there is one thing the government probably *doesn't* need, it's an online counsellor. Are we ready?' She keyed in the query.

The screen clears, then scrolls text.

‹*I have returned in signs and characters – this shape delights you best?*›

Versatile program. She approves.

'Let us see,' Johanna says, 'what you really would do, left to your own devices, Baltazar. Consult the oracle. Ask it.'

She sat back, staring him down, smiling. If he asks it, he is obeying her. If he refuses any part of this, he looks a coward in front of her daughter. These little double-binds are simple to set up, wonderfully effective in play.

'No?' she says, after a minute. 'Then let me. I wish it had been an artificial *intelligence.* It could be controlled far more effectively. One can't get a straightforward answer out of it – more like a novel than a slot machine.' She smiles, devil's advocate. 'One gets out of it what one is capable of understanding, rather than objective knowledge. Almost an artist's perspective. Which makes it harder to misuse.'

'Of course it can be "misused",' Valentine snapped. 'It's a purely liberal superstition to think that anyone who can comprehend what Art is telling them must be moral. Art isn't a democracy. I don't think an Artificial Unconscious is any more moral than a rabid dog. It just does what it does.'

The fat man knelt up to the table, entered codes on the keyboard, crashed, swore, re-booted, re-booted again; and sat back on his stockinged heels. Text scrolled rapidly across the nine-inch screen.

Her daughter smiled wryly. 'Oh – *I* get it. In the form of a screenplay this time.'

‹INTERIOR, SAN FRANCISCO APARTMENT, DAY

A young VALENTINE BRANWEN turns away from the 26th floor window. Behind her we can see San Francisco and the Bay.

VAL: Casaubon, I'm going to need the main monitor.

CAS: Hrrrrhmm …

VAL: *Now* will do!

The young BALTAZAR CASAUBON slouches on a swivel chair that creaks under his bulk, the VDU remote-control vanishing in the flesh of one hand. We see CASAUBON put his free hand on his shoulder and cover VALENTINE's fingers lightly resting there, without looking away from the wall-screen.

CAS: Inna minute …

VAL: Are you test-running – oh, what the hell! *Cas*aubon!

We see CASAUBON chuckle, the motion rumbling through his flesh. VALENTINE's fingers tense. CASAUBON clicks the remote control, absently, morse-fast, his eyes flicking across the divided screen. We can see on the split screen a page of novel-text surrounded by technical diagrams (the heroine's starship), time-lines (following a single character through the story; it gives spreadsheets on two minor villains at the moment), a video of the landscape over which a star-battle is taking place, with soundtrack; and selected chunks of the author's biography.

VAL: You're not still viewing that tripe!
CAS: We-ell ...›

Johanna looked up. The fat man's pudgy finger rested on the *Hold* key. His eyes were bright.

'Pleasant memories?'

Her daughter raised her head from reading upsidedown, and said softly, 'An amalgamation, I think?'

'Yes ...'

‹*CASAUBON reads effortlessly and holistically: skipping from battle-scene to the love-scene preceding, forward to one of the heroine's tragic deaths; running a rock video of the soundtrack, pausing to take in a scan of all other titles dealing with similar matters, fiction and non-fiction; and inserting top right a tv interview with an academic critic.*
CAS: Just a little relaxation, my Rose of the World.
VAl: I need the monitor. And you need to be using this properly! Any time this *year*, Casaubon.
VALENTINE reaches over his shoulder and removes the remote control.
VAL: I know that one. It's the pirate version of *Sun Magic*. It isn't relaxation, it's tripe, pure and simple!
CASAUBON lifts his head lazily and pulls VALENTINE down to kiss her. He rubs his cheek against her shoulder.
CAS: This from the woman I found making a novel out of the hyper-indexed version of Machiavelli's *Prince*?
VAL: That's different!
CAS: Splicing in it, as I recall, with segments from *The Three Musketeers* and the Olivier *Richard III* ...
VAL: Yes. Well.
If someone resting over a man's shoulder can be said to shuffle, VALENTINE shuffles. She bites at his ear. CASAUBON winces.
CAS: Now.
CASAUBON stands up. The chair's metal screeches as he uses it for support. He stretches his arms, then tugs off his vest.
CAS: I suppose one had better change for company.›

It is better than she supposes, when she looks up. Tears are running down the man's motionless features, dripping from his chins.

‹*CASAUBON unbuttons his trousers and kicks his feet free of the crumpled material. He removes a pair of crimson underpants, patterned with butterflies, and faces her, naked.*
CAS: At least I waited to undress. I thought you'd given up collecting little girls.
VALENTINE grins at him, and sighs between amusement and admiration.
VAL: You know damn well I think you're magnificent.
CASAUBON strikes a pose, hipshot, nude: hands clasped at the back of his head.
CAS: *And* magnificently endowed!
VAL: How would you know? I've seen it a hell of a lot more recently than you have!
CASAUBON flirts his eyebrows at VALENTINE, reducing her to giggles, and picks up a pastel pink cotton shirt. Surveying it, he sniffs, shrugs, and wrestles his arms into its sleeves.›

'It could have happened like that.' He does not touch Johanna's daughter but he looks at her. 'In Neal Street. Little one ...'

‹*VALENTINE hooks the cloth free of CASAUBON's elbow and buttons the shirt across his swelling belly.*
FX: DOOR BUZZER.
VALENTINE picks up the entry-phone and listens. We see her frown. She puts the receiver slowly down.
VAL: It's a woman. I think she says her name is 'Izumi Teishi'. She says she needs to speak to you?›

Quietly, without annoyance, her daughter reaches over and shuts down the notebook PC. 'I think that's enough.'

'Do you?' Baltazar Casaubon wiped his streaming face. 'Little one, I could read it all day, if I didn't hurt so much.'

'I think that's kind of the point.'

Her daughter Valentine has red-brown eyes, but there is no seeing them behind mirrorshade lenses that glint, and reflect the pale surfaces of stripped-pine tables, and the blue sky curving outside the window.

Johanna leaned forward. 'And now you're going to listen to me while I tell you the second thing that you need to know. Or do you need to know? I think, in any case, I need to tell you.'

She lifted the apple-tea and sipped. The hot ceramic brought a welcome warmth to her hands. She held the mug cradled while she spoke.

'Valentine. I have your fingerprints, and your DNA coding. I have your retinal prints. I have several years worth of statistical analysis of your computer-use styles, which makes them perfectly identifiable. And I have access to police and MI6 files, Home Office and credit-card databases, Social Welfare and hypertext journalism.'

Johanna drank again, and the apple-tea scalded her throat. Tears started in her eyes. She stared at them: the small red-haired woman and the large man. The early sun cast their shadows across the polished wooden table.

'Valentine, I may not be able to stop you hacking into the occasional bank for food money, but I'll get you thrown out of any accommodation. I'll make sure you never have credit or a cheque-book. I'll make it certain that you never get a job again. That you never hold any kind of professional status. Never get any State benefit. Never get through Customs.' She switched her gaze to the window, briefly. 'I'm making sure that the only place you have left to go is the pavement, with the other refugees.'

Johanna looked back. She made a small, snorting chuckle; very quietly.

'I'm not a complete monster. I won't interfere with the children going to Izumi Teishi. You may even see them occasionally – provided that you visit me at the same time. I don't think that's too much for a grandmother to ask, do you?' She allowed a calculated pause, and added, 'Your ex-husband can be employed at the Alexandria Library. He at least *can* work, whereas you never will. I regret the inevitable friction this will cause between the two of you.'

She sees them look at each other.

Is it triumph she feels? Or is it merely relief at the shifting of such a long-term, dead-weight, Gordian knot? Johanna Branwen drains the mug of apple-tea. She inhales the last incense-heavy scent of it, and puts the cooling ceramic mug down. Her gloved fingers shake very slightly.

'And that's all.' Johanna pushed her chair back. The legs screeled across the floor. She stood, staring down, and caught the gaze of the fat man. Baltazar Casaubon had his head cocked to one side.

She met his eyes, expecting customary benevolence.

She blinked with sudden shock.

*

Miles Godric paused for human interest footage on his way home through Charing Cross station, listening to the conversations under the noise of a harpsichord playing something cold and tinkly on the PA system. A few men in medieval costume seemed to be having an argument, in broad south London accents, over where their passports were, and how would they get across the GLC border *now*?

His gaze, flicking across the crowd, caught sight of a woman at the coffee stall. Orange hair. Broad shoulders. A head taller, even, than most of the male commuters around her.

Dorothea Casaubon, on her own.

He glanced up at the Departures board. A Channel train leaving in nine minutes ...

Dorothea Casaubon. A big woman wearing a suit: ivory silk jacket and skirt. With earrings composed of hawk feathers and tiny polished bones. Her wrist-deep massy hair down about her shoulders.

Knowing all objections: the woman one of *that* family, ten years older than himself at the least, and not particularly a friend of his. Bad beginnings, and no more than the stirrings of attraction to put against that. And what is she capable of, being *his* sister?

Knowing all this, Miles scrubs a hand through his beard, blinks pale eyes, and – the first decision, but not necessarily the hardest – walks across to speak to her.

'That is *not* all.' Baltazar Casaubon rose, magisterially, to his feet; still cradling the plate of lemon cheesecake.

'"Johanna is not a woman of her word",' Johanna quoted, standing facing him. '"It's past time I settled down, because otherwise I shall have done nothing but wander." Baltazar, you *want* this. The sweet fruition of an earthly crown. You want the Library.'

The big man gazed down at her. The first sun shone in through the café window on his stained cravat's creases, and knee-breeches, and the shoes slung around his fat-rolled neck.

Baltazar Casaubon rumbled, 'It's a bad error to think a person stupid beyond contempt, simply because they are the scum who have taken your daughter from you. You never took the time to discover adequately how I think. Yes, I want this position. No, I won't take it.'

He has the look of a man hearing bolts and bars collapse, a door swinging open. And then, with a sudden uncertainty, he finishes, 'But trying to make your daughter a non-person ... I confess I did not expect that.'

At last she looks at her daughter.

Expecting shock. Expecting that blind, beaten expression that is Valentine's fury from small child to teenager. Whether that is a current expression of her daughter's Johanna doesn't know, not having been with her in so many years. Certainly it is not the way she looks now.

'Is that a challenge to me – beat the system?' Dancing, her daughter's eyes; and suddenly Valentine swivels around in her seat and puts her heeled shoes up on the table, and stretches her arms as if they will crack. 'I *won*der ... And in any case, it can't be done. You can't do it. Jesus Christ, Mother. How many times have they lost *your* medical records? How many times has someone stolen your bank code? The higher the technology level, the more there is to fuck up, be honest. You can't make me a non-person, you don't have the control over the information.'

Valentine smiles.

'Especially not *now*...'

'Haven't you been listening to anything I've said!' Johanna quiets her voice and breathing.

'Of course.' The fat man sounded hurt by the imputation. 'Of course she has. You said something about sleeping on pavements...'

'Valentine, you have nowhere to go! You *have* to come to me.'

'Do you really think there won't be a subculture of the information have-nots?' Valentine says. 'I've slept on pavements before.'

'And a lot more people will be sleeping there because of you!' Temper gone now, leaning clenched fists down on the table, Johanna spits out the words. 'Prices, inflation, crashes ... Have you any idea of what life is going to be like with *this*? I think you've finally succeeded in shocking me. The economy's gone, and how long before it's the telephone network off, and water, and power? How long before London is part of Former Europe, without even the benefit of a *war* to cause it!'

'You don't know that it will be a total collapse.'

'You don't know that it won't!'

Johanna's bones ache with the early morning. She has had the victory and it aches somewhere down deeper in her bones. The mental readjustment to ambiguity takes hardly a blink; she has had to do more and harder in her time. Still, there is time for one more effort. To make her daughter *see* the position she's in. And then: '*Why*, baby? Why? What you've chosen to do is ... unforgivable.'

'It's nothing of the sort,' Valentine said. 'Or maybe it is, but it wasn't a choice. It wasn't a choice between good and bad, order and anarchy. It never is. It's a choice between the good of the powerful and the welfare of the powerless. Look at what you *can* do – even legitimately, you control the legislation, the army, the police, the money. Who else has that kind of power? Not me. Not anyone else I know. We never will.'

Johanna manages a sceptical smile.

Valentine leaned forward. 'The choice is between things getting worse for just the powerless, or things getting worse for everybody. It's rock bottom pragmatism. I choose the option where everybody suffers, so I can include those in power. Because otherwise only the powerless suffer.'

'You arrogant little girl,' Johanna said.

'Of course it's arrogance. I know how to create knowledge. I made the Non-P algorithm possible. If I can do that, I have some responsibility to decide what happens when I've done it! If I can. If I have the chance. I had the chance, this is it, make what you like of it. I thought, this way there's a chance something better might come out of it. As opposed to no chance at all.'

'It's too late to stop the chaos of a world with no privacy.' Johanna blinked. 'Which may be worse than the fascism of a world with invasive mind technology.'

'Risk isn't better than security but it's the only possible choice. History's on the side of the random hacker. You might call what I've done fighting fire with small tactical nukes!' Her daughter's gaze is, at last, hers. 'But it's better the powerful and the powerless should both be in the shit, when the only other choice is just the powerless in the shit.'

Johanna's clenched fist does not dent the notebook PC, merely rattles it across the café table. Her daughter places sallow fingers on it. Vivaldi on the café sound-system is replaced by Pachelbel.

'As for me ... ask yourself what the Artificial Unconscious can do,' Valentine said. 'It can answer questions we haven't asked yet. It can give amoral, pragmatic solutions to political problems – but it won't give them secretly. It can't keep a secret.'

She paused and leaned her chin on her fingertips.

'It'll make one hell of a military computer. What happens to battle simulations when you can process infinitely more data and come out with a real-time answer? Does it become possible to process a genuine war while you fight, and win because there are, now, no unforeseen actions? What happens when you do it, fully aware of enemy movements, and they fully aware of yours?'

'What will you do, now?' Johanna asked. 'Will you come home with me?'

'I thought it was so easy. Life the way it was. I'd built up a reputation in the entertainment industry ... Baltazar had just built up a reputation!' She grinned, and then grew reflective, studying the fat man's features. 'And I knew where you were if I should ever want to see you. Which I didn't.'

'Answer the question!'

'I'm going back to the Confederate military,' Valentine said, 'because they need me now. I'm going back to do something about the specifically military applications of direct neural input and the Artificial Unconscious – God knows, someone has to. It has to be someone who's not afraid of dirty hands. And I know how the military mind works.' She, for the last time, curved her mouth in that grin that is always Valentine's. 'I do have responsibilities, you know.'

'I begin to see how this works. I can always find you,' Johanna says, 'glass walls work both ways.'

Neither of them appeared to have heard her speak.

The fat man tugged at his costume breeches, casting a speculative eye at the morning outside, and began to pull on what was (now he unfolded it) a deep-cuffed, many-buttoned frock coat.

With a dignity that even Johanna had, as spectator, to admit, he said, 'Haven't I proved that you can trust me?'

The red-haired woman looked up, crossed heels still resting up on the table. 'I told you you didn't understand, sweetheart. You frighten me even more, now. What sort of people are we? What are we capable of?'

'I love you, little one.'

'You love a lot of people.'

'I do. Not the way I love you.'

Johanna, acidly, put in, 'This is very touching – from a married man.'

Her daughter Valentine acknowledged that with a quirk of her mouth. 'I guess ...' She scratched under her arms, through the linen shirt. 'It isn't that simple, I guess. But, give it a year or two and we may sort ourselves out. I have hopes.'

'"A year or two".' The large man thoughtfully folded his napkin about his remaining cheesecake slice, and tucked it squashily into one voluminous pocket. 'I'm coming with you to California. Now.'

'No. Not yet.' One hand steadies the scabbard of her rapier, the other reaches up to touch his arm. 'Soon. When things have changed.'

Baltazar Casaubon beamed. 'Ah, but I never did do what you told me to, did I?'

Johanna steps out into the air that is bitter, not with the bitter cool of sunrise in stone streets, but bitter as wormwood. Faustus is dragged down by devils in the end, no matter whether they be theological or interior demons. Undefeated on the field of battle, even Tamburlaine at last just – dies.

Pigeons wheel up towards the blue and pink sky.

She looks down at the paper that her hand, fiddling in her pocket, turns between curious fingers and brings out into the bright sunshine. Part of Godric's printout. It is the Epilogue speaking at the end of *The Spy at Londinium* when all (in a most unJacobean and unMarlovian device – an Artificial Unconscious can be most creative) are, from spy to clown to lady, narrowly escaped from death.

Johanna Branwen halts by the back railings of St Martin-in-the-Fields. A young man looks up from filthy blankets crusted with summer dust and says, routinely, 'Spare some change, please?'

Johanna reads aloud to him.

'Epilogue: *Kit Marlowe* speaks:

"Pleasures and pastimes in the city prove
Grave danger and great joy excite the mind.
Some narrowly escape the reaper's blade –
One in a tavern, brawling with a spy,
Escapes to vaunt the pleasures of old age.
The blade drew blood but failed to take my life."'

She takes a breath. The line of sunlight creeps down St Martin's spire.

'"Thus come I, visioning a greater city.
Closed London's river, bright as Hellespont,
Makes a wide strait between the past and present.
This London's people flow its mighty streets.
Themselves a river, in a city chang'd –
Though hungry earth would huddle me in death,
I preach no city of the afterlife
(Though after, life is chang'd beyond recall),
I prophecy no virtue, nor repentance!
My future's drawn in colour, with blood's scarlet,
The black of death; withal, the gold of power,
For after Kingship beggars will still strive."'

And now she smiles.

'"Of all, delight in hazard most endures;
Power's pleasures do not live with certainty,
They rise from danger as the Phoenix's fire:
As we, her children, burning, mount still higher.
– *Omnia mutantur nos et mutamur in illis* –"'

The young man stares at her. 'What the *fuck* use is this, lady?'

'It's price is above rubies,' she says cheerfully, handing him the screwed-up paper, 'but, unfortunately, mine is not.'

Is her Swiss bank account already dry? Has the PM seen her encrypted files? Does she still have security clearance to the Ministry of Defence building? Ah, two can play at those games. And doubtless will.

'What's the foreign stuff?' the young man calls after her.

'"All things change",' Johanna Branwen translates, '"and we change with them".'

Finding her own kind of freedom in the presence of risk, Johanna Branwen walks cold into the dawn down Adelaide Street, through to Trafalgar Square, where among fountains, with rotors turning, the military helicopter waits.

BLACK MOTLEY

A hand rapped the rickety dressing-room door.

'Ashar! *Two minutes!*'

In no apparent haste, Ashar-hakku-ezrian leaned forward to the mirror and applied greasepaint. The fly-spotted silver reflected his dusty yellow hair, guileless blue eyes, and a baby-fat face marked with kohl – lines that it wouldn't acquire in flesh for ten years or more. He preened a wispy almost-beard.

'*Ashar!*'

He straightened, easing the sash around the middle of his black robe to conceal his plump waist, and twisted himself to check right profile, left profile ... His thin tail coiled about his ankles. Its plush fur dappled brown and a darker blond than his hair. As he pulled on his gloves, he flicked dust from his hem with the whisk-end of his tail.

'I'm here.'

He pushed past the tumbling act, trotting through the dark and cluttered backstage area, and halted in the wings as the compère's voice rang out:

'And now, ladies and gentlemen! All the way from the world's end, and brought here at great expense – for your delectation and delight: the Katayan with the marvellous mind, the master of prose and genius of rhyme – *Ashar-hakku-ezrian!*'

Saturday night, all the week for a reputation to build ... In the dazzling space beyond the naphtha footlights, applause roared.

'Good introduction,' the small female engineer-conjurer remarked, waiting in the wings beside him.

'It ought to be. I composed it.' Ashar flashed her a grin, tightened his sash, and walked out on to the music-hall stage. Applause hollowed the high spaces of the auditorium; the stalls crammed full of workers in worn doublets and patched knee-breeches.

'Ladies and gentlemen, you see me *honoured* to appear before you!' He swept a deep bow. Beyond the row of naphtha footlights, bottles and pewter cutlery shone. Smoke-haloed and dazzled, easily five hundred men and women stared up at him; those there from earlier in the week banging their fists enthusiastically on the scarred tables.

'This evening my poor talents are at your disposal, entirely at *your* command—'

Close to the front of the stage, one woman wiped her mouth with her doublet-sleeve; a man bent across to whisper to a friend. Beaming, Ashar advanced downstage.

'—I will rhyme for you, I will compose for you; each monologue of mine is, as you know, *completely* extempore – no one like another, no night like the last!'

He swung his gaze up from the smoke-filled stalls to the circle. Merchant families slumming in factory-new finery; frockcoats and periwigs; one man laughing loud enough to drown him out. He fetched voice-projection from the pit of his belly:

'And to prove it, sir, to *prove* what I say, you may give me any subject and I'll begin – *any* subject that you please! Yes, you, sir! And *you.* Anyone!'

He backpedalled, hand ostentatiously to his ear. Raucous voices prompted from the stalls. Ashar crossed upstage, light glittering from the silver braid on his black robe, pointing randomly and encouragingly into the auditorium: waiting for his previously-rehearsed subjects to arise. He backed far enough to get the boxes into his line of sight – unprofitable, most evenings; and sure enough, either side of the stage, both empty.

No. *Not empty.* One box occupied.

'Do us a monologue about the Queen!'

'Naw, make it Lord William, the bastard!'

'—one on pretty girls!'

'As you command! Wait, now.' He held up both hands until silence fell, then stood straight under the spotlight. Piano accompaniment rose from the orchestra pit:

'Lord *William* treats her Majesty
Like a meeting in Hyde Park:
Harangues and preaches, talks and teaches,
Not a word of cheeks like peaches,
Shining eyes or love's bright spark.
Lord *Benjamin* with trembling lip
Speaks soft and low of legislation:
Handsomely sighs, bats his eyes,
Compliments, flatters – I can't say, lies –

And governs the whole nation!'

Under cover of the loud applause, Ashar slid a swift glance left into the Garrick Box. Naphtha flares dazzled his sight. Jewelled sword-hilts glinted in the interior of the box.

'Want one on *love*!'

'What about the pawnshop?'

'What about my missus here!'

A tall black Rat leaned up against the carved pillar at the back of the Garrick Box. Some five foot ten or eleven inches tall, with a lean-muzzled face, black fur scarred with old sword-cuts; and a plume jutting from his silver headband and curving back over translucent, scarred ears. The Rat wore the plain harness of a swordfighter.

Devilment spurred him. Ashar clapped his hands together. 'Lord Benjamin *again*, did I hear? Yes! yes, *and* —?'

Other Rats had crowded into the box. Not unusual to see a drunken Rat lord sprawled there some evenings, slumming, but this ... They wore the sleeveless blue jackets that are the livery of the Queens' Guard.

Ashar hooked his tail up over his arm, bowed to the stalls, and held up both hands for quiet.

The music-hall auditorium hushed.

'In honour of our esteemed visitors.' His hand swept out grandly to indicate the box. The black Rats faded back into further shadows. He grinned. 'I give you a completely new monologue, concerning our noble Lord Benjamin, minister to our Queen—'

'Gawd bless er!'

Ashar bowed expansively to the stalls at the interruption.

'—Lord Benjamin, together with that most delicate of sweetmeats, that most rare *candy*—'

'*Ashar-hakku-ezrian!*'

A female Rat's voice cut him off. He drew himself up, mouth opening for his usual response to hecklers; then shaded his eyes as he stared down into the stalls.

A Rat pushed between the dining-tables, her sword already drawn and in her long-fingered hand. Her white fur gleamed in the reflected footlights. Leather sword-harness crossed her silver-furred breast, and she wore a sleeveless, belted black jacket. She stood lightly on clawed hind feet, scaled tail out for balance, staring up at Ashar challengingly.

He glared back, uncharacteristically bad-tempered. 'Damn you, Varagnac, I warned you! Wait and see what you'll get for interrupting me.'

'I'll give you a subject for a monologue,' she shouted. 'A renegade Kings' Memory! *Take him!*'

Long-clawed feet scrabbled as the Guards leaped the low wall from the box to the stage. Steel grated from scabbard. Ashar swung round, open-handed, weaponless. A brown police Rat blocked the nearest wing, sword drawn; others blocked the far side. He turned. Varagnac shoved two tables aside and grabbed for the edge of the stage.

A black Rat Guard walked tentatively out on to the exposed boards towards Ashar, one slender-fingered hand up to keep the spotlights from his eyes.

'You're under arrest!' Varagnac shouted over the growing noise. A bottle crashed past from behind her and shattered on the stage. Feet stamped. Men and women hung over the edge of the circle, screeching abuse. Those in the stalls backed away, unwilling to confront Rat Lords. A child shrieked.

Ashar halted, dead centre-stage. 'I—'

He put his fists on his hips, sucking in his plump belly, and glared at the chaotic auditorium. Noise defeated his attempt to speak. He scowled, and stamped his left heel twice on the boards.

The stage trapdoor fell open.

He plummeted through, robes flying, arms and tail upraised; knees already bent for the mattress-landing below.

'Stop him!' Varagnac heaved herself up on to the stage and leaped forward. One of the Rat Guards threw himself down into the gap. She stopped on the very edge and stared down into darkness. 'Have you got him?'

A chop-bone from the auditorium clipped her shoulder, smearing grease on her white fur. She straightened, speaking to the other Rats. 'Keep this lot quiet. Clear the building if you have to. You down there! *Well?*'

From the open darkness of the trapdoor, the black Rat's voice drifted up.

'Nothing, ma'am. There's nobody down here.'

The woman sprawled back in her chair at the crate serving for a desk, one booted heel up on the heaped cash-books; her fingers steepled. Dawn air nipped her chin and nose. Through the open warehouse doors the river air gusted in, loud with the shouts of dock workers unloading clipper ships.

She tucked her hands up into the warm armpits of the black redingote, slightly too large, that swathed her.

'Have you found him yet, Master Athanasius?'

Her husky voice penetrated above the efforts of men wheeling trollies, women shifting crates; shouts and grunts; all the bustle of the warehouse being stacked full. Athanasius Godwin spared a glance at the high brick interior, the stacked wooden shelves, and bit back his resentment at being summoned to a warehouse.

'I regret to say – not yet. Madam.'

'I've heard *not yet* until I'm very tired of it. For the best part of ten days.' Jocelyn de Flores sat up. Grey streaked her shining black hair, that curled to her collar; and she looked up with a confident and capable smile.

'Now walk with me, sir, and I'll explain something to you, and *you* can explain it to the Academy of Memory.'

Athanasius Godwin pulled his cloak more tightly around his thin shoulders. The damp morning spiked rheumatic pains in his hip. Leaning on his silver-headed cane, he followed the woman through the crowded warehouse – she calling directions to left and right, not pausing in her stride – and came up with her out on the quayside. She stepped back against the warehouse wall, out of the way of a carter and his team. A Percheron huffed warm, equine breath

'Madam, I also was a Kings' Memory, before I retired to teach. I remember what you said at our last meeting. *There is a contract at stake here, Master Athanasius. The way that the world is going, you may wake up one fine morning, and find yourselves more* Merchants' *Memories than Kings' Memories. Remember it. Though I mean no disrespect to our Queen, God rest them.* The Academy of Memory is not unaware of that.'

She nodded at his word-for-word recollection.

'Perfect as ever, Master Athanasius. I believe you don't have to tell me you're good. We wouldn't use the Academy of Memory if it failed us, too much—' Her bare hand swept out, taking in the dock, the forests of sail-hung masts, and the tarpaulin-shrouded cargoes. 'Too much depends on it.'

'You have no choice about using us. We are all there is.'

'I would to God I was allowed to write down words, as I'm licensed to set down figures in my account-books! But the world isn't made as I like it.'

'Written words have too much power.'

The early sun brought out crow's-feet around her eyes. Light gilded her sallow skin. Her shadow, and the masts' shadows, fell all toward the west. She thumbed a silver watch from her waistcoat pocket, flicked it open with a fingernail.

'I can't spare you much time. I'll be square with you. You Kings' Memories set yourselves up to be the records of this country. You set yourselves up as trained and perfect memories, to hear all agreements and contracts and recall them at demand. Now, when one of your people goes renegade, and runs off, and takes with him the only proof of *my* contract—'

A call interrupted: 'Madam de Flores!'

Opalescent light shifted on the river, the east all one lemon-brilliant blaze. Athanasius Godwin narrowed his eyes and squinted. A fat black Rat strode along the quay, cloak flying. Dock workers got out of his way without his noticing.

'Ah. The *nouveau* poor.' The woman gave a slight smile, partly self-satisfaction, partly contempt. 'You've met my business partner, haven't you. Master Athanasius Godwin, of the Academy of Memory. Messire Sebastien.'

'I know you.' The Rat nodded absently at the old man while plucking darned silk gloves from dark-fingered hands. His embroidered cloak hung from his broad furred shoulders, swirling about his clawed hind feet and his scaled tail, that shifted from side to side. Lace clustered at the throat and wrists of his brocade jacket. A silver headband looped over one ear, under the other; and carried in its clip a dyed-scarlet ostrich plume.

'The 'Change is busy this morning.'

'Have you seen the Queen?'

Sebastien shrugged. 'With what in view? The Queen is as displeased as we are.'

He tucked his gloves under his sword-belt. A swept-hilted rapier dangled at his left haunch, and a matching dagger at the other. Plain, cheap weapons. The sword's velvet-covered scabbard had once had gems set into it, now the metal clasps stood levered open and empty.

'I say we should see their Majesties.' De Flores folded her arms. 'It's in the Queen's interest that we have this contract back in our hands immediately, before someone else finds him. Surely even you can see that!'

The Rat looked sourly at her. 'Madam partner, when they

permit such as you into the audience chamber, then do *you* go to see the Queen. Until such time as that, permit me my own judgement as to what is wise.'

He lifted a lace-wristed hand, pointing. Athanasius Godwin winced back from the accusing gesture.

'Master Athanasius, *find* this young man. Quickly. This is the height of foolishness. This Ashar-hakku-ezrian – he should never even have been acting as Kings' Memory to *begin* with!'

Nathaniel Marston ran up the cobbled hill from the docks. Towards the brow of the hill he stopped, breathing heavily, and leaned up against a wall, unlacing his doublet.

Indubitably, Madam de Flores, you don't know all your employees by sight, even if you claim you do!

He reversed his jacket, so that the plain hemp-coloured lining was replaced by rich blue velvet; wiped disguising dirt from his face, and rubbed a thumb over the calluses on his palm that shifting crates had given him.

But unless I miss my guess, the Academy of Memory didn't have good news for you. They haven't found Ashar-hakku-ezrian yet. And no wonder.

The sun, risen higher now, brought moisture to his fair-skinned face. He scrubbed his sleeve across his mouth. Sweat tangled stickily in his close-cropped beard.

A few men walked past, coming or going from early factory shifts; a coach with Rat Lords' heraldry on the door jolted down the hill. The city fell away in oak-and-white-plaster houses and spiked blue-tiled roofs, to the docks. Sun burned off all the spring's dawn cold. Haze clung to apple-blossom, white in gardens.

He moved off again, this time less hurriedly.

Narrow streets closed him in between barred doors and shuttered windows: a scarecrow-thin man in rich blue jacket and breeches, his hands heavy now with gold rings; and his dark red hair tangled down to his collar. Shadow slanted down. A quick turn into an alley – beyond that, he stepped from congested streets into an enclosed square.

Dust skirled across the great courtyard between sandstone walls. Thin ogee-arched windows flashed back the light. Wisteria, some eighty or ninety years old, spidered purple blossom all across the carved and decorated facade of the east wing. Students clustered on the steps leading up to the great arched entrance, talking; or ran, late for seminars.

'Nathan!'

A lead-paned window creaked open on the first floor and the Reverend Principal Cragmire leaned his elbow on the sandstone sill. The tall man beckoned. 'Get yourself up here, man! I want to know what's happening.'

Conscious of curious student eyes on him, Marston nodded acknowledgement, straightened his back, and strode up the steps and into the building.

This early, the corridors were full. Anglers and curbers waited to be led out for practicals in the city. A false beggar sat in a window embrasure painting on a scar. Two graduate nips and foists stood discussing the finer points of dipping pockets with a research professor.

'Excuse me.' Marston eased between a doxy and a mort, answering the latter's practised smile with a pinch on her buttock; and slid thankfully through into Cragmire's room.

'Come in, Nathan, come in. You look as though you've had a busy night.'

Sun gleamed on the panelled walls. He caught a wing-armed chair, pulled it up to the Principal's desk, and sank back into it with a grunt. 'Damn busy. What *I'm* worried about is my teaching load. Who's taking care of that while I'm watching Ashar-hakku-ezrian?'

The tall bearded man grunted. 'Sulis is taking your class in knife-fighting. Chadderton can handle the sessions on dangerous drugs and poisoning; and I've given first-level card-sharping and basic disguise to young Dermot. Ah ... the administrative work you'll have to clear up yourself when you get back.'

Nathaniel Marston grunted. 'I thought as much.'

'So what's happened?'

'I really *don't* know what that young man thinks he's doing. If I were Ashar-hakku-ezrian I'd stay under cover and pray to ship out of the city. *He's* making himself a career on the stage! Last night he didn't even bother to use a false name.'

'He's still at the Empire?'

Marston scratched the hair at the back of his neck and chuckled.

'Not after last night! We were right – they've put Varagnac on to the boy. A misjudgement, I'd say; but then, we know Varagnac better than they do ...'

'She found him?'

'Even she couldn't miss him. I'd have stepped in, but there wasn't any need. If Ashar-hakku-ezrian wasn't a Kings' Memory, I'd sign him up for us tomorrow. I'll swear he was about to spill the whole thing on-stage, Lord Benjamin and all – at any rate, Varagnac thought he was. She all but pissed herself.'

Cragmire frowned. 'To go renegade is one thing. I could almost understand that, with the particular contract that he's carrying in his head. But then, Nathan, wouldn't you hide, if it were you? And what does he do?'

'He goes on the stage. Under his own name.' Nathan shook his head, marvelling, amused. 'He's quite good. No, I do him a disservice. He's very good.'

There was a pause.

'If Varagnac's people found him yesterday, then they'll find him again. Ten days ago I would have said it was to keep him alive. Now ... Lord Benjamin may be having second thoughts.'

'It may be.' Marston shrugged.

'What about the commercial cartel?'

'De Flores has no idea where her missing contract is, and neither does the Academy of Memory. But they will, of course, if he goes on like this. The question is, what are *we* going to do about it?'

'There is the question of what the Queen ...' Cragmire scratched at his dark beard. 'I think you'd better keep a friendly eye on Ashar-hakku-ezrian. Protectively friendly. While you're doing it ...'

He stood.

'I'll call an emergency governors' meeting of the University of Crime.'

Far beneath the advancing morning, Ashar-hakku-ezrian stripped the black stage robe off over his head. His hands scraped the top of the brickwork tunnel.

'Shit!' He disentangled himself and sucked grazed knuckles. Cobwebs trailed lace-like across his plump belly and chest. He squatted down, sorting through the heap of stolen clothing at his feet, and hooked out a pair of black knee-breeches.

Unseen outside the circle of his dim lantern, a black Rat continued to follow him softly down the disused sewer tunnel. Blue livery caught no light. She paused, translucent ears and whiskers trembling like taut wire.

One thin, strong-fingered hand went to her belt, drawing a loaded pocket-pistol. She raised it and sighted.

In the lantern-light, the Katayan knelt, ripping out part of the breeches' hind seam with a pen-knife. He sat back on bare buttocks, lifting his feet and drawing on the breeches, and reaching in to adjust himself: close-furred tail hooked out through the slit seam. The watching Rat grinned.

A scent bitter as ammonia stabbed her nostrils.

Copper blood in her mouth, brickwork slamming her face and body as she fell; hands that caught and made her descent soundless – all this before she could recognize the scent and taste of pain.

A man lowered the Rat's unconscious body to the tunnel floor. He tucked his lead-weighted cudgel away under his belt.

After a minute's thought, he dragged the dead-weight back into the tunnel's darkness.

Ashar-hakku-ezrian stood, belted his breeches, and shrugged into an over-large shirt. He flicked his cuffs down over his callused fingers. The lantern cast his shadow on the wall. He turned, checking silhouettes, and combed his hair back with the whisk-end of his tail.

Whistling softly, he picked up the hurricane lamp and walked on through the disused sewer.

'Any mask put on will, after long enough, grow into the skin.'

Lord Benjamin, Prime Minister and Home Secretary both, stood looking down into Whitehall. A lone carriage and pair clattered past, rattling over the cobbles. Parliament Clock struck one.

He added, 'A surprisingly short time elapses before one cannot tell which is which.'

The silver-furred Rat standing beside his desk grunted. Benjamin turned to face her. One of his pale hands played with the scarlet and orange cravat at his neck. His other thumb hooked into the pocket of his embroidered waistcoat, pushing back his sober black frockcoat. Where one trouser-cuff pulled up an inch, a red sock was visible.

'But this isn't to the purpose. What happened to the young man?'

Varagnac leaned one furred haunch up on the desk, reached across, and struck a match on the casing of the ornate desk-lamp.

Her slender, longer-than-human fingers manipulated flame and a thin black cigar. She blew out smoke. Her scabbard scraped the side of the desk, scarring the veneer.

'You don't intimidate me. You never have.' Her lean-muzzled face was sullen. 'You're an outsider, and you play the fool – the Queen's fool. And you play it well. But you forget one thing. You're human. You'll always be here on sufferance.'

A springy dark curl fell across Benjamin's forehead. He flicked it back. Some glance passed between himself and the female Rat, and he put his hands behind him, clasped at the back of his frock coat, and let the smile surface.

'For now, you take my orders, Madam Varagnac.'

'For now, I do, yes.'

'And so – our young Katayan friend.'

The Rat stubbed out her partly-smoked cigar on the polished desk. She straightened up: something close on five foot ten or eleven, all whipcord muscle: her silver fur shining. 'Do you know, he's making songs in the music-halls? If I hadn't stepped in last night, I swear he'd have put the whole contract into rhyme, and let the scum hear it!'

Impassively unimpressed, Lord Benjamin said, 'And?'

The Home Secretary and the officer of the secret police looked at each other for a while.

'Well,' Varagnac said at last, 'he slipped away. We had to step in before everything was ready. My people are already paying for that one. I give it three or four days before he surfaces again. Then—'

She stopped. Benjamin schooled his features to order. In his luminous and large eyes, devilment shifted.

'Then?' he prompted, demurely.

Varagnac scowled. 'Do you want him dead? It could happen, resisting arrest.'

'There is the difficulty, you see, of needing to control the proof of contractual agreement, while needing *not* to have it made public... I think you had better take him into our private custody. I'll give you my own authorization. But if that seems too difficult, and time is short, then it may be better if he dies.'

Varagnac's lean face altered, in some way not readily decipherable. She bit at one claw nail. 'If you told me the details of this contract, I could tell you if it's worth keeping him alive?'

'No.'

Thoughtful, the middle-aged man turned again to look down from the baroque-facaded building into Whitehall.

'Whatever I may be, madam, I'm trusted. I endeavour to continue to deserve it.'

The theatre manager sorted through a cluttered desk, fidgeting among painted picture-playbills, seat-tokens, account-books, and a laddered silk stocking. Ashar-hakku-ezrian waited.

'Sixth on the bill,' the plump woman offered.

'Not good enough.' He stroked his wispy beard with his thumb. 'You know I'll get seats filled. I should have at least third billing.'

The fair-haired woman sat back and tugged at her bodice, sweating in the afternoon heat. Her lined eyebrows dipped. 'Yes, my chick, and I've heard of you from Tom Ellis down at the Empire. Half the Guard you had turning his place upsidedown. Oh, you'll put bums on seats all right... but if you do it here, you'll do it under a stage name.'

Ashar, sublimely ignoring dignity, hitched up his over-large breeches. The late afternoon sun slanted in through the high garret window and into his eyes, only partly blocked by the rear of the man-high letters spelling out ALHAMBRA MUSIC HALL outside the glass.

He protested, 'Who'll come to see an unknown?'

'Oh, word'll get round, my pigeon, don't you worry. I'll risk *that*, for the few nights that'll make it worth it. After that, you're on your own.'

Ashar-hakku-ezrian grinned. 'I want more than a twentieth of the door-take. I'm *good*.'

'No one's as good as you think you are, dearie.'

'No one except me.'

'I'll start you Thursday matinée. Don't come back here before then. In fact, if I were you, I'd keep out of sight entirely for the next three days.'

At the door, her voice made him pause:

'Ambitious little bastard, aren't you?'

'Of course. What I can't understand—' Ashar-hakku-ezrian looked at the woman over his shoulder. '—is why they won't all leave me alone to get on with it.'

Athanasius Godwin walked along the colonnade, drawing his robes about him in the evening chill. The shadows of pillars fell in regular stripes across the paving. His feet scuffed the worn stone.

The feet of the man walking with him made no noise.

'He's one of you. A Kings' Memory. Damnation, man, what's happened to him?'

Godwin didn't choose to answer immediately. Outside the colonnade, students of the Academy of Memory walked the courtyard. Most young, all with preoccupied faces and intense vision: all memorizing, as Athanasius remembered doing in his youth, the *loci* of the place as a structure for meaning.

One brown-faced girl paused, placing in the palaces of her interior vision the words of a speech given by her older companion. She squinted, eyes shutting, mentally walking the memorized rooms; recalling placed images and their associated words. She repeated exactly what he had dictated.

A low mutter filled the air, other students repeating back complicated sequences of random numbers; long speeches; random snatches of conversation.

Athanasius, through shrewd and rheumy eyes, looked up at the bearded, bald man. 'Master Cragmire, you have all the University at your disposal. If your sturdy beggars can't find him, being on every street-corner, nor your doxies who hear all bed-gossip, nor all your secret assassins – how am I to be expected to find one young man?'

Without detectable change of expression, Cragmire said, 'I lied, he is found. Rather, we know where he is *going* to be. That may be too late. Tell me about him, Master Athanasius.'

'So you can predict his actions? Oh, I think not.'

Irritation grated in his voice. Athanasius Godwin gripped his hands together behind him as he walked, turning his face up to what was visible above the Academy roofs of the orange western sky. Slanting sun showed up the peeling plaster on the walls; the water-stained, cracked pillar-bases. He picked words with a desperate, concealed care.

'Young Ashar ... what can I say to you about him? A phenomenal memory. Very little application ... No application. He became Cecily Emmett's pet. Cecily – but of course, you were there when that happened. Sad.' Godwin sighed over-heavily. 'The young man was on his last warning here. His very last. Another few weeks would have seen him sent back to South Katay in disgrace. Which disgrace, to my mind, would have no effect on Ashar-hakku-ezrian whatsoever. Of all the irresponsible – *this* is characteristic, this going into hiding in the city! You wait, Master Cragmire. A week or so and he'll surface, charm his way out of trouble, smile sweetly, and begin to cause trouble all over again!'

A genuine anger made him breathless. He glared at the Principal of the University of Crime.

'You sound reluctant to have him back.' Cragmire shrugged. 'What will happen to our young Katayan friend when you throw him out of here? Do Kings' Memories resign, Master Athanasius?'

'We have techniques to dim the memory. Drugs.'

Godwin brushed his hand against a pillar. Sun-warmed limestone was rough against the pads of his fingers.

'It is untrue, and cruel, to accuse us of turning failed students into idiots and fools. Young Ashar would lose nothing but a certain ability to concentrate.'

One set of footsteps echoed back softly from the colonnade. Godwin stopped. Silence fell. He did not look at Cragmire. Above, the sky glowed blue; all the motes of the air coloured gold.

'Do you have any idea,' the man's voice said, 'how badly we could hurt the Academy of Memory?'

'Or vice versa?'

Aware that tears leaked from the corners of his eyes, Athanasius Godwin reached out and grabbed the man's doublet, gripping the soft leather with age-spotted fingers.

'Ashar is a stupid child. Remember that.' His ability to hide desperation vanished. 'Cragmire, he's *not* to be hurt. If you want your University of Crime to continue visible with impunity – he is a boy, he is not to be hurt in any way, he is to come back here to me where he's safe: understand that!'

Cragmire reached down and detached his grip. Athanasius Godwin stared at his own hand, flesh cramped and white; and not at the forgettable face of the other man. Breath rushed hot and hollow in his chest.

Principal Cragmire said, 'If you can do anything, do it now. Your "stupid child" is in intense danger. I think we don't even have another day.'

The crowd outside the Fur & Feathers thinned now. A distant church clock struck midnight. Ashar-hakku-ezrian leaned both forearms on the bollard, and his chin on his arms, and flirted his eyebrows at the fair-haired human girl. 'But *when* do you get off work? They can't keep you here all night.'

The human girl bundled her skirts back between her knees, shifting the bucket; scrubbing brush in her other hand. The wet tavern step gleamed, the slate clean now of spilled beer and vomit. 'Can't they, though?'

He squatted, sliding down with his back against the metal pillar, twitching his tail out of the way of the road.

'Leave this. Come with me. I'm going to be famous.' The plush-furred tail slid across the air between them, nestled gently at the nape of her neck, between her caught-up hair and shabby dress.

'Oh, Ash ... I don't know you hardly.' She rubbed the back of her wrist across her forehead. 'You better get gone before the old man comes out. Get along now!'

'I'll see you back there.' Ashar-hakku-ezrian nodded in the direction of the cobbled alley opposite the public house.

'Well, I don't ...'

'Yes you do. You will. You *must*. For me.' He kissed her as he stood, grinned, and loped across the road. The noise of music, and quarrelling voices quieted as he entered the alley.

A slight thud sounded.

Curious, he turned. Several other alleyways split off from the main one, none lit, all now quiet. One of his eyebrows flicked up in momentary puzzlement.

He shoved both hands in his stolen breeches pockets and walked on, tail switching from side to side; debating whether the fair-haired girl was a sure enough bet to wait for, or if the Pig & Whistle would repay a visit.

Six yards up a side alley, an unconscious brown Rat's heels jolted over the pavement as Nathaniel Marston dragged him into concealment.

'Her Majesty is receiving the Katayan Ambassador,' the brown Rat major-domo said. 'If my Lord Benjamin would care to wait.'

Benjamin inclined his head to her. 'I shall always have time at her Majesty's disposal, I hope.'

He walked across the corridor to the arched window, tapping his folded gloves against his trouser leg, whistling softly under his breath. Light slanted down from above. Red, blue, gold, white: rich colours falling through a black tracery of stone.

The brown Rat appeared again, opening the antechamber's high door as a portly black Rat in lace and leather arrived.

Benjamin moved smoothly forward, stepping through on the heels of the visitor with a nod to the doorkeeper, calling ahead:

'Messire Sebastien!'

The pudgy Rat turned, unlacing his cloak and dropping it for the anteroom servants to pick up. 'Benjamin. I – you – that is, my duty to her Majesty—'

Benjamin met the gaze of bead-black eyes and smiled only slightly. 'How interesting to find you here, Messire Sebastien. Perhaps we arrive on the same business, hum?'

'I don't think so. I'm sure not.'

'How prescient of you, messire. I don't believe that I mentioned what my own business might be...'

The black Rat's eyes gleamed, set deep in his fat and furry cheeks. He folded his arms across his broad, velvet-doubleted chest; scaled tail sweeping the stone-flagged floor. 'Now you take good notice of one thing, *boy*. When all this scheming comes out, and has to be denied by certain highly-placed people, no one of *us* is going to stand the damage of it. For that, they'll pick a human. I'll let you speculate about which human it might be.'

'"Speculation" is not a word you should be using at the moment,' Benjamin said.

Squat white columns held up the anteroom's vaulted ceiling. Two men in Court livery scuttled away with coats and cloaks. Benjamin glimpsed through the square window the finials and carved facade of the palace courtyard.

Sebastien tugged his doublet down, pulling the lace at the wrists forward over his ringless fingers. 'I'll use what words I please, boy, and you'll have to show me a much better return on my investment before I stop. Damme, I don't believe you ever intended to go through with this mad scheme, it's all just to line your own pockets!'

'I think you should carefully consider what you're saying.'

'We've suffered you too long, in any case; and it's the last straw to be *cheated* by—'

Benjamin raised his hand and struck the Rat a stinging blow across the face.

'I will not be insulted by some down-at-heel has-been with a grudge and the brains of a mayfly! Will you complain? Do so. Do so! And the next time I see you I'll carry a horsewhip, and give you the thrashing you deserve, public scandal or not!'

The black Rat waddled back a step, long jaw dropping; made as if to speak; abruptly turned and flung out of the exit, pushing the doorkeeper aside with a furious oath.

Lord Benjamin stared, fabricated anger subsiding; sucked his skinned knuckles, and broke into a coarse laugh.

'Do you think the Prime Minister is going to fight with you in the streets like a barrow-boy? Such *stupidity.* Ah, but it has its uses. It does. I can well do without your company here today.'

The further anteroom doors stood shut, great black iron hinges spiking across the oak-wood. They slid at his slight touch, gliding open, and he walked through. He stood a moment while his eyes accustomed themselves to the gloom.

The great arched throne room opened up before him. Traceries of white webs snarled the walls, spindles of spider-thread curtaining off other doors and the lower, blacked-out windows. Webs dripped from the arched ceiling. One torch burned low in a wall-cresset, soot staining the already black masonry.

Kneeling priests flanked the walls, each at a low mausoleum-altar. Benjamin crossed himself thoughtfully, walking past them towards the high end of the hall. The Ambassador was gone. Perpendicular windows slotted down a little light. Upon the dais at the end, where all windows had been bricked up, a great mass of stonework stood. Close up, this could be seen to be an immense baroquely-carved and decorated tomb, Latin inscriptions incised in silver below the legend SAXE-COBERG-GOTHA.

'Your Majesty!' Lord Benjamin beamed effusively. 'To see you in such health is a privilege – to see your beauty, a delight given to few men in any age of the world.'

Below the tomb, on the granite platform, a profusion of black silk cushions lay scattered. Small stools had been set amongst them. Nine slender black Rats lay asleep, or sat sewing, or with folded hands and melancholy eyes gazed up at the tomb. They wore black silk robes.

On a larger cushion in the centre, attended by a brown Rat page, the nine Rats' tails rested, coiled into an inextricable and fifty-years grown-together knot.

Some of the Rat-Queen looked at Lord Benjamin.

A slender Rat who sat sewing at a sampler left off, extending one long-fingered dark hand. Benjamin bowed over it, kissing the narrow silver rings.

'We welcome your presence, Lord Benjamin. We were thinking of our departed Consort, and I fear falling into a sad melancholy.'

'Your Majesty might marry again. Such beauty will never lack admirers.'

'We could not be unfaithful to the memory of our dear husbands, Lord Benjamin. No, we—' She bit off a thread between front incisors. A more bony and angular Rat seated at her feet raised her lean-jawed muzzle:

'—could not think of it. What news have you for us, dear Lord Benjamin?'

Benjamin pondered *Only that the world misses you who are its sunlight* and decided to leave that one for another occasion. A third Rat-Queen shifted around so that she sat facing him, this one with something of a sardonic gleam in her eyes. He bowed again, floridly.

'I should ask news of you, dear lady, you having most recently spoken to the Katayan Ambassador, or so I hear.'

The third Rat-Queen frowned. 'They came to protest the siting of another garrison on their north coast, even though we are only there to protect them. Really, it is—'

She reached out to the tray of tea being offered by the brown Rat page. The Rat-Queen who had resumed her sewing completed:

'—most provoking. Do not make that the subject of your visit, I pray you. Dear Lord Benjamin, we have been giving serious consideration to your suggestion for our Accession Day Festival.'

'And your Majesty desires?'

'We think that we will indeed have a theatrical performance in the palace—'

'—by our command, this performance—'

'—because it will please the dear children,' another, more bony and angular Rat-Queen, cut in. 'And therefore we should have theatricals, songs, tricks, jugglers; all drawn from our great capital's theatres and places of entertainment. What—'

'—do you say to that, Lord Benjamin?'

'Admirable. Stunning! Quite the best notion I have ever heard.' His large and liquid eyes shone.

'So you should say, when it was your own.' The sardonic Rat-Queen smiled. 'We see through you, dear Lord Benjamin. But we know—'

'—that you have our best interests at heart.'

A tiny echo came back from each word, the Queen's high voices reverberating from the Gothick stonework. Further down the hall a torch guttered, and the scent of incense came from where the priests constantly prayed.

'A celebration would be much in order,' Benjamin said.

'We have drawn out a list—'

'—of those performers we hear are suitable. Our noble friend the Ambassador of South Katay recommended one young person, who sounds most amusing.'

He reached out to take a paper from one of the Rats laying amid the silk cushions, bowing as he did so; casting a rapid eye down the list until the name *Ashar-hakku-ezrian* leaped out at him.

'Yes, your Majesty.'

He rubbed an ungloved hand across his forehead, slick with a cool sweat, and smiled.

'And something else most intriguing came from our meeting with the Ambassador.' The Rat-Queen lowered her sleek muzzle over her sewing. 'We hear—'

'—interesting things of this most new discovery of the lands about the East Pole. We wonder—'

This black Rat fell to grooming the fur of her arm. The bony black Rat beside her opened onyx eyes:

'—whether we might receive ambassadors from them, as we do from South Katay. A peaceable treaty might lead to much trade, Lord Benjamin—'

'—do you not think so?' the first Rat concluded.

'Indubitably, madam. I'll be only too pleased to discover, for you, how this may be brought about.' Lord Benjamin, flourishing his yellow gloves, bowed himself out of the throne room.

A horse-drawn carriage took him back to Whitehall. He sat with his chin on his breast, slumped down in the seat, no expression at all on his face. Not until he stood again in the office overlooking Whitehall did he break silence.

He picked the telephone-mouthpiece off its stand, dialling a confidential and automatically-connected number.

A click, the phone picked up and answered. 'Varagnac.'

He nodded once to himself, silently, said 'Kill the contract. Immediately.' And put the telephone back on its rest.

'I tell you, Benjamin will sell us out!'

The fat black Rat slammed his fist down on the makeshift crate accounts desk, his voice cutting through the noise of work in the warehouse.

'Every penny I have is tied up in this, and as for every penny I *don't* have – I'll be ruined.'

Jocelyn de Flores sank her chin lower in her greatcoat collar. Slumped in the chair, so low as to be almost horizontal, she moved only her eyes to look up at Sebastien. 'So?'

'So we ought to destroy all trace of our ever having been involved in this scheme. Especially the contract. Gods, woman, even a sniff of the *candy* trade and we'll end up in Newgate!' The Rat moved from clawed hind foot to foot, rolls of fur-covered flesh shifting. He pulled out a darned lace kerchief to dab at his mouth.

'I trust our friend Benjamin as you do.' Jocelyn remained still. 'That's to say, not at all. Master Sebastien, do try not to be stupid – please, listen. I think we ought to have that contract safe. Very safe. Remember, it isn't only we two that it implicates.'

The black Rat began shakily to smile. 'Benjamin.'

Jocelyn de Flores came to her feet in one movement, coat swirling, striding out towards the quay and the chilly evening.

Ashar-hakku-ezrian passed the clock shop's window, paused, stepped back, and stared into the dark glass. After a moment's thought he brushed his blond hair further back behind his ears, preened his beard, and tried a left and then a right profile, gleaming his eyes at himself in the reflection with a grin.

'You could lose a little weight but you'll do.'

The glass reflected plane trees behind him, planted in a triangle of earth at the junction of two streets, their leaves rustling in a spring gust. He turned away, towards the main road further down, seeing noon and horse-drawn carriages and the corner of the Alhambra, and a man shifted out of the next doorway.

The man gnawed absently at a knuckle, among gold-ringed fingers. His greasy dark-red hair and beard straggled down over the collar of his royal-blue coat.

Ashar smiled very pleasantly, side-stepping. 'Can I help you?'

'A word with you, master. I've got a message from your sister.'

Coldness stabbed him just in the pit of the belly. Ashar shrugged. 'Which one? My father has ten wives, that gives me a number of sisters to choose from—'

'Not half-sisters, Master Ashar. Full sister. Ishnanna-hakku-ezrian.'

'How do you know about her?' Ashar stopped. The spring wind

blew through the thin weave of his stolen shirt. He clutched his arms across his chest. 'Who are you? Have you seen her? Where is she? Is she all right? What does she say?'

'Don't listen to him,' a woman's voice cut in. 'All Katayans look the same to him anyway. He hasn't got any message. Have you, Nathan?'

Ashar looked away from the red-haired man. A woman walked up the cobbled road from the direction of the Alhambra, her black coat open, its hem swinging about her calves. She stopped, hooking one thumb in her waistcoat pocket, and inclined her sleek head momentarily to him.

'Nathan?' she needled the man.

'I find your presence, madam, entirely superfluous.'

'On the other hand.' Grey eyes shifted, caught Ashar's gaze, and he blinked at that impact. 'The University of Crime has a way of finding out most information, even that the elusive Ashar-hakku-ezrian had a sister.'

Ashar made a jerky bow. 'Madam de Flores.'

'You remember me. For a moment I was worried about your memory – not that it isn't much on my mind in any case.' She smiled mordantly.

Her remark barely irritated him. He stared at the man. A lean, pale face; not to be read easily. Words cascaded through his mind, all of them drying up before they reached his mouth. He shook his head, shivering.

The thin sun showed up grey where it shone on de Flores' hair. She thrust her hands into her greatcoat pockets. 'How old are you, young man?'

Ashar swallowed. 'Sixteen. Ishnanna's – she was twelve.'

'You're old enough to make judgements. I want you. I want what you have in your head, and I want it safe.' Jocelyn de Flores shrugged. 'I can't say the same about Marston here. He's been hanging around my warehouse for the past fortnight. One of Cragmire's men – that ought to give you some idea. Come with me now.'

The man Marston shook his head. 'He goes with me.'

'*Do* you know anything about Ishnanna?' Ashar shuddered. 'I don't think so. I really don't want anything to do with this contract. It's boring. I don't know what you're all making a fuss about.'

Uncharacteristically abrupt, he shouldered between the two of them and walked on down the street, feet knocking clumsily against the cobbles and making him stagger. The wind smelled of dust and horse-droppings. He sensed rather than heard them stride after him.

He wanted – momentarily wanted so hard that he could not breathe – the dusty rehearsal rooms of the Alhambra: the piano with one key missing, the dancers' discarded stockings, sunlight through the brick-arched windows; sweat, effort, repetition.

The two called his name behind him. He broke into a run, swinging towards the corner stage-door; dodging between two passers-by, jigging a yard left to avoid the matinée coaches pulling up at the kerb.

Movement and mass in the corner of his eye made him stumble, shy away.

Neatly, hands went under his armpits from behind.

'*Hey—!*'

Two thick-set brown Rats in blue livery bundled him towards the nearest carriage's open door, his heels skidding across the cobbles, head ringing from a shocking blow. Steps, seat, and floor scraped his hands as he thudded across the carriage's interior. Cloth muffled his head. A horsewhip cracked. The carriage jolted into immediate motion.

A red-headed man and a woman in a black coat walked moderately rapidly in the opposite direction to the carriage, heads bent concealingly against the cold spring wind.

The theatre manager stared down from her office window at the carriage pulling away and resignedly tore up the sticker to be stripped across the night's billboard:

SPECIAL ATTRACTION!!! WORLD-FAMOUS KATAYAN MONOLOGUIST – ONE NIGHT ONLY!!!

A Rat's voice said, 'You're dead.'

The copper taste of blood soured his mouth. Ashar rolled over, the shackles that hobbled his feet to an eighteen-inch stride clinking. Metal cut his bare ankles.

'Should I feel unwell, do you think?' he said lazily, pressing up against her haunch. 'Being dead, I mean.'

Varagnac, leaning against the bed's headboard, reached out with one sinewy arm and slid it under his, gripping his body, pulling him up closer. Ashar kneaded his hand in the sleek fur of her shoulder, feeling her muscles bunch and shift.

She said, 'Dead as far as anyone else is concerned. You're mine now.'

Ashar-hakku-ezrian smiled. It cracked his split lip open again, and a thin thread of blood seeped down his chin. He wriggled his hips deeper into the rumpled bed sheets. Outside the inn window, a vixen shrieked.

'Well, boy?'

Candlelight gleamed golden on the timbers and beams of the room, on the bare floor and the bed. Shadows danced in cobwebs in the corners of the blackened ceiling. A cold draft shivered his bare spine. He pressed closer in to her warm pelt.

'Damn you, say something!'

'Rubbish. And you know it.'

Livery coat, sword-belt, and feather plume lay strewn across the floor, discarded. Ashar-hakku-ezrian eased the silver-furred Rat a little over on to her side and began to manipulate and knead the tense muscles of her back. She grunted deep in her throat.

'You know something about my sister.' He read the giveaway message of stress through his fingertips. 'You do! I always thought so. From the very first time I came asking!'

Her arm pushed him flat. Long grey-skinned fingers traced a line down his chest, claws leaving the thinnest trail of reddened skin. It patterned across other scored lines, raised and swollen. Her bead-black eyes shone, reflecting candlelight.

'You won't keep me,' he said softly. 'Even now you're thinking: *it was a moment's mistake, how can I get back to the city without being spotted, how can I put it right?*'

He smiled. It had no malice in it. His fingers plunged into the softness of her fur: throat, chest, belly. He curled up and lay his head across her chest.

'Which is not impossible. If it finishes all this, and it means I can get on with doing what *I* want to do, then yes! I'll tell you what to do to get out of it.' His breath pearled on her fur. He sensed her lean forward: sharp incisors just dinted his bare, scarred shoulder.

Ashar knotted fists in soft fur. 'What just happened was fun; but why did you think you had to go to all *this* trouble?'

Varagnac sat back and laughed.

Her chest vibrated. Ashar straightened up into a sitting position, shackles chinking. The Rat, head thrown back, wheezed for breath between paroxysms of laughter; at last reaching out and putting her hands on his two shoulders and shaking him, a half-dozen times, hard.

'Damn you! Well, and what do *you* suggest, if you know so much?'

'Ishnanna-hakku-ezrian.'

'Yes, I know what happened to her.'

Toneless, no hint in the voice; no clue in the language of her lean body. Ashar sat back on his heels, his tail coiling about hers.

'Tell me that and I'll tell you ... what the contract was.' He grinned. 'You were there. Well, almost there. Present, shall we say; even if you didn't know what went on—'

Her claw-nailed finger touched his lips, silencing him momentarily.

'Fast talker.'

The long-fingered hand straightened, patting his cheek hard enough to redden the skin. Her lean, long body shone in the yellow light; shadows lining jaw, eye, and translucent ears.

'At least I had you.' Varagnac chuckled in her throat. 'For a short enough time. It may be just as well. You bid fair to be unbearable.'

Ashar grinned. 'And then I'll tell you how we go back to town.'

The wind guttered the candle. Below, horses stamped in the stables. The silver-furred Rat grunted, rolled over, and retrieved her livery jacket from the floor, diving into the pocket for a thin black cigar. She tilted the candle to light it.

'So.'

'So ... it was hot.' Ashar rubbed his bare arms. 'You may not remember. I, obviously, do. Two weeks ago, at the official opening of the Royal Botanical gardens ...'

... The ribbon being cut, now, the assembled dignitaries wandered between tall lines of palms and ferns in the main body of the Palm House, few climbing the spiral iron staircases to the higher balconies.

Ashar stared at the thermometer in a pained manner. Spring sunlight through several thousand panes of glass added to the underfloor heating. The thin silver line topped out at 95 degrees Fahrenheit. Humidity quickened his breathing, put black sparkles across his vision.

'Ashar!'

He flicked his tail down to push aside a palm-frond. Wetness sprinkled his shoulders. Five or six people walked on this high-railed balcony. The elderly Kings' Memory Cecily Emmett, at the rear of the group, beckoned furiously. 'Come here!'

He smiled as he approached her. 'I'm listening. You don't really need me for this, you know. I could just slip away and not be bored—'

Cecily Emmett stepped back and grabbed his arm. Her weight startled Ashar momentarily. He braced himself as the large woman's support.

'I'll be bored, then.'

'You'll pay attention!'

A short, slender man in a black frock coat stood with one hand on the balcony rail, the other gesturing. Curling black hair fell across his sallow forehead. His cravat was wide, striped candy-pink and white; and his top hat sat rakishly cocked to one side. Ashar, fascinated, caught the man's eye across the intervening yards.

'Two Kings' Memories?' the human queried.

'Ashar-hakku-ezrian, your lordship. My apprentice.'

The man signalled acceptance with a hand in which he held sweat-stained white gloves. 'I understand. Very well.'

A slight wheeze hissed in Cecily's undertone. 'That ... is Lord Benjamin himself. Sebastien you know. De Flores you know.'

Lord Benjamin's light, penetrating voice cut through the humid air. 'Forgive me if I take advantage of this official opening for us to meet. It seems secure, and opportune.'

Ashar saw, over Lord Benjamin's shoulder, the hard jaw-line of a familiar face. Jocelyn de Flores. The fat black Rat Sebastien stood beside de Flores, talking across the trader to one well-dressed black Rat, and two brown Rats.

Ashar leaned his elbows on the balcony.

Below, out of earshot, stood a silver-furred Rat in plain leather harness and the indefinable air of covert authority that argued security police.

The Rat lifted her head. Varagnac.

Varagnac and he stared at each other.

Cecily's voice hissed in his ear. 'Listen to me, boy. You're on parole already. I want this meeting repeated back word-perfect from you; as perfect as my official record, *is that clear*?'

He beamed. Varagnac turned away.

'Of course,' he said.

A brass band played on the lawns outside the Palm House.

Music came muffled through the arching glass walls. Here, the fronds of giant ferns swept down to shield the balcony from sight of the main part of the hall. Isolated by height and occasion, the group halted.

'Master Cragmire.' Cecily introduced a tall, bearded man; balding, dressed in a plain frock coat; whose image would not stay in the memory for more than seconds. 'From the University of Crime. And not an ornament to any of these discussions, Ashar, at least as far as we're concerned.'

The dark-bearded man laughed. 'I'm not prolix. A little verbose, perhaps. Veritably, that's the worst criminal infringement you can accuse me of, Cecily.'

'Will you *listen* to him.' Amused, the fat woman shook her head.

Ashar stared between his booted feet, through the open iron-work floor of the balcony, looking directly down on water and the wide leaves of water-lilies. He lifted his head. White-painted iron chairs and tables stood on this wider part of the balcony, and the sallow-skinned Lord Benjamin already sat at one table, pouring out tea from a silver service.

'Gentlemen. Ladies.'

The trader, de Flores, fell into the chair beside Lord Benjamin, pulling at her high collar to loosen it. Sweat pearled on her face, and her grey-streaked hair plastered to her forehead.

'*Damn* stupid place for a meeting, my lord.'

'It has its advantages. Messire Sebastien?' The Home Secretary passed a fragile china cup up to the fat black Rat. Messire Sebastien shook lace ruffles back, and took the cup in fat, ringless fingers.

Cragmire drew out a chair for Cecily Emmett to sit; then seated himself beside her. The three Rat lords took chairs. Ashar hitched himself up to sit on the balcony rail.

Lord Benjamin lifted an eyebrow, then sipped cautiously at the hot tea. 'Well, now ...'

Prompted, Cecily Emmett looked up from arranging her long skirts and surreptitiously loosening her bodice. She blinked against the refracted sunlight. 'I speak now, officially, as the Academy of Memory directs. *You are heard.* What is said now, will be remembered. What is recalled by Kings' Memories is valid in law, in custom, and in the eyes of the gods. You are so warned.'

'I believe that is what we are met for. If someone would like to outline the proposition ...?' Benjamin set his cup down on the white-painted iron table, and leaned back with his arms resting along the spiral chair-arms. His large eyes moved from the Kings' Memory to the rest of the group.

Ashar hooked one ankle about the balcony strut he sat on and, balanced, leaned back into open space. Sword-bladed palms shone dully green around him, trunks rooting a dozen yards below.

Jocelyn de Flores said, 'For my part, it's simple. I want to open up trade with the newly-discovered East Pole. Since one of my skippers came back from there a month since, I've realized it isn't as simple as sending a clipper-ship and a cargo.'

'Your ship?' Cragmire queried.

'The *Pangolin.* The master is a man I trust.'

A Rat in a red jacket with gold epaulettes bowed, frigidly, to Jocelyn de Flores. 'You have described this new territory to us. Savages, ruled by theocrats.'

Inattention; a sudden quarter-inch shift of balance – his every muscle from ankle to thigh locked. Heart hammering, Ashar leaned forward and slid back down on to the balcony floor. His tail coiled about one strut. Across the group, he locked eyes with Cecily Emmett as the elderly woman wiped her sweating face with a handkerchief. Paleness blotched her skin.

'And the Queen?' another Rat asked. 'Lord Benjamin, it is common knowledge that you – make yourself agreeable – to her Majesty ...'

The sallow-skinned man smiled. He waved one hand expansively. 'Messire, I flatter the Queen, and I lay it on with a trowel. The Queen is not fool enough to believe me.'

'So why do it?' Ashar asked. Cecily Emmett glared at his daring to open his mouth.

'The Queen's pride is to see through me. I am quite transparent about it, you see. A rogue may get away with much, when making no pretence to be anything else but a rogue.' Lord Benjamin turned to the brown Rat. 'Have no fear of her Majesty. The Queen is always interested in new territory.'

'The lands that lie about the East Pole are *rich.*' A raw edge scraped in Sebastien's voice. The sun through the glass shone on his plump-jawed muzzle, glinting from his bead-black eyes. The light showed scuff-marks on his sword-belt and scabbard inexpertly concealed with polish.

'Rich,' Sebastien repeated. He tugged at the faded lace at his throat. 'Benjamin, you know all this: we can import enough in herbs, spices, and exotics from the East Pole to make all our fortunes ten times over. We'll never do it. Not while their Church of the White Rose is in power. The Heptarch wants nothing to do with foreign lands: *he* says, they need nothing from us, and will give us nothing.'

'And bribery?' Lord Benjamin looked to Jocelyn de Flores.

'Tried and failed, my lord. Their peasants have done nothing for centuries but toil and worship; and the Church nothing but *be* worshipped. Money doesn't mean anything to either.'

Here she shifted down in her chair, the collar of her shirt rucked up around her neck with the movement.

'Let me hear your suggestion again,' Benjamin asked mildly. 'For the record.'

'The question is, what do we have that they don't? And the answer's simple, if not obvious. We have this.'

Jocelyn de Flores took her hand out of her breeches pocket and stood a small phial upright on the table. Her black eyes gleamed, looking around the circle.

'I see you gentlemen don't frequent the docklands. This is called *kgandara.* More commonly, *candy.* I always have trouble with my deckhands using it. It comes from Candover,' the women said thoughtfully, 'and it is an extremely addictive drug.'

Lord Benjamin stretched out an ungloved hand and took it back without touching the phial of yellow powder.

'What does it do?' one of the nameless Rat lords asked.

'To your people, my lord? I don't know. It gives us dreams.' Again, that smile. Ashar blinked. Jocelyn said, 'Dreams are always better. I don't use *candy* myself. I have known men kill for half a gram of it. Once introduced into the new territories, we have a market that will *always* exist. After that, I think trade might move very briskly, and we might set our own prices for what we pleased to sell and buy.'

Cragmire sat forward, his heavy hands dangling between his knees. 'Part of the price being that the White Rose, also, sell *candy* as middlemen.'

'Oh, yes.'

The bearded man sat back. One of the anonymous Rat lords asked, 'Are you serious?'

Lord Benjamin shrugged. 'It is no worse, I dare say, than introducing muskets into Candover; which as I recall my predecessor undertook to do. With some success. Cragmire, you can supply what is necessary?'

'Indubitably, my lord. The University has connections with the *candy* trade.'

Ashar reached across Cecily Emmett's fat shoulder and helped himself to a cup of tea, now pleasantly cold. Sweat trickled down between his shoulder-blades, and he scratched at it with the tip of his tail. The several unnamed but unmistakably influential Rat lords bent their heads together in conversation. De Flores whispered to Sebastien.

Ashar squatted briefly beside the elder Kings' Memory. 'What a bitch of an idea.'

Cecily Emmett coughed. 'It's your business to remember. Not judge.'

'Not even admire?'

'More trade means more employment, of course.' Lord Benjamin nodded approvingly to de Flores. 'Now, as to my own part—'

Cecily Emmett's elbow slammed across Ashar's hands.

The china cup flew, splintered on the iron balcony floor. He put a foot back, tail hooked out on the air for balance; and caught her arm as she slumped across him. Her chair tilted and fell. The fat woman's body fell, pressing him against sharp angles of chair, table and balcony as the group sprang to their feet.

'Madam Cecily!' Ashar got his shoulder under her back.

The weight lifted suddenly as Jocelyn de Flores and Cragmire cradled the Kings' Memory and eased her down against them.

'Fetch a doctor!' De Flores thumbed up Cecily Emmett's half-closed eyelids, and rested a hand against her throat. 'Quickly. My lord, if you call—'

Cragmire said tersely, 'A stroke.'

Lord Benjamin stepped back from the balcony. Beneath, the clatter of running footsteps already sounded; Varagnac's voice yelling orders. He held up one hand.

'Messires, my people will see the woman to hospital, and notify the Academy of Memory.' His wide-nailed hand shifted to point at Ashar. 'This meeting should not be interrupted, being so hard to bring about. Messire Ashar-hakku-ezrian, you will act as sole Kings' Memory now. I'm sorry you have to end your apprenticeship in this abrupt manner.'

'I – yes.' He stepped back, not remembering standing up; watching in horrified interest as men and women from Lord

Benjamin's staff stripped off frock coats and, in their shirtsleeves, began to lift and manoeuvre the woman down the spiral iron staircase to the exit.

'Kings' Memory!'

Ashar-hakku-ezrian turned, hands thrust deep in his breeches pockets. 'I'm listening.'

'My last words?'

He met Lord Benjamin's gaze. '"More trade means more employment, of course. Now, as to my own part—"'

'Excellent.' The flamboyantly-dressed man took a last look over the balcony, and reseated himself beside Jocelyn de Flores. 'You need have no fear of her Majesty's disapproval. Let them wink and say they saw nothing. When "Empress of the East Pole" is added to the Queen's other titles, I think you'll find yourself rewarded well enough.'

He steepled his fingers. 'My notion is to float a somewhat larger company than you at present can, Madam de Flores; invite investment, and then further investment when the market proves itself open. The initial capital will come from these gentlemen here—'

He nodded at the Rat lords. One sniffed, adjusting an epaulette.

'—and the returns will be, I imagine, quite magnificent. It wouldn't do for her Majesty's approval of the *first* part of this scheme to become widely known; therefore, I think, we make secrecy one of our prime concerns.'

'It'll take cash to finance the introduction of *candy*.' Jocelyn de Flores glanced at Cragmire. 'I won't enquire into the University's methods, but you'll want funds.'

'Among other things.'

'Government resources.' De Flores looked back at Lord Benjamin, who spread his hands.

'As you say, dear lady, government resources. Which you will have. The House will approve it as part of the confidential budget, my colleagues here assure me.'

Jocelyn de Flores looked at the shabby black Rat, and Sebastien inclined his plump head. 'Well then. The University of Crime will undertake to supply *kgandara*, for a substantial share in the East Pole Trading Company. We'll handle transportation and trade. Lord Benjamin will—'

'—as I have said, expedite matters,' the flamboyant, sallow-skinned man cut in. 'Kings' Memory, do you hear?'

Outside, the brass band shifted into a martial tune played in three-quarter time. Under a blue sky, the sun blazed down on crimson and blue flowers in ranked beds. Ashar-hakku-ezrian slitted his eyes. Light shattered in through glass and ironwork. A fragile fern brushed damp against the skin of his sweat-damp upper arm. 'I hear.'

'I set my word to this as a binding contract: Benjamin.'

The black-haired woman licked the corners of her mouth. 'I also set my word to this as a binding contract: Jocelyn de Flores.'

'And I, Sebastien.'

'My word is given for the University: Cragmire. This binds me.'

Ashar cocked his head, gazing at the Rat lords.

'Seznec: this binds me.'

'Ammarion: this binds me.'

'De L'Isle: this binds me.'

The Lord Benjamin nodded once, sharply. 'So. It is remembered.'

'... and that's all.' The Katayan leaned his elbows back on the thwarts.

Varagnac shipped oars and held up long fingers for silence. The stolen wherry grated on shingle. She stared up at the underside of the river bridge. The estuary tide being out, they beached some thirty feet from the bank.

'You did it. We're home.' She heard the admiration a little too ungrudged in her own voice, and chuckled throatily. 'I don't have to ask if you remember what I told you – the procedure in case we become separated?'

Ashar leaned over the edge of the boat.

'I'm going to get my feet wet. You couldn't get this thing further inland?'

'No!' Varagnac swore. She vaulted over the side, landing lightly on mud-slick shingle. 'Move.'

The wind, bitter cold from the river, blew in her face. Her ears twitched. She loped across the shingle to the shelter of a pillar, tail out for balance. Her sword-belt bounced against her haunch.

'Now.'

Only pale hands and face visible, the black-clothed young man slid out of the boat and ran towards the bank. A soft noise triggered her reflexes in the same second as Ashar-hakku-ezrian swore and sat down heavily in the mud.

'*Damnation*—!' A scream sounded over his whisper.

Varagnac sucked her fingers, where the tip of her throwing-knife had caught on leaving her hand, and widened her eyes. Night sight showed her a slumped body at the foot of the embankment. She caught the Katayan's wrist and threw him into the shelter of the pillar behind her.

A voice rang out above. '*Ashar-hakku-ezrian!*'

'Nearly home,' Varagnac amended.

The male voice came again. 'Ashar! I want to talk. We *must* talk.'

The young man shrugged easily. 'I can talk to him. Why not?'

Varagnac drew her oiled blade soundlessly from its sheath. She pressed up against the wet masonry, every knob of her spine grating on the stone, back protected. A glance showed her Ashar-hakku-ezrian on the river side of the pillar, watching the other direction.

From the bridge above, the male voice sounded. 'You know she'll kill you, don't you? She has her orders.'

Tidal water lapped the shingle. The stolen wherry lifted, rocked, settled. Moonlight strengthened as clouds dissolved. She met Ashar's gaze.

'Ask her!' The voice rang out above, some yards differently positioned. 'Benjamin ordered it. Yesterday. At five-and-twenty to six.'

A blink: Ashar's lashes covered dark, glowing eyes. 'That's a man called Nathaniel Marston. De Flores calls him that, anyway.'

Varagnac's mouth quirked. 'So the University of Crime are tapping departmental telephone lines.'

Varagnac reached out a hand to the Katayan, steered him running, miraculously sure-footed in the river slime, to the shelter of the next bank-ward pillar.

Another voice came from further down the bridge. 'Ashar! You know we don't mean you any harm. We want the contract preserved. We've got every reason to keep you safe.'

'Cragmire,' the Katayan muttered. 'I told you he was at that meeting.'

Moonlight shattered on the river. A bitter wind ruffled her fur.

'If I go with them, will they let you alone?'

It was said with a serious, pragmatic curiosity. Varagnac didn't smile. She said, 'All the University wants ... They want you – no, they want the contract – so they can extend their *candy* trade. That's all. You don't want that.'

'What the hell do I care about whoever these East Pole people are!'

'Your conscience does you credit,' she remarked acerbically.

'They're a long way away, and my friends are here and now. Mistress Varagnac, I'm going with Cragmire. If you wait until we're gone—'

'You'll do as I damn well tell you.' Varagnac stepped out from under the bridge support, left hand going up to her shoulder-sheath and forward in one movement. A high shriek echoed across the city, ripping at the bitter cold air, ringing from warehouse walls.

She caught Ashar's hand and ran five yards, pulling him towards the steps rising up through one arch to the road.

'Because ...' At road-level she pushed him down beside her where she knelt, in a wall's shelter, peering out. Every sense alert for sound or movement, she murmured, 'Because I can tell you about Ishnanna.'

'Tell me!'

'You must go *now*. When I say.'

'Varagnac ...'

Varagnac ruffled his brown-blond hair. It stuck to the drying blood on her hand. She winced, laughing. 'You know how to get there?'

'Yes.'

'Go in the way I told you and you'll miss the security systems. Once you're in, ask for that name: "William."'

He reached up one hand from where he crouched at her side, running his fingers down the long line of her jaw. She pushed him: he stumbled into a run, fleeing towards the warehouses, bare feet soundless on the cobbles.

She stood up from the stairs' concealment. The full moon flattened itself against a blue and silver sky, drowning stars, chilling the air, spidering the pavement with shadows. The lean Rat turned, silver fur shiningly visible. She hitched up her sword-belt and wiped mud from her doublet. There was no sound.

Varagnac bent down, scraped a match along the pavement, lit a cigar that made a minute red ember in the night, and let them come to her.

'A command *performance*?' Jocelyn de Flores sat up at her warehouse desk, incredulous.

Sebastien nodded, halfway between satisfaction and hysteria. 'Ashar-hakku-ezrian performing monologues in front of her

Majesty themselves. Madam, you think I'm a fool. Well, even this fool can guess what we'll hear from that stage!'

He had the satisfaction of seeing her quiet for a second.

'This is certain? He's alive?'

'The young man was found this morning by Lord William, in the grounds of the palace. He's keeping him as her Majesty's guest until tonight. The only place in the dominion where none of us can reach him!' Sebastien slumped down on the desk, tail shoving account books on to the warehouse floor. He pulled his headband off and scratched at his sweaty fur, looked at the broken plume, and threw it down vehemently. 'I'm ruined. I'll get nothing back from that bastard Benjamin. When this blows, we all go bankrupt, if not to prison!'

'You must shift for yourself,' the woman said coolly.

'*We're* ruined!' He hardly noticed the woman leaving until she was a dozen yards away. He looked up, opened his mouth to call, and, too dispirited, made no sound.

Outside the river lapped at the dock. He wondered to what distant port the *Pangolin* might be sailing next.

Staring across the crowded palace anteroom, Jocelyn spotted very few human faces among the assembled Rat lords. She pushed her way through towards a young man in a half-unlaced black leather doublet, leaning casually with one arm across a sofa-back, the other hand moving in rapid gestures. Several Rats leaned up against the back of the sofa – a sharp brown Rat in linen and leather, fidgeting with the point of her dagger; a slender black Rat in mauve satin; two of her sisters in black sword-harness – debating across his head, fiercely, on subjects of his devising.

'What do you think?' He and a buxom black Rat had their heads together over sheets of paper that, Jocelyn saw, bore line-sketches.

'Well, I don't know, Master Kit; I think it comes perilously close to the forbidden art of writing.'

'Oh, no. No. Not at all. It's graphic art. Wordless graphic art – silent comics.' He riffled through the pages. 'I don't know about this, though ... I had the artist do my signature-portrait three-quarter profile, but it makes my nose look big. Do I really look like that?'

Leaning over the drawing, comparing it with the original, the buxom Rat traced a jaw-line and nose with a slender claw; then raised her hand to touch the young man's face, presented for her inspection with a certain complacent vanity.

'Kit!'

He excused himself politely and turned, with a ready sweet smile. 'Yes, sweetheart?'

Jocelyn de Flores folded her arms, hands in the sleeves of her overcoat. 'Who's got the ear of the Queen right now? Who are they listening to?'

The young man reached up and took off darkened spectacles, blinking thoughtfully. His smile flashed. 'Well, let's see. Yes. There's the very person. Imogen!'

A striking and statuesque woman in black leather stood in the centre of another group, one finger raised, halfway through the conclusion of a reported conversation:

'... completely evocative: but I said to him, a battle of wits, yes; but why should I fight an unarmed man?' She halted, turning to the young man and speaking in a slightly breathless, husky voice: 'Yes, Kit?'

'Imogen, this is Jocelyn de Flores; she runs the East Pole Trading Company; Jocelyn, this is Imogen, wit, truly wonderful person, and... well.' Kit smiled and put his darkened-glass spectacles back on. 'What can I tell you? She'll know what you want to know.'

'I need,' Jocelyn said with a degree of determination, 'to see the Queen. Today.'

'Now let me see, who would do...' Imogen lifted her chin, lively eyes searching the assembly. Poised, questing, she mentally sorted through faces and names. 'She won't be giving an audience, as such: I was just saying to Vexin and Quesnoy.'

Jocelyn looked blank.

'Oh, you don't *know* them.' Rapidly, apologetic, breathless. 'Vexin is the woman who's owned by Seznec.'

'Seznec?'

'Seznec left Barbier for Chaptal.'

Jocelyn gave it up. She glanced back at the young man.

'Look, I have to go.' His gaze moved to the group of Rats at the sofa, the dynamics of which had shifted towards dissolution without him. 'Imogen will look after you. Call me if you need me; I'll be right there.'

Imogen, who had looked enthusiastically ready to continue the conversation, spotted a face across the audience chamber.

'*Ah.*'

She turned and swept off, Jocelyn stepping rapidly to keep up, and bore down on a small red-headed woman dressed in black. The woman stood talking to a brown Rat:

'... I said to him, *Why, this is the Invisible College, nor am I out of it*... Hello, Imogen.'

'Æmilia, you can do this for me, can't you? Jocelyn needs to see her Majesty. Sorry, I *must* rush. Hope it goes well for you, Jocelyn.' Smiling, breathless, a little hurried; she moved with utter confidence into the crowd.

Æmelia lifted a dark eyebrow. She wore black breeches, boots, and a shirt embroidered in baroque death's-heads. For a second she stood with her weight back on one heel, surveying the far end of the hall. The glass of red wine in her hand wavered slightly. 'Right... See that door there? In about three minutes you'll see the guard leave it. Go through. Got that?'

'He'll leave?'

The woman grinned. 'You watch. Have a little trust. Honestly, the things I *do* for people...'

Jocelyn stared after her, losing her among the crowd of tall black and brown Rats. The background noise rose. She sniffed, smelling sweat and fur and scent, not the spices and tar of the docks; and stared the Rat lords up and down with some contempt.

The Rat Guard turned his head as the door behind him opened a fraction. He nodded and strode away, businesslike, towards the entrance. Jocelyn walked without any hesitation up to and through the door.

The heights of the Feasting Hall opened around her.

Brown stone arched up into Gothick vaults, by way of carved niches full of figures of Rat saints, statesmen, monarchs, and lords of antiquity. Blue velvet drapes curtained the draft from the hall doors. A spiky-branched candelabra hung down from the peak of the ceiling, candles as yet unlit.

The Rat-Queen in their close group stood, some directing servants in their cleaning operations, some supervising the erection of the makeshift stage, one reading in a prompt-book. Brown Rat servants made rows of chairs, and two velvet-lined boxes: a theatre set up in miniature.

Jocelyn swept a bow that left her greatcoat brushing dust from the hall floor. Some of the Rat-Queen turned. A sleek-faced one gestured to the page nursing their knotted tails; he set down the velvet cushion.

'Ah. One of our merchant-venturers, we believe. We hear that you wish to see us, Madam de Flores.'

'Mercy!' Jocelyn de Flores, with a mental and ironic acknowledgement to Lord Benjamin, theatrically fell on one knee.

Another sleek black royal head turned, wearing an expression of bemusement. 'Whatever for, Madam de Flores?'

'I know something that I must tell to your Majesty,' Jocelyn said. 'A crime. Of which I myself am not entirely innocent.'

Ashar-hakku-ezrian looked down with an expression somewhere between embarrassment and searing relief. The girl's arms locked about his waist, her face buried in his chest: only the top of her head and buttercup-yellow hair visible.

'Varagnac told me where you were.' He tentatively stroked her back. Her plush-furred tail looped up and coiled snake-tight about his forearm. 'But I'd have got round to looking here pretty soon.'

He brought his free hand round and shifted her embrace, getting fingers to her pointed chin and forcing it up. The twelve-year-old leaned back slightly and fixed him with impossibly large eyes.

'*Sure* you would.' A head and a half shorter than her brother, with cropped blonde hair, brown skin dotted with a hundred thousand pale and minute freckles, a body whipcord-thin: Ishnanna-hakku-ezrian.

Malice flicked her inflected speech: the dialect of South Katay. 'Oh, and if you think that, tell me what I'm *doing* here. *If* you can.'

The midday sun shone with a new warmth on the formal gardens of the palace. Topiary yews cast shade over grass walks, and, where the two of them stood at the edge of the grand canal, the water reflected hedges, the palace's Gothick heights, and the blue sky of spring becoming early summer.

Ashar-hakku-ezrian ruffled her cropped hair. 'So what did you run away to be, shorty?'

The Katayan girl stepped back and held up her hands. Black gum smeared her fingers, palms, wrists, and one elbow. Ashar began tetchily to examine his shirt where she had hugged him. 'What the hell is that?'

'Cartographic ink.' Ishnanna's white-blonde tail whisked dew from the flagstones, dipped into the canal, and brought up water for her to dabble on her stained hands. Her big eyes gleamed. 'I'm nearly trained, Ash. The Queen's Mapmaker has five apprentices, but *I'm* the one he's going to send on the *Hawthorne* when it sails to look for the West Pole. Oh, can't you just think of it!'

'Miles of empty ocean, ship's biscuits, storms, uneducated shipmasters, no destination, *seasickness* – yes, I can think of it.'

'*Ash*...'

'Did I *say* I wouldn't come with you?'

The girl smiled, short upper lip pulling back from white teeth. She squinted up at him, against the sun. 'Well... it's not for a year or more yet. Ash, what are you doing here? Did you just come looking for me? How's Mother? Did she say anything about me? Why didn't you get here sooner? Why did Lord William bring you in this morning? Are you in trouble?'

'Who, me?'

Ashar-hakku-ezrian grinned and looked up past her, at the sprawling bulk of the palace that squatted black and spiked and perpendicular in the sunlight.

'We are *most* displeased.'

The Rat-Queen's tone was icy. Benjamin bowed deeply. 'Your Majesty.'

'An attempt to undermine the ruler of these East Pole lands – why, the man is a monarch! As we are. How dare you even contemplate such an action?'

Lord Benjamin put his hands behind his back, gripping his folded yellow gloves. Just to his right, the stout and sober figure of Lord William waited.

'I had thought to make your Majesty's dominions wealthy with trade.'

Nine pairs of eyes fixed on him. Some of the Rat-Queen folded their hands in their laps. Lean-jawed faces stiffened, stern.

'And what example will you give the mob, Benjamin, if you begin by bringing a monarch down from his god-given station in life? How will the rabble out there think of *us*? Would you have us condescend to explain—'

'—our actions for their good, that they, being the common herd, cannot understand?'

High Rat voices reverberated from the white-cobwebbed walls.

'Or excuse ourselves—'

'—when our responsibility is solely to ourselves and the god that gave us this land to rule?'

'You may not do this thing! We are angry with you, Lord Benjamin. We think it best—'

'—that you conclude this sorry affair now. End it. Never more speak of it.'

One of the Rat-Queen laid a gloved hand on the edge of the baroque marble tomb, her face thoughtful.

'Lord William is to be our first minister in your place. We are sorry you should bring such disgrace upon yourself, my lord. Be thankful the punishment is no worse.'

Lord Benjamin swept a bow, turned, and, as he passed Lord William on the way out, murmured to those impassive, craggy features, 'Make the most of your turn in favour my lord. While you have it.'

Ten thousand candles illuminated the Feasting Hall. The naphtha jets stood unlit. A heavy scent of wax and warm flame filled the air.

Varagnac eased at the sling cradling her fractured arm, buttoned into her livery jacket; one sleeve hanging empty. She undid another button. Analgesic drugs buzzed in her head. She grinned lopsidedly, standing at the head of the steps and surveying the crowd.

Stage and royal box faced each other across thirty feet of hall space, the wooden framework bright with purple velvet coverings and the royal crest. Stage-curtains hung closed as yet. Some fifty plush chairs occupied the intermediate space, and between them Rat lords in evening dress and satins stood drinking green wine and talking. Varagnac eye-checked the positions of her plain-clothes Guard.

'Madam Varagnac.'

'Sir.' She walked down to join Lord William at the foot of the steps. Stout and stolid, he gazed across the hall.

Beyond the rows of seats, in front of the stage, Ashar-hakku-ezrian stood talking with Athanasius Godwin. The old man frowned. Ashar spoke, tail cocked, head to one side; and Godwin chuckled. Ears shifting, Varagnac caught a fragment of their conversation:

'... accept hospitality ... Academy ...'

The Katayan took the offered glass from Godwin, drained it, and wiped his wispy beard. Varagnac saw him grin, and vault up on to the stage and peer through the closed curtains.

She gazed up at Ashar-hakku-ezrian on the platform. In black evening dress, and with a silver sash slightly disguising his plump waist, the young man raised arched blond brows at Varagnac, and tipped her a twitch of his groomed tail.

'Isn't he something?' She shook her head and looked down at the stout man beside her. 'Sir.'

'Undoubtedly.' Lord William's tone was dry. 'However, he still carries dangerous knowledge. He knows more about certain people's business than is entirely wise for any of us.'

Varagnac rubbed lightly at her splinted arm. Through the crowd she glimpsed a red-bearded man leaning up against the empty royal box. His blue doublet had been abandoned in favour of formal dress; he moved stiffly.

'So Marston survives? Hrrmm.'

'Exactly. Watch the young man. I believe that that is all we can do. And I fear it will hardly be enough.'

Lord William bowed formally and continued to plough through the assembled dignitaries, towards the doors by which the Queen would enter. Varagnac circulated, checking more guard-points. She impressed in her mind the positions of Athanasius Godwin, and a small troop from the Academy of Memory; and Jocelyn de Flores and two other ship-owners. She searched keenly for signs of the visible Nathaniel Marston's invisible associates.

A voice some yards away said, 'I'm surprised that you're still here. After the fall of your patron.'

'Sebastien ...' She gave it a toothy emphasis.

'That's Messire Sebastien to you.' Fat and sweating in leather and lace, the black Rat narrowed his eyes in her direction. Varagnac chuckled.

'The security services are always here ... If you're looking for Madam de Flores, she's over with Lord Oudin. Or do you think that even a human won't welcome your company now?'

'Don't be insolent!'

'Don't be ridiculous.' She dropped humour and spoke concisely. 'My department has sufficient proof of your involvement. I know how deep in debt this puts you. If you're thinking of repairing your fortunes, go overseas to do it. You won't take a step here that I don't know about.'

The black Rat brushed her elbow as he strode off, sending pain up her arm and shoulder. She swore. Wax dripped down from the spiky chandelier, spotting the silver fur of her haunches. Her tail whipped back and forth a few irritated inches either way.

'Fool!' She clapped hand to her sword-hilt, avoiding spearing two black Rats in identical cerise silk, and took a few paces closer to the stage. Ashar-hakku-ezrian slid in between the closed curtains. She halted.

'Good god.' She failed to keep the amazement out of her voice. 'Lord Benjamin?'

Benjamin acknowledged her with a wave of his free hand. Resplendent in evening dress with a pink tie and cummerbund, curly hair shining with oil, he walked with a very young woman on his arm. Varagnac blinked.

'Varagnac, I don't believe you know my acquaintance of this evening. This is Mistress Ishnanna-hakku-ezrian. Queens' Mapmaker.'

Enormous dark eyes looked up from a level somewhat below Varagnac's collarbone. Freckled, darker, and with dandelion-fluff hair: the girl stood with all her older brother's aplomb.

'Apprentice Queens' Mapmaker.' Her tiny voice was husky, accented. 'You're the one Ash tells me about? *Mmmm ...*'

Hackles ruffled up Varagnac's spine. 'One of your family patronizing me is quite enough. Benjamin, are you mad? You shouldn't be here. She certainly shouldn't.'

'And for his own safety, nor should the lady's brother. I hold him no ill-will; what's happened has happened—' The ex-minister broke off. 'Speak to me after this. Ishnanna, look, there: her Majesty.'

'Oh, I've met her Majesty; they like me.'

A fanfare of silver trumpets interrupted, slicing the air like ripped silk; notes dropping a silence over the fifty or so Rat lords and humans.

Heels clicked across the tiled floors: the uniformed trumpeters retired. The great doors swung open. A line of three Rat priests padded in. Varagnac automatically crossed herself. Censers spilled perfumes. With a rustle of cloth, the crowd sank formally down on their knees.

'God save the Queen!'

Slender, pacing slowly in a close group, the Rat-Queen entered. Open-fronted black silk robes rustled. Diamonds flashed back the candlelight from rings, pectoral plates, and headbands bearing slender black ostrich plumes. Onyx mourning jewellery weighed down their slim bodies.

They spoke no words, only looking with black bright eyes at each other, and sometimes smiling as if in response. Some of the

Rat-Queen walked arm-in-arm, some with hands demurely folded before them. The royal pages carried the knot of their intertwined tails on a purple silk cushion.

'*Regina!*'

Varagnac narrowed her eyes. Nathaniel Marston knelt with only his dark-red hair showing, head bent. Two of Varagnac's officers flanked him, with another cater-wise two yards away. Lord Benjamin, kneeling next to Lord William, was muttering in the sober man's ear; Ishnanna-hakku-ezrian, peering everywhere but at the royal entrance, waved to someone—

To Ashar, looking out from backstage.

Guards unobtrusively shadowed the Rat-Queen down the hall and up into the royal box. Individuals approached to be presented by the major-domo.

Varagnac sighed with relief, surprised at the strength of her feelings. She got up, dusting the fur of her knees, and slipped between the crowd as they took their seats. She ducked around the curtained edge of the stage and into the backstage area.

A tall Rat faced her: blue livery half-unbuttoned, sword slung for left-hand draw; silver fur spiky with exhaustion. Lean, lithe; clawed hind feet braced widely apart, tail out for balance...

Varagnac moved around the conjuror's mirror.

Rails of costumes, trestle tables, standing mirrors, and a confusion of people crowded this blocked-off corridor. Varagnac stepped back as musicians piled past her, a furious argument in progress that stopped instantly as they emerged onstage.

'Ashar.'

'I'm here.' The Katayan drew the edge of a finger along his eyebrows, darkening them, and met her eyes in the make-up mirror. He grinned. 'House full?'

'Full of people who are dangerous.' The Rat ticked off points on long, claw-nailed fingers. 'I don't count de Flores, she's only lost one opportunity. Sebastien may hate the person responsible for his ruin, but *Sebastien* ... Benjamin will merely wait his turn out until he's in again. But you're a witness against the University, and I see Marston out there; and no doubt there are more of them here that I don't know.'

The Katayan stood and put his hands in his evening dress pockets.

Varagnac's left hand strayed absently to her splinted arm. 'Lord William's spoken to the Katayan Ambassador. You're going back next week.'

Music and song resonated through from the Feasting Hall. In a sphere of silence, she watched him.

'There are things even *you* can't do anything about, Ashar-hakku-ezrian. In a year or two it won't matter – some other company will have contracted to supply *candy* to the natives, and her Majesty will have been persuaded into turning a blind eye. For now, you're a serious embarrassment, and a high risk.'

He stepped closer to her, raising his chin so that he could look her in the eye. Varagnac stroked the side of his face. Cosmetic dust adhered to her long grey fingers.

'Rough night.' Without quite touching, his hand sketched the shape of her bandaged arm.

'Don't you hear what I'm saying!'

Head cocked to one side, he flirted eyelashes at her in a deliberate parody; she laughed; and he, soberly and easily, said, 'I've got it under control. Don't worry. Trust me.'

With the air of a respectable grandfather, he bent over her hand and kissed it. His fingers caressed the sensitive short fur under her wrist.

Varagnac remained staring after him until minutes after the young man had walked through on to the stage. She moved back through the side exit into the hall and positioned herself unobtrusively. Decorous requests for monologues were already being called out to Ashar-hakku-ezrian, poised on stage in the full light of two thousand candles.

He shone.

'Master Katayan.' The Rat-Queen's silvery voice cut across the theatre. 'Oblige us, please—'

Ashar-hakku-ezrian flourished a deep bow, tail cocked behind him. His eyes were brightly expectant. The candlelight dazzled on his black clothes and blond hair. Varagnac watched him spread his hands a little.

'I am entirely at your Majesty's disposal: command me!'

Two of the Rat-Queen looked at each other, relaxed, laughing; with the unconscious condescension of royal enjoyment. A slim Rat-Queen spoke. 'We know your skills are in spontaneous verse—'

'—but we find a great desire to hear a poem of yours which is somewhat famous.'

Ashar-hakku-ezrian bowed again.

'We would hear your rhyme of—'

One of the Rat-Queen unfolded a fan and hid her face. A bolder one continued, '—of the flea.'

Ashar snapped his fingers at the instrumentalists without even looking at them. He put his hands behind his back.

Varagnac's gaze shifted across the assembled company. Ammarion, Seznec, and De L'Isle. Commander-general. Speaker of the House. And First Lord of the Treasury. A cluster of judges, one with her pectoral badge showing four capital verdicts handed down. And merchants, businessmen, one theatre-owner; and Jocelyn de Flores with the literary mafia: Kit, Imogen, Æmilia.

For this second, all their eyes were on Ashar-hakku-ezrian. Obsessively she checked that her security officers were in their places ... Athanasius Godwin of the Academy of Memory had Nathaniel Marston seated next to him. She scowled, moving in their direction.

The drum beat: Ashar's voice filled the hall.

'Young Frederick, a famous flea,
Ambitions had to climb, you see,
Be bettered in the social scale,
And buy a better-class female.
He found a King whose mighty itch
Was for a—'

A silence fell. Varagnac glanced up at the stage.

Ashar smoothed back his hair with both hands. He glanced down at the leader of the musicians, nodded, and began again:

'A king whose mighty itch—'

He hesitated, stopped.

One of the Rat-Queen frowned, ready to pardon satire wittily expressed, but not ineptitude.

Varagnac's hand went to her sword, her eyes fixed on Marston.

The red-bearded man's mouth opened in a momentary, amazed O.

She looked rapidly back at the stage – Ashar-hakku-ezrian stood, red under his cosmetics, one hand still outstretched as if he could summon up the words: a royal Fool become a plain fool, evening dress become motley.

'—and so to scratch—' He wiped the back of his hand across his wet forehead. A shiver constricted Varagnac's spine. She dropped her gaze, not able for sympathy to look at him.

'I …' Ashar's voice faltered. His eyes narrowed, dazzled by candles. He stared into the fallen silence. 'I don't … don't remember it.'

From a mutter, the buzz of voices grew louder, masking his. One unidentified woman laughed, loud and coarsely. 'Nothing but a child with stage-fright!'

Varagnac's hand clenched. A movement in the row of seats beside her caught her attention.

Athanasius Godwin put his hand into his lap and then took it away. A cut-glass phial rested on the brown velvet folds of his robe. A tiny glass: empty.

Nathaniel Marston threw back his head and added to the laughter. Varagnac moved soundlessly to stand behind his chair, and overheard:

'Your Academy believes in precautions, doesn't it? Just as well, Master Godwin. Trying to hold him as a threat over us would have been dangerously stupid.'

The red-bearded man pushed his chair back and, under cover of the noise of people talking, changing seats, calling for drinks, and flocking around the royal box, walked past Varagnac towards the exit.

The heat of a myriad candles and gnawing pain from her arm dizzied her. She smiled, the expression turning sour. Weariness hit every muscle. Left-handed, Varagnac buttoned one more jacket button and straightened up.

Ashar-hakku-ezrian stood in front of the purple silk curtains. Sweat plastered his brown-blond hair to his face. He ignored a persistent hiss from the wings to come off, hardly seeming to notice.

'How can they?' Ishnanna's tiny gruff voice sounded beside her. Varagnac looked down. The pallor of anger showed up the girl's thick robin's-egg freckles. Tears stood in her eyes. Varagnac rested a sinewy furred arm across Ishnanna's shoulders. 'It's for the best—'

And then she saw it.

A split-second exchange. Ashar's head lifted slightly, his face red and sweating, and his gaze searched out and found Athanasius Godwin. The old man from the Academy of Memory sat serenely. And the slightest movement curved Ashar-hakku-ezrian's mouth into a momentary smile. He gave an almost imperceptible nod of recognition and thanks.

'Damn me.' Varagnac re-checked, glimpsing between Godwin's age-spotted fingers the glass stained with an unmistakable residue. *And people have ways of testing that.* She looked up again with something approaching respect.

Ashar-hakku-ezrian very quietly walked off-stage.

'It's for the best – trust me,' Varagnac finished.

WHAT GOD ABANDONED

What God abandoned, these defended,
And saved the sum of things for pay.
Epitaph on an Army of Mercenaries, A.E. Housman

There had been no rain for a month and the ground was hot iron under Miles' bare feet. Running, his bones pounded the earth. He bled. Dust rose, choking.

'—take him!'

The camp stretched away, apprehended in a single moment of time smaller than sundial or chronometer could measure. All its white tents, pennons, smoke from the cooking fires in the sutlers' quarters, shouts of muleteers, bellows of drill and countermarch, sun, dust and heat blanking out; narrowing down to just two things.

Two yards behind him the ratcheting-cogwheel snarl of one hound; the other four dogs running silent, without breath to waste, jaws dripping white foam on to the dust.

Half a world away (half the camp away) the glint of sun on metal: great-barrelled cannon and ranked organ guns; men playing cards on an upturned drum in the meagre midday shadow of the artillery field.

The provost's voice shouted again:

'Seize *hold* of him, rot your guts!'

Miles threw himself forward, legs pumping; healing muscular changes going on at cell-level, fibre-level... To think, now, in the heat of panic; to change anatomies without meditation or preparation – predator's instincts cut in. His muscles hardened, swelled, and drove him surging forward. A dog snarled, heart-stoppingly close, and then swerved, its bay rising a register into distressed yelps at changed flesh. It doesn't like my smell, Miles Godric thought, smiling despite everything. The baring of teeth became a snarl and he held back the instinct to turn and rip the animal's throat out.

The hounds' smell was sharp in his nostrils, like vinegar or stale wine. Below lay the slow burn of anger, his pursuers' pheremones on the still air. And below that the stench of the camp: sweat, undercooked food, bloody cloth bandages, gangrene and lice, wine, dung from the herds of sheep and cattle, and somewhere the smell of women, camp-followers with their scrawny arms deep in washing-tubs, the tang of menstrual blood so at odds with the blood shed in battle.

He loped, now, in a pace that ate up distance like a wolf's sprint, the tents and the open ground flashing by. His chest heaved deeply. The hounds fell back, outdistanced.

'Sanctuary!' He pitched on to his knees, on the rutted earth, throwing his arms round the carriage of the nearest cannon. 'You're my countrymen – sanctuary!'

Sun-hot metal burned his cheek. He made his chest heave as if panting, dizzy with effort; releasing the sudden changes of flesh. As his body subtly altered, he clung to the culverin.

'Hand him over!' The provost, shouting. And the baying of his accusers:

'The witch! Give us the he-witch!'

'—demand the justice of the camp, and execution—'

'—I'll gut him like a rotten fish and leave him stinking!'

'Sorcerer – man-lover!'

'Who do you want?' That would be the artillery master. John Hammet: the English mercenary and a stickler for camp law.

'He,' the provost said thickly. 'The big Englishman there. Godric.'

'He has right of three days' sanctuary, he has claimed it.'

Miles lowered his head, resting it against the barrel of the cannon, not looking round. The earth under his body breathed heat out, and dust whitened his shabby clothes, and a thirst began to rasp in the back of his throat.

The provost's voice sounded, close at hand. 'Very well. Three days only. I know the sanctuary of the artillery fields – he must move no further than twenty-four paces from the gun, or he is mine for the high justice.'

The master of the artillery train chuckled down in his throat. He removed his pipe from his mouth and spat. The spittle hit the earth a yard from Miles' sprawled body, darkening the dust. 'Take him now and I'll take my guns out of the camp, I swear it on God's bones and the Virgin's heart. And then you may fight your next battle with your pike and shot, and may all the saints help you to a victory without us! Sweet Lord, ten weeks since Maximillian's paid us, and now you come sniffing about to maintain justice in *my* own camp–'

Miles rolled over and sat with his back against the culverin.

A blazing blue sky shone, as it had shone for most of the summer. Bad campaign weather. Plague ran through the camp on little feet, taking more men to God than ever the King of Bohemia's muskets and pikes had. He wiped at his sweating forehead. The card-players had turned away and had their heads bent over their gambling again. He raised his head and looked up past John Hammet at his accusers.

The provost with his staff of office: a burly man with the veins on his cheeks broken into a mass of red threads, and warts on his hands. A dozen other men, mostly from his own pike unit. Familiar faces blank with a fear not shown in battle.

'I will station a man here to watch. Three days, you. Then broken on the wheel, before the camp drawn up to watch you.' The provost spoke in a slightly stilted English: a version of the camp patois that was part a myriad German dialects, part French, Spanish, Walloon, Pole, and Irish.

'May God damn your soul, and may the little devils of Hell play pincushion with your balls.' Miles had the satisfaction of seeing the provost snarl.

The men turned away, muttering. Miles Godric could not help but look for those he would not see – the little French boy, beardless, hardly out of swaddling bands; his friend, who dressed as a southern German should but whose accent was never quite in one country for more than a day; and the big man, whom he had first seen after the battle a fortnight ago.

'Succubus!' a departing voice yelled. Miles suddenly felt chill sweat down his back. *Sarnac's* voice?

John Hammet hacked at the dirt with the heel of his boot. His face was red, either from wearing good English woollen breeches and doublet in this hellish heat or else from anger. 'Is it true? Have you turned witch? God He knows, the priests are burning enough of them now.'

Miles stared after the men walking away across the camp. The provost's leashed dogs bayed. His scent came to them still on this still air. His lip lifted a little over a sharp white tooth.

'Give me a drink,' he said, 'good John, and I'll tell you the truth, I swear.'

A week ago…

*

... A warm night. Thick stars shone above the makeshift tent. They lazed half in the shelter of its canvas, protected from a myriad biting insects attracted by the warmth of their flesh, and passed bottles of sour wine back and forth as they drank.

'But how will I believe you?' the French boy said. 'When Master Copernicus *proves* that the great world hath the sun at its centre, and we and all the lesser stars moving about it, and all this without necessity of star-deities to guide the planets in their courses.'

Miles rolled over and took the bottle from him. A young man, face spoiled from handsome by pox-scars; with lively eyes and magnetic sharp gestures. Miles was a little in awe of him: the admiration of the Weerde for a creative mind.

The third, older man said lazily, 'Was not what I showed you today sufficient?'

'I have seen instruments for searching out the stars, that's true, but I have seen nothing of what makes the stars move.'

The older man, who spoke slightly imperfect French (as he spoke slightly imperfect Spanish and Walloon, to Miles' certain hearing) took a deep draught from the bottle. He appeared to be fifty or so; broad-shouldered, strong, and sunburnt. Miles noted with half his attention that the man, Maier, did not grow drunk.

'Love moves the stars, as the Italian wrote.' Maier wiped wine from his thick spade-cut beard. 'Look you, Master Descartes, you asked me for such wisdom as I can give, and it is this: there are correspondences between the earth and the heavens, such that all living things are subject to influence from the stars, and it is with the help of star-talismans that I draw down influences and perform healings.'

'And with such powers that you perform your alchemical experiments? You note I have studied your own *Arcana arcanissima* and *Atalanta fugiens,* Master Michael Maier. And for all this,' the boy Descartes said drunkenly, 'you ask no pay. A sad thing in a mercenary army. Much more and I shall truly believe you one of that Brotherhood that travels the world secretly, apparelled in each country as that country dresses, cognizant of secret signs, and practising the occult arts. But we are not—'

Descartes' beardless face screwed up in concentration, and he brought out:

'—we are not in an inn, neither are we under a *rose.*'

An interrupting voice took Miles by surprise so that his heart thudded into his mouth. The fourth man, Sarnac, said, 'Rosicrucians, is it, now? And will you have our Maier a member of that secret Order?'

He bellowed a big relaxed laugh. A look went between Maier and Descartes that escaped him. He has the intelligence of a bullock, Miles reflected. How can it be that I…

The big man's smell dominated the tent, blotting out all others. Miles lay on his pallet, picking at ends of straw; the breath shallow in his chest, breathing in, breathing in the male smell that dizzied him. And watching, in the campfire's shifting illumination, the curl of a lock of hair, the fall of loose wide shirtsleeves and buttock-hugging breeches, the knotted bare calves, the shape of broad shoulders and belly and balls.

Wanting to bury his face in soft and solid flesh.

He reached across Sarnac. His hand brushed the man's yellow-stubbled cheek as he grabbed a wine bottle, and the man swatted absently as if at an insect. Sitting up to drink, Miles shifted so that they sat hip to hip.

'Give me room, can't you?' Good-natured, Sarnac elbowed him a yard aside with one hefty shove. Miles spilt wine, swore, and slammed the bottle down to cover sight of his hands: shaking so that they could hold nothing.

Sarnac stood, took a pace or two to the other side of the fire, and hitched down the front of his breeches. One unsteady hand grabbed his cock. A stream of urine arched away into the darkness, shining in the fireglow.

'O wine it makes you merry,' Sarnac sang, 'O wine, the enemy of women; / It gives you to them, it makes you useless to them…'

Michael Maier lay with his upper body in the rough shelter of two sticks and a length of canvas, so that his face was in shadow. His voice sounded from the darkness. 'Come into Prague with me, Master Descartes.'

Miles Godric belched. 'What is there in a sacked city? That we haven't had already? The gold's gone to the officers, and there isn't a woman left virgin between here and the White Hill.'

Descartes ignored him. 'And see what, Master Maier?'

The bearded man pointed a stubby finger. 'You came searching for that Brotherhood in which you profess not to believe. If I tell you what is old news, that the city of Prague has been the heart of Hermetic magic since the days of Doctor Dee, then will you believe me when I say there is enough yet remaining that you would wish to view it?'

'Bollocks!' Miles snorted. 'There's nothing left. The fornicating Hapsburg Emperor's fornicating army's had it all.'

He settled back on his loot-stuffed pallet. The burghers of Prague had shown little inclination, last month, to stand a siege for their King after the battle of the White Hill. They threw open their gates to welcome the invading troops with indecent haste, but it did them no good: Maximillian of Bavaria and Tilly and the Imperial general Bucquoy ordered the city closed and gave the mercenaries a week to loot it bare. Truly, the troops should have robbed only the followers of the King of Bohemia, sparing those loyal to Hapsburg Ferdinand, but questions are not asked in the heat of plunder, and Miles Godric had little German, and the complexities of the German Princes' wars defeated him in any case, and Prague as it now was – burned, stripped, slaughtered and deserted – lacked only the scars of artillery fire to make it seem it had been taken after a six months' siege.

'Will you come?' Maier demanded of the boy.

Sarnac prowled back into the circle of firelight, his feet unsteady. He elbowed Descartes aside and went down on to his knees and fell into the makeshift tent beside Miles, face down, breathing thickly. The light shone on his white-blond hair.

Descartes said, 'Yes.'

'Don't leave without us,' Miles said. He studied the finger he had waved accusingly in the air with owlish curiosity. 'We'll come into the city with you. We'll come into ... what was I saying?'

He let himself slip back down on to his elbows, then rolled slowly sideways off his pallet, so that his back and buttocks rested snugly against Sarnac's chest, belly, prick and thighs.

Somewhere on the border of sleep, he smelled Sarnac's flesh tense.

The big man grunted, asleep and instinctive; throwing one arm across him; then rolled and kicked until Miles could only sit up, dazed, and say, 'You're a plague-take-it unquiet bedfellow, Sarnac!'

And lay awake and aching the rest of the night, not daring even to relieve himself in dreams.

Morning came welcome cold, the hour before dawn.

Miles stood with feet planted squarely apart, lacing the unfastened front points of his breeches to his sleeveless doublet. Between his feet, scabbarded, lay an arming sword and a foot-and-a-half dagger.

The sixteen-foot pike that was most of the rest of his equipment still rested across two notched sticks, supporting the tent-canvas. He absently picked at a rust-spot on its blade with a pared fingernail. The fingernails he had not pared with a dagger grew white and hard and more pointed than might be expected.

Momentarily he covered his face with his hands to hide the Change of stubble vanishing and leaving him clean-shaven.

He buckled on sword-belt and sword. Dew damped down the dust. He squinted across the waking camp, seeing the French boy on his way back from the sutlers with his arms full of bread and raw meat. Miles turned to build the fire in the fire-pit hotter, and sanded out the inside of his unlined helm, and filled it with water to boil.

'Beef?'

'Beef,' the boy agreed, kneeling down and spilling his load on to the earth. 'Out of Prague. We didn't eat like this before White Hill.'

Experienced, Miles said, 'We won't eat like it in a month, so eat while you can. Did you hear ought?'

'The usual rumours. We're to strike and move towards Brandenburg, to catch Frederick's Queen who's there with child; or else march on Mansfeld's mercenaries – but he'll turn his coat if we offer him pay, they say – or else we're to sit here and wait while the German Princes decide which one of them'll rebel against Hapsburg Ferdinand *this* time.'

Miles grunted. The morning had brought no sign of the woman and two boys he'd hired as servants to carry his plunder. He suspected the company captain had added them to his growing entourage. 'I'd happily winter here.'

Prompt on that, Sarnac groaned inside the tent and crawled out with his fair hair all clotted up in tufts, and sleep-grit in his eyes. Miles reached down and, with the hand that would have thumbed clean those eyes and lashes, handed the big man a pot of mulled wine.

'Urrghm.'

'And God give *you* a good morning, also.' Amused, suddenly warmed and confident, Miles chuckled. He ruffled Sarnac's long hair roughly enough for it to count as horseplay, and walked a good distance from the tent to piss, standing for long moments cock in hand and squinting his eyes against the lemon-white blaze of sunrise. On his return (the smell of boiling beef rank on the air) he found Maier about, dressed, armed, and neat as ever.

He remembered, with one of the flashes of memory which come in the dawn hour, Maier elbow-to-elbow with him in the thick of the line-fight; his pike raised up to shoulder-level, a yard of sharpened metal slamming into enemy eyes, cheeks, throats, ribs. Not neat then. Splashed red from chest to thigh, doublet and breeches soaking. A bad war, White Hill. The boy Descartes had vomited most of the following day, and Miles had also – but then, he could smell the gangrenous wounded two leagues away, and hear them too; and to excuse his reaction had drunk himself into a stupor, and woken – yes, woken to find himself beside the big drunken Frenchman from another pike unit, a man in his thirties, smelling of sweat and grass and blood: Sarnac. Sarnac.

He rescued some of the beef from the boiling helm and gulped it down hot, ripping the fresh bread apart with his strong teeth. Preference would have given him raw fresh beef, too; but the teaching held that such habits were unsafe. He chuckled under his breath. As for what the Family might say about *this* appetite ...

'God's teeth, man! You're not going looting without your comrades, are you?' Sarnac put his arm across Maier's shoulder. The bearded man (Swiss, could he be?) smiled. Young master Descartes sulked.

'Loot for the wit, Master Sarnac, not the belly or the purse.'

'What difference? We'll come.' His gaze fell on Miles, and his brow creased.

'God save us,' Miles Godric crossed himself, 'let's go to the city while we may. Tilly's thieving bastards have been there again, but they may have left something for thieving bastards like us.'

Dawn began to send white light across the camp. Pennants flickered into life on the officers' tents. The harsh bray of mules sounded. The four of them threaded a way through the rest of the pike unit with its drudges, wives, and servants; through musketeers, grooms, hawkers, children and quacks; past two sutleresses coming to blows over a stray sheep (Sarnac stopped to watch and Miles hung back with him, until the big man suddenly realized neither Descartes not Maier had stopped for the entertainment), and out through the ranked wagons that formed the military camp's walls.

*

Mid-morning found them in Prague, picking a way over blackened timbers, across squares and alleys choked with debris. Miles found a chipped dagger and shoved it under his belt. The rest of the ground was picked clean. Only the stench and the bodies heaped up for the common grave remained in the city. Refugees dotted the countryside for leagues around.

It seemed to Miles that wherever he stepped, flocks of crows rose up from the streets. He watched them wheel, wide-fingered wings black against the sun, and drop down, and stab their carrion beaks into sprawled limbs. Maggots, disturbed, rippled away like sour milk. The only things more numerous than the crows were the flies. He wiped his mouth clear of them.

'This ...' The French boy waved a hand vaguely, as if he had lost his sight. '*This!*'

Sarnac plodded back from the open door of an unburned house, empty-handed. 'Nothing! This quarter's been done over – I'll wager ten thalers it was that bastard Hammet's gun crews. I wonder they left food for the crows. Or if I heard they'd been selling this to the sutlers, and we eating it, it wouldn't surprise me.'

The boy retched and bent over, a thin trail of slime swinging from his mouth.

'This way,' Maier directed.

Miles, hot in brigandine and morion helmet but not about to go into even a sacked enemy city unarmoured, followed the older pikeman down between two stone mansions and out into an open space.

The gardens of Prague had not been deliberately sacked, but fire had raged down from the slum quarter and made a scorched earth of the palace grounds. Miles shaded his eyes, staring out across lines of blackened hedges at stumps of trees.

'There is enough left yet. Master Descartes! Here.' Maier turned and walked to where a terrace stood, the stone blackened, and stood staring out across the ruins. Miles followed him.

Descartes and Sarnac came some distance behind, walking out into the gardens, the boy with his hand on Sarnac's arm. Miles felt his chest tighten. He stripped off and threw down his mailed gloves, and swore.

'The Order of which that boy speaks,' Michael Maier said softly, 'has its rules, which are these. That each Brother of the Order travel, alone, through what countries of the world he may visit. That he in all things dress and speak as a citizen of the country he is in, whatever it may be, so that each man shall take him for one of his own. And also that he shall teach, as he goes, and not take life; but that last—'

Maier frowned, dreamily.

'—that last rule is not so strictly adhered to as is said.'

Miles Godric flared his nostrils, catching no scent even of a feral line, and smiled, showing clean and undecayed teeth. Cattle sometimes imitate their masters, all unknowing. 'Are you a Brother of the Rosy Cross, then, Master Maier? I'd heard Rosicrucians infested Prague and are half the reason the King and Queen fell into exile. Not a safe thing to be, if *concealment* is your rule. In this country they burn sorcerers.'

Maier grinned.

'And in this country, Master Miles, they burn sodomites. I think your big man there will not consent to your desires. I think him a woman-lover only – well, they have their peculiar superstitions, these men.'

'Yes,' Miles said. He watched Descartes and Sarnac climb up on to the ruined terrace. The big man wiped his sleeve across his face, mopping sweat; and Miles' teeth nipped his tongue.

'You may yet see the patterns of the knot gardens,' Michael Maier said, expansively gesturing. The sun flashed from his breastplate and morion helmet. 'Master Descartes, allow me to instruct you: *that* was the astrological garden, whose hedges grew in the shapes of the zodiac, and within the hedges the plants and herbs pertaining to each Sign. *That* was the garden of automata, and *that* of necromancy—'

'Necromancy!'

'You cannot stand in a sacked city and balk at the dead, young master.'

'But necromancy! But there,' the boy said, all his vitality momentarily gone, 'it is superstition, as my friend Father Mersenne tells me; and the Holy Church would not allow its practice, even were it a real danger.'

Maier asked acidly, 'And does your Father Mersenne instruct you in Logic?'

Miles left them quarrelling. Sarnac, idly wandering, hooked a bottle out of his half-laced brigandine and swigged at it, his back to the garden. Miles moved cautiously towards him.

Trails of soot blackened the masonry surrounding the garden. Something that might have been a rose-vine straggled up the wall, a dead bird crucified in amongst its thorns. Sarnac sat down with his back to the sun-hot wall.

The harsh calls of crows drowned Miles' footsteps.

The big man sat with his head thrown back, eyes closed. Dust grimed his corded throat. The bright curls of his hair showed under the battered morion he wore, the straps dangling loose; and sun shone through the golden hair on his chin and arms and bare shins, gleaming. A pulse beat in the hollow of his neck. Wine dried on his mouth and chin.

Cold to the belly, Miles sat down on his heels.

Sarnac opened his eyes. Light shone in them, as in brandy: brown and gold. He half-frowned.

'Sarnac.' Miles swallowed. The cold hollow under his ribs remained; and the smell of the man made him feel as if the earth had dissolved. He said, 'You must know I would lie with you.'

The briefest joy in gold-brown eyes; then Sarnac's face went blank, went white and then red. His voice came thick with disgust. '*You?* The Italian vice? Sweet saint's bones, you mean it for truth.'

Miles held up his hands in protest. He looked at his rough callused skin speculatively. 'Please ... please. Listen. I'm not as men are.'

The big man burst out into a laugh that began in scorn and ended in revulsion. 'So I've heard many say.'

'Sarnac, have you ever seen me unclothed?' He held the man's gaze. 'Or bathing in a river, or pissing?'

'No.' Puzzlement on Sarnac's face.

No, because you have been with the unit no more than a week. Miles bent forward, intense; using the Frenchman's own language. 'Because of my great desire for you, and because you should not think me capable of an unclean sin, I tell you my secret. I am no man, because I am a woman.'

The big man's mouth opened, and stayed open. His coarse brows dipped, frowning. A look began to come into his face: something between pity and lust and condescension.

'A woman soldier? One of the baggage train, tricked out in breeches – no, but I've seen you fight as no woman can! Are you one of the mankind sort, then, aping us?'

Behind him, Miles heard Maier's impatient raised voice:

'But I cannot prove it to you *here and now*! You *must* wait. Whether you will or no.'

Softening his voice, Miles held Sarnac's gaze. 'No, I wish for the privileges of no man; I would not have manhood if it were to buy. It is an old tale. I have seen such played on the public stage in London – a woman in boy's guise following her sweetheart to the wars. I dressed in male garments for safety and preservation of my virtue, and, when I learned he had died upon the field, stayed, and grew used to weaponry, since what else is left to me but to serve my Prince?'

A *very* old tale, Miles reflected sardonically. Sworn virgin warrior-maids are acceptable to him; this man had for country-woman three centuries gone that Jehanne who fought the English. Were I to say: I am a woman who loves fighting, who loves not the lordship of men, who will not wear petticoats – well then, Sarnac, would you lie with me? No, you would not.

Sarnac, still frowning, began to smile. 'Are you truly a she?'

Miles let out a breath he had not been aware of holding.

'Ay, ay, God's truth, and I'll prove it to you. Will you lie with me, and love me? Nay, not now, we're observed. Secretly. Tonight.'

Maier's voice sounded closer behind him, quarrelling with Descartes' importunate questions; but Miles did not move, still sitting forward on his haunches, the cloth of his breeches hiding his erection.

'Yes. Tonight,' Sarnac said.

Habit kept him outside the camp, in concealment. He lay up in a burned-out cellar near the walls of the city, eating crow-meat and less palatable offal; and at last sleeping the thick, heavy sleep of the Change. Shifting subcutaneous layers of body-fat, retracting testicles and penis, moving cartilage and hollowing muscle. Knowing what he would be when he woke.

The dark-lantern, its shutter half closed, made a golden glow in the cellar. Sarnac grunted. Straw dug sharply into Miles' back. She rubbed the slick length of her body against his, her breasts against the rough hair of his chest; shifted so that his hips and elbows were more to her liking and wound her legs about his hips. He thrust, penis finding obstruction (she had not, after all, forgotten the hymen) and then pierced her.

'Ah-h ...'

Miles Godric made deep noises in her throat. She buried her face against his shoulder, smelling the sweetness of his skin: sweat and dirt and woodsmoke. She bit at the bulge of muscle with her teeth.

'Wildcat!'

He pinned her. She shoved her hips up, taking him deep inside her; the tightness of a new vagina not wholly according to her plan, but still she held him, and thrust against his thrusts, and rolled over still holding so that she straddled him.

'Damn, but you're lively!' Sarnac, sweating, leaned up to nuzzle and suck at her breasts. 'Miles – no, what do I call you? What's your name?'

'Jehanne.'

The word came out unplanned; he, his eyes bright and heavy, never noticed. He mumbled the name into her belly, and pulled her down, one hand flat on the small of her back, pumping up into her.

'Woman!' he groaned.

She rode him as he climaxed, expecting nothing for herself, but the smell of him and days of wanting surprised her: she raked fingernails down his chest and bit his shoulder, drawing blood, with her own orgasm.

That day and the following she came back sweating and grinning from training fights, stepping lively and whistling, not caring who saw. For those who questioned, she told tales of a rare treasure looted out of Prague.

'You should have something for this,' she said expansively to Descartes, on the third day, sitting outside the tents. 'Didn't you fight at White Hill with the best of us? What will you take home to your sweetheart?'

The boy looked up from where he sprawled outside the tent. His deft fingers shaved a pen-nib, and a notebook lay open beside him. 'Pox, if I'm unlucky!'

'You're too young,' she teased.

'I was twenty-two when I left Paris,' Descartes said, naming an age precisely one-third her own, 'when I joined with Maurice of Nassau's men. It being my thought that, were I to be with an army, I would as soon be with confirmed victors.'

Miles rubbed more carefully with oiled cloth at the blade of her pike until it shone. She laid it down on the earth and stretched, and lodged one ankle over the other and leaned back on her elbows, surveying the evening.

'Nassau's bastards always win,' she confirmed idly. 'So what are you doing with Hapsburg Ferdinand instead of the Protestants?'

'I belong to Holy Mother Church. It's Maier who's the Lutheran. He's the one you should question. Or,' he quoted a prevalent maxim, '"So we serve our master honestly, it is no matter what master we serve."'

She squinted at the horizon, seeing thick pine forests darkening the mountains and, below them, white harvest fields burned black in the army's passing. 'You had that out of Sarnac's mouth.'

'Ay. Along with "In war there is no law and order, it is the same for master and man," and, "He who wages war fishes with a golden net".'

The boy rubbed at his scarred face, and rolled on to his side to look up at her. His small body had a kind of electric vitality to it; some spiritual equivalent of the wiry strength that made him train for the pike instead of (as he more properly ought) the musket.

'Master Maier showed me Tycho Brahe's famous astronomical apparatus, in the city, before the – before it was taken away.'

Miles snorted. 'Before the Rosy-Cross Brethren had it?'

'You don't believe in them.'

She shrugged, looking down a longer perspective of history than the human. 'I don't know what I *do* believe in, boy. I doubt, therefore I must think: and if I think, I cannot doubt that I am; what else is there?'

His eyes glowed. 'Much! Master Maier is instructing me. I write it all down here. Listen.'

In a sudden expansive affection for the boy and all the world, Miles Godric sat and sharpened the blade of her dagger, and listened to him declaim on analytical geometry, alchemical marriages, and other subjects worth not a penny beside the colour of the hair on Sarnac's belly.

On the fourth night, Miles stayed in the cellar after Sarnac departed. The big man kissed her, left the lantern, and at the doorway turned with one last puzzled look.

'You should let me guard you back to camp ...' His voice trailed off. She could see in his face how he could not take in the idea of a woman who was neither to be raped nor protected against rape. 'Are you content, lass?'

Miles nodded. 'I'll return later, as I have before.'

She listened to him go, hearing his footsteps halfway across the ruined city. Owls shrieked, and rats scuttled; and she curled up with her chin on her forearms, eyes dazzling in the lantern's yellow glare. She reached out and extinguished it.

And for tomorrow's drill? she thought. Sword and falchion I can use in this shape, and have; but for the pike should I Change and be a man? The weight may be too much to bear...

And if not, still, there's risk of discovery. Not as Family, but as woman, and then what? The baggage train, washing and whoring. I might stay concealed a woman soldier, as I have seen many do, with only a few of her comrades knowing and keeping secret.

But too many of *my* comrades have already seen me male.

She was not a small thing, laying there in the starlight; only her skin was a little smoother, for the layer of fat beneath it, cushioning the muscles. Her eyes gleamed flat silver like pennies. One hand stroked her breast, and she closed her eyes and slid down into the sleep of Change.

And so did not wake when they came.

'But *when* will you show me? *When?*'

'Soon! Be patient. You had patience enough to spend two years searching us out. Have a little more.'

The voices finally woke him. Miles shifted uneasily, rolled over, grabbed breeches and brigandine and – old habit of many night alarms – stood dressed and armed before he properly woke.

The cellar was dark, the door silver-outlined. On silent feet he slid out into the ruined moonlit alleys, shaking his head against sleepiness and chill. Voices, familiar voices, but where? And he—

Miles grabbed inelegantly, discovering himself awake and male. And the voices ... he slid the morion briefly from his head and cocked an ear. The voices were not as near as night-bemusement had made him think. But nonetheless familiar voices.

Maier and Descartes.

He glanced at the constellations. Two hours to dawn. The way to camp would be clear, and the dead-watch not prone to querying brother soldiers (if, indeed, they were not risking execution by dozing on duty). But then there was curiosity, and the question of what the French boy and Maier might be doing here, now, of all times.

Miles padded through rubble-choked alleys, silently climbing shifting burnt beams, avoiding pits, the pupils of his eyes wide and dark. The small winds of night brought him little but the stench of decaying flesh. For that reason he didn't realize Maier and Descartes were not alone until he heard boots scratching at stone.

Half an hour's solitary backing and tracking brought him to where he could observe. He eased into the shadow of a fire-blackened tree stump. Dry ferns brushed his face. He eased up a little, looking over the bank, and blinked momentarily at the space opened up before him.

Far below, the river shone silver. The town ran up in steep banks to either side. No lanterns, no movement; the darkness shrouded destruction.

Directly ahead, the towers of a palace rose up, almost untouched. The Emperor Ferdinand's banners now draggled from its spires, and men were quartered in its far chambers; but this part, overlooking the formal gardens, had no occupants that his hearing could detect. The only living beings – four of them – moved in the gardens below. Miles slid on his belly over the bank and down, moving soundlessly despite armour, his dagger drawn and carried in his left hand, ready.

He moved silently through burned gardens, past a hundred blackened and overturned marble statues, into what had been the centre of a maze.

'I had such dreams, last winter.' The boy, Descartes, stood with his arms wrapped in his cloak, hugging it around his body. His sharp, unhandsome face caught the moon's full brilliance. Miles saw the moon reflected twin in his eyes.

'Dreams. Nothing to do but winter over in Bavaria with the rest of Nassau's soldiers, get drunk and have women. I wondered, why did I ever leave Paris? Why did I ever join the God-forsaken Protestant cause?'

Softly, so that even Miles could hardly hear him, Maier prompted: 'But the dreams?'

'Of the black art which is called Mathematics.' Enthusiasm in the boy's voice, that faded with his next words. 'I dreamed that mathematics answered all, accounted for all, *was* all. That nothing moved on this breathing earth but mathematics could account for it, down to the final atom ... They were dreams of terror. They had no God in them, or if they did, removed far off and become watchmaker to the world: winding it up and leaving it until the end should strike. There was no magic.'

Unguarded, his French was of better quality than that heard in the camp, and Miles with difficulty adjusted his ear to it.

'And then I began to read pamphlets published out of Amsterdam and Prague. The *Chymische Hochzeit Christiani Rozenkreutz*, the *Fama Fraternitatis*. And broadsheet appeals to the Brotherhood of the Rosy Cross, to come out into the open, to share their secret knowledge of how the world works – how everything that is, is living and magical. *Everything*. How rocks, gems, trees, and stars share souls, as men do. How the alchemical transformation can change all our spirits to gold, and bring again the Golden Age of which the ancients wrote! And how a great instauration of magical science will come on the earth, and the bond be knitted again between the Lutheran Churches and the Roman Church into one great Christendom.'

Someone sighed behind the half-burned hedges. A woman, Miles realized. He felt bare-handed to see what cover he lay on, detecting no twigs to snap; and slid up on to one knee and then on to his feet. He reached down and loosened his sword, thumbing it an inch out of the mouth of the scabbard.

'And all this is words!' Descartes' voice snagged on pain. 'I must have proof. *Is* there such a Brotherhood? Do you have such magical knowledge? And is it truth, or charlatan tricks?'

Miles flared his nostrils. The sweet stink of rotting flesh covered all other scents. He could hear heartbeats, indrawn breath; but the four of them so close blurred his senses, so that he could not tell where the last one stood, or how near he was to the woman. The moonlight blinded his night vision. Using an habitual trick he searched the shadows with only peripheral sight.

There?

Michael Maier put his hand on Descartes' shoulder. He carried his cloak bundled over his left arm, leaving free the hilt of his military rapier, hood covering the glint of his helmet.

'That is a poor world you have in your dreams.' Maier's voice softened uncharacteristically. His French was adequate, not as good as the boy's; but as good as his Italian, or Spanish, or (if it came to it, Miles knew) English. 'I will give you *magia* for your mechanical universe, if you will.'

'*Magia?*'

'Platonist magic, sometimes called the Egyptian or Hermetic Art. It is easier explained if you have first seen. Hold in your mind the thought that all you have read is true. I have stood in these gardens on the day when statues spoke with human voices and moved with the spirits inspired into them; when the sick came and left healthy, and the dead with them – believe it – and the sacred marriage of the rose and the dew made bud, blossom, and fruit grow upon these same trees all in one hour.'

Miles heard the rustle of cloth. He stepped easily between sharp twigs and pressed his hand over the woman's mouth, his dagger-point denting her skin. He pitched his voice to carry no further than her ear. 'Cry out and I'll rip out your throat. What do you, here?'

This close to her he smelled satin, sour flesh, dirty hair, but no fear whatsoever. Maier's voice sounded again, and Miles could feel the woman strain to hear what came so clearly to him.

Michael Maier said, 'All this through *magia*. All this because our souls and our flesh are one, and at one with the living universe. We are demiurges upon this earth, and all of it from stone to sea will obey us, if a man but know the prayers, words, actions, and sacrifices necessary for it. We of the Brotherhood may speak to each other across vast distances, travel the sky and sea unhindered, heal, create gold, and pray down the wrath of the Divine upon the Divine's enemies.'

Miles Godric showed teeth, amused: one of the Weerde hearing – despite the searing belief in the man's voice – the old lie from a human mouth.

Descartes coughed. 'You may say so.'

Miles heard the fourth heartbeat now, not so close as he had feared. A dozen yards away in the wrecked maze.

'I say so!' Maier shouted. The empty gardens echoed, and Miles saw him look about, startled. More quietly, the burly man repeated, 'I say so.'

'But your true Alchemical Marriage, your Rosicrucian Kingdom to be founded here in Prague, where all this is to come about; where is *that* now – now that the city is sacked, and the King and Queen exiled or dead?'

'That hope is not ended.'

The woman breathed hard against his body. Her hands hung limp in the massive folds of her gown. Stiff starched lace rasped against Miles' face, and he felt the small coldnesses of gems in her hair. Listening hard, he momentarily ignored the sensations of his skin.

A soundless blast lifted Miles and threw him.

Stone and gravel scarred his palms. The world dissolved. Miles shook, his mouth full of blood, head ringing, hands and face afire. Mortar fire, or cannon? His left hand hung bloody and empty; he did not recall drawing his sword but the fingers of his right hand locked about the hilt.

Neither sword nor shot, but the suddenly-loosened power of a human mind seared the marrow in his bones.

'Maier!'

The voice he did not recognize as his: a bewildered and outraged child's shriek. He cowered, one hand over his head, sword thrusting aimlessly into the dark. Voices screamed and shattered around him; and he stood up, and the sky laughed as his sight cleared.

The night glowed blue.

Rich blue and gold, and the stars above were gone. The night sky over Prague shone with figures: planetary gods and zodiacal beasts, figures with swords and flaming hair, balances and spears, winged feet and bright eyes that shone no colour of the earth. The tides of power rocked the sky, and Miles fell down on his knees. He stared at the spade-bearded man. He heard the French boy cry out, and could not tell whether it were joy or terror.

'Maier!'

The older man laughed.

'What, Miles, you here? Well, then. See. See with clear eyes. Master Descartes, the Rosicrucian Kingdom is not ended, albeit the city has fallen. Look with clear eyes upon the Marriage of the Thames and the Rhine, the Winter King and Queen, Strength and Wisdom, *sophia* and *scientia.* Look upon the true Alchemical Union: Frederick the heir of the Germanies, Charlemagne's heir, Barbarossa's son; with Elizabeth the Phoenix Reborn, the daughter of Jacobus and heir of Gloriana, England's Virgin.'

The oldest of Weerde fears pierced him.

'Oh God I am most heartily sorry that I have offended Thee.'

Miles buried his head down against his knees, mumbling. The hot stench of urine made his eyes water. He rocked, holding his bloody hand to his gut, gripping the hard hilt of his sword; even in this extremity giving to his fear the name humanity in this age knew. 'I am most heartily sorry; preserve me from the Devil; preserve me from Him who walks up and down among men; dear God, most holy Lord ...'

Maier's hands gripped his shoulder, shaking him. 'Miles!'

Miles Godric at last lifted his head. 'Is it you who are doing all of this? Don't you know you'll call him, you'll call the Devil down on us? On *all* of us?'

Maier, kneeling behind him, put his warm arms around Miles' shoulders. 'Is *that* anything to fear? *Look*.'

Miles whimpered.

The two figures walked out into the centre of the maze. A woman and a man. Now the sound of their hearts beat against his ears, deafening him. A man with a plump face, dark hair and soft dark eyes; dressed in cloth-of-silver doublet and breeches, the Order of the Garter at his knee, but crowned in nothing save rose-coloured light. And a woman in cloth-of-gold farthingale and stomacher and ruff, a fashion two generations out of date, but her sharp-featured face the living image of a greater Queen. Frederick and Elizabeth: Winter King and Queen of Bohemia.

Not being human, Miles had only to gather his wits – thinking Yes, they escaped the battle! – to see the truth of it. A shabby man, a woman in a torn kirtle; their faces the pinched faces of refugees. The power that beat about them was not theirs.

But a power nonetheless, that brought the beasts of the night – foxes, wolves, wild boar – creeping to their feet, eyes shining. The rose-light gleamed with images of lion and stag and pelican piercing her own breast. Fireflies darted across the suddenly hot air.

In the false living tapestry of the night sky the Lords of Power bowed from Their thrones. Roses seemed to bud and blossom from the garden's blackened twigs. A petal brushed Miles and he shuddered uncontrollably, *feeling* it against his skin.

'How can they ...' The French boy knelt beside Maier, his face wide and wondering. 'How can they still be here, and their armies defeated and the city taken?'

'Because they are not defeated. Because they only wait their time. Which I – and you – will help to bring about. Nay, speak to them. Question them. I will be your warrant for it.' Maier stood and pulled Descartes to his feet. 'Come.'

The boy wiped his hair off his face, with the gesture seeming to take on years. He stepped forward. Something in his expression commanded: not the wonder, but the confirmation of knowledge.

'Is it so?' he said softly. 'And is it true, this union and this harmony?'

The woman spoke. '*Witness. We would have you witness, for you are the child of Our marriage. You are herald to the ages to come of what we proclaim: the union of man and beast, spirit and matter, soul and substance.*'

The man spoke. '*Witness Us as We are. Yours is a great soul, such a pivot as the world turns on, and We have called to you these two years that you should witness Us, and proclaim the Rose and the Cross openly to the world. So all men may be as We are.*'

To Miles' ears they mouthed rote-taught words badly. But the boy grinned, sucking at his still ink-stained fingers; and opened his mouth with the light of debate in his eyes.

'No!' Miles shielded his face with his arm. Shaded from that illusory light he could stagger to his feet, gain balance in the shifting world.

Time split now into clock-ticks, each one for ever, as time changes on the field of battle into a thousand non-sequential *nows*. He saw Their lips move, and Descartes' face shining. He saw Maier with arms folded, standing as a man stands who controls all circumstance. He saw the maze now blossoming with a hundred thousand red and white roses, their scent choking him with sweetness. And he heard, on the edge of consciousness, something else: the metallic clash of Legions marching, lost Legions, led by the Devil, and coming here to feed – he sobbed laughter – attracted like moths to a campfire. Attracted to the Light.

Small whirling bodies crisped in flame...

Miles Godric beat at his clothes with bloody hands. His sword fell, discarded, and stuck point-down and quivering, a bar of silver fire. The French boy took another step forward, holding out his hands. Miles strode forward and grabbed him around the body, lifting the boy and making to throw them both backwards away from Maier and his illusion of a mystical Marriage.

Descartes struggled. The boy's head jerked around. Miles stared into his eyes: eyes as dark blue and wide as a child's.

It seared into him, the origin of this force. Not Maier.

Not Maier, no more creative than a Weerde, but one of the human minds that is bound to change an age, whatever age it is born into; a mind only requiring, like a sun's beam, to be focused for it to burn. This boy's mind, tapped all unknowing, so that he spoke to the figures of his own desires – his own, and Michael Maier's.

Miles staggered, this close to the boy, all barriers permeable now, even the barrier between soul and soul.

Memory filled Miles Godric: memory not his own. The Family's memory. A vast coldness seared him, and a vast dark; and then the darkness blazed into a light more unbearable because in that light he saw one speck of dirt, himself, standing upon another speck of dirt which is the turning world; all circling a match-flame sun, one more in a swarm of firefly-stars. And between earth and suns, between stars and stars, such an infinite predatory emptiness and *appetite* that he whimpered again, eyes shut, himself and the boy curled foetally together on the garden earth, choking back tears in case they should be heard.

'*No!*' Maier screamed. His hands pried at Miles. 'No! Give him back to me! I want him for this—'

In a kind of battlefield calm, Miles knelt up and supported the boy across his thighs. He pried back one eyelid to study the boy's dilated pupil. 'Want must be your master.'

The approaching tread of the Devil's legions beat on his ears. Miles lay the boy down and stood up, grasping and recovering his sword.

'Well, I will have him for this in any case, and damn you,' the older man said. His voice held all the blindness of human belief. He knelt down, efficiently scooping the boy up, the thin body slumping forward, and drew his knife. 'I've waited for this conjunction of stars – and They have waited also, my King and Queen there – and now I shall give Them what They need to make Them actual, in this world, for ever.'

The irregular tread rasped in Miles' ears. He rubbed one sweat-sticky hand across his eyes. Movement in the Rose Garden, now. The tread of Legions ...

The moon, distorted by the boy's mind, made a false *magia*-light in the Garden. A white figure seemed to come into the centre of the maze, moving jerkily and swiftly towards Miles. The light shone on stone armour, full Gothic harness, and stone sword, and stone features; and shone upon limbs where white marble flushed now with the rose-and-gold of incipient life.

Reacting instantaneously, Miles feinted and slashed, backed two steps and then came forward, his blade swooping under the marble statue's sword and hitting with two-handed force where the armour gaped vulnerably under the arm.

His sword broke against the motionless statue.

His fingers fell open, numb. Metal shards shrieked and whirred past his face. He shouted, his voice ringing across the broken city gardens. Other white things appeared to move in the moonlight: all the stone warriors of the garden, breeding like Cadmus's dragon's teeth.

Miles stumbled back, no longer sure what illusion might become truth, given such an outpouring of the mind's power. He caught a heel against Maier's outstretched leg and staggered.

The older man bent over Descartes, his dagger carefully bleeding a vein in the boy's left wrist. With the blood and his fingers, he drew sigils on the hard earth. The spirals of psychic force tightened, tightened; building higher. Miles saw the boy's eyelids move and finally open, saw him look up into Maier's face. Saw him realize the open conduit, his soul drained to power visions, illusions, that Maier demanded become reality. The boy shrieked.

'Put an end to this.' Miles kicked Maier accurately and hard in the side of the head. The older man's dagger stabbed up and pierced his thigh. He sat down heavy, staring at the bleeding. Maier groped around for the boy's arm, and Descartes crawled crab-wise away from him on the burned earth.

'Stop it. *While we yet can.*' Miles hoisted himself up and sat down again, heavily, one leg no more use to stand on than water. He began to drag himself towards Maier.

Roses seemed to grow up from the ground and twine around his legs and arms. Their thorns bit deep into his flesh. He threw back his head, teeth gritted, straining. The vines held. Twisting, he for one second found himself staring into what he had avoided seeing.

In the heart of a rose and gold light, two naked and winged figures are embracing. Man and Woman, they are becoming more; draining the power of a human mind to become Lion and Phoenix. Their faces are radiant. They are a beacon of joy.

A beacon that can be seen for how great a distance?

Miles Godric lifts himself up again, as the rose-brambles bind him to the earth. The ground shakes with the approaching tread of Legions. A yard or two away, Michael Maier picks up his dagger and positions it under the French boy's ear; lifts his elbow to thrust.

The night explodes.

Nose and mouth bleeding, head ringing, eyes dazzled with the vanishing of a Light beyond all lights, Miles Godric lays among tangled dead briars and watches the moonlight shine on battered helms, scruffy brigandines, one smoking musket, halbards, and the excited faces and shouts of Maximilian of Bavaria's army.

'What was it, a quarrel over loot?' Sarnac shifted his body, pulling Miles' arm further over his shoulder. Miles slumped against the big man. 'Christ's bones, I didn't think there was enough left in the city to burn! You could see that fire clear from the camp.'

'Fire?'

'It's gone now. Odd.'

Miles felt the cold night air sting on his face. He glanced down. The moon's light showed him dark patches on his breeches and hands, and his leg was numb still. He groped at his head. Something sticky matted his hair.

'I don't…'

Only moonlight. Grey matter and dark liquid spattered his doublet. The memory of a musket-ball taking one side of Michael Maier's head off came back to him, and he tried with a dry mouth to spit into the road, knowing how inaccurate muskets are.

There was a bustle of soldiery around him and someone somewhere shouting orders and the road to the camp shone white and dusty.

'Where's the boy?'

'Vanringham has him. Living, I think. God's death, what were they quarrelling for?'

'I… forget.'

Sarnac's body-heat warmed him, and Miles conscientiously tried to stop shivering but without success. He would have sent men to search out the man and woman if he could have spoken – or if he could have been certain they had survived the illusions.

The march back to the camp seemed at the same time long and over in a heartbeat. Prague's ruined walls gave way to dawn and the ranked wagons of the camp, the provost and one of the company commanders, all of it happening somewhere far away. An hour passed in a minute.

Straw rasped against his back.

An early light shone in under the makeshift canvas tent.

Weakness pressed him down. He could not focus his eyes on what lay beyond the immediate circle of earth, fire-pit, and scattered equipment. He tried to moisten his dry mouth, swallowing. Sarnac, his back to Miles, boiled soup in someone else's upturned helmet.

'I... need a surgeon.'

'Do you, lass?'

Miles tried to make himself wake, move, protest. He saw Sarnac turn, face beaming with well-meaning.

'Think I'd let 'em treat you and discover you for a woman?'

'*No...*' He managed to raise his arms and grab Sarnac's hands. Knowing himself safe with surgeons, the surgeon's tents a cover for the many-partner marriages of the Weerde, and besides a necessary means for taking dead Weerde bodies from a battlefield.

'No: that's right.' The big man frowned down at him. 'I'm going to treat those wounds. Christ's little bones, woman, you're bleeding like a pig with its throat cut!'

The effort brought sweat out on Miles' face. His hands shook with the effort of holding Sarnac away. At some level of cell and blood he called on strength, knowing it was no use to call on Change; but the big man deftly slipped his grip away, stripping off Miles' doublet and breeches together and pulling at his shirt.

'Damn but you women always have some vapouring quibble. Haven't I seen you naked bef—'

Miles giggled faintly. The sheer bald shock on Sarnac's face made him splutter, not wishing it; robbing him of any words. He thought muddily, What words could there be?

The man bent over him, freckled shoulder close to his face, and Miles breathed in the smell of him through swollen and blood-choked nostrils; felt the big hands slide down the skin of his chest and belly and move as if stung from his cock and balls.

'But you *can't* be—'

The hot morning slipped a cog-wheel, reassembled itself into an absence of Sarnac and somewhere a voice shouting.

'*Succubus! Witchcraft!*'

With an effort that brought blood streaming from his thigh, Miles Godric crawled out of the shelter, pulled up breeches and doublet, and staggered away from the tent. The voice shouted. A dog bayed. His head came up and he searched the stirring camp, forcing his body to walk; to run...

...John Hammet sat beside him, back resting against the gun carriage.

'And thus I thought of you,' Miles finished, 'being a country-man of mine. And Family.'

Swallows and bats flew against the darkening evening sky, snapping at gnats.

'Pox take it, it's the world we live in that gives such schemes life.' The artillery man spat tobacco into the sun-dampened grass. 'I would the Family might change it. But witness our attempt to rid these lands of their superstitions – now half of the German principalities are burning witches, and half of their inquisitors are protestant Lutherans. Such was never our intent.'

Miles hunched his shoulders against the dust-clotted wood of the carriage. Heat stung his hands and face, blood now scabbing on their flayed skin. He tightened the bandage around his thigh.

'Will they burn me, think you?'

Hammet ignored the question. 'I talked to your French youth when they brought him in last night. I've seen men regain their rightful sense and speech, with less courage and spirit than he. Yet if I mistake not, he will fear "magic" all the days of his life. Do you know, kinsman, I think I would much like to live in his mathematical world. I would like a world where there are no devils and spirits in men, to risk calling down the Dark on our heads. It would be a peaceful one, I think, Descartes' world.'

Miles Godric shivered in the summer heat. Crows called.

The artillery man said, 'They will either burn you or break you on the wheel for a man-witch. So the provost orders. You had best shift your shape this night and join another unit.'

Remnants of fear chilled Miles Godric's bones. A vision came before his eyes of Sarnac's face loose in the concentration of pleasure. 'And leave Sarnac?'

Desire moves in his body for the man Sarnac, will move in it no matter what shape he wears; as if his mind were merely carried in this fleshly machine, a passenger subject to its will.

'How we love these may-flies,' he said ironically. 'Well, and in a while I may change flesh again, and find him again.'

'If he lives,' Hammet said. 'What is it draws us to wars?'

Miles Godric leaned his head against the metal of the culverin. Thinking of the heat of metal, firing case-shot; of pike and musket and the long sharp blades of daggers. Watching the evening dusk come on. 'We don't begin them. We only follow the drum.'

He got slowly to his feet, adding, 'We have few enough pleasures that we can afford to miss that one.'

In months to come he will hear rumours of Frederick the Garterless King – the royal boy having mislaid that English Order in his flight from Prague – and see him represented on satirical broadsheets with his stocking falling to his ankle. The drawings will show a plump young man and a hard-faced woman tramping the countryside in old clothes, trying to whip up support for their lost Bohemian kingdom. But support never comes.

In years to come Miles Godric will think of the taking of Prague, first bloodshed in thirty years of grinding war; and hear of Elizabeth's son Rupert fighting bloody battles in England, that civil war also engulfs. Word will come to him that Elizabeth, in exile, has the no-longer young Descartes at her court at the Hague, and that he has dedicated his *Principia philosophiae* to her. He will wonder if the man remembers what the boy once experienced, in Prague, in a garden, among roses.

And, being of the Family of the Weerde, he will live long enough to fight in most of the wars of the Age of Reason, that Cartesian dualism will usher in.

But for now it is a summer evening and Miles Godric is earning his reprieve; forgetting all else to stand, wounds stinging in the surface Change of stature and feature, and laugh, and anticipate the next battle.

THE ROAD TO JERUSALEM

Banners cracked in the wind and the hot grass smelled of summer. Sweat stung Tadmartin's eyes. Long habit taught her the uselessness of clashing mail gauntlet against barrel-helm in an attempt to wipe her forehead. She blinked agitatedly.

Sun flashed off her opponent's flat-topped helm; that brilliance that gives mirror-finish plate the name of *white harness.* A momentary breeze blew through her visor. Unseen, she grinned. She cut the single-handed sword down sharply, grounding her opponent's blade under it in the dirt.

She slammed her shield against the opposing helm. 'Concede?'

'Eat *that,* motherfucker!'

Knowing Tysoe, Tadmartin's unseen grin widened. She slipped back into fighting-perception, apprehending with the limited peripheries of her vision all the tourney field (empty now, the formal contests down to this one duel), the ranked faces of the audience, the glitter of light from lenses. A soughing sound reached her, muffled through arming-cap and helm. Tournament cheers.

Tysoe launched an attack. Tadmartin panted. Both moving slow now after long combat.

Strung out so tight, nothing real but the slide of sun down the blade, the whip of the wind coming in on her left side; foot sliding across the glass-slippery turf, heat pounding in her head. The body remembering at muscular level all the drills of training. Tadmartin moved without thought, without intention.

She felt her hand slide on the grip, the blade's weight cut the air – Tysoe's two-handed sword smashed down, parried through with her shield, her own blade cutting back; Tysoe's wild leap to avoid the belly cut – all slowed by her perceptions so that she watched it rather than willed it. Felt her body twist, rise; bring the thirty-inch blade back up and round and over in a high cut. Metal slammed down between Tysoe's neck and shoulder. The impact stung her hand.

'*Shit!*'

Tysoe dropped to one knee. Now only one hand held the

greatsword; the other arm hung motionless. Tadmartin stepped in on the instant, footwork perfect, sword up:

'Yield or die, sucker!'

'Aw, fuck, man! OK, OK. I yield. I yield!'

Tadmartin held the position, shield out, sword back in a high single-handed grip, poised for the smash that – rebated blade or not – would shatter Tysoe's skull. Through the narrow visor she caught the lift of the marshals' flag. A sharp drum sounded. Instantly she stepped back, put down the shield, slipped the sword behind her belt, and reached up to unfasten the straps of the barrel-helm.

'Fuck, man, you broke my fuckin' arm!'

'Collarbone.' Tadmartin pulled off the helm, shaking free her bobbed yellow hair. Sound washed in on her: the shouting and cheering from the stands, the shrill trumpets. A surgeon's team doubled across the arena towards them.

'Collarbone,' Tadmartin repeated. 'Hey, you want to use an out-of-period weapon, that's your problem. That two-hander's *slow*.'

'It's got reach. Aw, fuck *you*, man.'

Tadmartin held the barrel-helm reversed under her arm. Casually she stripped the mail gauntlets off and dropped them into the helm. She shook her head, corn-hair blazing against the blue sky. Conscious now of the weight of belted mail, hugging her body from neck to knee; and the heat of the arming doublet under it, despite the white surcoat reflecting back the sun.

'Tysoe, babe.' She knelt, and put her helm down; awkward with the blunt sword shoved through her belt; reached in and undid the straps and buckles holding Tysoe's barrel-helm on. The steel burned her bare fingers. Gently she pulled the helm loose. Tysoe's arming-cap came away with it, and her brown hair, ratted into clumps by sweat, spiked up in a ragged crest. The woman's bony face was bright scarlet.

'Shit, why don't it never *rain* on Unification Day?'

'That'd be too easy.' She loosened the taller woman's surcoat. Tysoe swore as the belt released the weight of the mail coat, and leaned back on the turf. 'They're going to have to cut that mail off you, girl. No way else to get to that fracture.'

Disgusted, Tysoe said, 'Aw, *fuck* it. That's my hauberk, man. *Shit*.'

'Gotta go. See you after.'

The drum cut out. Music swelled from the speakers: deliberate

Military Romantic. Tadmartin, not needing the marshals' guidance, walked across the worn turf of the stadium towards the main box. Breath caught hot in her throat. The weariness not of one fight, but of a day's skirmishing in the heat, knotted her chest. The muscles of her legs twinged. Bruises ached; and one sharp pain in a finger she now identified as a possible fracture. She walked, head high, trying to catch what breeze the July day might have to offer.

The PA blared: *'—the tournament winner, Knight-lieutenant Hyacinthe Tadmartin—'*

It's PR, she reminded herself. The Unification Day tournament; blunt weapons; a show; that's *all*. Aw, but fuck it, I don't care.

The applause lifted, choking her. She walked alone; a compact woman with bright hair, looking up at the main box. A few of the commanders' faces were identifiable; and her own Knight-captain with the white surcoat over black-and-brown DPMs. Tadmartin saluted with all the accuracy left to her. The steel mail hauberk robbed her of breath in the suffocating heat. She plodded up the steps to the platform.

Spy-eyes and bio-reporters crowded close as Marshal Philippe de Molay, in white combat fatigues with the red cross on the breast, stood and saluted her. He spoke less to her than to the media:

'Knight-lieutenant Tadmartin. Again, congratulations. You stand for the highest Templar ideal: the protection of the weak and innocent by force of arms. The ideal that sustained our grand founder Jacques de Molay, when the Unholy Church's Inquisition subjected him to torture, and would have given him a traitor's death at the stake. The ideal that enabled us to reform the Church from within, so that now our relationship with the Reformed Pope at Avignon is one of the pillars upon which the Order of the Knights Templar stands. While there are women and men like you, we stand upon a secure foundation. And while we stand upon the past, we can reach out and claim the future.'

Tadmartin at last gave in to a long desire: she smeared her hand across her red and sweating face, then wiped it down her surcoat. The grin wouldn't stay off her face. 'Thank you, sieur.'

'And how long have you been in the Order, Lieutenant?'

'Seven years, sieur.'

Questions came from the spy-eyes then, released to seek whatever sightbites might be useful for the news networks.

Tadmartin's grin faded. She answered with a deliberate slowness, wary in front of camcorders and Virtual recorders. Yes, from a family in Lesser Burgundy, all her possessions signed over to the Order; yes, trained at the academy in Paris; no, she didn't watch the Net much, so her favourite programmes—

A blonde woman, one eye masked by a head-up Virtual Display, shoved her way between Tadmartin and the Marshal of the Templar Order. Philippe de Molay's long face never changed but his body-language radiated annoyance.

'Knight-lieutenant Tadmartin,' the young woman said, with a precise Greater Burgundian accent. 'Louise de Keroac: I have you on realtime for Channel Nine. Knight-lieutenant Tadmartin, will you confirm that you were in charge of the company responsible for the Roanoke massacre?'

5 July 1991
One estate over, the houses and the cars are newer and there's more space between everything. Here the cars are old, knocked about, and parked bumper-to-bumper. Heat shimmers off pavements. Terraces and semis shoulder each other. Pavement trees droop, roots covered in dog-shit.

'Hey, Tad!'

Both Hook and Norton wear old Disruptive Pattern Material combat trousers, the camouflage light brown on dark brown; and Para boots. Hook's hair is shaved down to brown fuzz. Norton grinds out a cigarette against the wall.

'So what about the Heckler & Koch G11.'

Tad ruffles Norton's hair; he catches her arm; she breaks the grip. Time was when bunking off school left them conspicuous in the empty day. Now there are enough anomalies – unemployed, sick, retired, re-training – that they merge. Tad with braided hair, jeans; pockets always full.

'Caseless ammo. Eleven millimetre. This one *really* works. Low penetration, *high* stopping power – they want to use it for terrorist sieges.'

Tad knows. She can remember the excitement of knowing the litany of technology. The skill in knowing all measurements, all details; all the results of firing trials. She can remember when it was all new.

Tad and Hook end up in Norton's house, watching films on the old VCR. The living-room smells of milk and sick, and there are dog-hairs on the couch. Someone – Norton's older sister, probably – has left a clutch of empty and part-empty lager cans on the floor, along with stubbed-out cigarettes.

'So what's he say?'

'About training camp?'

Tad snorts. 'Of *course* about training camp.' Norton's brother is in the forces, and sent somewhere we don't talk about. Not if we want Norton's brother to remain the healthy, brutal, nineteen year old that they remember him.

'He says he nearly couldn't hack it.'

There is an awed pause: Norton's brother transformed from the squaddie in uniform to the sixteen year old that Tad remembers from summers ago. Word came back to Tad that Norton's brother and his mate done a runner from basic training; later she will know this is not true. Not and stay in the Forces. Which Norton's brother does for five years – until, in fact, some New Amsterdam paramilitary unit fires a rocket launcher at a garrison. The rocket goes literally between the two squaddies on Norton's brother's truck, giving both of them a bad case of sunburn: injuries from the rocket-motor. Norton's brother is inside talking to the on-duty watch, and there isn't anything of him left to find.

Tad, two years from knowing this, says, 'But did you *ask* him?'

'Yeah. He says you'll get in. They'd take you.'

Norton goes quiet after this. Hook prods him with one of the endless arguments about the stunts in the aerial sequences of *Top Gun*. Tad sprawls against the broken sofa. She is among clutter: a folded pushchair, someone's filthy work jacket, Tonka toys. She makes three separate efforts to join the argument and they exclude her. She feels bewilderment and hurt.

Remembering that hurt, it comes to her that they shut her out because they can see what she, at that moment, still cannot. That she will be the one to do what they never will – follow Norton's brother.

And more, that she has always meant to do this.

'I have nothing to say.'

The blonde woman spy-eye persisted. 'You were at Roanoke, Knight-lieutenant? You *were* at Roanoke at the time when the incident took place?'

Tadmartin let her face go blank. 'Nothing to say. You can talk to my company commander, Demzelle Keroac. I have no comment.'

'Will you admit to being on service in the New World at that time?'

'You can't expect a junior officer to comment on troop movements,' Philippe de Molay said smoothly. 'Thank you, Lieutenant Tadmartin.'

She saluted smartly. Shoulder and arm muscles shrieked protest, stiffening after exercise. She about-faced, trod smartly down the steps; heard the woman's voice raised in protest behind her as the security detail closed in.

Lights and camcorders crowded her face as she stepped off the platform into a crowd of reporters.

'Just a few words, Knight-lieutenant—'

'—you think of the European Unification—'

'—opinion on the story breaking in New Amsterdam; please, Demzelle Tadmartin?'

She knew better than to react. Still, *New Amsterdam* in that colonial accent made her blink momentarily. She looked between jostling bodies and memorized the face of a tall man, wispy-haired, with a tan skin that argued long Western service or Indo-Saracen blood.

'And your view of the Order's investment holdings in the New World—?'

She wiped her wrist across her nose and grinned at him, sweaty, breath eased from the long combat. 'It isn't my business to have financial or political opinions, sieur. If you'll excuse me, I have duties to attend to.'

Voices broke out, trying for a final question, but her patience and control ran on thin threads now.

'Yo! Tysoe!' She broke free and jogged across the field to the surgeon's van. The large, gawky woman waved her uninjured arm, beaming groggily through pain-suppressants.

'Wow, man. You look fucked off. What did they give you, six months' hard labour?'

Tadmartin heaved the buckle of her belt tighter, gaining more support for the mail hauberk. Disentangling herself from mail was an undignified operation – arse-skywards and wriggling – that mostly required help, and she was damned if she'd do it for an audience on the network. She swung herself up to sit on the van's hard bench seats. The orderlies snapped Tysoe's stretcher in place. Tadmartin saw they were ordinary grunts.

'I'll go back to base with you,' she stated, and pointed at one of the orderlies. 'You! Get my squad leader on the radio. I want him to supervise the clear-up detail here. I said *now*, soldier.'

'Yessir-ma'am!' Tysoe said, in a broad Lesser Burgundian accent. 'Boy are you pissed off. What happened?'

'I'll tell you what happened, Knight-lieutenant Tysoe.'

Tadmartin leaned back against the rail as the van coughed into gear. The sun slanted into the stadium, ranked faces still awaiting the final speeches that she need not sit through; and a granular gold light informed the air. She wiped the sweat-darkened hair back from her face.

'Someone wanted to interview me about Roanoke.'

Tysoe grunted. Pain-suppressants allowed a shadow of old grief or guilt to change her expression.

'That was settled. That was accounted for.'

'No,' Tadmartin said. 'No.'

5 July 1992

Tad hits cover at the side of the track, body pressed into the bank. Her body runs with sweat. She stinks of woodsmoke survival fires. Listening so hard she can hear the hum of air in the canals of her ears. She risks a glance back. She can't see the four men in her squad who are down the track behind her – which is how it should be. They can see her. Their responsibility to watch for silent signals.

Looking up the track she can see Tysoe, Shule, and Warner flattened into bushes and behind trees. On ceaseless watch, Tysoe catches her eye: taps hand to shoulder in the sign for *officer* and pats the top of her head, *come to me*. Tad immediately slips up to join her.

'We've *got* to move up. What's the problem?'

Tysoe: all knees and elbows, face plump with puppy-fat. She shrugs. 'Warner and Shule. You put them on point. They keep going into cover.'

'Jesu Sophia!' Tad, bent double, dodges tree-to-tree as far as Shule, who's belly-down behind soft cover. 'For fuck's sake *move*!'

'The scouts—'

'*Just fucking move!*'

She picks up Shule bodily by the collar, throwing him forward. He opens his mouth to protest. She slams her rifle-butt against the back of his helmet. His head hits the ground. He and Warner move off. She signals the squad forward in file, settling in behind point, shoving Shule on every ten or fifteen yards. Too late to change point now: Tysoe would have been better, but she needs Tysoe as her other team leader, so – command decision.

At low volume she thumbs the RT. Out-of-date equipment, like so much else here. 'Sierra Zero Eight, this is Oscar Foxtrot Nine. Give sit-rep, repeat, sit-rep. Over.'

No voice acknowledges. The waveband crackles.

'Sierra Zero Eight, do you copy?'

White noise.

'*Fuck.*' She looks back to catch Tysoe's eye, signals *close up* and *move faster*; slides the rifle down into her hands and jogs off at Shule's heels. The kevlar jacket weighs her down; her feet throb in her boots; and the assault rifle could be made from lead for all she knows.

Running, she can hear nothing.

The forest is a mess of brushwood, high trees, spatter-sunlight that's a gift to camouflage; noisy leaves, her own harsh breath in her ears; sweat, anxiety, frustration. Her eight-man squad moves tactically from cover to cover, but all of it soft cover. No time to check her watch but she knows they've exhausted all the time allowed for this flanking attack and then some.

'Fuck it!' She skids to a halt, signals *cover* and beckons Tysoe. The young woman spits as she hits cover beside Tad.

'What?'

There should be silent signals for all of this: she's forgotten them.

'We haven't got time for this! We're leaving the track. I'm taking them down through the wood; we'll come out above the camp and take them from there. Pass it back.'

She hears Tysoe go back as she moves forward to Warner and Shule. The woods are still. Not a crack of branch. And no firing from down by the base-camp. Nothing. A hundred square miles and there could be no one else there . . .

'Move!' she repeats, throwing Warner forward bodily. He stumbles into the brush. Giving up, she takes point; ducking to avoid snagging her pack on branches. One look behind assures her Tysoe – thank God for Tysoe! – is taking the back door and moving the squad up between them by sheer will.

Sacrificing tactics for speed, she cuts down a steep pine slope, over needles and broken branches; pauses once to thumb the RT and hear nothing but white noise; hits a remembered gully and slides down into it, feeding Warner and Shule and Ragald on and past her.

Just turned sixteen, Tad is not yet grown; a young woman with her hair under the too-large helmet shaved down to bootcamp fuzz. She hooks her neckerchief up to cover her mouth and nose and crawls down the gully, placing each of the eight man squad at intervals.

Now she can hear voices, or is it the fool-the-ear silence of the Burgundian woods? Let it ride, let it ride... and yes: a voice. The crackle of a voice over an RT, muted, a good twenty-five yards over the far rim of the gully. She gives the thumbs-down for *enemy seen or suspected,* points direction, holds up three fingers for distance. Looking down the line, she sees Tysoe grinning. All of them acknowledge. Even Shule's smartened up.

Eight sixteen year olds in soaked and muddy combats, weighed down with packs and helmets, assault rifles ready.

She signals *stealth approach.*

Up to the edge of the gully, assault rifle cradled across her forearms, moving in the leopard-crawl. One hand lifting twigs out of her way; not resting a knee until she knows the ground is clear underneath.

Concussive explosion shatters the air. The rapid stutter of fire: still so noisy that she hardly believes it. She flattens down to the turf, the camp spread out below her, anyone who so much as glances up from the APCs and tents can see her—

The basecamp grunts are hitting dirt and hitting cover behind the gate barrier. Tad grins. There goes the diversionary attack, in on the gate. Blanks, loud and stinking.

She jerks her arm forward, and the dummy grenades go in; then the squad, charging, yelling, running as if they carried no weight at all. Firing on automatic.

Tad never sees the end of it.

A stray paint-pellet rips open across her stomach, splattering her scarlet. It is assumed the attacking grunts' blanks mostly miss. It is established that the training sergeants' pellet guns rarely do. The impact bruises. Tad goes down.

The wilderness training range echoes with gunfire, shouts, radio communications, orders, pyrotechnic explosions. She lays on her back. Men and women run past her. A smoke grenade goes off. Orange smoke drifts between the trees. Tad, with what she assumes for convenience's sake to be her last conscious effort, puts on her respirator. The choking smoke rolls over her. The firing continues.

An hour later, exhausted, dirty, hungry; Tad calculates that, within the confines of this exercise, the medivac team failed to reach her before she became a fatality. She resigns herself to latrine duties.

'Sieur Tadmartin.'

She grins. 'Sarge.'

The sergeant kicks the food-pack out of her hands; she's up, outraged; he hits her fist-then-elbow across the face. 'You're a dead grunt – *sieur*. Why? I'll tell you why. Because you're a shit-stupid, dumbass excuse for a soldier. What are you?'

'A shit-stupid dumbass excuse for a soldier.' Sergeants run armies; she is not, even at sixteen and in officer training, stupid enough to answer back the company sergeant.

'And just *why* are you a shit-stupid dumbass excuse for a soldier, Tadmartin? Speak up! These people want to hear you.'

'Don't know, Sergeant.'

This time she sees it coming. When his fist cracks across her face her nose begins to leak dark blood.

'Because you set up an opportunity and you blew it. You took your people in like fucking *cowboys*. Next time you start a stealth attack you keep it up until you're in charge distance, you don't fucking *waste* it, you pathetic bitch, do I make myself clear?'

'Yes, Sergeant.'

'Coming in from the gully was good. You weren't spotted at all until you broke cover. Not,' he raised his voice to include the trainees guarding the base, 'that that should particularly surprise me, since none of you fuck-stupid *officers* can see your arses without a map and searchlight. Now you're going to clean up the area and *then* you might eat. Move it, fuckheads!'

The next day they repeat the exercise.

And the next.

The mess hall still had the smell of new buildings about it. Pre-stressed concrete beams, plastic benches, tables bolted to the floor; all new. Only the silence was old. Tadmartin, changed back into the white fatigues of a Knight-lieutenant, ate with the Sergeant Preceptors in the familiar silence. She fell into it as she fell into combat-perception: easily, as a body slides into deep water.

The bell for meal's end sounded.

'Knight Brothers and Sergeants of the Convent. Every perfect gift comes from above, coming down from the Father of Lights and the Mother of Wisdom, Christ and Sophia, with whom there is no change nor shadow of alteration.'

The *frère* at the lectern cleared his throat, addressing the grunts in the main body of the room.

'The reading today is from the bull of Pope Innocent-Fidelia. "For by nature you were children of wrath, given up to the pleasures of the flesh, but now through grace you have left behind worldly shows and your own possessions; you have humbly walked the hard road that leadeth to life; and to prove it you have most conscientiously taken up the sword and sworn on your breasts the sign of the living cross, because you are especially reckoned to be members of the Knighthood of God."'

Tadmartin sat easily erect on the hard bench. Sunlight slanted down from the clerestory windows on shaven heads, DPM fatigues. The smell of baking bread drifted out from the kitchens: the esquires and confrères working in silence except for the clatter of pans.

The words slid over her and she busied herself remembering equipment maintenance and duty rosters; found herself looking down at her hands in her lap: short-nailed, callused, and with a perceptible tremor.

The bell took her by surprise. She rose, saluting with the rest, about-faced and marched out.

'Tad.' Tysoe, arm strapped, fell into step beside her. 'You know where the rest of the company are now?'

'They were split up.' She didn't break stride.

'We should talk.'

'No.' She walked off without looking back at the taller woman.

Once in her quarters, she ripped the top off a can of lager, drank, and vocalized the code for network access. The cell's viewscreen lit up with the public channel logo.

'Search *Tadmartin*,' she said morosely. 'Then search *Roanoke*. Backtime forty-eight hours.'

The small viewscreen beeped and signalled a recorded sequence. Green leaves. Shells: the flat thud of one-oh-fives. A soundtrack:

'Here in Cabotsland, in the Indo-Saracen states, gunfire is an everyday sound. Terrorist explosions mingle with the artillery barrages of brushfire wars between settlements. For generations there has been no peace.'

The shot pulled back to show a spy-eye reporter standing below the walls of Raleighstown. Sun, swamp, forest, and mosquitoes. Tadmartin smiled crookedly. The reporter was a blonde woman in her twenties, eye masked by head-up Virtual Display.

'This is Louise de Keroac on Channel Nine, at Raleighstown. Centuries of settlement – our reformed Gnostic Saracen settlements imposed on the indigenous Indian population – have brought about not the hoped-for melting-pot of civilization, but a constant boil of war for land and hunting rights. The Crusades suppress this temporarily. But, as we all know, even if governments are reluctant to admit it, after the troops are withdrawn, the fighting breaks out again.'

The woman's visible eye was a penetrating blue. She spoke with a breathy, cynical competence. Tadmartin raised the can to her mouth and drank, the alcohol pricking its way down her throat. She raised a thoughtful eyebrow. The alcohol combatted the cell's official 55°F.

De Keroac's voice sharpened:

'But Roanoke is different. Five years after the unexplained deaths of fifty-three civilians, as well as fourteen Knights Templar and thirty-three Knights Hospitaller, here in Roanoke, rumours continue to grow of a quasi-offical shoot-on-sight policy. None of the soldiers wounded in that battle have ever been available for interview. Official sources have always spoken of "surprise heathen attacks". But now, finally, New Amsterdam is demanding an official enquiry.'

A shot of the shitty end of the settlement; Tadmartin recognized it instantly. In the arms of a great forest, dwarfed by trees, the wooden buildings hug the ground by the river. The palisade fence winds off out of shot. The stone crenellations of the Templar castle came into shot as de Keroac's spy-eye panned.

Tadmartin rested her chin on her chest as she slumped back, watching Raleighstown. Bustling, full of men and women in short flowing robes and buckskin leggings, veils drawn up over their mouths against the mosquitoes and the White Fever. Crowded market stalls, with old petrol-engine taxis hooting against herded buffalo in the streets; women with children on their hips; the glitter of sun off low-rise office blocks. The camera caught *Franks go home!* and *To Eblis with Burgundy!* graffited on one wooden wall.

'This is the garrison. The locals call it the garrison of the Burgundian Empire—'

Tadmartin groaned.

'—rather than that of United Europe. Whether partisan attack, terrorist bombs, or one lunatic with a grudge was responsible for the destruction of half its troops has never been known. Now, however, new evidence has appeared.'

'It's the sakkies.' A man leaned up against the door of Tadmartin's cell. Tall, young, broad-shouldered; and with the Turcoplier's star on his collar.

'Yo, Vitry.'

'Yo.' He stubbed out a thin black cigarette against the concrete wall and walked in. 'That one's all bullshit. You want Channel Eight realtime.'

'Eight,' Tadmartin said. The video channel flicked obediently.

'—ever-present knowledge that the European governments could bomb them back into the Stone Age.' A bio-reporter looked to camera: the man with the faded skin, Indo-Saracen blood. 'Talk to the Templar grunts and sergeants. They call them *sakkies.* Their word for Saracen. No one I've spoken to will believe that a small paramilitary group of sakkies could destroy a trained Knightly garrison—'

'Bollocks.' Vitry squatted beside Tadmartin's armchair and reached for her can of lager. 'Every damn local régime gets lucky some time or another. We all know that. And that's the answer he'll have got. Lying bastard.'

'—attempted to talk to the winner of this year's Unification Tourney; the lieutenant who, as a junior officer, found herself in charge of this Burgundian frontier outpost; Knight-lieutenant Hyacinthe Tadmartin.'

She regarded the screen morosely, watching the stadium from a different angle than the combatants saw. Dust covered the mêlée in the main field. Vitry peered closely at the screen.

'There's you – and there's me, look!' He lifted his voice without looking away from the screen. 'Yo! You guys! We're on the network!'

'Jesu Sophia!'

She watched herself walk down the steps from the main box. The mail hauberk glittered and the stained surcoat's red cross blazed. The camera zoomed in and held the image of her face: oval, youthful until the eyes. The Knighthood of God. She thought that she looked both older and younger than twenty-six: fitter in body than most, but with weathered crow's-feet around her eyes.

She snapped her fingers to mute audio, not being able to stand the sound of her own voice; bringing it up again only when the camera cut back to the bio-reporter.

'Hiding within the strict rules of the Templars – a Templar *frère* may never "disclose the House", that is, give out information on Templar activities, on penalty of losing their place within the Knighthood – hiding under this cover, no one can cross-examine this member of Burgundy's most elite force—'

'Yo!' Vitry roared. 'That's one for the Hospitallers. *We're* the most elite force!'

The rest of the mess, crowding Tadmartin's narrow cell, swore at or yelled with Vitry according to temperament.

'—no one can even establish who did command at Roanoke; even less what happened there, and why. Moves are being made to take this to the High Council of Burgundy when it meets with Pope Stephen-Maria V in Avignon later today. But will the truth, even then, be brought to light?

'This is James de Craon, for Channel Eight—'

Talk broke out, the Templars dispersing back to the mess.

'Ah well. Bullshit baffles brains.' Vitry shrugged. 'You never had an overseas posting as far north as Roanoke, did you.'

Since it was not a question Tadmartin felt no obligation to give an answer. She snapped her fingers to kill audio and video. As the crowd moved away from her door, a grunt anxiously saluted her. She returned it.

'Yes?'

'Message from Commander St Omer, sieur. He'll see you in his office at oh-six-hundred hours tomorrow morning.'

5 July 1994

'Fine brother knights.' The Preceptor Phillipe de Molay clears his throat and continues to read. '*Biaus seignors frères*, you see that the majority have agreed that this woman should be made a *frère*. If there be someone amongst you who knows reason why she should not be, then speak.'

The dawn sun hits the mirror-windows of Greater Burgundian office blocks and reflects back, slanting down through ogee arches into the chapel, failing to warm the biscuit-coloured stone. Tad, at attention, can just see her instructors – in formal black or brown surcoats – to either side of her. The stone is bitter cold under her bare feet. The Preceptor's voice echoes flatly.

'You who would be knightly, you see us with fine harness, you see us eat well and drink well, and it therefore appears your comfort with us will be great.'

And so it does appear to Tadmartin, used now to being provided with combat fatigues, formal uniforms, assault rifle, all the technology of communication and destruction.

'But it is a hard thing that you, who are your self's master, should become the serf of another, and this is what will be. If you wish to be on land this side of the ocean, you will be sent to the other; if you wish to be in New Amsterdam, you will be sent to Londres ... Now search your heart to discover whether you are ready to suffer for God.'

One does not go through the specialist training – the suffering for man? Tad wonders – to refuse at this late stage. But some have. When it comes to it, some have refused in this very ceremony.

Outside, the deep blue sky shines. She can hear them drilling, down on the square. Voices, boots. Here in the cold chapel, the commander and turcopliers in their robes stand side-by-side with the medic and psychologist – to certify her fitness – and the solicitor.

'... Now I have told you the things that you should do, and those you should not; those that cause loss of the House, and those that cause loss of the habit; and if I have not told you all, then you may ask it, and may God grant you to speak well and do well.'

'God wills it,' Tadmartin says soberly, 'that I hear and understand.'

'Now your instructors may speak.'

De Payens is first. A short, dark-haired woman; worn into service; a sergeant who will do nothing else but train now, although Tad knows she has been offered command of her own House.

De Payens' warm voice says: 'She passed basic training at 89 per cent and advanced training at 93 per cent. We consider this acceptable.'

Six o'clock mornings, runs, workouts, assault courses; field-stripping weapons and field-stripping your opponent's psychology; all of this in her memory as de Payens smiles.

'Advanced strategic and tactical studies,' St Omer concedes, '85 per cent, which we accept.'

'Combat experience,' de Charney's voice comes from behind her.'No more errors than one might expect with a green lieutenant. I don't give percentages. Christ and Sophia! She's here, isn't she? And so are her squad.'

The preceptor frowns at that, but Tad doesn't notice. The cold of the chapel becomes the cold of fear. Brown-adrenaline fear, and the boredom and the routine; and the training that takes over and takes her through rough southern days fighting mercenaries on the Gold Coast.

The preceptor commands, 'Appear naked before God.'

Her fingers are cold, fiddling with the combat fatigues, and it is a long moment before she strips them off and stands naked. The chill of the stone reverberates back from walls and weapon-racks and the altar crowned with the image of St Baphomet. Her skin goosepimples. She has learned to ignore it, resting easy in her body, unselfconscious with their eyes on her.

The preceptor, de Molay, searches her face as if there is something he could discover. Waiting long minutes until the other Templars stir impatiently.

At last he asks, 'Do you wish to be, all the days of your life, servant and slave of the House?'

She meets his gaze. 'Yes, if God wills, sieur.'

'Then be it so.'

He doesn't look away. She takes the white livery with the red cross from de Payens, who helps her rapidly dress; she signs the document the solicitor gives her, assigning all possessions now and for her lifetime to the Order; she takes the congratulations of the officers relaxing into informal talk. All the time, de Molay's eyes are on hers.

She does not – cannot – ask him what he sees. Woman, *frère*, special forces soldier; none seem quite to account for that look. As if, before the altar of God, he sees in her what God does not.

'Roanoke was Border country, sieur.'

'You might as well say bandit country and be done with it.' St Omer spoke quietly and rationally, not looking at her. 'It's still a devil of a long way from being an explanation.'

'I know that, sieur.'

A truck rumbled past outside the window. The dew was still on the tarmac of the camp; grunts doubling across wide avenues to kitchen and latrine duties. Tadmartin ignored her griping stomach. The commander's office smelled of photocopier fluid. Three of the six telephones on his desk blinked for attention.

'Emirate Cabotsland...' Knight-Commander St Omer sighed. 'I'm formally warning you, Knight-lieutenant, that it may become necessary for an enquiry to be held.'

'Permission to speak, sieur.'

The middle-aged man responded tiredly. 'Speak as God bids you.'

'The Roanoke House already held such an enquiry, sieur. Report dated 10 July 1997. You can access it above rank of captain, sieur.'

Tadmartin stared at a middle-distance spot six inches to the left of the commander's eyes, wondering what particular circumstances had left him manning a desk while other, younger knights gained field promotions ... She steered herself away from seeing her image mirrored in him.

'You misunderstand me,' St Omer corrected. 'It may become necessary to hold a public enquiry. I suspect that that's what Avignon will come to, ultimately. You're to hold yourself in readiness for that event, and, if it should come about, act in all things in accordance with your vows of obedience to us.'

Tadmartin stared. Caught, for the first time in five years, unprepared. She dropped her usual pretence of just-another-grunt-sieur and responded as Templars do. 'They can't ask me to disclose the House!'

'Normally, no, but his Holiness Stephen-Maria may release you from that vow. Publicly.'

'That – sieur, excuse me, even his Holiness can't reverse a vow made before God and the chapter!'

St Omer stood and walked to the window. He remained facing it, a black silhouette against brightness. Tadmartin returned to staring rigidly ahead.

'The *magister Templi* requires me to inform you, Knight-lieutenant, that – if necessary – you will answer questions on the secret history. Is that clear? Of course,' the level voice added, 'what you perceive as a necessity will prove of interest to us all.'

Maps of Cabotsland's settled east coast on the walls, satellite photos of its Shogunate west coast; network terminals, old mugs half-full of coffee; the commander's office is one Tadmartin has often stood in, on many different bases. And there are the insignia on the walls, of course. Banners of campaigns. Some traditions do not die.

'You'll leave at oh-nine-hundred for Avignon; you will be accompanied at all times by a security detail; you will report to me immediately on your return. Go with God. Dismissed.'

*

5 July 1995
Tadmartin hefts the sword in her hand. It's lighter than she expects, no more than two or three pounds. A yard-long blade, a short cross-guard, a brazilnut-shaped pommel.

This is a live blade. Bright, it nonetheless has the patina of age on its silver. But a live blade, with a razor edge, and it slides through the air as slick as oil. It flies, it dives. The weight of it moves her wrist in the motions for attack, parry and block.

'And that's the difference.' The combat instructor takes it back from her reluctant hand. He replaces it in the weapons rack. The sun from the gymnasium window lights his sand-coloured, whitening hair.

She wants to hold it, to wield it again. She has the height and strength now of adulthood; a woman of slightly less than medium height, with strong shoulders. She wears new white combats, with the Templar red cross above the breast pocket.

'You, however, are going to use this for today.'

He hands her, single-handed, a greatsword.

Two-handed grip, wide cross, forty-four inch blade. Tadmartin takes it, coming into guard position: the balance is good. But it weighs as much again as the single-hander.

Probably her body-language broadcasts impatience: she would rather be out on the ranges. Possibly he has had to deal with other recruits to the House of Solomon. The instructor, Sevrey, shifts into combat speed; and she is left defenceless, holding the grip in sweating hands, as his blade swings to cut at face, belly, groin: the blunt edge barely touching the cloth of her combats each time as he stops it. Ten, twenty blows.

'It's a discipline. *The* Templar discipline.'

A yard of steel, rebated or not, is an iron bar that can break and crush. She freezes – after all her training, *freezes,* like any green conscript or civilian – and the blade flashes back brilliance.

'We've never broken this tradition. From the first Holy Land until now.' He stops, sudden but smooth; he is not breathing any more strenuously. When he wields the sword he becomes something other than a forgettable-faced sergeant. The sword and the body are one.

'It's what we are.'

She has seen him fight. Nothing of grace in it, unless it is the grace of chopping wood or driving stakes; the whole body weighing into the movement.

'I'll teach you,' Sevrey says. 'At the moment you're thinking about it. Where's the blade coming from, how do I move to parry, can I block that, where shall I attack? Train. Train and practise.'

'And then?'

As he speaks she moves out on to the mat, gripping the sword, swinging it through the drill movements of parry and blow. Sometimes the blade is inert. Sometimes it moves like running water.

'*Sword* and *intention*.'

She will understand intellectually but not in her gut. That comes later. With some it never comes at all.

'The sword is not part of you. You have an intention to use it.' Sevrey moves out on to the mat with her. They circle. She watches, watches his grey eyes, the blade. Later she will learn not to watch any particular point in her field of vision, but to see it all, central and peripheral, simultaneously.

'First comes *no-sword*,' Sevrey says. His blade comes out of nowhere, feints; she pulls back from a parry and his sword connects firmly across her stomach. An inch and a half behind the peritoneal wall coil thirty yards of intestine, and how much pressure does it take on a razor-edge to split muscle?

'No-sword: when the sword becomes an extension of yourself. You don't move the sword. You and the sword move.'

She flips the blade back, lets the weight carry it over; and he cuts behind her cut and parries her through, the steel clashing in the echoing gymnasium.

'And then—' the first break in his stream of words as he almost follows her feint; gets back in time to block '—if you're good, then *no-intention*. You'll have done so much fighting that in combat you don't even think, you don't even see an opening. You just watch the sword come down and cut home – it'll seem *slow* to you. No-sword, no-intention. But for that you're going to have to spend a lot of time at it, or be naturally good, or both.'

If he says more, she doesn't hear, the fight speeds up now. Combat speed.

In three months she will find herself fighting in this same gym, in a multiple mêlée; she will – and she only realizes it after the moment, and stands still in mid-combat and is cut down easily – strike down one opponent to her right and, in a reverse movement, block a stroke coming at her from behind with a perfect glissade. Nothing of it conscious. Nothing. But to the end of her days she will hear that back attack connect with her blocking blade, and hear Sevrey's profane astonishment at her getting it there.

Air-conditioning hummed in the room without windows.

His Holiness Stephen-Maria V sat at the centre of the horseshoe-shaped table. He intently watched a small monitor, resting his chin on his gloved hand. Two priests stood in readiness behind his chair. Incense drifted from their censers, whitening the corners of the room and smelling of sandalwood.

Tadmartin came to attention the prescribed three yards in front of the table and knelt, bowing her head. The heavy material of her white surcoat draped the floor. She noted with detachment the shoes of the others seated at the horseshoe-table: officers' boots, politicians' shoes, and the fashionably-impractical footwear of the media. Everything impinges itself on the detachment of combat-vision.

'Rise, demzelle.'

She rose easily. Only her eyes moved, checking the faces. Civil servants. Priests. Mostly unknown: these would be the power-brokers, and not the men put there for show. Military: the heads of the Templar and Hospitaller Orders. And two other known faces – Channel Eight and Channel Nine seated side by side, all rivalry gone; James de Craon bending his ruddy countenance on her blind side as Louise de Keroac murmured some comment.

Outwardly calm, Tadmartin waited.

'I think we may offer the demzelle a chair, don't you?' His Holiness Stephen-Maria glanced at one of the dark-suited men on his right.

'I prefer to stand, sieur.'

Outside the claustrophobic secure room, Avignon's baroque avenues and domed cathedrals shone with rain, the last of it dampening Tadmartin's red-crossed surcoat and white combats.

The Pontiff leaned back in his chair. Fluorescent lighting glittered from his white and golden robes, stiff with embroidery. He shone against the beige walls like an icon. His small owl-face creased with thought.

'Knight-lieutenant, will you summarize for the board of enquiry the purpose of the Order of Knights Templar, please.'

At this moment and in this place, a minefield of a question. Tadmartin responded instantly. 'We're a trained elite force, sieurs. Founded in 1119 AD, in the first Holy Land. We do undertake Burgundian missions where necessary, but we see action primarily overseas in Cabotsland. We operate out of the Templar fortresses down the east coast. Our main objective is to keep the pilgrim roads clear from the coast to New Jerusalem. It's therefore necessary for us to keep civil order.'

The bio-reporter De Craon raised his head. The priest at Stephen-Maria's side signalled assent.

'Lieutenant Tadmartin.' De Craon turned to her, the room's fluorescent lights shining in his wispy hair. 'These fortresses are garrisoned with Templars?'

'Yes, and with lay-brothers.'

De Craon smiled. Skin creased lizard-like around his mouth. 'There is another Order, am I right, who assists you in this?'

She kept her eyes from the Knight-Brigadier of St John. 'The Hospitallers provide auxiliary services, yes, sieur.'

'But they also see action?'

'After a fashion, sieur, yes.'

An almost imperceptible lifting of Stephen-Maria's hand and the bio-reporter became silent. The Pontiff, amiably smiling, said, 'Demzelle de Keroac, do you also have a question?'

'Sure I do.' The woman planted her elbows on the table. Her curled hair glittered yellow in that suffocating light. She fixed Tadmartin with a brilliant blue eye. 'You know your Templar organization also provides a banking service for the United governments?'

'I know that one exists.' Tadmartin paused. 'I don't know how it functions, demzelle. It never occurred to me that it was my concern.'

The woman twitched a muscle in her cheek. The spy-eye whirred into zoom, closing on Tadmartin's face. 'Do you know just how rich the Templars are, Knight-lieutenant? Do you realize why that makes them close advisers to presidents?'

'I don't know anything about banking, demzelle. I don't have any money of my own.' Momentarily amused at the disbelief on the woman's face, she added, 'The Order provides my housing, uniform, food, and equipment. Anything I owned was signed over to them when I joined the Order. I never handle money unless I'm getting supplies from the locals round a garrison.'

Louise de Keroac snorted. 'You're telling me soldiers never go out drinking, or to the local brothels?'

'We are the Knights of God.' Tadmartin, not able to hear the tone in which she quietly said that, was surprised to find the room silent. 'Some backslide, yes; if they do it repeatedly they lose the House.'

A movement snagged peripheral vision. Tadmartin turned her head. Not the Templar Marshal de Molay, sitting still and expressionless. The stout man next to him in black-and-red DPMs and Knight-Brigadier's insignia.

'Harrison, Order of St John,' he introduced himself briskly to the media. 'What *is* your view of the Knights Hospitallers, Demzelle Tadmartin?'

Dangerous. She refrained from saluting, which was some return for the *demzelle*. A coldness touched her which was not the air-conditioning. Thoughtfully, she said, 'I suppose there's a competitive spirit between all the knightly Orders, sieur.'

'But between Hospitallers and Templars? Wouldn't you call it more than "competitive"?'

She looked towards Stephen-Maria's small, bland face. 'Competition is strong, yes, sieur. The Hospitallers being under worldly jurisdiction.'

Abruptly Stephen-Maria snatched off his gold-rimmed spectacles, leaning forward and pointing at Tadmartin with a gloved finger. 'Knight-lieutenant, do you ever think of the young Indo-Saracen women and men whom you fight? Although they are terrorists and heretics, do you think of them as people, with souls? Human feelings?'

Tadmartin gave that due consideration, relieved at the change of subject. 'Not really, sieur. I don't think you can afford to. I tend to think in terms of target-areas.'

'But you are aware of it.'

'Yes, sieur.'

'One should thank God for it. Since there is wheat among the chaff – innocent civilians among the terrorists.'

His eyes were an exact faded blue. It was not possible to tell his age. Tadmartin remained easily at attention. The security detail at the entrance to the building had relieved her of her automatic.

'Under what circumstances is it permissible to kill, Lieutenant?'

'I do my job, sieur. It's a professional job, and I've been trained to do it very well. Yes, it says in the holy texts *Thou shalt not kill.* It also says *Suffer not the enemies of God to live.* Sometimes that has to be done, and it's better left to trained personnel.'

'Pariahs for the Lord.' Stephen-Maria smiled. It was not, despite his creased face, a gentle expression. 'Who are the enemies of God in Cabotsland, Lieutenant?'

Knowing he must know all, Tadmartin nevertheless blinked uneasily at that question. 'Indo-Saracen terrorists, sieur. Natives. Tokugawa-backed paramilitary groups.'

'Yes ... and *only* those. Lieutenant, remember one thing. Your Order answers to no president or government on this earth. It answers to us. We think it would be as well if you answer us truthfully.'

'Yes, sieur.'

How much for the media? How much for the anonymous suited men and women around the table? And who is to be the scapegoat? Tadmartin relaxed imperceptible muscles so that she still stood effortlessly to attention under their scrutiny.

'Lieutenant Tadmartin, you know what is meant by *the secret history*.'

'Yes, sieur.'

'Will you give us your understanding of the term, please? For the benefit of these people here.'

Tadmartin cleared her throat. 'It's a traditional term for the Cartulary of a knightly monastic order. It contains the full details of campaigns.'

'Full details?' Louise de Keroac pounced. 'So what's given to the outside world is censored?'

Tadmartin politely took the offensive. 'Not censored, demzelle, no. Condensed. Would you want all the details of how many water-bowsers were sent to which port and when; how many aerial refuellings took place on any given mission; how many sergeant-brothers were treated for blisters or heat exhaustion—?'

'Just how condensed *is* the history for public consumption?'

Stephen-Maria V said, 'Demzelles, sieurs, you can judge for yourselves. Knight-lieutenant Tadmartin, we're going to ask you to answer according to the secret history. We want your own account of the Roanoke incident. You were there. You were, however temporarily, the officer in charge of that company. Regrettably, innocent people died. The reports the public can access through this—' Stephen-Maria tapped the computer console. '—are official. You now have our order to speak without reservation.'

For whom does one tell the truth? Tadmartin let her gaze go around the table, seeing bankers and politicians and the media; and she did not let her gaze stop at the Templar knight Philippe de Molay in his white and red. No question. Finally, there is no question at all.

Tadmartin said, 'No, sieur.'

'We,' Stephen-Maria V said, with a deliberate gravitas, 'are granting you absolution from your vow.'

Unspoken, his gaze tells her this is enough of the obligatory refusals.

'You can't absolve me from the vows of secrecy, sieur, no one can. I'd lose the House and the habit.'

He scowled at her stone-wall morality. 'My daughter, there have been public accusations made, that the Order of the Knights Templar operates a shoot-on-sight policy in the emirate lands. These talks are to give an equally public refutation of that accusation.'

But truth is a seamless whole. Part told, all will be told. Tadmartin shrugged. 'Sieur. You don't understand. If I speak, I'll have to leave the Order; I couldn't stay – I couldn't face them.'

The Supreme Pontiff remained silent, but the priest at his left hand said quietly, 'For refusing to obey the supreme head of your Order you will lose the House, demzelle. I remind you of this.'

'Yes.' Tadmartin did not say *I know.* She let the media frustration wash over her, standing steady, her gaze fixed just slightly to the left of the Pontiff's head.

James de Craon interjected. 'What have you got to hide, Lieutenant?'

'Nothing. This isn't about me. It's about the Rule of the Knights Templar.'

Pope Stephen-Maria V said, 'Will you speak?'

Tadmartin shook her head. 'No.'

'You must.'

She allowed herself the luxury of showing, in full, what she felt in part. 'Sieur, I can't!'

For the first time her voice varied from its reasonable calm. A soldier's voice, roughened with shouting over the noise of firefights; a woman's voice thinned by the heat of bandit country. Now she heard her voice shake.

'We're Templars. We are what we are because of how we behave. You don't break vows. You *don't.* We're not just any body of fighting men. Sieur, you *must* understand, you're the Pontiff. I can't obey the order you're giving me.'

The priest leaned forward and murmured in the Pontiff's ear. 'I warned you, your Holiness. The men won't speak, the officers won't speak; it was most unlikely you could persuade a junior officer of the Templars to speak out in open court.'

'We are the head of the Order!'

Tadmartin made as if to say something, opening her mouth, but her throat constricted and she was silent. All muscles tense, as if her body urged her *speak out!*, but she literally could say nothing.

Am I really going to do this? she thought. Am I going to let them – no, am I going to *make* them throw me out of the Order? Jesu Sophia! I'm too old to go back to the regular army – and they won't take me anyway.

'For God's sake, sieur.' She at last appealed to the Templar Marshal seated midway down the righthand side of the table. She spoke doubly: in her role as stolid knight, and with her own secret knowledge. 'I've got nowhere to go if I leave the Order. I couldn't even buy civilian clothes! Don't let them force me out. Sieur, please!'

'There's nothing I can do, Lieutenant.'

De Molay's tone let her know he was aware of duplicity. The man's face was flushing a dull red: anger at her display of emotion, anger at his own embarrassment. Not until he looked away from her to the Knight of St John, and then back, did she catch his expression properly. Seen once before, in a chapel, one cold dawn.

'Get rid of these people!'

The Pontiff swore at his attendant priests and shoved his chair back, rising. The chair clattered over. The swirl of his robes as he turned caught a censer, tipping out burning sandalwood coals. One black-suited man stamped furiously on the sparks. Stephen-Maria stalked out.

The men and women at the table rose, caught by surprise. Talk broke out; the media people checking recordings; the rest debating uncertainties.

Tadmartin stood, undismissed. Even now, hoping against knowledge for a reprieve. Praise, even, for her steadfastness. Nothing came.

A quartet of military police officers filed in to escort her out.

5 July 1997

When it comes to a question, which do you choose?

There is no question.

The truck jolts and her ribs slam against the rim of the cab-window. The road to New Jerusalem winds up into the high lands, white under the moon. An exposed road, here.

The Hospitaller APCs judder past, tracks grinding white dust that falls wet and heavy from their passing.

'What's the intelligence report on hostiles?'

'They're saying up to sixty hostiles, heavily-armed. Fucking sakkies.' Tysoe spits.

Tadmartin has never seen that trail's end. Has never been posted to that tiny Vinland settlement where, one millenium since, Sophie Christos came to preach her gnostic gospel and reap the reward commonly given to reformers. But Tadmartin has, on the same chain as her dog-tag, a tiny fragment of the Second True Cross embedded in clear plastic.

'Give the Hospitallers sixty minutes dead,' she directs Tysoe. 'If they can't get their half of the ambush set up by then, fuck 'em.'

'*Bastards.*'

Brown camo-cream distorts the angles of moonlight on Tysoe's face. She's leaner than she was in training, five years ago; a long-jawed, bony woman.

'Something you should have reported to me, girl?'

'Pfcs Johannes Louis and Gilles Barker aren't on duty.'

The captain absent, Tadmartin is senior of the four lieutenants at the garrison. Tysoe has Squad One, Cohen Two, and Ragald has Three; sergeants are keeping the fort secure. Close on a hundred men, a company-size operation. Needless to say she has not commanded at this level before, or not officially, and not under combat conditions. It tends to blur the minutiae.

She notes now that Squad One has a replacement man on heavy-weapons support, and a woman Tadmartin recognizes from the garrison taking the RT. She misses Gilles Barker's snap-on laconic radio technique. Johannes Louis will be missed by no one, realistically, but that's not the point; he was part of the squad.

'Brawling, wasn't it? They're both on the medic register.'

The exigencies of ambush take her away from the vehicle for a minute, sending Two Squad and Three Squad up into position to approach the valley. Trees sway and creak. The night is uneasy, and the full moon an annoyance. And all the time that white, white road runs east away from her, dusty with the feet of a million pilgrims, trudging or riding broken-down trucks from Templar fort to Templar fort, all the way to the end of the trail.

She hauls herself up into the back of the truck.

'We'll move out in five.'

Tension. Final checks of equipment – grenade launchers, heavy machineguns, flamers, assault rifles – and the mutters of *shit* and *fuck* and *Jesu Sophia!*, and the churning gut that always comes with action; the fear that stops the breath in your lungs. Tadmartin puts her head down for a second, inhaling deeply, and straightens with some electric excitement replacing breath.

'Barker and Louis.' Tysoe says, joining her. 'Hospitallers jumped 'em last night.'

'Sophie *Christos*,' Tadmartin says, disgusted.

Raleighstown, a spring night, Tadmartin new in the *outremer* territories; she and the other Knight-lieutenants gone drinking. In downtown bars where the whisky is rough and cheap, and there are the young men and women who naturally congregate around military bases: who know what to offer and what to expect in payment. But Tadmartin tells herself she is only there for the drink. And Tadmartin, leaning out of a bar door and throwing up in the street, is hit in the kidneys from behind, sprawls face down in her own vomit, white DPMs stained yellow and brown.

'Fuckin' Templar *cunt*!'

Tadmartin does nothing but come easily up on to her feet. Head clearing, the night slipping past in freeze-frames: herself on hands and knees, herself standing, three Hospitaller squaddies grinning – a red-haired man and two sharp-uniformed women.

'Yo,' she says softly. Turns smartly, unsteadily, on her heel and walks back into the bar, where Tysoe and – names? names forgotten, but the company lieutenants are there, and two sergeant preceptors, so there are six of them; and out into the night, where one of the Hospitaller women is still visible down the road, and off and running into the downtown quarter. Following her down the road at a sprint, street-lights failing, and swinging down one alley and across into the next—

Where there are thirty Hospitaller squaddies waiting. The woman's buddies. Tadmartin finds out that they even call it *Templar-bashing*.

Arrests and enquiries do not follow, not even for a shit-stupid dumbass excuse for a lieutenant. Templars and Hospitallers have to police the same territory, after all. There are nominal noises of disapproval on both sides. She is out of hospital in a matter of months and feels pain in her hands for two winters after.

'Stupid *cunts*. Aw, shit, Tysoe, girl!'

Warnings go out from the company captain's desk, strict

warnings with penalties attached. *Leave the Hospitallers alone.* There will always be grunts who regard them as challenges, or a matter of pride.

'Louis'll be back.' The woman puts on her helmet, clips the strap, checks the internal RT. 'They blinded Gilles Barker. Left eye. Going to be invalided out.'

'*Christ.*'

Implications flick through her head. For a shared op.

'Where's the report on this?'

'It's on your desk.'

'Shit. OK—' Too late to change the plan now. All she can do is keep a closer eye on Squad One. 'OK, I'll come in with you guys; Ragald can take Three up the road. That's time – let's roll.'

Out of the truck and into the forests. Maybe a mile to cover, but a mile in silence. They melt into night and quiet, each one; going down into a silent crawl, shifting twigs and branches as they move, falling into the rhythm of clear ground, move elbow, clear ground, move knee ...

Fifty minutes.

The terrain changes. Leaving the forest for wet heather, and then up along drained hill slopes and into pine. Tadmartin moves in the night, combats soaked, warm with the weight she carries. Slow, slow. Cold breath drifts from her mouth; camo-cream is cold on her skin. She crawls past a fox. Unspooked, it watches her go. The night wind moves the creaking pines.

'Delta Alpha, sit-rep, over?'

'*This is Delta Alpha, in position, out.*'

'Hotel Oscar, sit-rep, over.'

'*Hotel Oscar to Romeo Victor, say again, over?*'

'Romeo Victor to Hotel Oscar, sit-rep, say again, sit-rep, over.'

'*... Victor, in position, do you copy?*'

'Hotel Oscar, I copy, out. Sierra Foxtrot, sit-rep, over.'

'*In position, Romeo Victor. Out.*'

She curses the moon. Too much light. It blotches the ground under the gnarled pines, splashes the jutting rocks at the edges of the deep valley. Low-voiced zipsquirts over the RT assure her Tysoe's got Squad One in position along the cliff-top. Three's further up; Two covering flank and rear.

Tadmartin moves up, assault rifle cradled, crawling silently from cover to cover. She edges on her belly into the brushwood that overhangs one jutting rock.

The night wind is cold against her eyes. At least the noise will screen movement – but that's a two-edged weapon. She stares down into the valley.

A bright flicker of light is moonlight on the stream, thrashing in its rock-strewn bed. The road winds along the valley floor, sometimes beside the river, sometimes crossing it. The overhang she lays on is fifty yards upstream of a bridge. Nothing moving down there yet. No sound of engines. She merges into the stripes of moonlight and brushwood, thinking *tree.*

And across the other side of the gorge a glint of light shows her someone using night glasses. She sub-vocalizes for the helmet RT and zipsquirts:

'Romeo Force to Juliet, repeat Romeo Force to Juliet, do you copy? Tell your men to lay off the night scopes, they can see 'em back in *town,* for fuck's sake! Over.'

There is the split-second time-delay of zipsquirt transmission, then:

'Juliet Force to Romeo, wilco, out.'

Curt to the point of abruptness. Tadmartin grins but it stiffens, becomes a rictus on her face. Thinking of Johannes Louis and Gilles Barker.

She lays on her belly and stares across the gorge, idly pinpointing the more unwary of the Hospitaller troops. The ambush will lay fire down into the valley and nothing will walk out of it. Assuming that the hostiles come down the valley and not around it. Assuming that intelligence is right and an arms-shipment is due. Assuming.

Always assuming.

'Romeo Victor, this is Sierra Foxtrot. We have a possible contact, repeat, possible contact at Falcon Station. Advise, over.'

'Sierra Foxtrot, this is Romeo Victor. Confirm sighting and advise numbers. Let them come past you. Out. Romeo Force to Juliet—' She swallows, continues with a level voice. 'Possible contact at Falcon Station. Over.'

'Juliet to Romeo, I copy, out.'

Each of the valley bends has been assigned a name. She listens to the zipsquirt transmissions: Falcon, Eagle, Duck, and Crow all passed, and then the sound of engines is clear to her. She blinks up visual enhancement, closing one eye and staring down the valley. Patches of moonlight blot and blind. She blinks enhancement off and relies on one eye's night vision.

There.

Nosing around the corner of the gorge, one ... two ... three closed trucks, rolling with the movements of heavily-loaded vehicles. An artic, straining at the gradient. Three more trucks, and a battered old limo. The engines shatter the silence of the woods.

'Romeo Victor to all units, confirmed sighting at Bluejay Station.' Sliding the assault rifle up the length of her chilled body so that it will not catch on the rock. The way behind her is clear for retreat. The gorge in front of her is one killing zone. 'Hold your fire until I give the signal—'

Silence shatters. The night coughs a throat of flame. The abrupt noise stutters her heart. The limo at the rear of the line swerves in a pall of fire, hits the edge of the stream and rolls half-over. Shouts and screams come from the valley, the advance trucks gun their motors.

'—*fuck!*' Tadmartin rolls over on her side.

Muzzle flashes burst down the whole other side of the valley: the Hospitaller troops opening fire.

'OK. OK. Take out the front vehicle!'

Two of the rear trucks accelerate into the shadows of overhangs. Inside seconds there is the rattle and crack of small-arms fire. The flares blaze in. Tadmartin hears the *whumph!* of a grenade launcher and ducks her head into her arms, comes up and looses off suppressive fire down towards the rear of the column. There is the amputating roar of claymore mines as hostiles abandon the trucks.

Explosions deafen her. Hot air hits her cheek, splinters of wood spatter the rock-face. The grenade explosion takes out a chunk of the bank and starts fire in the brushwood.

'Heavy weapon! Tysoe, take that truck out!'

Tysoe's yell from ten yards away: 'Assault team move up!'

'Romeo Victor to Sierra Foxtrot, close up the back door, repeat, close up the back door. Out. Romeo Victor to Hotel Oscar, Cohen, cover our fucking arses, we've got an illegal firefight going on up here, watch our backs, out; Tysoe, do you copy? Repeat, do you copy, over?'

Now there is no answer.

'Romeo Victor to all squads. Bottle the bastards up. Out!'

Two rounds clip the branches above her head and she swears, sprayed with exploded fragments of pine wood. The stink of resin fills the air, sickly-sweet with cordite and woodsmoke. She glances over her shoulder at the brushfire.

'Move 'em down!' She falls into cover, finding Tysoe a few yards ahead. In the valley, one of the trucks swings around in an impossible turning-circle and accelerates back towards the bridge. Someone screams. 'Medic! Squad One Medic – through there.'

She pushes the medic on down through the trees and leaves him squatting over a grunt with a shattered face. Hair blown back, face glistening red, eye and jaw mincemeat. There is blood on her combats to the elbow, she doesn't remember touching him.

'Where's it coming from?' Tysoe and the assault team hit cover beside her. 'It ought to be a fucking turkey-shoot, where's it *coming* from?'

'You!' Tadmartin grabs the woman with the heavy weapon: a shoulder-fired rocket launcher. 'Take that bridge out – *now.*'

The grunt belts past her, kneels. Two successive blasts shake the air. Flame shoots from the rear of the rocket launcher as the missile fires. Line of sight into the valley is obscured by flare-lit shifting smoke. Muzzle flashes gleam through it, and the roar of brushfire whipped up by the night wind. Tadmartin hears voices screaming – on the banks? in the valley? – and the *whoomph!* of a truck going up. Hot air blows against her face. She smells the charred stink of cooking meat. Rounds whistle through the pine trees. Belly-down, crawling; and then there is a hollow concussive sound from the end of the valley and a cheer from the assault team.

'Bridge is down, L.T. We cut off the retreat.'

'Good. Lay down fire into the valley—'

There is a *crump!* and the night lights up like Christmas. That one landed *behind*: a cut-off shot. The pine trees burn like pitch torches and the night is hot; she is sweating and covered with black ash and her hands are blistered.

'L.T., that came *across* the valley!'

'Give me a range and direction!'

'Fifty metres, two o'clock.'

'Lay down suppressive fire. Tysoe, take 'em down the south side of the valley. *Now.*' Tadmartin falls into cover behind a rock outcrop. The stuttering cough of a heavy machine-gun vibrates through the earth. Flashes of light strobe the night: give her lightning-strike views of branches against the night sky, grunts running, a casevac team with a bodybag. Her face bleeds. 'Romeo Force to Juliet, do you c—'

'*They're* firing on *us*. The fucking Hospitallers!' Tysoe, camo-cream smeared with blood, stands up waving the assault rifle. 'For

Christ's sake tell them to cease fire!'

'Romeo Force to Juliet, repeat, Romeo Force to Juliet. Cease firing on friendly targets. Repeat *cease fire on valley wall.* Juliet Force, do you copy? You're firing on us! Do you copy? *For fuck's sake answer me.*'

Her dry throat croaks. She is aware of her split lip, bleeding in the night's chill. The helmet RT has insufficient power in this atmospheric muck; the woman with the RT was the casevac case; and Tadmartin pushes up from her cover and leans round the outcrop, spraying the far valley wall with undirected fire. 'Cease fire! *Cease fire!* We're in a fucking killing zone here!'

The rifle is hot, magazine almost exhausted; she with swift precision removes it and snicks another one home. She feels the slick, greasy heat of shit down her thighs.

'Squad One reform and move up!' Tysoe bawls. She dips for a split second beside Tadmartin. 'They're asking for it – they're asking for it! We're going to take them out! It's the only way!'

Another shell lands behind, up the valley wall. Rock splinters shrapnel the woods. Pull out? The way's blocked. Back to basic procedure: fight through.

Tadmartin yells, '*Take* the fuckers out. Go!'

Squad One are gone, pounding through the brushwood. Tadmartin goes a step or two after them and then falls into cover. The situation's sliding out of control, and she's got two other squads to contend with and the hostiles in the valley: let Squad One go do it. Cut losses.

'Romeo Victor calling Delta Alpha, move up into position at the valley wall above Bluejay Station, I repeat, move up into position at valley wall above Bluejay Station. Fire at will. Out. Romeo Victor to Hotel Oscar – get your asses up the south side and give Squad One covering fire. Move it!'

At daybreak she will walk through the floor of the valley, past burst and burnt-out trucks, when dawn glitters through the trees and off the stream. The track is puddled with red mud for two hundred yards. There are bodies and bits of bodies in the vehicles, charred and black. There is meat hanging from the trees.

She will walk the far side of the valley wall and watch the casevac of Hospitaller troops. Flying out to the same field hospitals as her own troops. She will hear the Hospitaller captain's oddly apologetic offer of help; an offer that vanishes when it emerges his troops are chewed up twice as bad as the Templars.

What will she feel? Satisfaction, mostly. Righteous satisfaction.

Daybreak, and things become visible.

There aren't half a dozen rifles together in the column. Of course, it wasn't a shipment of arms. Nothing for a stealth ambush to make an example of. It was, it later transpires, thirty families of paramilitary terrorists being shifted out from an up-trail district (in secrecy) into Indian territory. For their own safety.

Families with a small guard. Civilians.

Anything more than a quite minor investigation and it is unlikely Templar and Hospitaller troops will be tenable in the same territory. When it comes to a question, truth or something you can live with, which do you choose?

5 July 2002

'Did you hear? They want to cancel the Unification Day parade next year.' Knight-lieutenant Tysoe leans morosely against the door-frame of the cell. 'Because *the ordnance damages the streets,* for Chrissakes! Fucking government shit. When they start worrying about tanks chewing up a few roads, then you know you've lost it.'

Tadmartin ignores her. The cell containing only a small mirror, she is studying her full-length reflection in the metal door.

'Shit ...'

A woman something under medium height, shoulders stretching the cloth of her demob tunic. Blonde hair far too short for a civilian. A young woman with a sunburned face; moving uneasily in the heeled shoes, smoothing down the plain cloth skirt.

'Who'd be a fucking Templar? You ain't missing nothing,' Tysoe assures her uncomfortably.

Tadmartin looks.

'Well, *fuck*, man ...'

'It's all right,' Tadmartin says. 'It's all right.'

'*We* know what you did.'

Tadmartin hefts her small shoulder-bag. Gifts, mostly. Face-cloth, toothbrush, underwear, sanitary towels. 'Write or something, will you?'

It is a momentary lapse. Some lies are easier than others. Tysoe says 'Sure!' and ducks her head uncomfortably, waits a moment in the face of Tadmartin's calm, then shrugs and leaves.

Little now to do. Tadmartin reaches up to the weapons rack on the cell wall and takes down the rebated eleventh-century sword.

The tv snaps on, on auto-timer: she ignores the whispering voices.

Tadmartin sits on her bed, her back against the wall, the rebated sword resting with its hilt against her shoulder and the blade across her body. She rubs microcrystalline wax into the metal with a soft cloth, the movements rhythmically smooth.

It is the last piece of equipment she will return to the armoury.

She finishes with maintenance, stands; holding the hilt and letting the blade flip up into first guard position. The sun shines into the monastic cell. There is just space enough to lose herself in the drill of cut, parry, block...

The blade moves smoothly in the air. The solidity of the grip, the heft of the blade; moving in a balance that makes it all – edge, guard, grip, pommel – a singularity of weapon.

She loses herself in it.

Becoming *no-sword*, one culminates in total resignation, abandoned to the skill of the blade. Nothing matters. One cannot care about winning, losing, survival, dying. One cannot care, and act right. She enters the complete, balanced resignation of the fighter: dead, alive, alive, dead. No matter. No difference.

The face on the tv screen focuses in her combat-widened peripheral vision. The fair-haired woman, de Keroac; capable and triumphant. Tadmartin hears her speak.

'The government's denial of accusations that they are operating a shoot-on-sight policy in emirate Cabotsland was further complicated yesterday by the breakdown of the Avignon talks.

'Talks broke down when a Templar officer, Demzelle Hyacinthe Tadmartin, refused to give any eye-witness evidence whatsoever about her command at Roanoke. Claims will now continue to be levelled at the government that the civilians killed at Roanoke were innocent casualties of what is, in all but name, a war in the New Holy Land. It is five years to the day since the Roanoke massacre claimed fifty-three civilian lives. This is Louise de Keroac, for Channel Nine.'

The words are heard but they do not matter.

She is a sword, a sword now out of service. But held in the balance of that resignation she knows, *no-intention* will carry her far abroad. Alone. Away from bystanders who she may, instinctively, hurt.

Tadmartin walks out of the cell, putting the first foot on the pilgrim road – unrecognized as yet – that will take her, solitary and one day in the far future, to the New Jerusalem.